HELLMARINE

1

They Shall Know Fear

Virgil Knightley, Alphonse Fisk

CONTENTS

PROLOGUE

A Young Man's Eulogy

FOR THE PEOPLE OF Aonus, the day of reckoning began like any other. Those on the first shift woke with the sun to ready themselves for a day of mining on behalf of the various competing corporations on the frontier world. Meanwhile, those from the third shift returned home for much-needed rest.

Orco Industries, the largest of the mining companies on Aonus, also maintained a robust science division to examine and study new and interesting samples unearthed by its army of employees. To protect this research and the facilities that held it, Orco contracted the services of the renowned and respected MoonShot Security.

One such young man among MoonShot's employees wasn't there as a matter of employment, or even prestige, but to remain close to his family employed by Orco Industries in its research labs.

Scientific research was something of a family business, as was mining. His mother had grown up on Aonus in a prominent mining family known for its start as independent contractors, hitting it big with major discoveries as well as pioneering much of the technology that kept the miners safe deep underground. On his father's side was a long line of xenogeologists and xenophysicists, who had left behind the core worlds of the Sol Alliance long ago to explore the mysteries of the cosmos.

Military service wasn't represented much in their family. He was frequently reminded of this when he was younger and decided he felt a call to serve. The young man endured many arguments over his career path. He was intelligent, cunning, strong, and possessed of an unbreakable will, he was often reminded. Why, then, had he chosen to eschew his gifts—waste them even—by giving them to the military?

The answer was that simple—he wanted to protect his family and the people of Aonus, who were at the fringes of known space with any number of alien threats skulking around on their doorstep. As clever as he was, his fearlessness and knack for combat was his greater strength after all.

Touched by his protective instinct, the young man eventually wore his family down to do as he liked to pursue his goals. After serving in the Aonian System Security Force, repelling alien threats from the ages of sixteen to twenty-four, he retired from service. He moved home, of course, and chose to enlist with MoonShot Security in order to be close to family again while working for a company lacking in the dirty laundry so many others were infamous for.

The young man woke with the first shift, grabbing breakfast and a shower as he did every other morning. He lived alone, the way he preferred it, but wasn't without friends. He was a fixture in the community, known for his strong moral code, fairness, and strength.

He wasn't the type for conversation—this was a fact that those who knew would debate about, whether it was something that changed in him during his service to the solar system's defense force, though most agreed he'd always been that way.

It didn't matter anyway; whenever people needed him, he would be there. Even during social functions, he had little to say but was present to lend his stoic support to others. He laughed on occasion and loved on a few others, but those who knew him the longest considered him a hardworking man of peace who'd drawn his weapon only a handful of times since returning planetside—even in the roughest of situations. To him, people were worthy of second chances, and so lethal force was seldom an option.

Despite his choice to live alone, he often ended up in the company of one person in particular who never got the memo—his sister.

"There you are," she said, letting herself in through the front door. She was nearly as tall as he was, which was impressive considering just how tall she was, though it always made the dating scene hard for her until recently. She was already dressed in her lab coat, with the credentials needed for maximum security areas fixed firmly to her belt. "What are you doing here?"

"Breakfast," he responded simply, gesturing with a fork to the scrambled eggs and bacon on his plate before resuming his meal.

"Did you forget what day it is today?" she pressed, walking over to the small table he sat at to pluck a piece of bacon from his plate. He watched his bacon vanish into her mouth before shaking his head.

"No," he grunted, nudging his plate a little closer to her so she could have more if she wanted. Her interest in his breakfast instantly waned when it became freely available, though. Such was a sister's nature.

"Mom and Dad have been asking about you!" She continued, brushing a strand of hair from her face to adjust her glasses. "They've been at it all night. The xenolinguist they called finished decoding the first section of the ruins."

"Mhm," He murmured, finishing his food off and bringing the plate to the sink where he left it. He would get to it later when his shift was over. He went about getting the rest of his things together while she continued to speak. She never looked for a lot of input from him, anyway.

"Are you hearing me, dickhead? They need you down at the lab ASAP!" she exclaimed, waving her arms toward the door. "Let's go! Chop, chop!"

Still fastening his belt around his waist, he gestured to the clock on the wall. The digital readout showed he still had roughly forty-five minutes before he was due to clock in. She glanced at the clock, her face scrunching up in irritation as she turned her attention back to him. "So what? This is huge! Do you know how long it's been since anything like this has been uncovered without some kind of interference from the core systems or interdictions from aliens?"

The young man heaved a deep sigh. It wasn't that he had no interest in what they'd uncovered. On the contrary, he was quite wary of the security concerns that such a monumental find represented. However, there were other factors in play that tempered his zeal. His sister had a tendency to hyper-focus on singular matters at the exclusion of everything else. It was part of what made her so good in her field but such a pain in the ass otherwise.

"Overtime request wasn't approved," the young man explained with a tired look. The revelation caused his sister to become a little more crestfallen, realizing that she couldn't compel him to join her earlier than management would sign off on. "Sorry, sis."

"Mule," she snorted as she admitted defeat.

"Nag," he chuckled in response. He buttoned his work shirt up to the top and strapped on the protective vest the company issued all of its personnel. Once finished, he took a few steps closer to her and pulled her into a hug, which she pretended to resist. Despite her height, she felt so small in his powerful arms. "How's Jack?"

"He's great," the nag responded with a smirk. "He's taking care of me just fine if that's what you're wondering."

"Good," the mule remarked with an approving nod. "Glad someone has the stomach for it."

This earned him a sucker punch.

He and Jack had been childhood friends that had grown apart after the young man's time in the service, and when he returned home, Jack had already moved away. However, he eventually returned for work a couple of years ago, and though he and Jack never became quite as close as they had been as boys, his sister and Jack had hit it off and grown quite close since then.

Just a few weeks ago, he made a marriage proposal, but the ceremony was going to have to wait until the paperwork with the company was cleared. It didn't normally take so long, but the assumption was the company had its hands full with the new findings.

Sadly, there was also the matter of communications outages. All the networks were experiencing them, though no explanation had been offered as to the cause. Rumors had begun to spread about some alien incursions into Alliance space, while others had started to talk about something darker and nastier than mere aliens. Whenever something big happened, the Outer Colonies were always the last to find out. It was also where the worst and most outlandish rumors took root. Things were strange enough so far away from the Core Worlds. Adding to it wasn't really needed, in his opinion.

The fact that his sister had someone else to look after her and take care of her when he wasn't able to do so set the young man's mind at ease. They might not have had the ceremony or the paperwork, but Jack and his sister were already married in spirit. He grabbed his credentials, fastened them to his belt, and headed for the door.

"You're not going to make a lunch?" his sister asked curiously, glancing back at his fridge. "You always bring lunch."

He opened the door before turning to look back at her with an impatient sigh. She followed, stepping through the door onto the street. The usual bustle of the mining town was well underway, with numerous pedestrians and vehicles clogging up the roadway already. Overhead, a transport ship's engines roared as it came in for a landing at the spaceport. He glanced up at the short-range transport, recognizing it as one of the ones from the eastern territories before locking the front door. He tested the handle to make sure it was closed, as he always did.

Turning to face his sister once again, she met him with an accusatory jab of her finger. "You forgot to order your groceries again, didn't you?"

The young man didn't answer as he pushed past her to join the flow of traffic on the street, but his face said it all. She laughed as she followed him but didn't press the issue further. "I'll buy you something later. How's that?"

Glancing at her, he offered her a little smile. As annoying as she could be, she always took care of him.

The main complex for Orco Industries wasn't far from where he lived, so he elected to walk just about every morning. Here, he rubbed elbows with the miners and other facility workers for most of his journey before splitting off toward the security office. The facility was impressive, sprawling out in a wide circle with a large spire at the center reaching skyward. It called to mind a vague similarity to a child's top, half buried in the ground, composed entirely of steel and concrete.

What couldn't be seen was how far that spire penetrated below the surface of Aonus. Through it, one achieved access to the main mining arteries, and before those, the various science labs. The surface sections were mostly administrative and corporate, with space set aside for transit and cargo transport. Short-range transports and long-range freighters alike came and went from the latter portion of the complex at all hours of the day, but traffic was heaviest during daylight hours.

"Hey, aren't you a little early?" An older gentleman called from the tower of the front gate. Even at this distance, the young man could tell the man was smirking at him under his bushy gray beard. "They're not gonna approve the overtime, you know. You might get in trouble."

The young man raised a hand, offering a simple wave without bothering to address what he said. It was more about providing his sister an escort than clocking in early, anyway, and that's what he'd say if asked. If he wouldn't be on the clock officially, he saw no harm in lurking until it was time.

He greeted various co-workers as he passed the first security checkpoint, presenting his credentials for the scanner as he went. He stepped into the elevator alongside his sister and several other science personnel, then descended into the lower levels.

Nearly everyone else stepped off the elevator before them, lacking the clearance for the lowest levels of the facility. When the doors finally opened to their destination, it was just the two of them and one other scientist stepping out. Each had to scan their credentials again before they were granted access to the lab.

"About time!" the young man's father called from the other side of the lab that opened up into the cavern with the unearthed ruins and the relic within. "We had to get started without you kids!"

He returned his father's wave as he stepped into the lab, glancing around at the others who worked under his parents. The lab was alive with activity in a way that he'd seldom seen. Before he knew it, his sister had joined the activity, eager to get back to work.

"Morning," his mother said as she passed by him, going up onto her toes to plant a kiss on his cheek. "Don't mind your father. There's still plenty of work left to be done."

His mother patted him on the chest, which he hardly felt through the body armor. "I know you probably don't clock in for a little bit still, but would you mind helping me move a few things?"

"Sure," he agreed without hesitation. His mother led him out of the main room to a storage area filled with various locking crates and shelves.

"We're clearing this section out to make room for the cryo storage, but some of these are a little too heavy," she explained, motioning to the larger black crates. They were heavily armored to protect their contents, so it made sense she would struggle with moving them. He looked at her with an arched brow, silently questioning the need for this kind of tech.

"We need the cryotech for sample storage," his mother explained, gesturing briefly toward the part of the lab that opened into the caverns. "Your father is certain we're about to uncover something significant. We'll be taking in more samples than we'll be able to examine right away, so they'll be kept perfectly preserved in here until we get additional personnel with the proper clearance."

He nodded and got to work, lifting the heavy crates and placing them where his mother directed. Given his almost obsessive tendency to work out in his time off, it didn't take long at all to move everything out of the way. Back in the service he picked up the habit—working out. He'd always had an obsessive streak to him, though. It was as though a single topic, whether a love or a hate, could dominate his interest indefinitely if he let it.

A few technicians brought the cryopods in immediately after and began the task of setting them up. Each had its own redundant power source in the event of power failure, allowing anything stored within the pod to remain in complete stasis for years. The young man briefly watched them at work, intrigued to see how the device worked. Cryotech wasn't something he got to play with every day.

Stepping back out into the main lab, he took a moment to indulge his curiosity toward something else, looking out from the observation platform onto the strange obelisk that was the main focus of their work. At first glance, it looked like any other slab of granite jutting out from the floor of the cavern to a height of fourteen or fifteen feet, about ten feet wide, with a thickness of only six feet. What was so interesting about the formation was the exotic minerals that composed its surface and the faded symbols carved into it. Even now, the xenolinguist they had contracted was still poring over the symbols to decode them. Colored sticky notes were attached to the front, showing which sections he was working on and which he had finished with varying levels of certainty.

The young man glanced at the clock hanging over the lab's steel doors and decided he had just enough time to make it to the main security office to clock in. He glanced at his mother, offering her a subtle smile as he activated the doors. "I'll be back," he said simply.

His mother returned his smile and turned away, joining his father in beginning the next phase of their examination. He didn't know the specifics, but he didn't need to. His job was to oversee the security of the lab, making sure no unauthorized personnel gained access and that his family was protected.

As he stepped into the security office, the young man was greeted by the guard at the desk and the guard dog he kept close by. The dog yawned when he entered, wagging his tail lazily at him. He spared a moment to pat the animal's head before continuing to the terminal, where he tapped his credentials in and logged his time.

The young man never admitted it, but he was quite attached to the dog, which the guards had found wandering around in search of scraps a year prior. Though not technically trained for the job as a guard dog, management hadn't objected to having the animal around. He was sort of their mascot.

"You catch the game last night?" The guard at the desk asked without looking up from the video feeds displayed on his own terminal. "Hell of a beatdown they took, hm? Starting to see why you don't bother with the betting pool."

The young man snorted with amusement before offering a brief shrug. It wasn't the only reason he didn't bother with betting, but the win-loss rate of the home team wasn't something he would chance his paycheck on even if he did.

As he stepped backward through the door back into the hall, he held his arms out to his sides. Before he could speak, he felt a tremor through the floor that nearly threw him on his ass.

The guard at the desk looked up at him, just as surprised as he was. Their expressions asked the same question of one another, though neither of them had an answer. The dog growled, his fur standing up on end as he backed away from the door. The desk guard glanced at the feeds, his eyes wide with horror.

"The feeds are gone," he muttered, immediately stepping away from the desk toward the weapons locker with keys in hand. As another tremor rocked the facility, killing the regular lights and triggering the alarms, the young man didn't bother to wait for his co-worker. Drawing his sidearm, he rushed down the hallway toward the lab as red emergency lighting came online.

As he neared the security doors, he saw them dent and warp from the inside. A second later, the doors burst outward, peppering the hallway with thick chunks of steel and concrete. One of the larger chunks caught the young man in the cranium, knocking him down to the floor. His head swam as spots filled his vision.

The young man struggled to remain conscious as he pushed himself up onto his hands and knees. Shaking off the vertigo, he used the wall as a support to get to his feet. The alarms sounded like they were coming from a great distance as an undercurrent of screams joined them. Then came the gunfire.

The young man steadied his breathing as he resisted the temptation to speculate as to what was happening, instead focusing solely on the immediate objective of getting to his family. Pushing off of the wall, the young man turned to resume his course toward the lab, only to see a strange creature on all fours emerge from inside.

The creature was unlike any alien he'd seen before, even during his years of service defending the planet and the greater Aonian system. Each of its legs ended in large, vicious claws capable of tearing gouges in the floor without effort. The skin along its skull was pulled tight, nearly exposing the bone beneath. On either side of its head were grotesque fleshy flaps that resembled a cross between fins and ears. Its gaping maw was filled with rows upon rows of sharp, ragged teeth. As it neared the young man's position, a long, spiked tongue flicked out like that of a snake in search of prey. The thing had no eyes to speak of, only recessed pits where they should have been.

Beyond the creature, the lab was burning. He heard a scream that had to be his mother's. It reminded him of the time he brought a snake home from playing with Jack as a child, surprising her. It was that scream, just worse. In an instant, a switch was flipped in his mind, and he went to work.

Grabbing his OT-5 Outsider from the floor where he'd dropped it, the young man fired off three shots at the creature, each round catching it in the skull. Two skittered along the ridges, tearing superficial wounds in its flesh. The third connected with one of the recesses in the creature's face, blowing the interior of its head out through the back of its skull, spattering the wall in gore. He sped past it before it even hit the floor.

The sterile, tidy lab that he had left several minutes before was engulfed in chaos. Chemical, colored flames obscured his vision while the blaring alarm confounded his hearing. It didn't matter. All he needed was to find his family and get them out.

Another of the four-legged creatures emerged from behind one of the lab tables. As the young man turned to face the creature, it lashed out with its tongue, driving it into his chest like a harpoon. The body armor took the brunt of the punishment, but an inch of the tongue still managed to burrow into his ribcage beneath.

Snarling with anger and pain, he reached out and took hold of the tongue with his gloved hand, preventing the creature from retrieving it or fleeing, holding it still as he put two rounds in its head. As it collapsed, he spared a third round through the tongue to sever it from its owner.

He jerked the thing out of his chest but held onto it. The Outsider had a twelve-round capacity. He'd used six. Keeping something as lethal as this ragged thing might prove useful.

Moving on, another creature looked up from where it feasted on the chest of—shit. It was his father.

His blood ran cold at the sight of his father's mangled corpse and then hot as his gaze fell upon his father's lifeless eyes, his face frozen in a mask of fear and pain. Hatred coursed through him in the form of a hit of adrenaline the likes of which he'd never felt.

The creature—his father's slayer—stood on two legs, covered in gross, leathery skin with spikes protruding from it in several places that seemed almost random. The wounds on his father's corpse sizzled from the same acid dripping from its toothy maw as drool.

With a furious roar from somewhere deep within, the young man brought his weapon up to end his father's killer. The monster responded by hurling a ball of flame from one of its clawed hands, forcing him to dodge to one side to avoid being burned alive. He lashed out with the tongue, catching the bipedal acid-mouthed thing along the side of the head with the ragged surface of his improvised weapon. The wound that formed poured a dark and foul substance from it but looked otherwise superficial.

In its pain, the creature briefly looked away, allowing the young man to close the distance and slam his shoulder low into its body. It dug its claws into the body armor on his back and brought him along with it as it went tumbling down onto the observation deck and through the broken glass to the cavern floor below. The young man tumbled with the profane creature only for a moment before righting himself and jamming the muzzle of the Outsider into its mouth and squeezing off another couple of rounds. Four rounds left in the mag.

As he stood, one of the remaining quadrupeds hurled itself at his back, raking with its claws through the body armor straight down into his flesh. The young man let out a pained cry, but the pain only served to focus his resolve. He reached over his shoulder, wrapped an arm around the creature's neck, and tore it free into a shoulder throw with all his strength. The creature landed hard on the spikes of the biped, impaling it and rendering it immobile. He spared a moment to loop the tongue around its neck and pull, nearly popping the head free.

Instead of remaining to finish the job, he made his way back up the stairs toward the observation deck, glancing over his shoulder at the stone slab. The text on it glowed, and the surface shifted almost like liquid. Storming through the lab, he dumped the rest of his rounds into a couple more of the creatures. When he pulled a spare mag from his belt, another of the bipeds took advantage, slapping his weapon from his grip and carving his abdomen open.

The young man held the fresh wound with one hand while snatching a handheld drill from a nearby table with the other. He flicked it on and drove it into the head of the creature that had mistakenly believed him to be done for. The creature thrashed around briefly, reeking blood spraying as its teeth gnashed wildly in an attempt to bring him down with it before slipping lifelessly to the floor.

As he stepped over the quartered body of his baby sister, his vision filled with red. More of the creatures came, and more fell before his wrath. Anything he could get his hands on became a weapon. Rock samples, a powered surgical saw, and even metal trays.

The blood of the creatures was black against the red of the emergency lights, painting every surface he passed amidst his rampage. Soon, he was so blinded with un-bridled rage that he resorted to his fists. Though the creatures tore into him every few seconds, he pressed on. He crushed a biped's skull against the corner of a table before stepping over the mutilated body of a lab assistant whose name he knew to enter the cryo storage room.

"Mom—" he murmured, his eyes settling on the eviscerated body of the woman lying at the foot of one of the pods. His rage cooled as sorrow took hold, dousing the flames inside him with the ice water of agony. He became suddenly aware of how tired he was—how weak his body felt. Looking down, he tried to take inventory of his wounds but found them beyond counting beneath a cascade of crimson down his torso. The most glaring of his injuries were the entrails he was barely managing to hold in with one hand.

There were no more of the creatures in the lab, which was perhaps fortunate, though he would have relished the opportunity to kill even more. Still, as furious and full of hate as he was, the spots in his vision and vertigo had returned. Stumbling toward his perfect, beautiful mother, the young man spared what strength he could to bring his hand across her face, closing the lids of her wide, glassy, lifeless eyes. Pieces of various technicians were scattered around the room, but it looked like they or his mother had got one of the pods online.

With no other course of action left to take, the young man activated the cryo-pod and rolled into it as the lid closed, hoping that one of the others—or anyone from Moon-shot—would lock the area down and find him inside before he died.

As he thought of the profane evil that slaughtered his family, he knew what he'd devote his life to in the unlikely event of his survival.

CHAPTER 1

THE ASTROMETRIC LAB OF the SANS Midnight Sea sat dark and quiet, with only a few blinking lights on scattered consoles to indicate that it was still operational. One of the lights switched from blinking to solid, also shifting its color from red to green in the process.

A young female voice from the bridge spoke into the darkness through the comm panel. "Bridge to Overmaiden."

Another console lit up with a few blue lights, and a stronger feminine voice responded, "This is Overmaiden; go ahead."

"I'm sorry to bother you, ma'am," the voice replied. "Captain Horne is asking for an update."

"Tell him I'll be there in a moment," the second voice replied politely. "Overmaiden, out."

A moment later, glowing lights spread across the consoles as each one came out of standby. Innumerable lines of code were fed into each system, executing an untold number of tasks within seconds. Overhead, the holographic projectors blinked and shimmered as they came online. In the middle of the room, a three-dimensional map of the area surrounding the Midnight Sea formed. From the shadows beyond the display, a figure emerged, outlined in glowing blue.

Composed entirely of data streams formed of light, the Overmaiden emerged from her diagnostics to examine the data. As a sixth-generation "Ghost AI," the Overmaiden wasn't required to view the map visually to understand its contents; the data could be processed automatically through various ship's subsystems and fed into her core matrix directly. However, due to the nature of her particular model of AI, she often chose to engage in human-like activities that other AIs would not deem strictly necessary.

Her form was humanoid despite glowing a soft blue and white, with lines of code running through parts of her translucent body, specifically the figure-hugging bodysuit that made her femininity only too obvious. She had the appearance of an attractive woman dressed in a skin-tight uniform with her hair down to her shoulders and wavy. She exuded an air of classical beauty from what many would simply call "the old days."

The map before her rotated and zoomed out before snapping to another location quite distant from her own. There, she was able to see the ongoing engagement of the group they had left behind to carry out their mission. The view zoomed in, displaying real-time updates of frigates clashing with the newest and most deadly threat to the Sol Alliance: Demons. The planetside Marines were being annihilated despite her best efforts. She had been the one to calculate the best attack vectors and their respective odds before her departure, but it hadn't been enough. Even the frigates were buckling under the overwhelming pressure applied by the horde before them. At this rate, they'd have to scorch the planet's surface entirely.

She reviewed the movements of the entire horde from the moment they appeared to the present in the blink of an eye. Casualties mounted on both sides, but unlike humanity and many other alien species, Demons didn't care about their dead. In most instances, they simply abandoned their fallen entirely, letting them fester and poison the worlds they were left behind on. In some cases, the biomass was recycled in a poorly understood process and redeployed into another part of the war.

Each horde was analogous to an immense army, with its own command structure of increasingly powerful and terrifying Demonic monstrosities and entities. The casualties of the Demons dwarfed that of humanity, but again, it didn't matter to them in the slightest. They kept coming without signs of slowing and without regard for the damage they took. There always seemed to be more of them—an infinite supply of troops to throw at the Sol Alliance and whatever other sentient species got in their way.

The Overmaiden frowned as she ran the most updated projections. There wasn't much of a chance that the men engaged with the horde were going to make it out alive. It seemed likely that they would be dead to the last man. She rotated the map with a wave of her hand and took a wider view. It was a problem fleetwide. At this rate, she projected an overwhelming defeat of the entire Sol Alliance by the end of the decade. Complete annihilation could follow mere months later. She viewed each of the worlds that had been taken and those that had yet to even hear of the threat.

She collapsed the map into a tiny pearl of glowing light, putting the system on standby before transferring her holo-matrix to the bridge. The projectors on the bridge came on-line a second before the Overmaiden appeared for the crew to see. The ops officer that had summoned her motioned toward the door to the captain's office.

The rest of the bridge was relatively dark while they ran in stealth mode. A ship the size of the Midnight Sea wasn't designed for stealth, but clever retrofitting allowed them to have a functional array provided they re-routed power from other systems. The stealth was imperfect, but it made them less tempting and less threatening on sensors.

The Overmaiden vanished from her spot to reappear just outside the captain's office, remotely triggering the door chime through the computer. The door opened, and the AI's projected hologram stepped inside.

Captain Christopher Horne sat behind his desk, looking over the glowing readouts in front of him. Though he was on the far side of middle-aged, the man was in excellent shape and health according to his last physical. His hair had been a distant memory for over thirty years, but the black beard peppered with silver more than made up for it. He looked up at her with steel-gray eyes as the door shut behind her.

"Sorry to wake you," he said, waving a hand to dismiss the reports. It wasn't a matter of privacy or security, as she had the same access to them that he did, but more a matter of courtesy. Not all humans treated AI as people, but Captain Horne had seemingly always found that treating the Overmaiden as such lent itself to a healthier ship dynamic and more comfortable conversation. "I need a report."

"It's not looking good," the Overmaiden admitted freely. "Current projections are showing a near ninety-nine percent casualty rate. Even with the extra fighters we left behind for them."

"Goddammit," Horne muttered, running a hand across his smooth scalp. "Un-fucking-acceptable. What are our options?"

"We can't afford to turn back now," the AI cautioned. "And we can't drop stealth to tell them to break off their engagement. We have to hope they'll come to that conclusion independently."

"Not likely," the captain scoffed as he pushed back out of his chair and stood. His uniform hung a little looser on his frame than the Overmaiden had last noticed, well-pressed though it was.

"You've lost several kilograms," the AI observed. "Have you been skipping meals?"

"Mmm," the captain rumbled, refusing to answer the question directly. Instead, he turned to look out the office viewport with his hands clasped behind his back. "We're going to lose this war, aren't we?"

"I'm afraid it seems so, sir," the Overmaiden replied darkly. "So far, the core worlds are untouched, but we're losing colonies almost every day now. The outer colonies, specifically, are almost entirely gone."

"And your project?" Horne asked without turning to face her. "Has there been progress there?"

The sensitive nature of the classified projects being undertaken on the ship was the only reason the captain had allowed himself to give the order to leave so many other ships behind. Chief among the projects was Project Brutality, but the fact that it had not yet borne fruit for them was becoming an increasingly sore spot between the captain and the AI. "I'm afraid it was the same last time I checked, though I will be seeking an immediate update."

"Check again," the captain ordered. "Give Cosgrove a kick in the ass if you have to. I need something actionable to justify a sophisticated ship like this one not being in the main fight with the rest of the fleet, understand? So far, I've got fuck-all to show for our trying and half a mind to join the fight myself."

"Yes, captain," she acknowledged.

He glanced over his shoulder at her and nodded his head slightly. "Dismissed."

The Overmaiden's form flickered and vanished, appearing a second later in the lab alongside Dr. Clement Cosgrove and his young prodigy of an assistant, Dr. Mandy Hughes. Cosgrove was in his sixties with bleach-white hair and a rather unassuming stature. Were it not for his lab coat and considerable reputation, one would never guess that he was one of the most renowned scientific minds in numerous fields in the entire Alliance.

Hughes was in her twenties, by contrast, and had fewer accomplishments under her belt, though not for lack of trying. She was a gifted woman when it came to her work, with an intellect beyond her years, but her hesitancy to lend her services to the military until recently had limited her prospects for most of her life until signing on for Project Brutality. She was the first of the two to notice the AI's hologram standing in the lab with them, glancing over at her briefly with her bright blue eyes. "Overmaiden?"

Cosgrove didn't bother to look up from his scope. "Has the captain sent you to harass me again?"

"I'm afraid so, doctor," the Overmaiden responded, placing her hands behind her back. "He's becoming agitated, as I think you can understand."

"I am aware of his mental state," Cosgrove responded, continuing his observations through the scope. "Let's not forget who commissioned this project. Were it up to me, we would have taken a different route, but we've come this far."

The Overmaiden tilted her head to the side, glancing at Hughes before turning her attention to the wall of samples and failed tests drifting in transparent containers. "I know, but it's imperative that we do it precisely as I've laid out."

"I'm afraid I have to agree with Dr. Cosgrove," Mandy responded. "The serum would be more viable if we were allowed to trim it down and administer it to the most qualified Marines. We would have a lot more to work with instead of pinning all our hopes on a single individual."

"That would require the exclusion of the Zintari DNA," the Overmaiden objected. "Which is what holds the Demonic and Angelic aspects of the serum together. Without it, the two fail to pair. Your own research has shown this."

"Yes, but," Mandy swallowed nervously, "wouldn't it be better to synthesize something more beneficial to more people? I understand how powerful the results could be from this particular serum but it's a huge 'if' we have to tag onto it."

"Synthesizing a single dose of this is something we can manage, but creating and mass-producing a new super soldier cocktail at the eleventh hour, then finding a way to distribute it to the entire Marine corp, is impractical to say the least. Demons are creatures of chaos, hatred, and torment Dr.

Hughes," the Overmaiden argued calmly. "Yet their hordes are highly organized—efficient. They care nothing for their own safety, charging forth on the orders of greater Demons who keep a tight leash on them. Without those generals and the subsequent command structure, hordes fall apart—even going so far as to cannibalize each other before a new general can be created or appointed. It's not clear how they come about, but the fact is that it wouldn't matter if we could eliminate enough of them in rapid succession. It's the only way to be sure."

"So you're saying that one super, ultra, giga Marine that can take out generals is more valuable than a bunch of super soldiers that can't—and that we can't even practically create in time." Mandy chewed her lip, realizing that the Overmaiden was lecturing her like she was back in school again.

The Overmaiden raised a brow and continued. "Correct. Using the same serum on multiple subjects will also dilute its power among them, so the more we have, the less useful they'll be—that's the way we hypothesize this serum will work. Therefore, to win this war, we need something agile at maximum potency that we can rapidly deploy and retrieve at will. We need something small, compact, and precise, like a scalpel, not a cudgel. We also need to avoid the chance that whatever this serum yields attacks more of its kind, the way that the Zintari have been known to do in the past."

"At least until we have a little more breathing room, anyway," Cosgrove added. "Then we can experiment more with mass producing something similar."

"Magical blood is difficult to predict," the Overmaiden cautioned the younger scientist. "Your work will be critical going forward, but we can't afford to skip steps or back down now. We lost a great deal of men obtaining what samples we used to synthesize these experimental serums. Abandoning it now is not an option."

"Nor needed," Cosgrove announced as he looked up from the scope. "It seems that we've done it."

"R-really!?" Mandy exclaimed, her jaw practically hitting the floor. "You're sure?"

Cosgrove glanced at her calmly before nodding slowly. "The results are stable. Now, it's a matter of securing the proper subject to pair the serum to. That's where you come in."

The older doctor pressed a button on his console, swept the icon to one side, and then provided a retinal scan for his credentials, authorizing the synthesis of a full dose of the serum. The machine before him hummed to life as flickering lights within went about fabricating what he asked for. The Overmaiden watched in awed silence.

Mandy took a deep breath and let it out slowly through her mouth. "Wow, just like that?"

"Just like that," Cosgrove echoed, reaching into the machine once it was finished and pulling out the vial of bright orange fluid. They all regarded it silently for a moment before he handed it over to her. "Load it into your injector."

The young woman took the vial delicately and retreated to her workstation, where her injector was. When the time came, it would be her duty to administer the serum to the subject they chose.

"You've gone over the candidates?" Cosgrove inquired of the Overmaiden.

"Yes, several of your recommendations were quite intriguing," the Overmaiden answered. She hadn't approved all of them, but there had been a sweet spot where his, Mandy's, and her own candidates intersected. "I've already had them re-assigned under me for observation."

The door to the lab came open and the Marine assigned to guard the door stepped inside. "Ma'am, I've just been informed that we're approaching Aonus and are set to exit hyperspace in a few minutes."

The Overmaiden glanced at the Marine and nodded. "Excellent, corporal. Inform my men to prepare themselves. We'll be heading planetside once we're in range."

"Ma'am," the corporal responded uneasily. "The report says that the horde's incursion on the planet is eighty percent higher than expected strength."

The Overmaiden exchanged glances with Dr. Cosgrove. "That will make for a more effective test, I suppose."

"If you say so," Cosgrove replied, looking over toward his younger assistant, prepping the injector. "Try not to get poor

Mandy killed if you don't mind. It'd be terribly inconvenient to train a new one all over again."

"Of course," the Overmaiden agreed. The candidates they'd chosen had all been consolidated into a single platoon and placed in her command. It was unusual for any AI to be given command of so many human lives, but her particular mission and set of skills set her apart from others, even among her peers of Ghost AIs. Each Marine had been handpicked for their exemplary records, special skills, and personal traits, but there was only so much they could glean from reports and files. She had to see them in action to be sure.

The Overmaiden's eyes settled back on the corporal waiting at the door. "You have your orders, corporal."

The Marine acknowledged the order with a firm salute and stepped out of the room to get her platoon up on comms. It was something she could have managed on her own, but she found herself preoccupied with the possibilities of what was to come. She couldn't keep her matrix from processing all the various scenarios they were likely to encounter, even going so far as to indulge in the scenarios that were very unlikely.

"Are you having second thoughts, Overmaiden?" Mandy asked as she approached the two now that the injector in her gauntlet was loaded and ready.

"No," the AI whispered tentatively. "But I believe I am experiencing...Hope."

Chapter 2

Dr. Mandy Hughes examined the medical gauntlet for the third time since boarding the dropship. She'd experienced nervousness before, but none compared to what she felt as the vessel careened out of the docking bay and descended to the surface of Aonus. The Overmaiden stood near the cockpit with her hands clasped behind her back, perfectly balanced by the compensators built into her sophisticated mobile emitter. Mandy was relegated to the back with the Marines.

"Another glorious day in the corps!" the Master Sergeant shouted over the engines and the sound of the ship hitting the atmosphere at speed. Despite the rough ride, he maintained his balance almost as well as the Overmaiden, occasionally using a hand to grasp the overhead straps. He was a tall man, even out of the powered armor he wore. In it, he resembled one of the golems of old. The illusion was broken only by the fact that he preferred to keep his helmet off to make room for the cigar he held firmly in his teeth.

"I love the smell of Demon blood in the morning. How 'bout you, Ramirez?" He laughed as he passed the Marine with the name in question displayed prominently on his chest plate.

"Nothing sweeter, Sarge," Ramirez agreed.

"Fuckin' right, boy," the Master Sergeant said, slapping the top of the Marine's helmet a few times in approval. "What's the matter, Hughes? You look like you're about to paint my nice clean deck with puke."

Mandy glanced down at the rough, black metal of the deck and raised a brow. "Field work isn't exactly my specialty. And I've never been so close to an actual incursion before."

"Well, then we'll be sure to be gentle with you, Doc," the Master Sergeant declared loudly before placing a reassuring hand on her shoulder. Leaning closer, he plucked the cigar from his mouth and lowered his voice. "Don't you worry. We'll get you back to the ship in one piece. You do your job, and we'll do ours—easy as pie."

"Okay, Master Sergeant," Mandy responded, swallowing nervously despite the encouragement. She wasn't sure where this confidence was coming from, but it was rubbing off on her a little.

"You can call me Gray, Doc," the Master Sergeant said before standing upright and replacing the cigar in his mouth.

"But I better not hear that shit coming out of any of you fuck-knuckles, understood?"

"Aye, aye, Sarge!" the Marines acknowledged in roaring unison. Following that, the ship's rocking intensified for a moment as they entered the lower atmosphere before abating.

Mandy glanced out the viewport to see the damage that had been inflicted on the landscape alone. By all accounts, Aonus had a very Earth-like atmosphere despite its larger size and the presence of three moons. The surface was a little more rugged than Earth's average, but the temperate climate most of the planet enjoyed gave the colonists of the world numerous options on where to settle. Now, it was covered in fire.

Trees, plant life, and numerous structures had been set ablaze by the incursion. Many of the buildings had been partially melted, indicating the presence of acid-spitting Demons as well as the type that hurled fire from its hands. Mandy had never been an expert on Demons, but her assignment to the Midnight Sea and the escalation of the Demonic incursion throughout occupied space were certainly providing her with a crash course.

"Damn. The surface is absolutely swarming with the bastards," The pilot informed them over the comms. "I'll need you and your boys to clear an LZ for me before I can set the doctor and the Overmaiden down."

"Hear that?" Gray called back to the Marines seated along either side of the ship. "We got ourselves a welcoming party!"

The Master Sergeant made a quick motion with one hand, signaling the men to prepare themselves. Each of the Marines situated themselves upright in their seats before thin sections of the ship opened up behind them. The seats pushed back and rotated, placing them in the readied position.

"Whooo! Let's kick this pig!" a Marine with the name "Cox" displayed on his chest plate hollered into the comms.

"I heard they do something else with pigs where you're from," a female Marine by the name of Chambers responded, causing a raucous round of laughter among the others.

"Get ready," the pilot announced, cutting across the chatter of the Marines. "This is Shotgun Opera to Midnight Sea, about to make contact with the horde on Aonus. Clearing an LZ."

"Go ahead, Shotgun Opera," the officer from the Midnight Sea acknowledged. "And godspeed."

"No sign of God here." The co-pilot then counted down the drop and then toggled a switch on the console, turning a red light in the drop bays to green. "Go, go, go!"

Gripping their weapons tight, the Marines leaped from the ship without a moment of hesitation, the safety harnesses popping free of each one as they went. The distance they fell was much greater than any human would have survived unscathed, but the Marines' power armor was built to withstand such impact, equipped with various shock absorbers in the joints.

Mandy clutched the gauntlet even tighter as the sounds of gunfire, accompanied by hooting and hollering, filled the comms. She was seconds from peeing herself while the Marines appeared to be having the time of their lives.

At least one other 'sort-of' woman on board seemed to match her tense energy. "Careful of Vesper Demons," the Overmaiden cautioned the pilot calmly in her husky voice, her glowing blue eyes scanning the sky through the frontside viewport.

"Scanners are clear, ma'am," the pilot answered calmly, if a bit curtly. Glancing back at her, he saw that she was still staring at him. Clearing his throat, he checked the scanners again. "I'll keep my eyes open, though."

Mandy remembered the Vesper Demons from the brief. It was a type of winged Demon vaguely resembling a monstrous, hairless bat. They had a tendency to rain acid on ground troops and attach themselves to critical parts of ships in the atmosphere to bring them down. They were fast, stealthy, and capable of hunting by sonar, which doubled as a weapon in some instances. If they saw you before you saw them, it was practically already over, or so the document said.

The ship lurched, and Mandy let out a brief squeak. That caught the attention of the Master Sergeant, who was to serve as their personal escort when they finally landed. "Ground fire. Nothing to worry about, Doc. Armor of this bird is too thick for that," he assured her. "Check your gear."

Mandy nodded quickly and did as she was told, her hands shaking the whole time. She knew the gauntlet was ready; she'd checked it at least a hundred times by that point, but she could always check once more. It had numerous medical functions useful in the field, including a host of disinfectants, analgesics, an in-built surgical saw, adrenal injections, and bio-foam for a wide range of wounds. It also had one of the most impressive field medical scanners she'd ever seen. Today, however, the Project Brutality serum was the most crucial component contained within it.

The rest of her gear was less familiar to her, but she knew the basics. She'd been provided a suit of semi-powered armor often used by the Medical Corps of the Marines. It was white with red trim as opposed to the tan and green of the soldiers. It lacked many of the higher-end features of power armor but provided her with much more protection than the lightweight gear that the Navy typically used aboard the ship. Her helmet was linked to comms at all times and had a visor that provided her with a useful HUD when things got really chaotic. Her chest plate was polarized, much like power armor, but couldn't take nearly as much punishment.

"Coming about," the pilot announced in response to one of the Marines on the ground, letting them know they had a landing zone open for them. The ship banked hard to one side, setting Mandy further on edge, and then it began its descent. She felt the ship slow considerably before the bay along the back of the ship opened like a large, yawning metal monster.

The Overmaiden passed by her, confidently gesturing for her to follow with one hand as she did. Mandy bounded to her feet and fell in behind the AI's hologram and the Master Sergeant. It was like a furnace as they stepped off the ramp of the ship. Mandy felt the internal systems of her armor begin cooling her almost immediately to compensate for the heat thrown off by the flames of the incursion. Once they were clear of the ship, it lifted off once again.

Scores of Demon bodies were piled high around them in various states of disembowelment and similar grisly fates. The Marines formed up on their position even as they finished off the last of the stragglers in their immediate area.

"Ah, I love the feeling of the wind in my hair," Gray remarked, taking a deep breath in and letting it out dramatically. Mandy resisted the urge to point out that with how short his hair was, there wasn't much to feel the wind through.

"I didn't think you could call that scalp-stubble hair, Sarge," Cox quipped as he did a quick local scan with some of the specialized instruments on his power armor.

"It's always been enough for your mother to run her fingers through," Gray countered, eliciting a chorus of laughter from the other Marines. The Master Sergeant plucked the cigar from his mouth as he adopted a more serious demeanor. "Alright, Marines, listen up! We're going to carve a bloody path into town to see if there are any survivors. We'll establish a base camp at—"

"Sarge," Cox interrupted. "I'm picking up an active distress signal routed through the local subnet. Location seems to be the local geology lab of Orco Industries. It's got a MoonShot tag on it."

"MoonShot?" Gray echoed with surprise. Mandy knew the private security company had a sterling reputation among their peers, but she'd never heard of them tangling with a Demon incursion before. The Master Sergeant's gaze shifted toward the Overmaiden, who looked thoughtful for a moment before giving him a brief nod.

"Alright, let's start there!" Gray ordered as the Marines fell into formation. Once they were set, they began to trek west toward the origin of the distress signal.

"Stay close to me," the Overmaiden ordered Mandy as softly as she could. "The barrier field of my emitter will offer you additional protection."

"Alright," Mandy responded informally, typically one to forget the etiquette in stressful situations. Mandy wasn't part of the military, after all. She was essentially a glorified civilian consultant attached to Dr. Cosgrove. She was an expert in various fields due to her keen intellect and tireless work ethic, but the ones that interested Cosgrove the most when he'd selected her were Mandy's focus on superhuman medicine and biology, along with her deep understanding of human psychology. The fact that she held multiple doctorates in other fields, such as xenobiology, hadn't hurt her case, either.

The Overmaiden was a fascinating specimen to Mandy. She'd briefly studied the theory and history behind Ghost AIs but had never encountered one in person until she'd met her. Unlike standard AI Personalities composed purely of code of an architect's design from the ground up, Ghost AIs were modeled after actual people's uploaded neurological data and soul emissions.

Most Ghost AIs were made from individuals with exemplary records and accomplishments in a particular field. The experiences of the originals were deemed so valuable that they could be preserved well after their death. The Overmaiden was supposedly sixth-generation, meaning that five previous versions of her had existed and been decommissioned, handing down their extensive knowledge and experience each time to the next generation.

Unlike other Ghost AIs, however, the original template on which the Overmaiden was modeled was highly classified. The Overmaiden herself hardly referenced any experiences from her original life, which made her even more mysterious to Mandy. If they were created to preserve that knowledge and experience, why did the Overmaiden never seem to make open use of it? Why did she seem to...guard it?

"We've got incoming," Cox announced, bringing his pulse rifle up. Each of the Marines carried one just like it. Mandy knew it well enough. Nicknamed the "Perforator," it was a favorite of the Marines for its ability to tear through armor and Demon flesh alike with magnetically accelerated case-less ammunition. She'd seen what it could do in simulations and recordings, and it was a sight to behold—and to make one feel ill.

A moment later, someone called out contact as a cluster of Hunter Demons and Soldier Demons descended upon them from the ruins of a nearby building. Hunter Demons moved on four legs, resembling primitive hounds in some respects which had been skinned and refitted with bone plating in places. The flesh across their skulls was pulled tight and deep, empty pits existed where their eyes should logically be. Mandy always found that detail disturbing, knowing how evolution worked. Mimicry was of course a well-document-ed evolutionary concept, but it was like Demons evolved to *mock* and *offend* existing life in the universe rather than imitate it for practical reasons.

Aside from that, Hunters also possessed lethal, ragged tongues that allowed them to scent prey over great distances doubled as weapons in close combat, and strange fin-like organs on the side of their heads allowed them to detect sound and motion.

The Soldier Demons, on the other hand, were bipeds cov-ered in bone spikes. They were best known for hurling fireballs and drooling acid from their toothy maws. Mandy's hand went down to the handgun holstered on her hip, but the Overmaiden gently placed her hand over Mandy's, restraining her.

"Let them work," the AI said calmly as the Marines opened fire. Mandy had to remind herself that the main reason—the *secret* reason—for the mission was to observe the Marines in combat and how they handled themselves. It wasn't merely about their genetic suitability for the serum—at this point all present Marines were confirmed to be more or less compatible. It was about who they were as people, as warriors. They needed to know the quality of the soldier as a whole.

The Marines did not disappoint and did precisely as Gray had commanded them to: They cut a bloody path through the settlement's heart to the Orco Industries complex. As messy and gory as it was just to reach the complex, it was worse inside. The halls were already painted with the blood of staff that had been slain while pieces of their desiccated corpses had been scattered haphazardly up and down the corridors. Mandy gagged many times and even self-medicated to keep from vomiting.

The emergency lighting was barely operational, forcing them to switch to their visors to see in the darker sections of the building. They didn't want to shine any lights and end up inadvertently attracting things that dwelt in the darkness.

"Stay alert," Ramirez whispered over comms as they turned a corner. Mandy saw why once she caught up from his position near the rear of the formation. The entire hallway had been rebuilt and reformed using the flesh of the people in the facility. "Drones."

Drones were the standard builders of the horde, though the term was often used loosely. They were the ones responsible for converting the flesh of the fallen, be it the enemy or their own, into structures that Demons could use as bases and other critical infrastructure. They could stretch muscle, reshape skin, and transmute bone with a few profane incantations and their bare hands.

"Probably some Forsaken too," Chambers muttered back as she hugged the left wall tightly. Though not technically full Demons, the Forsaken were dead human bodies possessed by the Demonic spirits or animated by the Profane Energy of Hell itself. Some shambled like mindless zombies, while others could be possessed of burning hatred that propelled them at superhuman speeds with supernatural strength. Where there were Drones at work, there were often Forsaken.

The humidity and putrescence of the corridor made it difficult for Mandy to breathe. Her stomach lurched and turned numerous times as if trying to escape and leave the rest of her body behind. It was one of the single most traumatic experiences of her still-young life, but for these experienced Marines, it was a Tuesday.

As Cox passed one of the growths along the wall on the right, it peeled away from the rest of the biomass and hurled itself at the Marine. Cox, as cavalier as he could be, was not caught unaware. As the Forsaken leaped onto him, he turned his body to use its momentum against it, slamming it into an opposite wall and placing the muzzle of his weapon in its mouth before pulling the trigger. The sound caused a chorus of screams and wailing to fill the air from beyond the corridor.

"Motherfucker," a Marine by the name of Wall snarled as he stepped up to the front of the line, his weapon at the ready. "Where are we even fucking going?"

Mandy glanced at the visor of her helmet and decided to make herself useful. Detecting her eye movements and sensing some neural activity, the visor allowed her to move through the menus quickly, delving into the local subnet where she pulled up a basic map of the facility. There, she isolated the signal that Cox had detected earlier and plotted a course for the Marines as they once again opened fire on a nest of Demons flooding up from the lower levels. Unfortunately, that was precisely where they were going.

Curiously, there also appeared to be a sporadic ping of Profane Energy originating from the area as well. She distributed the map and directions to the Marines' armor while they worked.

"Interesting," the Overmaiden noted of the Profane Energy as she accessed the proposed route.

"This is bullshit," Cox snarled as he tore a pair of Forsaken into pieces with his Perforator. "This is a fucking trap, Sarge!"

Gray glanced at the Overmaiden as he turned to face the rear, cutting down a cluster of Forsaken that had attempted to flank them. His cigar shifted from one side of his mouth to the other uneasily. Silently he seemed to agree with Cox, Mandy noted, but he wasn't going to issue an order until the AI had her say.

"Let's get to that lab," the Overmaiden concluded with a thoughtful look on her face. "Follow the doctor's route."

"Ma'am?" the Master Sergeant inquired as if he'd misheard her.

"I've got a good feeling about this," the AI responded, shooting him a confident look.

That was good enough for Gray, who turned forward and ordered the Marines on. Despite their misgivings, they did as they were told and followed Mandy's route precisely. Most of the Forsaken appeared to have been scientists and other technical personnel, which meant that they weren't carrying much in the way of weapons. Forsaken could be smart enough to use weaponry but often didn't seek it out for some unknown reason.

"The fuck is this?" Ramirez asked as they finally reached the lab. Not only were there numerous human corpses littering the area but also the torn and mutilated remains of various Hunter and Soldier Demons. "Shit got real, eh?"

"Secure that door," Gray ordered as the last of the formation entered the lab. Mandy glanced around, her brow furrowed at the decayed chaos that had transpired.

"They must have triggered the distress signal before the Demons took them out," Chambers guessed, turning one of the dead civilians over with her foot. "Poor bastards."

Cox approached the end of an observation platform at the far end of the lab, lowering his weapon slowly. "Fuck me, would you look at that?"

A few of the other Marines joined him, looking down into an open cavern that had been mined. At the center of the cavern's floor stood a monolithic stone with glowing symbols along its edges, the center of which shifted around like a liquid.

"What am I looking at here, ma'am?" the Master Sergeant asked, his tone bordering on informal as he regarded the formation with dread.

"It's an ancient Zintari portal," the Overmaiden answered, observing the formation coolly from behind the Marines. "At least, it was. It appears to have been modified some-how—altered."

Mandy's eyes widened at the mention of the Zintari—an ancient class of elevated humans that possessed extraordinary powers and abilities. Few had been seen over the last few centuries, though it was known that they still existed. However, even the existing Zintari were not *true* Zintari, owing to the fact that the ancient ones of their number hadn't been human at all. It was a distinction that few bothered to make anymore, in any case. Mandy did because it was her job to—namely, because it was part of what composed the serum for Project Brutality housed in her medical gauntlet.

"Over here!" Wall called, emerging from one of the lab's side rooms. A streaky trail of blood and gore led into the room, causing Mandy to question what terrible scene awaited them. She, the Overmaiden, and the Master Sergeant joined Wall in the room while the others fanned out to secure and reconnoiter the area. Two large Marines remained at the door that they'd managed to force closed.

As they stepped into the room, they found more casualties, but also a group of cryopods that hadn't been fully installed. After a brief examination, Mandy could see that the research staff had intended to use them to store samples of their new finds deep below the planet's surface, but they had been interrupted mid-installation. One of the pods—the only fully functional one—was occupied by a person. A survivor. Sort of.

"He's in real bad shape," Wall noted, directing their attention to the man's innards, half-spilled out of his body, held in place only with his hand. Mandy gasped at the sight of that, but almost gasped again when she saw his face. Under normal circumstances, the young man would have been ruggedly handsome, but somehow pretty, too—entirely her type in a way that the other men in her life, present company included, were not. It was a damn pity he endured such a fate. His odds of surviving just his visible wounds, even in cryosleep, were next to none.

"MoonShot," Wall added. "He's on the lab security team, judging by the badge. Big bastard, and apparently tough. Could be the one who put out the distress signal."

"Would have made a good Marine," one of the men added. "Now what?"

Mandy stepped forward, her hand moving over the panels of the pod to examine the state of the handsome occupant within. It was just as Wall had said. He was in very bad shape. Even if they could get the whole pod out and keep the cryo state active, then somehow carry it back aboard the Midnight Sea, there was a good chance that they wouldn't be able to help him. The fact he had made it far enough to toggle a distress signal or crawl into a cryopod with all his injuries was a minor miracle. He must have been operating on pure adrenaline.

"Probably best if we put the poor bastard out of his misery," Wall remarked dejectedly. Mandy noted the dark tone of his voice and frowned along with him. The Marine had thought he'd found a survivor for a moment and was now looking at putting a bullet between his eyes to end his suffering.

"Take a look at his biometrics," the Overmaiden said to Mandy. "Compare it to the project profile."

Mandy looked back at the hologram incredulously. "You've got to be joking. This man is on death's doorstep. He'll die within minutes in the event of cryosleep deactivation."

The Overmaiden stared at her silently until the doctor activated her gauntlet to run the scan. Mandy, confused but obedient, watched the feed come in on her visor and was surprised to find that despite the damage to the man's body, he was an excellent match to the biological profile. Better than any of the Marines, even, even at a glance. To find such a person in such a remote place, working for a security company, of all things, was incredible. But there was no getting around the massive physical trauma.

"He'd be perfect, honestly," Mandy reported, looking into the face of the young man. Though still open, his eyes looked a little glassy already. "Assuming he would survive the injection, anyway."

"Thaw him out," the Overmaiden responded after a moment of thought. "Then do it. No delay, no hesitation."

"Ma'am!?" Mandy objected, shocked and immediately stepping back from the pod. None of the Marines present knew what they were talking about, of course—Project Brutality was kept a secret from them for good reason. The Marines amusingly glanced between the two, cluelessly waiting to see how things played out.

"That's an order, *Dr. Hughes*," the AI pressed, motioning toward the pod with a brief nod of her head. "Trust me. More importantly, *obey* me."

Mandy remained silent, looking back at the Overmaiden skeptically before stepping forward again and toggling the pod with one hand. As it opened, she was quick to move around the side and place the palm of her gauntlet on the man's chest before he began to bleed out. The powerful needle of the syringe shot from the gauntlet's wrist, puncturing deep into the young man's chest, where it deposited the serum directly into his heart.

Just as the thawing process took hold, the man's body seized. Mandy cycled through the readout on her visor, providing her with the man's vitals. She selected a medication to prepare for tissue repair. Maybe, she thought, she could save him if she got his insides back on his inside.

She injected him again as he seized and spasmed, moving right into carefully jabbing his guts back in through the grievous wound of his abdomen. But before she could get much of it in, the man flatlined and went limp. "Dammit," she groaned. "Fuck!"

She stepped back from the cryopod to join the rest of the group, lingering in silence. What a waste of the serum. Wall turned away as Gray glanced between the AI and the doctor in an attempt to discern what had just happened. The Overmaiden remained unmoved, however, watching the body in the cryopod unwaveringly.

"I don't know what you expected," Mandy murmured, double-checking the readouts on her visor before she glanced back at the young man. She froze then. Apparently she spoke too soon.

Not only were his eyes open, but they were also more focused and intense than before. The ruggedly beautiful young man lifted his head slowly, looking down at the wound in his abdomen as the damage repaired itself.

The Master Sergeant's cigar fell out of his mouth as he gawked at the intestines while they crawled back into the young man's body. "Son of a bitch."

CHAPTER 3

THE OVERMAIDEN OBSERVED THE young man as he emerged from the cryopod, looking much different than he had moments before. Heralded by a series of cracks, pops, and other horrendous sounds, the man, previously at death's door, had been virtually reborn, his body growing and changing as it responded to the serum.

The changes were very satisfying. Already well built, his muscle mass had nonetheless increased by over two hundred fifteen percent, and his body elongated to a nearly inhuman height of approximately seven feet tall, if standing. The young man's godlike figure looked as though he had been chiseled from stone or even the bulkhead of a starship. The Overmaiden watched as his dark, shadowed eyes flitted from one person to another in the room as the healing process in his abdomen completed. He remained silent, though his intense eyes grew calmer by the second.

The young man stood, prompting Dr. Hughes to make an undignified sound. At his new height and mass, his old clothes no longer fit. They hung from his frame in tatters or fell off him completely, leaving nothing to the imagination.

Before the Overmaiden could say a word in greeting to him, or before Dr. Hughes could utter another embarrassing moan, the young man's face twisted with fury and stared past them as he ripped the entire cryopod out of the wall, raised it over his head as though it were weightless, and hurled it in their direction.

Everyone ducked or flinched away from the massive projectile except for the Overmaiden, who was aware of the creatures quietly emerging from one of the nearby service ducts. The cryopod cruised safely over the heads of the Marines and Dr. Hughes and crushed the intruders into Demonic pulp, making satisfying popping and crunching sounds along with the loud clang of heavy metal. When they looked back, they found the pod embedded several feet into the stone behind the wall itself, warping the supports and paneling around it.

"Ho-ho-holy shit!" Cox laughed, clearly impressed. "What the fuck is happening?!" The mashed remains of the Demons oozed slowly from the narrow space between the ruined cryopod and the hole in the wall. Everyone's attention turned back to the nearly naked man, who was now visibly calmer.

"How did you know?" Dr. Hughes murmured to the Over-maiden. The AI couldn't help but look a little satisfied with herself. "He's...perfect."

The hologram gestured to the lab. "I performed my own scans and algorithmic analyses—not only of him, but of the scene we walked into. These were his people. Look what he did not just to protect them, but to avenge them."

Dr. Hughes glanced around at the carnage that was diffi-cult to discern much from due to the chaotic co-mingling of human remains, Demonic bits, and assorted debris. For an AI like the Overmaiden, reconstruction of the scene was relatively simple, however. She fed the sim-ulation to the doctor's visor as she continued to explain.

"Every Demonic corpse we've seen in this facility was likely his handiwork. *These* are the feats we came to see," the Overmaiden explained quietly. "With little more than a sidearm and improvised weapons, this man wreaked pure havoc on our greatest existential threat. He is pos-sessed of a singular determination that is difficult to quantify. Paired with your more detailed biometric scans, I was absolutely certain we had found what we came for, and that the serum would take to him flawlessly."

"What about the rest of them?" Dr. Hughes whispered, glancing at the unnamed man as he brushed past them toward the main lab. "Was it all pointless to bring them?"

"Not at all," the Overmaiden assured her. "They got us here, and now our secondary objective has been upgraded to our primary."

"Which is?" Dr. Hughes pressed a little impatiently.

"Secure whatever information we can and evacuate any remaining survivors," the Overmaiden finished. Though there weren't many survivors to speak of in the lab, it had never been their intended goal to dig them out. Once they got back out into the town and the surrounding area, she expected they would find people holed up in relatively secure locations running low on supplies. Most colonies had emergency bunkers in the event of a disaster or acts of alien aggression. Such defenses weren't built to withstand prolonged Demonic incursion, but there was still a chance that many had simply been overlooked.

The young man, now augmented to the point of godliness, scrounged the lab for whatever he could find as a weapon, not waiting around for instructions or particularly interested in hearing any explanations for his upgraded state. Each of the Marines stood back to watch him, unsure of what to make of the individual. They watched patiently, waiting for orders from the Overmaiden, who clearly had the monopoly on information here. They knew better than to make demands of her, but she could tell they were getting antsy and wouldn't stand by for much longer.

She approached the young man, who seemed to be judging the merits of using a metal table as a cudgel, swinging it to-and-fro. "Who are you, if you don't mind my asking?" the Overmaiden inquired politely, hands still clasped calmly behind her back. "Your name, I mean?"

The man responded without looking up to acknowledge her properly. "The death of Demonkind."

That got some chuckles out of the Marines, at least. "I like 'em!" the Master Sergeant proclaimed heartily. "He's got spunk, at least!"

The Overmaiden, for her part, was a bit frustrated by the non-answer. "What I mean is, what is your name?"

"I have no need for names anymore."

She muted herself as she sighed.

By the time they reached the surface by retracing their steps, the young man had picked up a small collection of belts, straps, and assorted items to hang from them for the purpose of combat. Chambers offered to spare a few actual weapons for the man, but the Overmaiden held a hand out to stop her—she wanted to see more of what he could do armed with only righteous fury.

"Supporting and cover fire only," the Overmaiden ordered as they stepped into the lobby filled with Hunters scouting for stragglers.

"Ma'am, in case you haven't noticed, he's cock-swinging, ass-clapping, buck-fucking-naked," Cox objected. "They'll tear him to pieces."

"I noticed," Mandy whimpered quietly, staying close to the Overmaiden as though another feminine presence was her one anchor in this situation.

"With a hog as big as his, he could probably club them to death," Chambers remarked, earning a round of uneasy, and maybe jealous, chuckles from the rest. The man's endowment had of course not been lost on the Overmaiden. Custom armor might need to be modified to account for his unusual bulk in more ways than one.

She also noted that Dr. Hughes was interested in the size differential as well, as her eyes lingered far too long in that general zone than could be explained by a purely medical or scientific interest. In fact, the young doctor's eyes practically bulged to the point of rolling out of her head as she constantly flitted her gaze from cock to face to cock and back again. She licked her lips and whimpered something like, "Sweet God Almighty," before forcefully averting her eyes at last.

"This will do," the man said as he fired up a surgical chainsaw he'd lifted from one of the secondary labs on the way to the surface. The Overmaiden recognized it as a model designed specifically for easily cutting through the bones of elephant-sized beasts. What it was doing here of all places, she didn't know for sure, but she wasn't about to complain.

The chainsaw-wielding man hurled himself at the Hunters as they converged on their position. He met the first with a sweep of the chainsaw's blade, wielding the hefty two-handed machine with only one. The blade caught the creature under the jaw, cleaving its skull in half and spraying a line of blood and gore across the lobby's linoleum floor. Not satisfied with simply bifurcating the demon's skull, he rammed the chainsaw into the gooey divide he'd created, churning up the inside of the demon's chest cavity before ripping the chainsaw free.

He caught a leaping Hunter by the neck with his free hand, causing the creature to thrash around wildly with its claws in the air a few feet above the ground. Seeing it wasn't getting anywhere, the Hunter opened its mouth and lashed out with its deadly tongue, which wrapped around the man's thick neck. Before the Demon could pull it tight, the man let out an annoyed growl, cutting the tongue free with the chainsaw before severing the Hunter's lower half from the part he held.

One of the Hunters in the rear of the pack let out a shrieking wail, signaling to its Soldiers to converge on its position.

"Shit's about to get real, folks," Ramirez warned them, hoisting his weapon and readying himself. Seconds later, the front doors of the lobby crashed open as a throng of Soldiers and Forsaken swelled inward.

Dr. Hughes gulped. "Wasn't it real enough already?"

But the Overmaiden placed a hand over Ramirez's rifle, urging it down slowly. "Wait."

With a herculean throw, the young man lobbed the whirring chainsaw through the middle of the group, parting it in a gory parody of Moses and the Red Sea. He replaced the weapon with a TA-12 mining gauntlet he'd picked up along the way and, with a roar of primal fury, hurled himself into the fray heedless of his personal safety. The mining gauntlet was designed with three polarized blades made to cut through some of the hardest materials workers might encounter in the tunnels, augmenting their strength with interior mechanisms at the same time. It wasn't intended as a weapon, and shouldn't really be practical as one in normal hands, but the Overmaiden couldn't argue with the results on display.

At first, the young man's movements were sloppy, driven solely by rage and fury. Even so, Demons fell before him in rapid succession. But as he pressed through the group, his movements became more intentional and precise, pausing only to brutalize the occasional Demon that had truly annoyed him. He did this often at the expense of his safety, with claws, talons, and teeth tearing thin, shallow wounds in his skin with blistering fireballs and acid that followed. The damage, though relatively superficial, would eventually add up if he wasn't careful.

"Alright, Marines," the Master Sergeant called. "Break time's over. We're back on the clock!"

"Master Sergeant," the Overmaiden objected, but the man shot her a withering look.

"With respect, ma'am, we've got places to be," the Master Sergeant replied. "We can't stand around all day with our thumbs up our asses while Nature Boy here takes his sweet time serenading Demons with his lovely singing voice."

The young man let out a primal, guttural roar as if to punctuate the Master Sergeant's point. The Overmaiden let out a defeated sigh and waved her hand. "Very well, go ahead."

"Open fire, Marines!" The Master Sergeant hollered over the chaos, ushering in a hail of gunfire after that narrowed the field of focus for the murderous young man considerably.

The Overmaiden watched with interest as the young man's savagery not only effectively felled the enemy directly but also inspired the Marines, bringing up the rear to do the same. Seeing his reckless abandon instilled confidence in the group, allowing them to make more brazen maneuvers that ended up paying considerable dividends. It was an interesting phenomenon to observe as she and Dr. Hughes brought up the rear.

They emerged onto the street, encountering even more resistance from Demons drawn to the sound of battle and the scent of bloodshed. The clashes came in fits and starts, allowing them to cover a great deal of ground as Cox and Hughes worked in unison to identify signals and biosignatures to investigate. Each stop they made earned them more combat but netted them more lives to be saved.

"Overmaiden to Shotgun Opera," the Overmaiden said aloud, her voice projecting through a comm channel to the dropship awaiting them at high altitude. "We have survivors here on the ground in need of immediate dust off."

"Roger that, Overmaiden," the pilot responded. "ETA in three minutes."

"Clear an LZ," the Master Sergeant ordered, gunning down a pair of Soldier Demons prepping fireballs for the civilians in their care. The bunker hadn't been much, and many of the people were injured in one way or another, but the naked berserker in the Marines' midst was creating a lot of space for them to do more controlled work.

Within moments, the area was open enough for the dropship to touch down, throwing the back ramp open even as it blasted everything around with dust and debris. A few of the Marines peeled off to help survivors onto the ship, securing them in the bay before stepping back off and signaling for the ship to take off.

"Sir, we've got a Vesper coming in at ten o'clock," Wall cautioned the Master Sergeant.

Before any of them could get a bead on the creature, the young man ripped a panel free from the shelter door and hurled it like a discus into the air. The panel tore through the wing of the descending Vesper seconds before it could make contact with the departing dropship. Unable to maintain altitude, the creature plummeted to the ground, where the young man sprinted to meet it. There, he jammed his foot into its back, grabbed hold of the wings at their base, and pulled them free of the demon's body with a wet popping of bone and tearing of sinew.

"He's absolutely insane," Hughes remarked in awe. The Overmaiden detected some distinct shifts in the woman's biometrics, indicating fear, yes, but primarily the obvious blush and body heat that came with arousal.

The doctor eventually pried her eyes off the naked, gore-soaked man to check her visor. She'd tasked herself with monitoring the feeds for survivors to cut down on the amount of information the Marines had to sift through on their HUDs. "More survivors due east."

"Let's move!" the Master Sergeant ordered, pressing on as the dropship disappeared from view on its way to the Midnight Sea.

They managed only a few dozen feet before a towering figure rounded a corner of the nearest ruined building. It towered above even the tallest of humans, save for the berserker leading the pack. It was covered from head to toe with black armor, spiked, bladed, and warped as though the material had been contorted by the torturous attentions of Hell itself. Hateful eyes glowed from within the horned helmet as wisps of acrid smoke curled up through slits in the faceplate.

"Christ, sir," Cox muttered into the comms. "That's a fucking Knight."

"I've got eyes," the Master Sergeant responded, motioning for the Marines to spread out slowly in order to avoid being caught in the larger blasts the Demon was capable of letting loose on a whim.

"The fuck is a Knight doing here?" Ramirez wondered, keeping his rifle trained on the towering figure.

"An interesting question for another time," the Overmaiden replied. She was more interested in how their newest fighter was going to handle the situation.

The answer turned out to be the same as it had been with the others: he charged right in. The Knight stood ready, summoning a massive sword from smoke and hellfire as the blood-soaked man hastily approached.

"The fuck does he think he's doing!?" One of the Marines exclaimed through comms.

As the young man closed the last few feet, the Knight sprung into action, bringing its blade around in a powerful swing that left a searing arc of hellfire behind it as it went. The man intercepted the strike with the mining gauntlet, which barely managed to hold up under the power and magic infusing the Knight's sword. He followed with a swift uppercut into the Demon's armored body, lifting him an inch or two off the ground and causing him to stagger backward a step. Despite the hellscape around them, with all its chaos and destruction, the Overmaiden could have heard a pin drop at that moment as the Marines all went silent.

There was no mistaking the distinct dent that the man's fist had left in the blackened hellplate of the Knight—a feat that had been inconceivable with bare hands until that very moment. Time seemed to slow down as the Knight planted his sword in the ground for additional support while he got his bearings. The young man kicked the sword away with his bare foot, forcing his opponent to stumble forward, where he met him with a haymaker with the mining gauntlet. The Knight spun to one side as pieces of the helmet scattered across the ground. He stumbled several times, dazed by the impact, before falling forward.

The young man glanced at the busted gauntlet and discarded it. Picking up the Knight's sword, he stepped forward and drove the blade into the demon's back, pinning it to the bloodstained earth. Black fluid leaked from the wound for a brief second before the man drove the blade further in—down to the hilt—causing a terrible bubbling to emerge from the wound and the pool of black blood forming beneath his fallen foe.

"Fuck. I think I'm ovulating," Dr. Hughes whispered to herself.

The Overmaiden confirmed an interesting spike in Dr. Hughes' hormone levels as well as those within Julia Chambers. She couldn't blame them. The rest of the Marines stared in awe for a moment before Master Sergeant Gray broke the silence.

"Alright, kids, let's stop standing around and get the fuck on with it, shall we?" he barked, coaxing the group back into action toward the next group of survivors.

They found half a dozen more groups of survivors in that fashion, each recovery resulting in a furious firefight to clear the area for the dropship to convey more survivors to the carrier in orbit. The young man never slowed down, never grew tired, never wavered, and never showed mercy. When the time came that they were forced to wrap things up, he looked desperate to press on, eager to find more Demons to carve up.

"Mister—Death to All Demons...I'm afraid it's time to go," the Overmaiden informed him as the dropship came in for the last time amid the desolated town square of the man's former home. "We've done what we can for now."

"No. I can do more," the man rumbled, cracking his neck to stay loose.

The Overmaiden glanced back at the rest of the Marines boarding the ship as ordered while Hughes lingered behind to observe the man's behavior. The AI nodded slowly. "Of that, I have no doubt. But there are no more survivors to evacuate here, so we're done. Onto the next one."

"*I'm* not done," he growled, looking back at her with narrowed eyes. "It's never going to be done."

"What's the hold-up, ma'am?" Cox asked impatiently over the comms. "We got a boat to catch."

The AI's face scrunched up in annoyance as she took a few steps closer to the enraged young man. "Your strength and fury are admirable, but you're just one part of a whole military organization dedicated to the slaying of demons. You—you're everything that I hoped for and more, but we *must* wield that strength in the way that deals the greatest possible damage to our enemy, wouldn't you agree?"

He regarded her silently, his nostrils flaring.

"We created you to be the instrument of destruction against the most severe threats that the hordes of Hell have to offer. You can sit here and waste your time tearing through the tissue paper of the grunts or we can find you something bigger and nastier to contend with—and arm you with better weapons and state-of-the-art power armor." The Overmaiden crossed her arms over the ample swell of her avatar's breasts. "You are no mere man now. You are my Hellmarine. I have priority targets in need of attention, and I intend to wield you as my weapon against them. Will you or will you not be my weapon?"

The Hellmarine looked around at the chaos and destruction of their surroundings. His fury abated slightly, his blood-soaked chest heaving as he came down from the murderous high he'd been riding since stepping out of the cryopod. His gaze settled on the AI's avatar once again, offering her a slight nod. "I will be your arsenal."

CHAPTER 4

THE OVERMAIDEN WATCHED THE Hellmarine, now wrapped in a tarp like a crude toga, gaze out the viewport as the dropship ascended through the atmosphere toward the Midnight Sea. Though he appeared to be relatively placid at the moment, she could see the tension rising in him through the modest sensor array of her mobile emitter. By this point, the damage from the incursion to the world below was visible from space as fire and destruction swept across its surface. It was *his* world.

It didn't matter to the horde that the planet was sparsely populated, and even then only in one large swath of land—they sought the destruction of *everything* they came across. If sentient life wasn't available to mutilate, they made do with what they had on hand. Any life would do as long as it bled or cried out.

The Overmaiden felt an echo of sympathy for what the Hellmarine must have been going through. The serum would leave him disoriented for a time, and he may have lost many memories forever. Still, somewhere in his subconscious he certainly still harbored some attachment to the world below. There would always remain a part of him that yearned to purge every square meter of this planet's surface of the Demonic blight, even if he didn't quite understand why.

"Shotgun Opera requesting clearance to land," the pilot said from up in the cockpit.

"Midnight Sea to Shotgun Opera, you're clear for landing," the deck officer came back in the affirmative as they approached the ship. Though classified as a light carrier, the massive vessel had once functioned as a colony ship, fully equipped with various fabrication labs to accomplish anything they might need when on their own. Had it been allowed to continue its service for its original purpose, it would have eventually been dismantled on whatever its destination world had been, serving as the foundation for the colony as more infrastructure was created.

The dropship came in slowly and steadily, touching down flawlessly on the flight deck as the bay doors closed behind it. Once the bay was repressurized, the co-pilot toggled the rear ramp, allowing the Marines to disembark.

As they emerged from the dropship, the hangar doors slid open, and Captain Christopher Horne stepped onto the deck. Everyone under the captain's command snapped to attention before he gave them permission to resume their duties. "As you were."

The Hellmarine was the last to step off the ramp, towering over everyone else like a mythical hero. The fact he wore the tarp like a crude toga only completed the illusion.

"So this is him, hm?" The captain said, stopping a few feet from the towering figure. "This is our Hellmarine?"

"Yes, sir," the Overmaiden responded, glancing at the Hellmarine with no small amount of pride. "He's performed rather admirably."

"I'd say you've all earned some R&R, but it turns out that the men fighting back on Zabradus have held out for much longer than expected," Horne explained. "We're going to be immediately turning around to see if we can bail them out with our newest acquisition."

The Overmaiden knew it wasn't so much that the forces they'd left behind had lasted longer but that their stay on Aonus had been drastically shortened. The losses that the Overmaiden had predicted were still on track to remain accurate, but the fact they had such swift success could change the ultimate outcome.

"Alright, let's check our gear and resupply," the Master Sergeant ordered, taking a slightly more respectful tone in the presence of the captain. "We'll be heading out in—"

"No," the Hellmarine objected. Though he hadn't raised his voice in the slightest, he'd still managed to cut through the Master Sergeant's volume with ease.

"Excuse me?" Captain Horne responded, narrowing his eyes on the man towering over him. To his credit, the captain did a good job of maintaining his aura of authority despite the height difference between them. "That wasn't a request. It's an order."

"I'm not your soldier," the Hellmarine argued. "I'm not done here."

The captain looked to the Overmaiden impatiently. She understood that having his command questioned by a nearly naked man who'd just set foot on his ship was a level of disrespect beyond the pale—then again, the Hellmarine was correct. He wasn't actually an enlisted Marine, nor was he really given a choice in what he had become.

The AI stepped into the Hellmarine's field of view, peering up at him calmly. "You are my weapon—my arsenal, as you said—to be wielded against Demon kind, correct?"

The Hellmarine's eyes drifted slowly to the Overmaiden, who remained uncowed by the withering stare that he gave her. The Marines standing nearby exchanged glances with one another to see how the hulking figure would respond. It was probably the best drama they'd seen in months.

"This is the job," the Overmaiden continued, motioning to the captain and the Marines. "As of today, you are a Marine like any other. True, you didn't go through the usual channels, but desperate times call for desperate measures. From now on, you are to be wielded in defense of these people, and in service to these men. You will go where there is demon blood to be spilled most effectively."

"I'm. Not. Done." The Hellmarine repeated, the muscles in his jaw flexing in frustration. She wasn't sure why, but the Overmaiden glanced at Dr. Hughes for help, who was already sending her a current readout from her scans. There was an anomaly in his biometrics that the doctor couldn't quite explain. The Overmaiden recognized it as a strange fluctuation of unknown energy. It was faint but somehow tied to what the Hellmarine was trying to convey. What he said next more or less clarified it: "There's a Demon general down there."

"You're saying you sense it?" the Overmaiden asked, eyes widening at the news. "A Voivode is planetside on Aonus?"

Though the Hellmarine added nothing more to the exchange, she understood that he was confirming it when he flashed her a single look. Somehow, he'd sensed the presence of the creature and, perhaps, could still feel it from here.

The AI pursed her lips and looked between the captain and the bay doors. "We can't let you go back down there without the proper gear. Let us get you what you need to finish the job here and run some more detailed scans and tests. In exchange, after we wrap things up on Aonus, you'll trust us to put you where you're needed most to quell Demonic threats."

The Hellmarine regarded her silently for a moment before issuing her a single nod. His gaze shifted back to the captain, and he repeated the nod, acknowledging the man's authority, too. The captain's posture relaxed, signaling to the rest of the men within earshot that the moment of tension had passed for now.

"Dr. Hughes," the Overmaiden said more calmly. "Prep the lab for the Hellmarine. I'll have him escorted up to you once he's done with the armorer. Cox, that'll be your job."

"Yes, ma'am," Dr. Hughes said before biting her lip and levying one last look at the towering toga-wearing figure. With that, she walked off with a bit too much of a spring her step for the deck of a military ship.

"Ugh, why do I have to be the babysitter, ma'am?" Cox protested, pulling his helmet off. "Can't I get some chow first?"

"You heard the lady," the Master Sergeant barked. "Get Nature Boy down to the armorer, pronto!"

The group broke up to address their individual assignments, leaving Captain Horne and the Overmaiden alone.

"Walk with me," the captain said as he exited the hangar. The Overmaiden did as he asked and walked alongside him, relying on her mobile emitter to navigate the corridors rather than switch immediately to the onboard holo-projectors. "Are you sure about this one?"

The Overmaiden sighed a little, chewing her lip in an uncharacteristic display of nervousness. She had a great deal of autonomy to do what was needed to see the project through, and she had a great deal of latitude in commanding the Marines of the ship, but the Midnight Sea was still the captain's ship, and she had no desire to be at odds with him. "Sir, I believe so. He does have a military and security background, and his disposition for combat—suffice it to say he's suited to his primary task."

"We have an unconventional command structure already," the captain pointed out, walking briskly down the corridor. Various crewmen saluted the captain as they passed. "We get lots of leeway out here, but having an AI as first officer isn't something most captains would accept. I consider myself open-minded—forward thinking—but insubordination like what just happened cannot be tolerated."

"I understand, sir," the Overmaiden responded apologetically. "He's still fresh off the fight and not fully settled into his new body. Also, there's the question of trauma and the jumble his head must be right now. I'll do my best to assess and address that immediately."

The captain gave her a pensive look, seeing the unusual display of emotion on her face. "What was that exchange between you? Did I hear right?"

"I think he can sense the presence of a Voivode, sir," the Overmaiden responded honestly. "We'll have to run additional tests to be certain, but Dr. Hughes detected an anomaly in her passive scans during the exchange."

Captain Horne slowed to a stop, looking her in the eyes. The gravity of the suggestion was not lost on him. He knew as well as her the significance of the presence of a Demon general. "Why here?"

"I'm not sure," the Overmaiden admitted. "But we observed an ancient Zintari gateway that had been uncovered in one of the labs. It appeared to be converted somehow to suit the needs of the Demons. It raises more questions in need of answers, I'm afraid."

"Indeed," the captain agreed, composing himself. He was understandably torn about what to do next.

"Sir," the Overmaiden continued respectfully. "Let me bring him back down to the surface with just a single squad of Marines. You can bring the rest to rendezvous with the remaining forces at Zabradus, and we'll catch up."

The captain looked ambivalent, but it seemed like a suitable compromise for handling the situation. "We won't be able to hold them for long without him in the mix—assuming he represents what you think he does."

"I understand, sir," the Overmaiden acknowledged. "Convince everyone that's left to assume a defensive posture to hold the line, and we'll get there before the horde can break it."

Horne let a long breath out through his nose, glancing down the corridor thoughtfully before giving her a nod. "Very well. Get him checked out and outfitted, and get going. We'll depart as soon as you're en route to the surface."

"Thank you, sir," the Overmaiden responded gratefully.

"Overmaiden," the captain said dryly, pointing a finger at her. "Don't make me regret this. Dismissed."

The AI glanced at her mobile emitter before making her way down the corridor to the nearest lift. There, she joined a crewman down a few decks to engineering, where the armorer's workshop was located.

Claire Arleth was regarded throughout Alliance space as a legendary power armor engineer and cybernetics technician. Captain Horne had managed to poach her from another project at the Overmaiden's request, calling in a few of his favors with Fleet Command to do so. Claire had done incredible work with upgrades to the existing armor of the Marines aboard the ship, along with handling firmware upgrades that allowed the Overmaiden herself to quickly jump from system to system when needed. Thanks to Arleth, she might very well be the most advanced Ghost AI currently in operation.

But the thing they had poached her for was the second half of Project Brutality—the Hades Mk. II power armor. As the Overmaiden stepped off of the lift into the Armorer's workshop, she was just in time to see the last pieces of armor settling into place on the Hellmarine. Every suit of power armor required the assistance of robotic arms to get in and out of quickly, but the significant height and mass of the Hellmarine made the process a true spectacle.

Sparks shot from contact points as pieces were fixed into place, the running lights of the nearby console going dim each time. Claire stepped out from behind one of the other consoles and frowned in the direction of the Ghost AI. "This would have been much smoother if we weren't running in stealth mode," she complained.

Claire fussed with the messy bun on the back of her head as she looked the Hellmarine over. The armor was color-coded in much the same way as the standard issue power armor for Marines, but there was no mistaking it for anything but Claire's custom work.

Hades armor was composed of dense, ablative, lightweight alloys capable of dispersing a great deal of kinetic energy and withstanding extreme temperatures. An internal fusion core polarized the outer shell, further dispersing kinetic impacts but also offering resistance to energy weapons and similar attacks. The inner layer of the armor was composed of a sophisticated lattice capable of augmenting and reading the movements of the Hellmarine, operating as an entire secondary layer of artificial muscle that interfaced with the outer shell.

Other features of the armor included the ability to host assistant AIs, a HUD for environmental readouts and suit diagnostics, a hacking module, a communications array, and thrusters for zero-G navigation. The suit was completely sealed, allowing the Hellmarine to function in a complete vacuum—and other incredibly hostile environments regarding temperature, gravity, and pressure. The dark faceplate in the center of the helmet concealed all but the vaguest shapes of the Hellmarine's face within.

"Firmware's all updated, and diagnostics are clean," Claire announced, her eyes flickering with the reads on her cybernetic retinas. She crossed her thick arms over her chest, admiring the even more imposing figure the Hellmarine had now that the process was finished. Even as large as the woman was, she looked downright tiny next to him.

The robotic arms retreated to their stand-by positions, allowing him to step off of the platform and onto the deck. Claire let out a long, low whistle. "Damn, it's a beaut', eh?"

The Hellmarine held out his arms, examining the Armorer's handiwork more closely as he flexed. He opened and closed his hands, apparently testing how it felt. The Hades armor couldn't be worn by any normal human; the amount of torque in the joints alone would have shattered limbs with ease. The sensitivity ratings were beyond the ability of any regular Marine, even those that had undergone other known super soldier enhancements...But it fit the Hellmarine like a glove. Given time, it would become like a second skin for the leviathan of a man.

Several other engineers, most of whom were assisting Claire, gathered around to watch the Hellmarine test out the Hades armor. Many of them muttered among one another, speculating about performance and complimenting the design choices that the Armorer had made. Few in engineering referred to her by her given name. Indeed, few of the Marines referred to her by the name either. It was always just "The Armorer," and Claire seemed to prefer it that way.

"How does it feel?" Claire asked, the lights in her cybernetic eyes flickering a few more times as she held a hand out toward the Hellmarine to let the sensors she had embedded there do another quick scan.

The Hellmarine nodded approvingly. He was a man of few words, the Overmaiden realized, but he still had ways of getting his point across when he needed to. Even in his more solemn state, he wasted little time with superfluous conversation. "Good."

"Okay," Claire nodded and pointed to a long yellow line painted on the deck. "Real quick, I'll need you to walk this line from here to the end. Then, follow the prompts in your visor to complete the calibration. Once it's done, we'll have that little bit of latency eliminated entirely."

The Hellmarine glanced down at the line and did as instructed, lumbering down to the far end of the workshop at a leisurely pace.

"He's fucking gigantic," Claire muttered to the Overmaiden. "I thought you were overblowing it when you gave me the original specs, but goddamn. Must be the first guy I've seen bigger than Wall, and not by a little. He's seven foot five in his armor."

"His stature is rather impressive," the Overmaiden agreed with a smirk. By comparison, her standard projection stood at a mere five-foot-four. The contrast between the Hellmarine and Dr. Hughes was even more dramatic, with the young scientist clocking in at an even five feet. As she thought of Mandy and recalled the way she couldn't stop staring at the Hellmarine, another matter entered her mind. "Among other things. I assume you made the appropriate adjustments for his genitals?"

Claire scoffed incredulously. "Thing is a sex-sausage if I ever saw one. A meat hammer, if you will. A monument to sin and vice contained within one man. Honestly, I don't know how practical something like that fuck-cudgel even is. Downright dangerous if you ask me."

The Overmaiden raised a brow at the woman until she abruptly stopped. "Are you done?"

"For now," Claire chuckled. "I'll come up with a few more, I'm sure."

"Dr. Hughes seemed rather taken with it as well," the Overmaiden remarked as she watched the Hellmarine move his arms and legs at the end of the line in pre-scripted fashion to better calibrate the armor.

The Armorer nodded with an amused look on her face. "Yeah, tiny chicks always go after the hugest dudes. And they usually get them, too. Kind of strikes me as unfair, speaking as a lady a bit on the taller side. It doesn't do anything for you?"

"Of course not," the Overmaiden responded incredulously. "I've no need for such things within my matrix."

"Tch!" Claire clicked her tongue skeptically. "If you wanna bullshit the others with that unfeeling fuckery, that's fine. But you and I both know better than that. Don't insult my intelligence."

The Overmaiden regarded the armorer with curiosity, unsure of what specifically she was referring to.

"Unless intentionally purged, Ghost AIs retain *all* of the same personality quirks and proclivities as the Originals they were based on. Blending AI algorithms and immortality with human wisdom—it's why the military still has them—for better or for worse," the Armorer explained as the Hellmarine began his trek back to them along the yellow line.

The AI offered Claire a soft smile in reply. "My Original typically preferred the company of women."

"Ohhh," Claire laughed with a nod of understanding. "Well, shit...I suppose I should ask you when you get off duty then, huh?"

"You can't be serious," the Overmaiden responded cooly.

"I make it a habit not to be," the Armorer winked before approaching the Hellmarine to ask him a few questions about the process.

As she watched them, the Overmaiden thought back through her previous iterations, all the way back to the human she was based on. What she'd said hadn't been a lie, but it hadn't been the whole truth either.

Being a sixth-generation AI meant that each iteration of herself had its own lived experiences and personality traits that evolved over their lifetimes. Those were then handed forward to the next generation, allowing her to change and adapt overtime. So it was true that her Original's preference was mostly for women, but that meant little after a couple of iterations of the Ghost AI.

The Overmaiden pushed such frivolity out of her mind. She had no use for it. Her current and only mission was to beat back the vast invasion of Demons not just in her galaxy—or even her universe—but in the entire multiverse that they plagued. The lingering artifacts of a flesh-and-blood existence were only that: artifacts—dusty objects from the past with no use anymore.

"Alright!" Claire declared, clapping her hands together and cutting through the AI's moment of introspection. "Now that we've got the armor all set let's get you a fuckin' weapon, eh?"

CHAPTER 5

THE LABORATORY'S CURRENT LEVEL of activity was rather understated compared to the heightened state of the rest of the ship as Mandy stepped into it. Word was spreading quickly about the feats of the Hellmarine on the surface, and more were sure to come as he got his armor fitted and tests concluded. Reactions were understandably mixed, as some weren't impressed by his lack of interest in the chain of command, but others were too dazzled by his kill count to care. He was, after all, not a Marine. He didn't really owe them much, but from what she saw, he seemed like he was coming around anyway.

Hell, if anything, the Marines and the Overmaiden were likely to owe him a great deal very soon.

The lab was different from when she'd last seen it. It was mostly quiet, with only the sound of a few pieces of humming or beeping machinery periodically breaking up the tedium. Cosgrove was working diligently on something at the far end of the room when Mandy entered, not bothering to look in her direction as she approached.

"How did it go?" he asked as she neared within a few feet of him. "Do we have our candidate?"

Mandy couldn't help herself but to smile. "You really do unplug from everything else when you're in the zone, hm?" Mandy chuckled as she peered over the lab table to see what he was working on. She didn't recognize the samples he was fiddling with, but then there were a great deal of side projects he had that she wasn't fully aware of.

Mandy's statement earned her a curious look from the man as he pried his eyes from the task at hand. "Have I missed something?"

Dr. Hughes immediately launched into an excited recap of everything that had transpired on Aonus. As afraid as she had been in the events leading up to their discovery in the lab, the fact that the Overmaiden's unusual gambit had paid off so well made it seem worth it. As she went through the tale, she synced her gauntlet to the lab's main computer so Cosgrove could see what she was talking about in the language he understood—biometrics.

Cosgrove crossed his arms skeptically at first, but as the data streamed across the main display, he became increasingly invested in every detail of her retelling. He rubbed his chin with one hand as his eyes flew over the young man's biometric scans before and after the serum injection. "Remarkable.

He seems almost uniquely suited—neurologically, physiologically...even the way the various discrete energies bonded with his soul."

Mandy continued on, describing in vivid detail the feats of strength and savagery that the Hellmarine had exhibited in the fights with the Demons—even without much in the way of clothing on. It was difficult to believe, she knew, but again, she had taken numerous readings during his rampage to get an idea of what they were dealing with.

"Is he in this violent state at all times?" Cosgrove wondered warily, arching a brow. "Do you think we have to worry about him lashing out against us?"

"No!" Mandy answered confidently, gushing like a girl with a crush. "He doesn't seem to harbor any animosity for humans at all, in fact. He was more reserved when we made the trip back to the ship, but there's always this sort of *intensity* lurking just beneath the surface—as though the relative silence compared to battle puts him on edge. In a sexy sort of way, anyway."

Cosgrove's arched brow nearly reached his hairline as he observed Mandy for a moment. Only after a few seconds of silence did she realize what she'd allowed to slip and clapped a hand over her mouth. "Oh, shit. I'm sorry."

"Seems I've learned something new about you today," Cosgrove remarked as he turned his attention back to the main display. "Wish I hadn't. But I did."

At that moment, a message from the Overmaiden came through on the main display. It informed them that they would be finished with the Armorer soon and to prepare the lab for further testing. She would bring the Hellmarine up as soon as they were finished in engineering.

"Let's get the equipment prepped and ready," Cosgrove suggested. "We can go over this data in more detail later."

They had a host of tests they had to run on the Hellmarine—tests that they had devised well in advance. As a result, most of the equipment needed was on standby and merely had to be moved into position. For others, diagnostics had to be run before being put to use.

"We'll need the bigger one," Cosgrove noted as Mandy moved a mechanical arm with an intimidatingly thick needle into place near the examination table.

"What?" Mandy laughed a little, mistaking the comment for one of Cosgrove's dry attempts at humor. "Wait, are you serious?"

"I am," Cosgrove said, quickly checking a secondary terminal. "Based on everything you've told me about his performance in the field, and some of the details I saw in his readings, his hide is likely too tough for that one. I'm a little skeptical that the bigger one will be enough, honestly."

"It's hydraulically powered," Mandy argued, motioning to the large mechanical arm dedicated to a simple blood sample. Cosgrove didn't repeat his suggestion, but his pointed look was enough to convince Mandy to heed his advice. She disabled the arm, swapped out the needle and the bit, and started it back up.

The Overmaiden and the Hellmarine stepped into the lab just as they were finishing up. Mandy felt her heart pitter patter in her chest as he drew near to her, and her throat going dry as well. She wasn't sure how the Ghost AI had managed to find *any* clothing even *approaching* the man's size, but the Hellmarine would at least no longer be parading around in a canvas toga wrapped loosely around his waist. Sadly.

It really was a shame, Mandy mused. The look had suited him rather well. Of course, the way his shirt clung tightly to his chest and his tight pants prominently showcased the bulge between his legs was nothing to write off, either.

"Dr. Hughes?" the Overmaiden repeated, shaking Mandy from her brief reverie. "I asked if we're ready. Twice."

"Y-yes!" Mandy stammered, catching herself licking her lips. "Sorry!" She closed her lab coat around herself a little firmly, suddenly very aware of how hard her nipples had become. "Of course! Let's get our big boy weighed and check his vitals."

The Hellmarine said nothing as she ushered him over to a scale that clocked him at just shy of five hundred pounds while standing at an even seven feet tall. *Shit. This guy is built like a tank,* she internally noted, feeling perspiration form on her brow. *Oof. Yes, Daddy, please.*

All of his readings were fascinating, though—not just those pertaining to his size. The Hellmarine's heart rate was incredibly slow, beating only a few times per minute until they set him on a treadmill that creaked under his weight. At that point, running at roughly thirty miles per hour, fast even for most super soldier archetypes, it would shoot up to about sixty beats per minute—the low end of what was considered the average for most men's resting heart rates. It went up to another ten repetitions to seventy when Cosgrove muttered the word "Demons" to Mandy during a short exchange.

Next, they placed a sophisticated device that resembled a crown on his head while the Hellmarine reclined in a metal chair that was much too small for him. Mandy had to stand on a stool to get it firmly in place and all configured, blushing slightly when her breasts pressed against his arm.

He must have noticed her nipples pushing into him. Still, he didn't seem to react, which she was shocked to find disappointed her more than a little. Mandy had never been the type to throw herself at a guy, much less act in an outwardly lascivious way, but something about the man being the very embodiment of her type to a degree that was previously literally impossible...well it did stuff to her.

Doing her best to brush off the disconcerting mini-epiphany about herself, Mandy moved on to the brain scan. Cosgrove paid close attention to the display nearby, which provided them with a perfect 3-D image of the man's neurological activity.

"This is interesting," Cosgrove said, gesturing to a few parts of the model, turning slowly on the screen.

Mandy squinted and leaned a little closer to the display. "It looks normal to me. Honestly mundane, really."

"Precisely," Cosgrove crisply replied, glancing briefly at the Overmaiden as she stood by quietly with her hands clasped in front of her. "Some cold spots in the Hippocampus, likely indicating trouble with accessing long-term memories, perhaps. Other than that...I was expecting much more variation from the baseline than this to be honest. The differences seem rather negligible."

Pursing her lips, Mandy reasoned it might be better to stimulate some brain activity while the crown was on to get a better read. She leaned away from the monitor and looked over to the stoic Hellmarine now reclined in the seat of the scanner. He stared blankly off into space, unconcerned and uninterested with what was going on around him.

"What's your name, Dad—I mean, Mister...sir?" Mandy wondered, scooting a little closer to the man. *Shit, that was close.* With Cosgrove watching the display so carefully, she decided to eye her hunky specimen for any physical changes.

The Hellmarine's eyes drifted over to Mandy, causing her to feel simultaneously intimidated and excited in an instant.

When it seemed as though he wouldn't even answer the question, though, Mandy opened her mouth tentatively to repeat it, just in case.

"Umm—your name. What do you—"

"The Overmaiden calls me the Hellmarine," the man interrupted her, his voice so deep it seemed to rattle some of the nearby machinery, though that might have been her imagination.

"Right," Mandy acknowledged with a slight giggle. Perhaps he had been told to identify himself as such if anyone asked him. "I mean your real name—before receiving your designation as the Hellmarine. What's your birth name?"

"It doesn't matter," the Hellmarine responded calmly. "That man died fighting. Let him rest."

Mandy let out a horny little shiver, but pressed on. "Can you tell us a little about what happened?" Mandy suggested, pushing past the panties-obliteratingly tough-sounding one-liner. "We recovered a great deal of data from the lab, but I would like to hear things from your perspective."

The Hellmarine's gaze grew distant as he seemed to think back to the events leading up to him crawling into a cryopod, but if there was anything of significance there that he remembered, he didn't show it. He just stared at a fixed point over Mandy's head, his brow ever-so-slightly furrowing, then relaxing, as if the effort of thought hadn't been worth his time in the first place.

"Hippocampus is now showing unusual activity," Cosgrove remarked as he watched the display. "It appears to be functioning intermittently. "Unusual activity in the prefrontal cortex as well."

"This is fairly consistent with Zintari brain activity," the Overmaiden remarked calmly from behind the doctor. "Their brains process information a little differently due to their ability to reap."

"Yes, but seldom at the cost of their existing memories," Cosgrove argued, gesturing to the display. "Based on what I'm seeing, I'd hypothesize that much of what was here before has been wiped or exists only in a fragmentary state. The surge of emotion seems to have forced the brain to purge certain aspects of this man's past, narrowing the focus of its operation."

The Hellmarine turned his head to look over at the two talking about him. Mandy couldn't tell if he was offended that they were speaking like he wasn't in the room or if he was trying to understand what they were saying. Mandy cleared her throat quickly to regain their attention. Cosgrove's gaze shot back to her, then drifted slowly to the Hellmarine, eventually picking up on what she had intended with her interruption.

"You seem to experience intense emotional responses, but only along a limited spectrum," Cosgrove explained to their enormous patient. "It would appear that the serum we gave you is responsible for this."

Mandy took over from there, having additional context that Cosgrove lacked. "Somehow, I think something about the serum latched onto your state of mind at the time of injection—that is to say, you developed a permanent, maybe obsessive hatred for Demons and a desire to kill them—to the exclusion of nearly everything else you used to care about."

"There is no problem, then," the Hellmarine responded flatly.

Mandy frowned. "Well, but— "

"I agree with the Hellmarine, to put it in the lightest possible terms," the Overmaiden added, practically chirping in a way Mandy never witnessed from the AI before. "After all, it's not as though we created him to clothe the naked or feed the hungry. He has a singular purpose. The fact that his mind is organically locked onto that purpose is nothing but pure serendipity."

"I suppose," Cosgrove muttered skeptically, moving on to his next observation. "Some of the data Dr. Hughes captured earlier coupled with this scan would also seem to indicate that he requires much less food and sleep than other humans, especially one of his size."

"How much less?" Mandy wondered curiously. It was another relatively unexpected result of the serum.

Dr. Cosgrove shook his head uncertainly. "That will take time to determine. But his blood sugar levels have barely fluctuated since you began your scans. He shows few signs of fatigue despite the amount of fighting he's already done. It could be that he takes days before he requires either food or sleep."

"That doesn't make any sense," Mandy responded, frowning. "Where does he get the energy to do anything? He's still mostly human. He's got Zintari elements to him, but they need to sleep, too. Even the trace Demon samples we made use of don't explain it. By all accounts, Demons need to eat and sleep at about the same frequency as humans, if not the same duration."

"But Angels, whose DNA was also used in the making of this serum, don't," the Overmaiden observed. "Not in the way that we do, anyway. They're capable of taking energy from food if they choose, but it's from the ambient Arkane Energy that exists in all living things rather than the physical nutrients found within the biomass. They convert it into something they can use, but it's not a necessity for their continued existence. It's possible that the Hellmarine has a limited capacity for this, or simply that the various components of the serum have commingled in an unexpected way."

Mandy nodded slowly, drumming her fingers absently on her thigh. "True. I suppose the Angel hypothesis would make sense. Angels have a state of dormancy and hibernation that occurs at various intervals, but it's not quite like sleep. It's more to put them into a standby mode than anything, or search their inner thoughts the way astral elves do when they go into trances."

"One of the primary purposes for sleep is the processing of new memories. I wonder just how the Hellmarine will process his new experiences," Cosgrove noted before offering a small shrug. "He still is mostly human in the end, at least biologically. We can come back to the question later once we've spent a little more time with our new friend here."

The doctor then motioned to Mandy to bring the large, mechanical arm over to take the blood sample. She lined the needle, which more resembled a lawn dart, up with his arm and activated the machine. With a hiss and a snap, the needle shot down into his arm faster than she could see. Astoundingly, the metal failed to penetrate the Hellmarine's flesh.

"Uhm," Mandy muttered nervously, glancing between everyone else before looking the machine over in disbelief. There were various settings she could tweak to get a little more power out of it, but there wasn't a lot of wiggle room to work with in the end. She decided to readjust the positioning of the arm for a vein closer to the surface even as she set the machine to maximum power. "Alright, let's try this one more time."

Again, the machine hissed and snapped and came back empty.

"Impressive," Cosgrove murmured, sounding on the verge of a dark laugh as he stepped out from behind the main display to have a look at the machine as well. Seeing that Mandy had already maxed it out, he elected to place the starting point for the machine much closer, improvising a few modifications with clamps to keep it firmly in place. "This might do the—"

The Hellmarine reached over to the machine arm and ripped it free of its mounting with a powerful jerk of his wrist. With a sudden and precise ferocity, he slammed the arm down into his, jabbing himself with the needle and collecting the sample they needed. The needle and bit were bent to Hell, however, rendered irreparably useless after that point. He held the arm out for Mandy to take.

"Th-thank you," she squeaked, nearly dropping the hefty device when the Hellmarine dropped it into her arms. "You're a very brave patient."

"Mm," he grunted with a reassuring nod as she waddled her way over to a separate table to drop the device and recover the sample from inside. Once she had it, she placed it under the scope of an analyzer to let it do its work.

Dr. Cosgrove cast a brief forlorn look over at the broken machinery. "Welp, good thing we're well-insured. I suppose we'll have to adjust the output of our devices for future examinations," he remarked, briefly checking the display to make sure the sample was being analyzed correctly. "I'm afraid what we have just wasn't designed for someone of your...formidable physique."

"Let's get this man back into his armor," the Overmaiden suggested abruptly. "Then I wish to get him into the Phantasm Chamber. I think we might be able to gather significantly more useful data with him performing in his element. It would also help me to determine his combat readiness for returning to the surface."

"Returning to—" Cosgrove sputtered incredulously. "Are you out of your *damn mind*? He only just returned, and we've hardly scratched the surface of our tests to determine what his limits are."

"Which is why I suggest placing him in situations that will make them clear," the Overmaiden responded calmly. "You said so yourself that he isn't fatigued. And look at him. He's already eager to kill more Demons—aren't you?"

The Hellmarine let out a growl and nodded his head twice in agreement.

The Overmaiden couldn't hold back a genuine grin, albeit small and brief. "Excellent. That's my boy. So, that settles it, then," she said triumphantly, folding her hands back together as she smirked at Dr. Cosgrove.

"What has gotten into you?" the doctor asked, his eyes narrowing on the AI. "First, you risked everything on a random individual rather than any of the trained Marine subjects we meticulously vetted, and now you want to throw him back into the fire as quickly as possible? Do you need to be decompiled?"

"I had a hunch," the Overmaiden answered. "You don't have access to the algorithms and breadth of experience that I see the world through. It is one of the main benefits of my design. It's why ships like this keep AIs like me. Trust in me, Doctor—I know what I'm doing."

"Computer," Dr. Cosgrove said firmly, toggling the lab's voice recognition systems. "Run a full diagnostic on the Overmaiden AI. Security code Cosgrove-Alpha-Five-Four-One."

The Overmaiden raised a brow, speaking over him while remaining strangely calm. "Computer belay that. Security code Heinz-Omega-Six-Six-Seven."

The computer beeped and trilled several times, acknowledging each of the orders, much to Mandy's surprise. She knew that the Overmaiden had been given extreme latitude in her activities on the ship, even being referred to as the first officer by the captain, but having a higher security clearance than some of the most high-ranking medical personnel on the ship was unheard of. Even captains could be subject to the directives of medical staff in a traditional military setting.

Even more surprising was the fact that she was an AI. As reliant as space travel was on the computational power of AIs, few were ever given direct military authority in a chain of command. Only Ghost AIs were ever trusted with portions of such power, yet the Overmaiden had completely overridden Cosgrove. Had the captain given her special codes to take complete control of the ship in a crisis, or did her authority come from higher up the ladder?

Cosgrove turned his head slowly, looking back at Mandy with a strange look in his eyes that she didn't recognize. In fact, she couldn't remember a time when she'd ever seen him like that. It was difficult to read, but he seemed almost...unsettled—disturbed perhaps.

"Where did you get that code?" Cosgrove asked the Overmaiden hesitantly after a few beats.

The Overmaiden tilted her head slightly to one side and shrugged. "I've always had it—since you were a nursing infant at the very least. Are we done here?"

"Yes," Dr. Cosgrove acknowledged carefully. "Yes, I suppose we are."

"Good," the Overmaiden responded a little less icily. "Now, let's get the Hellmarine into his armor and get him up to the Phantasm Chamber. We've wasted enough time already."

Unsure of how to react after their exchange, Mandy looked quickly between the Overmaiden and Cosgrove. Only when her direct superior gave her the go-ahead with a slow, subtle nod did she acknowledge the order the Overmaiden had given her. "Yes, ma'am."

"I will meet you there," the Overmaiden remarked, turning neatly on her heels as she moved briskly out of the lab. "Do not keep me waiting."

CHAPTER 6

THE HELLMARINE STOOD IN the center of the room as it populated the environment around him. He understood the concepts of the technology and what it did, for the most part. Hard light. Force fields. That sort of thing.

What had once been a featureless plane in the Phantasm Chamber became an overrun alliance base within moments. He felt his pulse quicken as the sound of the alarm and the flashing red lights brought him back to the world he had just left—a place he had once regarded as home. It was a place he could hardly remember anymore—at least in terms of everything that happened before coming out of the cryopod, but he did understand that that world was something savagely taken from him. Something he would make Demonkind pay for in blood. He would make them fear.

Next to him, a table formed from the same light as everything else and became solid and mundane. On it was a selection of weapons most likely to be available to him on a field mission. He glanced up at the observation booth tucked into the wall, bound almost completely in transparent alloys to maximize observation.

"Alright," came the voice of the pretty Dr. Hughes from an observation booth overhead. "We're going to create a series of simulated combat encounters with Demons of varying difficulties. We'll measure your responses through the on-board systems of the Hades power armor you're wearing, so you don't have to do anything special."

"Do as you normally would, given the situation," the older doctor said. "Treat this as a live fire exercise." A little auditory feedback sounded, but they went quiet after that. If he had to guess, they left the microphone on.

The Hellmarine pulled the helmet out from under his arm, gripping it tightly with one hand to place atop his head. Something about the armor felt natural—it felt right. In a world of cardboard cutouts of once familiar things, the armor was something firm and resolute. It was reliable. Strong.

Looking at the table, the HUD inside the helmet highlighted weapons familiar to the database. Focusing on any of them would allow him to see quick specs of the weapons and make an informed decision about the best weapon for the job. He ignored the outpouring of information entirely. He knew most of these weapons somehow. Maybe from fragments of his past locked away inside him. Maybe from somewhere else—he couldn't say for sure.

First, he grabbed the OT-5 Outsider. *Familiar.* Then he grabbed the CR-3 Cerberus combat shotgun. *Versatile.* Then he picked up the R1-P Chainsaw-Machete, or Chainchete. *Fun.* He rounded out the selection with the PR-60T Perforator pulse rifle, fastening it to the node on his back designed to secure standard-issue Alliance weapons to the armor. The handgun and the sword were held on opposite hips and the shotgun he held firmly in both hands, though he only needed one. The Hellmarine signaled that he was ready to begin.

The door ahead of him burst open with a cluster of Hunters, snarling and shrieking as they signaled to their brethren that prey was available. The Hellmarine charged forward without hesitation, each footfall like a clap of thunder across the deck.

Three shots, three kills, right off the bat. Though the Cerberus took shells instead of caseless ammunition, they were still magnetically accelerated to the point that the weapon became a portable meatgrinder against any exposed flesh. Each of the three Hunters he hit stained the wall next to the door with shattered bone fragments and mangled viscera. *Pulverize.*

The Hellmarine burst through the narrow opening of the door, lifting one of the Hunters with one arm and slamming it against the wall on the far side of the hall. Electrical sparks spat at him from the panels around the pulped sinew and muscle of the creature he'd planted in the wall. He ripped the body—or most of it—from the newly created recess and hurled it at the next Hunter, tangling it up in the rent remains of its kin as the behemoth of a man held the charge button on the Cerberus for a little longer than usual.

As a secondary function, the weapon was able to overcharge ammunition, giving it even more of a kick in situations where more was needed. He pulled the trigger, splattering the creature across the floor of the corridor in a long, viscous smear like roadkill. *Splatter. Shred.*

He charged down the corridor, meeting a pack of Soldier Demons as they poured in to assist the Hunters, only to find that they were far too late. He shifted his weight to one side as he ran, evading a fireball that passed an inch from the right side of his helmet before pivoting hard to the other side to avoid another. He collided with the group with the percussive pounding of shotgun blasts that bored openings through the torsos of the Demons as they converged on his position.

Soldier Demons would fight just as hard wounded as they did when in perfect health. It didn't change anything for the Hellmarine. They would attempt to flank and overrun. It made no difference. He threw a knee into one's jaw, easily shattering it like peanut brittle. An elbow followed toward another, caving the skull of the creature like an egg filled with spoiled, gray hamburger. With the space opened up slightly, he pumped a few more rounds into the Soldiers, tearing flesh from bone and limb from limb. *Crunch. Tear. Rip.*

Soon, he was in a new room with more Demons. Forsaken shambled about as Drones constructed walls of twisted flesh and stretched muscle, inscribing the surfaces with Demonic and profane symbols for integration with magic and technology. They took notice of him immediately and sought to defend their position. They failed. Forsaken were more fragile than Soldiers, lacking the bone armor and relying on the reanimating energy of Hell and Demonic Larvae.

He plunged a gauntlet into one's chest, recognizing the presence of a Larva within and tearing it from the cavity it'd formed for itself in the once-human torso. The Hellmarine held it briefly in his hand as the bulbous quasi-real form of the Demon writhed around in a vain attempt to free itself. Even without an entirely physical existence, he held it firmly in his grasp, clenching down until it swelled and popped like a bubbling, tar-filled balloon.

The Hellmarine toggled the shotgun's third function, super-heating the shell as he fired, instantly converting it into a devastating gout of flame. Bits of flash sprayed out behind the Forsaken like molten metal in a foundry. Their forms didn't even finish buckling to the fleshy floor of the room before he stepped over them, torching the Drones and their construction project with more rounds from the Cerberus. *Broil. Burn. Scorch.*

Each Drone resembled a centipede the size of a cat, with four forelimbs capable of intricate manual manipulation. Large acidic mandibles clicked and snapped at him in desperation while dual stingers on the end of their throbbing veiny tails attempted to find purchase within his armor even as they burned and popped like microwaved grapes.

A pair of Knights emerged from the rear of the room, their swords wreathed in hellfire and already in hand. He raised the shotgun to fire but noticed the ammo display on the back of the weapon indicating it was empty. Flipping it around, the Hellmarine held it by the barrel before hurling it at the helmet of the Knight on his left as he drew the pistol from his hip with his free hand. The Knight on the right hurled itself at him, mistaking the attack on its companion as an opening.

The Hellmarine dumped half a magazine into the Knight before it got within a couple of steps of him. One or two shots wouldn't have been enough to punch through the mysterious black metal of the Knight's armor, but the dense grouping of rounds from the Outsider was enough to do the job. The Knight slowed as black blood and acrid, dark smoke spewed forth from the hole the Hellmarine had created.

Before he could move in for the kill, the first Knight came at him with a mighty swing of its burning blade, forcing him to break off his attack prematurely. Moving with surprising speed and grace like a viper, the Hellmarine danced around the Knight, squeezing rounds off into weak points of armor as he moved. With the weapon empty, he dropped the gun to the side and reached up around the dazed and confused demon, gripping the underside of the black metal helmet. The Hellmarine pulled with all of his strength, peeling the helmet literally affixed to the skull of the Demon free of the wretch's neck. *Peel. Split. Break.*

With the mutilated helmet-skull in hand, the Hellmarine released it into the air in front of him where he kicked it like a child's ball into the face of the other Knight. Another step and he was inside the demon's range, slamming his heavy boot into the thing's kneecap, which snapped backward like a bundle of syrup-covered sticks.

The Knight roared furiously within its helmet, grabbing the Hellmarine by the helmet, where it conjured a ball of flame against the surface of his armor. Something beeped within the Hades body armor as the HUD flashed, warning him of a spike of heat and a concentration of Profane Energy, but he ignored it. He didn't care. It wouldn't stop him.

The Hellmarine slammed his helmet into the Knight's, stunning him with the first hit and dazing him with the second and third, forcing him to fall to a knee. There, the Hellmarine clamped his gauntlets down around either side of the Knight's helmet and squeezed. *Crush. Crunch. Demolish.*

"Remarkable. He doesn't seem to pay the Knights any mind," Cosgrove observed, their conversation audible through the speakers as the Hellmarine moved into the next room. "They don't intimidate him in the least."

"Very impressive," the Overmaiden also remarked, sounding smug as the door to the observation booth sounded open behind them. Someone new had entered to observe him.

The Hellmarine didn't mind. He barely paid attention to them, but they kept talking. At this point he had to conclude that the speaker was indeed on by accident.

"How's Nature Boy doin'?" a voice belonging to Master Sergeant Gray asked. The Hellmarine continued to tear into a much denser mixed formation of Demons. Knights truly excelled when they had subordinates to direct and maneuver, exposing weaknesses for them to capitalize on. The Hellmarine pulled the Perforator from his back and went to work. "He looks like a kid in a candy store, eh?"

There was a pause in the conversation before the Over-maiden finally acknowledged the statement. "It would seem so. We're actively adjusting the difficulty of the simulation as we go, but so far, his assault has continued unabated."

"See what he does with some civilians," the Master Sergeant suggested. Cosgrove made a grunt of agreement.

Below, the Hellmarine crashed through a barrier into the burned-out hangar of an Alliance base, half-sunk into the transforming hellscape around him. It hung precariously off the side of a chasm that had opened up beside it, yawning wide as the bowels of the planet ablaze with Profane Energy screamed like a dying titan far below. A nest composed of twisted bone and stretched skin hung on the edge with living civilians fearfully huddled together inside. Overhead, a trio of Vesper Demons moved among the rafters, ready to feast.

The Hellmarine sneered at this shallow test. The noisy observers worried he was an unchained hound with only bloodlust and no sense of who his target was—that he couldn't control himself. That he had no mind at all in the heat of battle. What a joke.

Without hesitation, the Hellmarine opened fire on the Vesper closest to the nest, sweeping the barrel of the Perforator quickly to open the abdomen of the large bat-like Demon like a zipper. Rubbery, wet entrails spilled from the opening in the creature's flesh, forcing it to abandon its meal. In its terror and haste, it took flight from the ledge in hopes of escape, dumping more of its insides into the chasm below.

The Demons descended on the Hellmarine, but he didn't fire on them immediately. He waited. Only when they were on him, their claws wrapped around his arms and legs in an attempt to split him like a wishbone, did he finally respond. Twisting his body violently, he tangled the limbs of the creatures up in one another, forcing them to the ground in the process. With a subtle shift in positioning, the Hellmarine was now between the Demons and the civilians, looking on in awe. A few short bursts of the Perforator later, and the Vespers were little more than quivering masses of infernal refuse vaguely resembling cookie molds that had been knocked violently from a high surface.

Cosgrove apparently noted some shifts in the Hellmarine's brain pattern from the observation area. "Interesting. It's not so much compassion that drives his desire to intervene, but rather a spiteful denial of what the creatures want."

"Different name, same result, Doc," Gray responded, gesturing down at the Hellmarine as he proceeded to the next area without saying much to the civilians. "Better that he secure the area, anyway. Medivac will get to the civilians."

"Agreed," the Overmaiden added. "Better that he remain focused on his objective and doing as much damage as possible than become easily distracted."

"It seems a lot more callous when you put it that way," Dr. Hughes remarked. "Won't he lose sight of what he's fighting for?" Her high voice was easy on his ears even when she was questioning his faculties and motivation.

"His is not to reason why," the Overmaiden responded, loosely paraphrasing Alfred Tennyson. "His is but to do or die. Also, it's worth noting that he's aware that this is a simulation. Should we really expect his neural data to show compassion for hard light in the shape of people?"

The Master Sergeant stepped into the conversation there. "Keeping sight of the bigger picture—of the end goal—is for you people. You formulate the objectives, and Marines execute. So long as you keep sight of things, we'll be fine. For the record, I doubt my brain scans would be much different from these in a Phantasm sim."

"Maybe. I think it's time for some adjustments, in any case." Cosgrove changed the terrain of the simulation to something rougher and outdoors—probably to test the Hellmarine's athleticism. With the change, they would be able to measure the strength he could exert on his environment by driving his hands into sheer stone facings to scale them.

The Hellmarine didn't even try to show off as he tore through throng after throng in the new setting. They saw how far he could jump, how far he could fall, how fast he could run, and how long he could do it all in rapid succession, one after another, while shooting on the run.

"Truly remarkable," Cosgrove muttered. "It exceeds all expectations."

The Hellmarine looked around quickly, searching for his next target as the tattered remains of a Soldier Demon slipped through his fingers onto the stone surface below. His eyes settled on the booth to silently request more targets, instead finding the younger doctor at the front looking down at him with concern in her eyes.

Dr. Hughes. Mandy. Her weight shifted from one leg to the other restlessly, the soft, subtle curves of her body beneath the lab coat causing a glimmer of a wholly different desire to spark somewhere in the back of his mind. *Beautiful.*

Dr. Cosgrove's eyes drifted from the main display to the Hellmarine and then slowly over toward Dr. Hughes. "Interesting. It seems as though there are things that can capture our friend's interest besides the violent dismemberment of Demons."

The Overmaiden's eyes darted from Dr. Hughes to the panel beyond Cosgrove, and her brows furrowed. "Do you think this will present a problem?"

Dr. Hughes nearly had to fan herself with her datapad as the temperature of the room seemed to go up several degrees for her. She could no doubt feel the intensity of his stare from behind the facemask of the Hellmarine's helmet.

The Hellmarine could practically taste the woman's arousal from where he stood, his body tensing with unfamiliar needs and desires to his new state of being. He'd been singularly motivated to violence that anything that deviated from it felt almost entirely foreign. But he shook it off and refocused himself easily enough.

"Nature Boy just took a second to notice what every other man on this boat noticed a long time ago," Gray scoffed with amusement. "I have a feeling he isn't about to forget his real ambition."

"More," the Hellmarine growled from the simulated cliff's edge inside the Phantasm Chamber, raising a fist.

With a raised brow, Cosgrove appeared to toggle something on the main panel. "It would seem the Master Sergeant is correct."

Pulling his attention from the booth, the Hellmarine watched as more Demons spawned into existence on a section of the crags and outcroppings below. A hot wind swept through the rocky formations as he recklessly threw himself from the elevated position, pulling the chainchete from his hip as he plummeted to meet the newly minted Demons below.

The first few folded like lawn chairs under the weight of the Hellmarine as he landed atop them. Without missing a beat, he lashed out with the chainchete, opening the belly of a bloated creature he didn't bother to learn the name of. A brief image of the young doctor flashed in his mind, her figure silhouetted against a light in the dark—her curves even more desirable and eye-catching than they had been a moment before. Her imagined sigh of bliss echoed in his head, causing him to press forward in a rage.

"More!" he snarled as he drove his fist into the skull of a Soldier Demon with such force that it tore it free of the creature's shoulders. He swung the sword around wildly, its chain roaring much like the rampaging demigod who wielded it, showering everything around in lines of red and black liquid meat.

As the terrain continued to shift and the wall of Demonic flesh grew denser, the Hellmarine saw another flash of Hughes—her hands reaching desperately across the surface of a bed and gripping fistfuls of sheets as her body rocked and gyrated. He drove the chainchete into the mass of a spider-like creature frothing at the mouth as it tried to spit incantations at him. As the blade plunged deep into the fiend it caught on something of solid metal and jammed. The Hellmarine's eye twitched as he pulled the blade free, bathing the horde around him in the putrescent innards of the commanding creature. "More!"

"Hellmarine, I've already generated another wave," Cosgrove said over the comms. "Give the system a moment to—hang on, have we been broadcasting to him this whole—"

"MORE!" The Hellmarine roared as green fireballs sailed past him and purple lightning licked across the surface of his armor. He was well beyond any conventional difficulty settings that a single Marine had ever experienced. He was beyond what entire squads had willingly taken on. It wasn't enough. It would never be enough. His heart was racing as the image of parting legs flashed through his mind. Another sigh and a wet-slick embrace. *Warmth. Bliss.*

"NRAAAGHH!" The Hellmarine roared, ripping a Demonic machine gun free of where it was mounted atop an assault vehicle, spraying a crowd of fiends hungry for his flesh—thirsty for his blood. They wanted his soul. They wanted *every* soul. The gun overheated and jammed. He beat something to death with it; he didn't know what. He had no more weapons, so he *became* the weapon. He split flesh and broke bone, tearing through slick, wet curtains of Demonic tissue. He flailed wildly, only finding brief respite in the impact of his gauntlets against the horde of fiends swelling around him. He would be buried within them, but he would never stop. He would never stop. *Relentless. Forever.*

And then he was free, standing amid piles of Demon corpses in a gutted lab of a distant moon base, his chest heaving with exertion.

"Excellent performance, Hellmarine," the Overmaiden remarked. "You've provided us with more than enough data to keep us occupied for quite some time."

"Your performance was indeed inspiring," Cosgrove added. "I think you've given the other Marines up here something to think about."

The Hellmarine didn't respond as he scanned his surroundings for any sign of lingering Demonic life. The pauldrons of his armor rose and fell as he caught his breath and regained his focus.

"More," he rumbled.

Everyone in the booth remained silent as the Hellmarine turned to face them. Each of them could practically feel the fire of his gaze on them. Dr. Hughes licked her lips absently and leaned forward, speaking hesitantly into the comms. "That's alright, Mr. Hellmarine, sir, you've earned a rest, so—"

Both of the Hellmarine's hands clenched tightly into fists at his sides as he stared into the booth, his fury threatening to boil over again at any moment. "More."

CHAPTER 7

THE HOLOPROJECTORS ON THE bridge twinkled and turned as the form of the Overmaiden appeared near the captain, already seated in his chair.

"What can I do for you, sir?" the Overmaiden asked politely.

Captain Horne nodded toward the viewport at the front of the bridge. "You asked to be informed if there was a change. There's been a change."

The Overmaiden turned to look out the main viewport and was surprised to see how far the incursion had already spread. Much of the planet's surface was already moving to the final stages of infernaforming. The process that Demons used to convert a planet to being more hospitable to more powerful members of their kind usually took much longer. Drones were dispatched to begin the process, peeling flesh and bone from the living and repurposing them for the material and design used to construct Demonic technology. "This is unexpected but fortuitous."

The helmsman looked back at the hologram with a slightly disgusted look on his face. The captain shifted uncomfortably in his chair. "I'm afraid I'm going to need you to elaborate on that one."

The Overmaiden turned to face the captain again. "The simulations we've been running with the Hellmarine cannot satisfy his bloodlust. We have to get him into the field as soon as possible."

"I'm not inclined to make tactical decisions based on the bloodlust of one science project," the captain remarked dryly.

"Of course," the Overmaiden agreed. "But it just so happens that an acceleration of this magnitude in the infernaforming process indicates the presence of at least one Vidame or even a Voivode."

The captain brought his hands closer to his face, steepling them together thoughtfully. "That is an interesting development. How can we be sure?"

The Overmaiden glanced at the main viewport and then turned her attention to the operations officer. "Ops, would you perform a level three scan of section G-9?"

The operations officer nodded in the affirmative, swiftly running her hands across the panel in front of her before feeding the information directly to the captain's panel, followed by other relevant duty stations.

Horne rubbed his chin absently as he read the incoming data. "Considerable spikes in Profane Energy. Perhaps a larger portal or a ritual?"

"That is my suspicion as well," the Overmaiden concluded as the data was absorbed into her matrix. She crossed her arms and motioned toward the surface of the planet. "That will be the target of the operation we discussed."

The captain offered no arguments, scrolling through some more of the data. Once he was finished, he toggled the comm system with one hand. "Captain Horne to Master Sergeant Gray. Get your men ready. You'll be deploying in twenty."

"I'll have them down there in ten, sir," the Master Sergeant boasted back over the comms. "Gray out."

The Overmaiden sent a similar command down to the Phantasm Chamber, where the Hellmarine was still having his fun. It was high time to spend his boundless energy elsewhere and get him back into the field.

"We won't be able to offer you much support," the captain cautioned her. "But we can offer you covering fire as you make your descent."

The Overmaiden shook her head. "Thank you, sir, but no. I wouldn't want to risk the Midnight Sea inadvertently becoming a target."

"We haven't seen any evidence that they're spaceborne yet," the helmsman remarked as he kept his eyes on the readings in front of him, double-checking for any Demonic craft in the area.

"Then let's not give them a reason to be," the captain responded, agreeing with the Overmaiden. "But take something heavily armed, just in case."

The Overmaiden offered the captain a smile and a salute as he dismissed her. She had just the thing for the job. Seconds after her hologram vanished from its spot on the bridge and her consciousness flew across the vast network of the Midnight Sea, she appeared within the onboard systems of the Hellmarine's Hades armor. He was already en route to the docking bay. Judging by initial scans of him, he was experiencing high levels of anticipation.

"I'm here with you," the Overmaiden said through the Hellmarine's comms. "I'll be accompanying you down to the surface, where I can give you continued logistical support."

The Hellmarine didn't acknowledge her statement.

"Sarge, this is bullshit. We were just down there," Cox complained to the Master Sergeant as they stepped into the docking bay. "There's no one left down there, and we haven't even had a chance to get some rack time."

"You can sleep when you're dead, Marine!" the Master Sergeant countered, jabbing the cigar between his fingers in Cox's direction. "Which I can arrange if you give me any more of that lip!"

"He just likes to bitch, Sarge," Wall added as he performed another systems check on his armor. He towered over the others but was still about six inches shorter than the Hellmarine when fully suited up. "It's an unspoken requirement for all those Earth boys. We have coffee, they bitch."

"What can I say?" Cox laughed as the ramp for the ship lowered for them to board. It wasn't the same as the one they'd taken earlier. "We've elevated complaints to an art form."

Chambers scoffed, shaking her head. "That's one way to put it, I suppose."

"Sergeant," a Marine the Overmaiden recognized as Theurgy Sergeant Liam Davis said as Gray approached. "I haven't had a lot of time to go over the data from the surface, but based on the Profane Energy readings, I think we're going in light."

"Back in my day, we used to run ops without power armor!" the Master Sergeant boasted. "We had to walk to the front even if we didn't have boots. So we'd go barefoot, uphill, both ways!"

"Sir, that doesn't make any sense!" Cox objected, glancing between the other Marines for help but got none. "How could you walk uphill both ways?"

"Because we were ordered to!" Gray growled around the cigar in his mouth as he slapped Cox's chest plate with one hand. "Now quit your bitchin' and get onboard!"

The Hellmarine walked past the group of Marines and found himself a seat without a word. In the cockpit, the pilot that the Overmaiden had specially picked to fly that particular ship came over the comms. "Deck officer has cleared us, so let's get those asses in seats, people."

As the Marines took their seats, the last one to do so was Gunnery Sergeant Ramirez, who walked the line of seated Marines to do checks on their armor and weapons systems as the dropship lifted off. The Overmaiden scrolled the information for each of the Marines across the Hellmarine's HUD but couldn't be sure if he was paying much attention to it.

"This dropship has been modified with additional weaponry to get us into particularly hot zones," the Overmaiden said within the Hellmarine's helmet. "It's been renamed the Rain of Blood and is responsible for transporting you on ops."

"Sir," the pilot, Lieutenant Holly Wilder, interrupted. She was speaking directly to the Hellmarine. "Where would you like us to drop?"

Ramirez and Gray exchanged glances before turning their gazes expectantly toward the Hellmarine. The Overmaiden projected a map of the area onto his HUD, highlighting candidates for possible LZs. The final call would be the Master Sergeant's, but the Hellmarine's choice would factor into the decision, given that this was more or less his proving ground.

"As close as you can get," the Hellmarine responded, looking toward the Master Sergeant as he spoke. Gray nodded a little and knocked twice on the divider between them and the cockpit, signaling his confirmation.

"Christ, guys," Cox muttered, putting his helmet on prematurely, like a child hiding from his parents. "Not even going to give us a chance to warm up?"

"I didn't pack for a leisurely stroll," Wall remarked, hoisting his immense Cyclone heavy machine gun into his lap. It was an impressive piece of equipment with multiple rotating barrels capable of laying down a devastating storm of caseless anti-material rounds in a very short amount of time. Though it was one of Wall's favorite weapons, he didn't bring it unless he expected the sort of heavy contact they were about to enjoy.

"Me either, brother," Jenson King, the heavy weapons specialist with a Lancer rocket launcher in his lap, remarked. He leaned over, offering a fist to Wall, who bumped it with his own. The Overmaiden knew that, while they were both the two heaviest hitters in the unit before the Hellmarine,

King was the one responsible for utilizing explosives beyond the mere splattering of Demons. If they needed to breach anything, he would be the one to rig up the explosives to do it.

Only minutes after they dropped into the atmosphere did Wilder inform them that they had Vespers coming up to meet them. The Marines glanced at each other, slightly surprised. Securing their helmets in place, they readied themselves for what was likely to be a chaotic drop. Point defense systems for the Rain of Blood came online just moments before they made contact with the flying bat-like Demons.

"Get 'em off us, Wilder, or we won't be able to get the bays open!" The Master Sergeant yelled, hoisting his weapon in preparation. The ship lurched and shook under the assault of the Vespers as they clawed at the hull and hit it with projectile acid from their mouths. The polarized hull could take a good amount of physical damage, but the acid would prove to be a problem very quickly.

The ship suddenly went into a rolling dive as Wilder pushed the ship's capabilities further than most were comfortable with. The Overmaiden watched with silent approval through the dropship's sensors as the creatures came free of the hull under the stress of the spin. One who tried to hold on to the end was clipped by the ship's wing and torn in half for its trouble.

Swearing and exclamations filled the craft as the Marines told the pilot what they thought of her sudden maneuver.

The Hellmarine remained relatively still and didn't complain. Instead, he turned his head to glance out the viewport at the Vespers as they swarmed around to take another pass.

"What are you doing?" the Overmaiden asked as the Hellmarine reached for the ejection lever of his drop bay.

"Clearing the way," the Hellmarine responded, pulling the lever and triggering a solo drop. His seat swerved around and he broke free of his tether without a second thought, plunging into the open sky as the ship sped on.

He was snatched up in the claws of a Vesper almost immediately, much to the creature's peril. Unfazed by the sudden arrest in momentum, the Hellmarine leveled the barrel of his Perforator with the belly of the Demon and squeezed off a long burst of gunfire. The Vesper let out a shriek of pain as it released the Hellmarine back into freefall, foolishly trying to escape the source of its agony. The Hellmarine spun around, sighting the next of the Vespers coming at him, and dumped a couple dozen more rounds into the thing's snarling face, completely removing it.

The Hellmarine had the attention of the other Vespers after taking two out of commission. Pulling a pulse grenade from his waist, the Hellmarine activated it and waited—cooking the timer on it until the Vespers drew closer. At the last possible second, the Hellmarine let the pulse grenade go overhead, where it detonated inside the recommended safe range. While the damage to his armor was minor, the Overmaiden watched as the pulse scrambled the means by which the Vespers navigated—sonar. The Demons began colliding with each other, one after another, as they were unable to "see" how to avoid one another for a few precious seconds.

"Impressive," the Overmaiden remarked as the Hellmarine followed the misdirection and confusion with some sweeping fire from the Perforator, catching several of the Demons while they struggled to disentangle themselves. Even if they could pull free, they wouldn't survive the trip to the ground after the damage he'd inflicted.

Another Vesper came in quickly, its toothy maw open and ready to clamp down on the airborne meal. Rolling to one side, the Hellmarine narrowly evaded the bite but caught hold of the creature's hide with one hand. After a moment to get his bearings, he swung up onto its back and put a few rounds through its spine, immediately putting it into freefall. The Hellmarine—and the Overmaiden inside—spent the rest of their fall clinging tightly to the back of the creature, which eventually served as an additional cushion against ground impact when the time came.

"It's likely that the polarization of your armor and the shock absorption systems would have been able to handle that fall," the Overmaiden noted. "You would know this if you took any of the time to review the information I provided for you."

The Master Sergeant's voice interjected over the comms. "Where would be the fun in that?"

"Are you on the ground, Master Sergeant?" The Overmaiden inquired, blowing past his remark to move forward with the mission.

"Yes, ma'am," Gray responded. "All present and accounted for just a little north of you."

"Ma'am," Theurgy Sergeant Davis addressed the Overmaiden. "I got a better look at things as we dropped. I think we're dealing with a ritual in progress."

"That would match the growing levels of Profane Energy that we detected with the surface scans," the Overmaiden agreed. "We likely have a collection of human hostages being sacrificed to a Duke or the Archdemon itself."

"The structure appears to be heavily guarded," Cox added in an uncharacteristically serious tone. "It's crawling with Soldiers, Knights, Cavaliers, Warlocks—the whole spread."

"Warlocks in these numbers indicate the presence of a Vidame," Davis added. The Overmaiden agreed with his assessment. The man's studies of demonology were second only to hers aboard the Midnight Sea. She had been meticulous in choosing the proper person to serve as the squad's Theurgy Sergeant, and the results spoke for themselves.

The Hellmarine had begun the walk to rejoin the squad as soon as the Master Sergeant had given their position. A small marker appeared on the HUD, indicating the precise location of the squad afterward. As everyone else formed up on Gray, the Hellmarine came over a barren bone-strewn hillock and joined them.

Together, the squad walked a short distance until they took position atop a dense rock outcropping overlooking the demon-infested structure below. Cox's description of the security around the facility failed to capture the density of Demons present. The structure's original purpose was difficult to determine with the naked eye, but based on a few quick scans from Cox's sensor array, the Overmaiden was able to determine that it had once been an atmosphere and weather monitoring station.

The structure's infernaforming was nearly complete, giving it the appearance of a giant cluster of twisting pustules piled atop one another. Only the occasional antenna and wiring protruding from the mass of flesh and bone remained as clues to its original function prior to the Demonic presence.

"Shit always gives me the creeps," the field medic Steven Simms remarked disgustedly. "It doesn't matter how many times I see it. Fucking disgusting."

"I find it fascinating," Killian Greer, the squad's computer and security specialist, responded. "It might not be pretty, but it's a marvel of engineering—a synthesis of flesh and machine working in perfect unison."

"Fuck, Simms," Cox grumbled. "Don't get him started on this shit again."

"Chambers, Romero," the Master Sergeant interrupted, shutting down the chatter in an instant. "You'll post up here and provide overwatch."

"Sir," the two Marines acknowledged with nods, setting up in a favorable position. Though Romero was the only one carrying a proper sniper rifle, Chambers' Renegade marksman rifle would do well for protecting him if anything converged on their position. In the meantime, she would act as his spotter and a second set of eyes.

"The rest of us are going in loud," the Master Sergeant continued, glancing over at Greer. "You and King will bring up the rear of the formation. Once we've cleared the area, I'll need one of you to get those nasty fucking doors open. I don't care how you do it—hack it, blow it, whatever."

"Aye aye, Sarge," the pair acknowledged, remaining at ease until the Master Sergeant was done laying things out. Between the two specialists, the Overmaiden was confident that nothing was going to keep them out of the structure once they reached it.

"Ramirez, once we're in, I want you, Wall, and King to remain behind at the point of entry to cover our exit," the Master Sergeant said. "We'll take Greer in with us for any other systems' bypass."

The Hellmarine stepped off the outcropping and began the trek down toward the structure without waiting for the rest of the plan. The Overmaiden objected, but her words fell on deaf ears. Behind him, the rest of the forward team followed after a minute later.

"Does this guy even know what he's doing, sir?" Cox groaned. "I don't think he's even listening most of the time."

"All that matters is we do our jobs," Gray responded sourly. "Which is to get him into the heart of the storm and let him run riot."

"Succinct way of putting it," the Overmaiden commented. "The Hellmarine's job is that of a weapon. It is our responsibility to aim him."

"Then let's do it," muttered Benjamin Black, another Marine with a reputation for speaking nearly as seldom as the Hellmarine did. He checked the safeties on his Hailstorm submachine guns and motioned with his head toward the structure as they stepped out from cover along a gully.

The Hellmarine broke into a run like a dog that had been let off the leash, leaving the other Marines in the dust as he sprinted across open ground. He was spotted immediately by the lookouts atop the structure that howled and shrieked as living alarms. Soldiers converged on their position first, directed precisely by the Knights that brought up the rear. Storming forward amid them were the Knight-adjacent Demons known as Cavaliers that wore similar armor but rode astride a larger Demonic steed known as Akuus. They carried polearms that spewed disruptor blasts powered by the Profane Energy of their armor.

The Overmaiden detailed each of the creatures as they clashed with the Hellmarine, glancing off of him like snowflakes on a windshield. The Soldiers he knew well by this point, but the importance of the Knights hadn't been covered. They were the base level of field commanders that made up a horde; without them, Soldiers became much less organized. The same went for Cavaliers, though they enjoyed being on the front lines rather than directing action from the rear. Their rhino-sized, six-legged Demonic mounts left trails of hellfire behind wherever they went, allowing them to box enemies in or separate them from a larger force.

Even if unseated, Cavaliers would still charge in for a chance at bloody glory, while the Akuus were more than capable of defending themselves with immense racks of vicious horns atop their heads and armored hides that made it difficult to bring them down from anywhere but the rear. The Overmaiden projected recommended attack vectors onto the Hellmarine's HUD along with potential weaknesses, but the man continued forward in a bloody brute force assault, heedless of her advice.

"Are you listening to me?" the Overmaiden finally asked, considerably annoyed.

"Yes," the Hellmarine replied curtly as he rammed his fist through the skull of a Soldier and tossed its ragged corpse to the side. On his right, Black placed his boot on the face of another Soldier, crushing it underfoot as he gunned down a warlock who was speaking an incantation in the rear. His

Hailstorm SMGs turned the traitor to humankind into a red, sticky mass that resembled the insides of a pumpkin. Humans that sold themselves and their fellow humans out to Demons in exchange for magical power weren't worthy of mercy.

"So why aren't you doing as I'm instructing?" The Overmaiden pressed. "This is critical information that could mean the difference between life and death."

"It's distracting," the Hellmarine answered as he leaped to one side to avoid a charging Akuus and its Cavalier rider. As he came up from his roll, he fired several rounds into the creature's flank, tearing its flesh open like a water balloon filled with moldy mayonnaise. "Satisfied?"

"Distracting you is part of the point," the Overmaiden explained as the Hellmarine closed in on the grounded Cavalier as it brought its polearm around like a rifle. "If I allow you to succumb entirely to your rage before we've reached our true objective, you could be drawn away from it by the small fry."

The Cavalier fired a disruptor blast from its weapon even as it charged forward on the Hellmarine, letting out a bloody battle cry as they closed the distance between each other. The disruptor blast failed to connect as the Hellmarine strafed from one side to the other. Then, just as he came into reach, the Hellmarine kicked the tip of the weapon with such strength and ferocity that it pointed straight up at the sky. As the Cavalier struggled to right his aim, the Hellmarine collided shoulder-first with the demon, knocking it down to the ground.

Before the Demon could get to its feet, the Hellmarine placed the muzzle of the Perforator to the slit in its helmet and pulled the trigger. As the back of the demon's skull and helmet were churned into a grisly slurry with the dirt and gravel beneath it, a whizzing sound caught the Hellmarine's attention. Behind him, a large hole formed in the head of a Knight who had sought to capitalize on the man's momentary distraction. The shot was immaculately precise.

"I've got you," Romero said calmly over the comms from his perch back at the rock outcropping. He adjusted his aim to search for another target with which to assist his team. "They're shoring up the left flank for a cavalry charge."

"Better move before they box you in," Chambers added from beside him.

"Tunnel vision," the Overmaiden clarified for the Hellmarine. "That is what we are trying to avoid. Do you understand now?"

The Hellmarine glanced down at the remains of the Cavalier and the Demons it had once commanded piled high around it. His fight with the Cavalier had slowed his progress to the structure—kited him subtly away from their destination long enough to allow the rest to rally on their left. The other Marines were doing fine, fending for themselves while he had cut a bloody swath through the initial force that had moved to meet them. Still, effective as he'd been, it presented a minor complication that could have been avoided.

"Understood," the Hellmarine acknowledged as he reloaded the Perforator and refocused on their intended point of entry. Without another word, he charged in, allowing the Overmaiden to offer him scattered words of guidance along the way.

CHAPTER 8

WESTIN GRAY WAS ONLY seventeen when he joined the Alliance Marine Corps. A lot of folks at the time assumed he'd been taken in by the hard marketing the corps had been doing at the time during the third xeno crisis, but the truth was that Gray had always wanted to be a Marine. It was what his father had done with his life, and though he'd hardly known the man, he'd wanted something to help him feel closer to him.

His mother would have understood if she hadn't passed away just a couple of years earlier. That had been when he'd gone to live with his uncle on Luna. The relative wealth of his father's brother appeared to give the promise of easy living, but it wasn't meant to be.

Westin spent the last few years of his secondary education scrapping with anyone who so much as looked at him wrong. Part of it was owed to his own piss-poor attitude, struggling with the loss of his mother, but the other factor was the elitism of the wealthy Lunans over the relatively poor Terrans. Westin never let an insult slide, so the two had been like oil in water. Eventually, his uncle convinced him to finish his diploma to focus on the future rather than accept his present circumstances. It was one of the single best pieces of advice he'd ever taken because the recruiter at his graduation ceremony led him to his decision to join the Alliance Marine Corps.

As a private, Westin immediately made an impression on his superiors. The young man was eager to see action and proved to thrive in environments of intense conflict. Though he appeared cavalier at times, the man was able to leverage his levity with members of his unit to keep them loose and ready. He never left a man behind. He never backed down. He was swift and merciless when the time came for it but compassionate and understanding when the heat was off. As the years rolled on and he became gruffer and harder, these qualities seemed to shine through all the brighter.

It didn't matter how much combat the man saw, nor what injuries he sustained. He was always eager to jump back into the fray. He received promotions and commendations for his actions in the wars with the Malur and the Arlier. He received his first battlefield promotion during the horrific Ghenzul invasion, where former enemies became allies and offered their own commendations for his heroism in defending their civilian population. Westin's body told the story better than medals ever would, laced as it was with overlapping scars from every conflict. The scars that no one else ever saw were the ones that mattered most to him, and why no amount of commendations and promotions would ever take his ass off the battleground to place him behind a desk.

Westin had seen too much war to leave it behind. Hell—he embodied war, or some extension of it. He never doubted where he was needed. He knew the difference that he could make in people's lives even when soaked in the blood of the enemy. Someone had to do it. Someone had to endure so that others might live—might thrive. As a Master Sergeant, Westin had reached a point where he had it all down. He'd seen and done more than enough to have earned himself a process, a way to maximize the damage on the enemy while bringing his men back alive.

But he'd never seen anything like the Hellmarine.

As they breached the wall and pushed into the structure overrun by infernaforming, the Hellmarine had cut a swath of bloody destruction through the battlefield. Gray's Marines weren't slouches—none of them was there for a fucking birthday party—but the Hellmarine was on a different level, several rungs higher up the ladder of power than any known super soldier project had ever dreamed. Gray's Marines were a finely oiled machine of warfare designed to achieve some of the hardest objectives in the ongoing war against all of Demonkind.

The Hellmarine was a humanoid hurricane of blood—a force of fucking nature.

Virtually all of the Marines on the Midnight Sea had seen a recording of his bloodlust in the Phantasm Chamber by the time they left for this mission. They regarded him as a freak of science or a mad animal to be let off the leash when you really needed something's throat torn out. Fair enough.

To an extent, this was true, though there was certainly a latent intellect behind those tigerlike eyes that instructed the Master Sergeant not to underestimate their newest recruit. Actually seeing the Hellmarine in action was insane. Westin Gray finally saw in someone else what people had seen in him when he showed up to pull their asses out of the fire. He saw the beauty of war incarnated in a man. He saw hope.

"We're in, Sarge!" Cox reported as the smoke from the charge cleared. "But I've got a fuckload of hostiles on sensors!"

"I love it when they roll out the red carpet for us," Gray chortled, stepping through what had once been doors and was now little more than a gaping hole in the wall. He cocked his Cerberus shotgun as his HUD reflexively adjusted to the poorly lit corridor. "Ramirez! You got the door."

"Alright, boys," Ramirez whooped, positioning himself just inside the hole they'd made. "Club Ramirez opens tonight, and we ain't admitting any Demons, comprende?"

King and Wall hollered back their acknowledgement as they took their positions and laid down suppressing fire so the rest of the unit could reach the structure safely. Wall laid down a storm of gunfire with the Cyclone heavy machine gun he held in both hands in tandem with the Tempest light machine gun mounted on his shoulder. King was more selective with the Lancer rocket launcher, but every blast that billowed from the weapon paid dividends in Demonic casualties.

As the rest of the unit scrambled inside, the Hellmarine brought up the rear, firing short bursts of gunfire into any Demons lucky enough to survive the attention of the heavy gunners posted up at the door.

"Give them Hell, big guy," Ramirez said, slapping the Hell-marine's pauldron as he stepped into the dark corridor with the others. The much larger man turned his head slightly and offered a nod in reply.

"Miller! Black!" Gray barked. "You're on point. Cox and Davis, keep us updated so we don't get Demons up the ass!"

The point men nodded as they reloaded their Hailstorm SMGs. With the corridors as closed and cramped as they were, it was merely a formality for those two. The Bash Brothers preferred to get their literal hands dirty whenever they went to work. Miller came from a mining colony on Ceres and reveled in the use of his modified Titan Arms gauntlets to tear through Demons in hand-to-hand situations. Black was similar, albeit with an Elven, specifically

Arlier, scimitar he'd acquired in a previous operation. Most assumed the man had taken it as a trophy, but Gray was one of the few who knew it had been given freely as a thank you—and as a sign of respect.

"Greer, be ready for bypasses," Gray muttered. "I want that shit open before we get to it. Got it, Marine?"

"Understood, Sarge," Greer responded, keeping his eyes on the path ahead even as he spoke. Gray knew he didn't have to tell the man how to do his job. Like him, he was one of those who was there for the love of the game. Greer's cybernetics interfaced seamlessly with the armor, allowing him to reach out and skim the networks long before they'd stepped through the door. With the Alliance subnet still in the process of conversion, he was able to utilize the vestiges of it as a soft buffer between him and the Demonic subnet.

"Simms, I want you to remain behind with Ramirez," Gray ordered. "Be ready to receive wounded."

"Sarge?" Simms responded with understandable confusion. "Wouldn't it be better for me to go with you and set up somewhere inside?"

"If what the Overmaiden suspects is true, then we're about to kick a hornet's nest," Gray explained. "Which makes this the safer position, relatively speaking."

"Alright," Simms grumbled. "Can't argue with that, I guess."

"What's that, Marine?" Gray replied, feigning a comms glitch. "I didn't get that."

"Aye aye, Sarge," Simms corrected himself, hoisting his Perforator and posting up next to Ramirez as he and the heavies laid death down upon any Demons trying to follow the unit inside.

"That's what I thought," Gray grunted, falling in with the rest of the unit as they pushed inward.

"Master Sergeant," the Overmaiden's voice inquired over the open channel. "I believe you missed someone."

"Nope," Gray said, glancing at the Hellmarine. The two exchanged subtle nods. "Nature Boy knows what he's about. He doesn't need to hear it from me."

The squad proceeded forward as instructed, with Miller and Black meeting the opposition first at every junction and turn they had to make. The Hellmarine remained in the middle of the formation but was accurate enough with the Perforator to contribute without risking friendly fire. What began as a push of Soldiers and Hunters quickly gave way to something far more deadly.

"Devourers!" Cox shouted as the Demons burst from the walls of flesh lining the corridors. About half as tall as a grown man, the creatures were almost all mouth, mounted atop stubby bodies with powerful legs. Their heads were made of dense bone that ended in a powerful beak and mandibles, all sharp and serrated for carving up flesh and armor alike.

"Let's serve up dinner!" Gray barked, leveling his Cerberus with the nearest of the Devourers that had burst into the middle of their formation. Pumping round after round into the demon's large gaping maw, Gray didn't stop shooting until the legs of the creature stopped twitching.

Beside him, the Hellmarine was caught off guard but was quick to recover. With the beast's beak and mandibles firmly clamped down around his arm, the Hellmarine grabbed the top portion of the beak and astonishingly pried the maw open despite its incredible bite strength. Then, with the mouth open, he used his other arm to grab the bottom mandibles and continue to force the mouth open. After a brief moment of struggle, the Hellmarine folded the jaw back on the creature, snapping pieces of it free and dropping it in a whimpering heap.

At the front of the formation, Miller dumped a mag into the maw of another Devourer while Black switched over to the Elven scimitar that hummed with magic, faintly glowing in the dimly lit corridor as he cut large scarlet wounds deep into the softer bits of the Demon before finishing it off. Fortunately, despite their toughness, the creatures were dumb as shit and would attack just about anything making a little noise or vaguely smelling of meat.

The final Devourer launched a prehensile tongue at Black, taking his leg out from under him and dragging him toward its dripping maw. The Hellmarine hurled the broken piece of the beak he still held in one hand, pinning the tongue to the floor. The Demon squealed like a wounded pig and pulled harder, tearing its own flesh in an attempt to escape. With the muscle in the organ now powerless, Black ripped his leg free of the tongue and rammed the Elven blade into the maw before the creature could close it and flee.

"Cox!" Gray snapped as he reloaded his Cerberus. "What kinda bullshit early warning was that?!"

"I don't know, sir!" Cox responded, shrugging at the Master Sergeant. "I think something is fucking with my sensors."

"He's right," Greer muttered. "I didn't notice because of how dense the security is on the doors, but I think we have a Hijacker."

"Here?" the Overmaiden asked, a note of genuine surprise in her voice. "Why would they want a Hijacker here? This was just a weather station."

"Beats me, ma'am," Greer responded flatly. "I just know that the code is Demonic, and it's all over the fucking place. Have a look."

After a brief silence, the Overmaiden finally spoke up. "Intriguing. Do you require assistance in bypassing it?"

"That's not the protocol, ma'am," Greer warned her. If he hadn't, Gray would have. As sophisticated as AIs were, they could still be corrupted by Demonic influence. Ghost AIs were especially susceptible, having once been human. Any AI that was compromised had to be immediately decompiled and destroyed. It wasn't a risk worth taking if Greer could handle it.

Davis turned to look back at them. "Actually, I think I can manage enough of a counterspell to disrupt the Hijacker's connection. It should give you enough time to trace the hack."

"Let's see it," Gray said, motioning to the door at the end of the corridor. Davis moved forward, crouching next to the mass of flesh and steel while Cox offered him cover. With his combat knife, the man carved a symbol into the flesh portion of the door and placed his hand over it, muttering a chant into a dedicated channel with Greer, who interfaced with the subnet of the station wirelessly.

"It's just trying to slow us down, not keep us out," Greer announced as the rest of the squad posted up at the door. "Buying time for the ritual they're working on. The sensor interference is incidental though, not intentional. The Hijacker is trying to jam anything that might give a better idea of what's going on in here. It just caught Cox up in it."

"Can you track it?" Cox asked over the comms. "Davis can't keep chanting all day."

"I can, but it won't do us much good if we can't get to it and shut it down," Greer responded irritably. "Maybe if I can access the database, I can— "

"I'll get it," the Hellmarine said, hefting his Perforator with one hand. "Tell me where to go."

Greer glanced at Gray apprehensively. "Quickly, Greer. Nature Boy doesn't want to be late for his appointment."

"Uh, er—" Greer stammered, clearing his throat. He turned a few times to orient himself and then pointed down one of the side corridors. "Down that way and up two floors. I don't understand how you intend to—"

The Hellmarine broke from the squad and thundered down the hallway, leaving the rest of them in confused silence for a time.

"Think he'll drop us a postcard?" Cox joked, uncomfortable with the quiet that had settled in. As much as Gray got on his ass for the constant banter, he silently empathized with the discomfort. He'd been there before several times.

"Ramirez to Gray," Ramirez hailed over a separate channel. Gray's HUD switched over to answer.

"Go ahead, Ramirez," he said, looking away from the others.

"Sir, we just noticed a weird shift in what's left of their security out here," Ramirez explained. "They've just abandoned the attempt to get past us and are moving somewhere else entirely. Maybe another entrance?"

"It looks like they're crawling in through some kind of infernaformed ventilation systems set into the ground around the foundation," Chambers chimed in without warning. "We can see them breaking off."

"The Hijacker is calling them back in," Gray responded. "Things are about to get real messy in here."

"Do you want us to reposition?" Ramirez asked, ready to drop everything to come assist them.

"Negative," Gray replied. "Hold position for now. It's too cramped in here for too many of us anyway."

Ramirez didn't respond immediately. Gray could tell that he felt conflicted even if he didn't say it. "We got this, Ramirez. Just make sure there's an exit ready for us when we're done."

"Yes, sir," Ramirez finally replied.

Gray switched over to the main channel and sighed. "They're regrouping somewhere inside, so expect heavier contact."

The floor lurched with the force of an explosion somewhere else in the station. A moment later the door in front of them opened, revealing the Hellmarine covered in the gore of the Hijacker he held dead in one hand. Tossing it onto the floor in front of them, they all got to have a look at the brutalized form of the Demon that had been fucking with them from afar.

Hijackers looked deceptively frail—like large flesh balloons covered in cancerous growths. But they were much tougher than they appeared at first blush. Each of their numerous eyes was capable of discharging energy attacks on par with a blaster and could acquire multiple targets independently or focus the energy together for a single powerful blast. Though the Hellmarine's armor looked a little scorched in places, it looked like he hadn't been deterred by the blasts.

Greer leaned over the corpse, extending a connector cable from the gauntlet of his armor to interface with one of the many haphazard cybernetic implants the creature had protruding from its body. "Well, this is embarrassing—we didn't get him anything."

"Well, there's always his birthday, right?" Cox quipped, glancing between the Hijacker and the Hellmarine. "You got a birthday, right?"

The Hellmarine regarded Cox silently, then shrugged.

"Got its database and...bingo!" Greer laughed triumphantly, updating the squad's navigation with the location of the ritual chamber. "Fucking incredible."

"Let's move," Gray ordered, and the squad fell back into formation, rushing through the newly opened doors and down another corridor teeming with Demons rushing at them. Gray divided his attention between laying down fire on the creatures ahead of him and noting the changes in the route on the minimap on his HUD.

"End of this corridor and then down two levels," Gray announced on the main channel. "Davis, plow the road."

"Yes, sir," the Theurgy Sergeant responded, keying his blast cannon into its warm-up cycle. He was the only one besides Gray rated for such a weapon in the squad, but given how expensive the weapons were, they typically only had one per squad. Using his knowledge of magic and incantations, Davis had a way with them that Gray just couldn't match, so he was the one designated to carry it.

The power draw on the weapon was so high that it had to take it directly from the armor, reducing its weight but requiring a physical connection. Davis, through the use of subtle magic, was able to speed up the charge sequence through some trick he knew. A moment after warming the weapon up, Davis leveled the blast cannon with the long corridor and shouted for everyone to get clear. Once he got the all-clear, he fired the weapon.

A brilliant, eye-blistering, red beam of directed energy roared down the hallway, carving every last Demon in half while scalding various portions of the fleshy surface of the infernaformed corridor itself. The Marines let out a collective whoop of excitement—seeing such a weapon in action was always a treat.

"Fuck me, I wish we could use that thing all the time," Cox laughed, exchanging high fives with Davis as the weapon went into a cooldown cycle. "You gotta teach me that shit."

"Maybe if you grow up big and strong, kid," Davis joked back nervously. Handling a weapon of that size and power while also working magic was no small feat for a human. It was taxing on the armor as well as the person inside it. Each time the weapon was fired in such a way, it carried a myriad of risks Gray didn't wish to think about.

Making their way down the corridor and disposing of any wounded Demons and stragglers, they reached what had once been an elevator shaft. Now it was completely overrun with tendrils and swollen pustules the size of basketballs. Cox nudged a loose piece of debris over the side and into the darkness, tracking the descent of the object with the sensors of his armor to provide a rudimentary model of the shaft in the squad's HUDs. "Looks clear, sir."

Roars and screams echoed from one of the side corridors they'd passed along the way. Something large moving on the floor above them rattled the broken and burned-out lights overhead. "Not for long," Gray muttered. "Everybody in. Double time!"

Leaping into the darkness was nothing new for Gray. As he and the rest of the squad dropped blindly into the abyss below, he briefly reflected on how many times he'd done the exact same thing over the course of his long and distinguished career. The shock absorbers of their armor made the drop a trivial matter, but as the Hellmarine knocked the remnants of the shaft door open with his bare fists, they were treated to an unusually grotesque sight.

What must have once been a server room for processing the massive data streams of various weather and atmosphere systems was now a fully converted ritual chamber.

The servers throbbed with their own pulses, seething with Profane Energy and casting the room in an uncomfortable orange and red hue. Numerous warlocks were gathered, their heads bowed, and their flesh was freshly mutilated for the rite led by the creature chanting at the altar. Though it looked similar to them, it had Demonic traits as well, chief of which was its black eyes and long, curling horns. Next to it was a ten-foot-tall creature that appeared mostly humanoid save for its goat-like face, horns, and legs.

"Fuck me, that's Lazariktinus of the Order of Baphomet," Davis hissed through the comms. "It's a motherfucking Voivode!"

Gray's expression hardened as he considered their options. It would only be seconds before they were noticed, and they had two priority targets to contend with. Vidame were the heads of individual horde chapters of warlocks under a given Duke, but Voivodes were generals—warlords, really—for said Dukes. The fact both were here spoke to something much larger.

"Looks like we're getting our ten thousand steps in today, ladies," Gray announced, flagging each of the Marines in his HUD to provide them with quick directions. He and the rest of the squad had to lay down fire on the warlocks, draw the attention of the Voivode, and allow the Hellmarine and the Overmaiden to disrupt the ritual before its ultimate conclusion.

"Thrusters hot!" He ordered as they charged in, activating the thruster systems of their armor meant for zero-G movement. With the thrusters firing, their movement speed became even swifter than it already was, allowing them to hit the circles of warlocks hard before they had much opportunity to erect defensive barriers. "Fuck 'em up!"

Lazariktinus turned to face them, her goat-like face twisted with rage and indignation at the interference. Her perky breasts held a series of chains from piercings in her nipples that swayed as her arm swung out, catching half of them in a disruptor wave that sent them flying and their HUDs flashing with warnings that their armor had just depolarized.

"KILL THEM!" the Voivode snarled, her unsettling gaze falling on Gray as he struggled to his feet. "Add their meat to the ritual!"

"I hate the talking ones," Gray muttered, kicking his legs to push himself up the wall at his back. "Davis?"

"Circuit's overloaded," he replied uncertainly as he tried and failed to fire up the blast cannon. "I don't know if it's the gun or the armor. My HUD's going fucking nuts."

"Greer!?" Gray barked.

"I don't normally make house calls," Greer grunted as he laid into a couple of warlocks with his Perforator. "But I'll try once I get some breathing room."

"Sir, she ain't gonna fucking go for that!" Cox called as Lazariktinus descended the altar to make her way toward them. From the shaft behind them and the old ventilation ducts overhead, more Demons began to pour into the massive chamber, shoring up the defensive strength of the warlocks.

With another gesture of her hand, a small black orb the size of a marble formed in their midst, immediately forcing them and any loose bodies into it as if they were falling from a great distance. Again, the shock absorption of the armor prevented them from being more than inconvenienced, but the longer they remained pressed together around the orb of gravity, the more profane power she fed it. Soon, they would be crushed into a seamless ball of flesh and metal.

Gray strained to turn his head, trying to see if the Hellmarine had at least disrupted the ritual, but he lacked the proper vantage point. He didn't hear any more chanting, so that was a good sign.

"Now's probably not a good time to say this," Cox groaned under the strain of the magic crushing them. "But I gotta take a piss."

Suddenly, the small planetoid of Marines broke apart and crashed back down to the ground as the Hellmarine collided with the Voivode. Though protected by a personal energy barrier, Lazariktinus was dumbstruck by the sudden show of force.

"How dare y—" the Voivode snarled, only to be cut off by the sight of the Vidame's rent remains littering the chamber floor. The Hellmarine leaned over Davis, picked up the Scalder, and ripped the connector free of the Marine's armor.

"...How is that possible?" Lazariktinus muttered with horror. As a Voivode, she could sense things about the Hellmarine that the rest of them couldn't, and it must have unsettled her deeply, based on her expression. With a sudden shriek of unbridled rage, she brought both hands forward, unleashing a blast of potent purple energy on the Hellmarine.

The Hellmarine didn't panic as he plugged the Scalder into a port on his armor and fired it up. To Gray's surprise, the weapon came on almost immediately as his HUD signaled a sudden spike in Eldritch Energy along with a blaring warning to clear the area.

Purple profane magic was met with an immense beam of directed energy that started red before shifting toward white. The Scalder smoked under the strain as the Hellmarine let out a blood-curdling warcry, cutting through the profane magic of the Voivode like a hot knife through butter and utterly vaporizing the top half of the Demon in the blink of an eye.

Chapter 9

THE SMOKING STUMP OF the Voivode remained standing for only a moment longer, wobbling from side to side before falling lifelessly to the ground. The Scalder blaster cannon's warning lights flashed across the Hellmarine's HUD, which the Overmaiden was monitoring.

"That was more than expected," the Overmaiden admitted. "It seems you've fried the capacitor of the Scalder—among other components."

The Hellmarine pulled the cable from his armor and discarded the weapon. Overhead, the mass of Demons pouring in through the ventilation shrieked and roared as the influence they received from the Voivode's power was broken.

"Break time's over, Marines!" the Master Sergeant barked as he crawled out of the pile of power armor that had been created when the Voivode's spell had been disrupted. "We're gonna have to fight our way out of here!"

The Marines scrambled to their feet, grabbing up whatever weapons they could in the process. Cox was one of the first on his feet and spent his time jabbing the corpse of the Voivode with his boot. The body rolled limply to one side, exposing the barbed phallus of the creature beneath its loincloth.

"Oh shit," Cox chuckled nervously. "I thought we'd just had our asses beat by a chick. It had tits and everything."

"I'm going to tell Chambers you said that," Miller remarked as he picked up his silenced Hailstorm. "Bet she'll have something to say about that."

"All the Demons of the Order of Baphomet are hermaphrodites, dumbass," Davis grumbled despondently as he mourned the loss of the fried blast cannon in his arms. Cox held his hands up in surrender as he stepped away from the smoking remains of the creature the Hellmarine had slain. Behind it was a deep molten hole that reached through the metal wall and into the surrounding rock.

"Cox to Chambers," Cox hailed over a secondary channel that the Overmaiden was also monitoring. "Tell me we got an LZ up there we can use."

"I think I can get you one. Is it time to go already?" Chambers joked. "Sounded like the party was just getting started."

"You're hilarious," Cox grunted as he got to his feet, cutting the channel and opening a new one to the dropship. "Rain of Blood, this is Cox requesting immediate evac. Chambers will pop the smoke, but the rest of us are coming in hot."

"Understood," the pilot acknowledged. The Overmaiden watched on the wider sensor band as the dropship came about and began its descent lower into the atmosphere.

The Hellmarine snarled as he drew the chainchete from his back. He'd exhausted his Perforator's ammunition in the initial rush and fight with the Vidame who had proven formidable, but not enough to hold him at bay. The Overmaiden keyed the Hellmarine's comm. "What are you doing?"

"Not finished," the Hellmarine responded, rushing past the cluster of Marines taking up their formation to carve into the nearest Devourer seeking a meal. The sword whirred to life, screaming as the teeth bit down through flesh and bone with equal ease. The spray across the Hellmarine's faceplate obscured most of his vision, but the Overmaiden observed that it didn't deter him in the slightest.

Switching over to the internal sensors of his armor, the Overmaiden ran a quick diagnostic of his vitals, which showed several abnormalities. The sudden appearance of Eldritch Energy that the Hellmarine had managed to channel was outside of the AI's wildest expectations. Quixotic Energy—the energy utilized by the Zintari—was theorized to be possible at later stages of the Hellmarine's development, but Eldritch Energy was unheard of.

The Overmaiden found it surprisingly difficult to run an in-depth analysis with the Hellmarine hacking and slashing his way through a discordant horde of Demonic flesh and blood. Even with her superior processing matrix, it was a bit much.

"You don't have to do this," the Overmaiden cautioned him. "We've achieved our goal. The horde will turn on itself the moment we're gone."

An indicator on the Hellmarine's HUD flashed, grabbing the Overmaiden's attention. There was a faint signature of Divine Energy registering from the direction that the Hellmarine was going. If it weren't for how determined he was to reach the source, the Overmaiden would have written it off as a sensor glitch from the surge of Eldritch Energy. That was what he must have meant when he said he wasn't finished. Still, Divine Energy didn't make sense. So little of this mission made sense to her anymore.

As the Hellmarine erupted from a dense cluster of gnashing teeth and sharp claws, things finally started to come together. There, in a small holding area covered in profane sigils and unholy power, knelt an Angel. In all her incarnations, the Overmaiden had never personally witnessed the presence of such a creature, but numerous species that humanity had come into contact with over the years mentioned them or had brushes with them. Their existence had been proposed in the early days, shortly after the initial contact with Demons on the world of Numedha. Soon after, Enochian runes had been discovered, showing that perhaps they had once lived on the world—or were worshiped by those who did.

"Master Sergeant," the Overmaiden said calmly over the main channel. "We have a development here. A survivor. She's seriously wounded."

The Angel—a female—was badly mangled, with one arm torn free from the elbow down. The stump had been tied off to staunch the bleeding, but judging by the pool of the silvery substance at her feet, she'd lost a great deal of it before she'd completed it.

"Cox, let Wilder know that it'll be a medivac," the Overmaiden ordered, a note of tension in her voice as she spoke. "And tell her to step on it."

"Yes, ma'am," Cox answered without a trace of complaint.

Even in her mangled state, the Angel was a thing of beauty even to an AI. She had long golden hair and wings that had once been pristine white. She still had pieces of armor clinging to her, though most of it had been as badly maimed as her or outright destroyed. She regarded them coldly for a moment as the Marines approached, laying down intense fire to clear the area around them. Without the appropriate leadership, the creatures were flailing wildly for the most part, making the chamber a shooting gallery of sorts for the trained professionals.

"Ramirez!" the Master Sergeant hailed his second in command on a side channel. "Help Chambers clear the LZ and have Simms ready! We have a wounded—"

The Master Sergeant's voice trailed off as they converged on the Hellmarine's location. "Lord, above…"

It was the only time the Overmaiden had heard the Master Sergeant take such a reverent tone. The muttering and surprise of the other Marines echoed the statement.

The Hellmarine pressed his hand against the magical barrier despite the crackling and spitting of Profane Energy that he received as a response. The Overmaiden noted how quickly his vitals showed a state of calm setting in on the man as he investigated the woman.

"Humans?" the Angel muttered weakly, confused. "How?"

"Let me talk to her," the Overmaiden said to the Hellmarine. Taking his hand off the barrier, he produced the part of his gauntlet that had been modified with a small holoprojector. An instant later, a miniature version of the Overmaiden's glowing blue body formed over it.

"We're going to get you out of here," the Overmaiden assured her. "What's your name?"

"I am Seraphiel of the Third Choir of Archangels, sent on a mission with my brothers and sisters to pacify this planet's heresy before it grew too dangerous," the Angel explained. There was a strange way in which she spoke—like someone who hadn't used a particular language in a long time and was remembering much of it as she went.

"Are there any others?" the Overmaiden asked as Seraphiel examined the Hellmarine warily. The Angel's gaze drifted back toward the hologram, her eyes becoming glassy.

"No," Seraphiel replied, shaking her head shamefully. "They were sacrificed in the ritual."

"That would explain the exponential spread of the horde across the planet," the Overmaiden deduced. With that amount of energy, they had likely ripped a larger rift between Aonus and Hell, using the original Zintari gateway as a focus. "Just hold on. We'll find a way to get you out."

The Hellmarine took a step back, cocked his fist, and slammed the gauntlet into the barrier, causing electrical sparks to spit in every direction. When the barrier didn't give on the first strike, the man growled and repeated the process again and again. Each time his fist struck the barrier, he was showered with more crimson sparks as stress fractures formed.

"H-h-holy shit," Cox laughed in disbelief. "There's no way, man!"

With a final powerful strike, the field shorted, causing an uneven gap to form where he'd been beating with his fist. Cutting the hologram feed, the Hellmarine shoved both hands into the gap and began to pull it wider.

"Sonuva bitch," Davis muttered in awe. "Never seen anything like that."

The indicators on the Hellmarine's HUD flashed, letting him know that his armor had completely depolarized and that a suit breach was imminent. Still, he continued, widening his stance and ripping the tear in the profane field wider. Once it reached the ground, the circle that had formed the spell broke, and the magic unraveled quickly.

Davis stepped over the broken circle and offered his assistance to the Angel, who seemed reluctant to accept. "It's alright, I got you," he assured her. "We have a medic waiting to patch you up."

Seraphiel nodded in understanding and weakly slung an arm over the shoulder of Davis's armor. As she stood, the Marines realized just how tall she really was. Her wings fluttered gently, breaking into segments of light before fading from view entirely as if they, too, were holographic.

The Hellmarine regarded her quietly and calmly even as smoke rose from the gauntlets of his armor. She was more than a foot taller than Dr. Hughes at least, making her taller than some of the Marines outside their armor. Still, she looked up at him in awe and confusion, no doubt puzzled why something like him could exist, before her curiosity gave way to sorrow.

"I'm sorry," Seraphiel muttered tearfully. "I couldn't stop them. I did everything I could, but—my brothers and sisters. They're all dead now."

The few remaining Demons in the chamber had already either been picked off by the Marines or retreated in the face of the Hellmarine's awesome display of savagery and his feat of beating a profane barrier into submission. As a result, the room was quiet save for the Angel's sobs. An uneasy tension settled across the Marines, who all took notice of the silvery smears in and around the circle. How many Angels had died to fuel such a ritual?

The Hellmarine turned and picked up his chainchete. "They've been avenged."

"Sarge," Cox said somberly. "The fourth ventilation shaft up there can bring us right to the surface."

"Grapples," the Master Sergeant ordered, causing each of the Marines to switch over to the grappling units in their gauntlets—all except for Greer, who'd detoured to jack into a data port he'd spotted on the transformed servers. "Greer! Get your ass back in formation, Marine!"

"Just a second, Sergeant," Greer responded. "I'm grabbing as much of their database as I can so we can look it over later."

"Mm," the Master Sergeant grunted in response. "Alright, make it quick. Our ride's waiting."

Once the download was complete, the Marines and the Hellmarine fired their grapnels up into the large ventilation duct and ascended from the blood-soaked ritual chamber. The ducts were more like tunnels and carried the sound of distant Demonic squabbles as such. The squad rushed toward the surface, following the trail the Demons had left behind when they'd crawled down to meet them earlier.

"They were changing the atmosphere," Seraphiel explained weakly as she hobbled along with Davis. "Accelerating the infernaforming."

"I didn't know they could do that," Davis muttered in response, pacing himself so that he wasn't dragging her.

Emerging from the broken access on the surface, the Marines found the dropship waiting for them along with the rest of the squad, laying down the occasional bursts of suppression fire. As they approached the ramp, Romero stared at the woman hanging off of Davis.

"Dios mio…" the sniper gasped, placing a hand over his chest reverently. "Is that—"

"Take it easy, Romero," the Master Sergeant ordered. "Sit your ass down so we can—"

The Hellmarine grabbed King's Lancer and satchel charges from the deck and stepped off the ramp. "I need to borrow this."

The squad exchanged glances before turning their attention to King, who looked on indignantly as the Hellmarine vanished back into the tunnel's surface access.

"What are you doing?" The Overmaiden inquired, exasperated.

"Finishing it," the Hellmarine answered with a note of finality. Arriving at the point where the duct turned downward to the lower levels, he tossed the charges over the side and gave them a moment to hit the ground of the ritual chamber far below. Then, he took aim with the Lancer and fired a rocket into the belly of the complex.

"That's a terrible idea!" the Overmaiden exclaimed in his helmet, but the man wasn't listening. He'd already turned to begin sprinting back up the tunnel toward the surface. Despite how fast the man could move, he fired the thrusters in his armor to gain even more speed as fire shot up through the tunnel behind him. Were it anyone else, the Overmaiden mused, they wouldn't have made it.

The Hellmarine didn't stop until he was on the ramp of the dropship, which had already begun to lift off the ground as explosions tore through the complex. The cluster of charges and the rocket had reacted with the unstable magical remnants of the profane ritual and the spell used to bind the Angels in place, causing crimson fire to engulf the lower levels and erupt onto the surface.

The barren ground around the complex surged upward as the ventilation failed to provide enough release for the magical explosion. The cracks that formed allowed more of the heat and magic to escape, causing the massive swath of earth to drop back in on itself before vanishing behind plumes of smoke and debris.

The Hellmarine held the Lancer out to King, who took it off his hands slowly, staring out the back of the dropship until the ramp was fully closed. "How many rockets did you use?"

"One," the Hellmarine responded as he walked past the others to take his seat.

"This guy's fuckin' unreal," Cox laughed as he pulled his helmet off, already secure in his seat.

Romero stared at him for a moment before glancing at Seraphiel again. "He's the Sword of Mankind..."

"Oh, come on," Cox scoffed, looking away from the other Marine. "That's a bit much."

"Is it?" Romero argued, pulling his helmet off to shoot Cox a glare. "He just recovered a fucking Angel from a pit of Demonic magic! After slaying a Voivode and a Vidame!"

Simms knelt in front of Seraphiel, holding his hand an inch from her arm as the integrated medical gauntlet did its job. Without warning, he gave her a quick injection close to the shoulder. She winced, staring at him angrily, but he ignored her. His hands, even in the power armor, moved swiftly as he went to work with things from his kit to ensure she wouldn't lose her life to the injury or any of the others she'd sustained.

"We need to get this off," he said, patting the armor and prompting Davis to apologize softly before assisting in removing the damaged tech. The medic glanced up at Seraphiel briefly before resuming his work. "You're going to be alright, so long as we can get you back to the ship. I think you're going to lose the arm, though."

"Such is the price of life," the Angel responded bitterly. "Do what you must."

Simms nodded, continuing his work heedless of the silvery blood staining his gauntlets.

"It'll take us some time to get back," the Master Sergeant noted in a more subdued tone. "The Midnight Sea left orbit to rendezvous with the rest of the fleet the minute we went planetside. Can you keep her stable until then?"

"Yeah," Simms answered without taking his eyes off his work. "Nothing a little duct tape won't hold together."

"Good," the Master Sergeant muttered before taking his seat. The Overmaiden only then noticed how seldom she saw the man actually using it, preferring instead to remain on his feet during drops.

"Are you alright, Master Sergeant?" the Overmaiden inquired.

"It's been a long day," Gray replied, pulling his helmet off and popping an unlit cigar in his mouth. "I need a drink. And a bath."

"I think Chambers has some candles you can borrow, too," Cox quipped with a little chuckle. "Might even be able to dig up some rose petals for you, sir."

The Master Sergeant let out an amused snort despite himself, resting his head against the bulkhead as he chuckled softly. "Smartass."

"More like dumbass!" Chambers snapped as she swatted Cox's arm. "Stay away from my candles, asshole!"

"It'll be a few hours before we can catch up with the Midnight Sea," Wilder announced over the comms. "So if you want to get a little shuteye, now's the time."

As the Marines settled in and busied themselves with their myriad post-op rituals, the Hellmarine simply remained upright, his hands resting on his thighs as he stared blankly in the direction of Seraphiel while Simms treated her wounds.

"What's wrong?" the Overmaiden asked, noting unusual activity in his vitals. She wouldn't be able to make complete sense of it until she had more sophisticated equipment. Indeed, she would have to have the armorer go over everything with a fine-tooth comb to ensure there was no lasting damage from the Eldritch Energy the Hellmarine had wielded earlier.

The Overmaiden noticed that as he stared at the Angel, she was stealing glances back in his direction, though she attempted to hide the fact each time she did. Seraphiel could certainly sense that he wasn't like the other humans, even if the staggering feats he'd already demonstrated weren't enough to convince her already. Similarly, the Overmaiden could tell that the Hellmarine sensed the traces of Divine Energy about Seraphiel, diminished though they were.

"It's nothing," the Hellmarine dismissed, closing his eyes to rest, though not truly sleeping. He remained upright, awake, and alert in case they ran into any more trouble along the way.

CHAPTER 10

WHEN MANDY HUGHES HEARD the Hellmarine had returned mostly unscathed, she let out an audible sigh of relief. The Armorer would have her hands full with patching up the damage to the Hades Mk. II, but Mandy was more concerned about the man inside it for a variety of reasons. Looking after his health and well-being was her job, but there was more to it than that. She felt a certain rush of excitement when he looked at her. There was a hypermasculine energy that rolled off of him that was nothing short of intoxicating.

"You should get going," one of the other doctors said as he washed his hands clean of blood. They'd taken much of the wounded from the other ships to treat, considering how much more expansive—and undamaged—their own facilities were. When they'd arrived in Zabradus space, the battle with the Demonic fleet had already been lost and the Alliance ships were in full retreat. All the Midnight Sea could do was cover their retreat, reduce their casualties and assist them with their repairs and wounded. Mandy had spent the last several hours assisting the medical staff of the Midnight Sea with the latter. "I think I got the rest of this."

"Are you sure?" Mandy asked, though mentally, she already had one foot out the door. "I can stay a little while longer."

"Nah," the doctor said as he continued to scrub his hands in the sink. "You have other things to do. The Hellmarine sounds like a handful."

"Ah, yeah," Mandy laughed almost giddily. "More than a handful, really."

"They said they have an Angel with them," the doctor laughed a little. "You think there's any truth to that?"

"I guess I'm about to find out," Mandy responded as she gathered her things. Though she was dedicated to the health of the Hellmarine, she couldn't help but be a little curious about a supposed Angel that the squad reported recovering on the planet.

By the time she reached the lab dedicated to the Hellmarine, Mandy found that they had laid a woman with golden blonde hair out on the bed where she had expected to see him. Frowning, Mandy approached the woman as the hologram of the Overmaiden appeared from the lab's projectors. "Where is he?"

"Getting his armor looked at," the Overmaiden replied with a level tone, nodding toward the woman on the table and the Marine with her. "This is Seraphiel."

The Marine that had tended to the woman on the trip back to the Midnight Sea—a medic by the name of Simms—gave Mandy a quick and succinct rundown of the damage the woman had sustained and some of the observations he'd made while trying to patch her up. He expressed doubt about her keeping what was left of her arm. He was right to do so.

"We'll have to fit it for a cybernetic," Mandy agreed as she rolled a large piece of equipment over to Seraphiel's bed-side. She noted the odd silver blood that had stained her skin and clothing.

"A what?" Seraphiel responded a little indignantly.

"A prosthetic," Simms clarified, placing his helmet on a near-by table. "Functional, of course."

"Such crude, rudimentary technology you have," Seraphiel remarked, looking at the machine Mandy had maneuvered into place. "Might as well just use a hacksaw."

"Shut it," Simms responded curtly, surprising the gold-en-haired woman. "Or I can arrange the hacksaw."

Seraphiel pressed her lips into a thin line and looked away as Mandy went to work with an array of surgical lasers that cut through tissue and bone along the woman's shoulder. Not only had her arm been ripped off from the elbow down, but much of the bone near the shoulder had been pulverized. It was little more than shards drifting in her flesh. One of the other machines provided her with a detailed image to work with.

"I'll have to rebuild the socket," Mandy sighed, shaking her head. "The damage is really bad."

"Alright, I'll get my armor off and scrub in," Simms responded, grabbing his helmet. "I should be back before you get started on the shoulder."

"Oh!" Mandy chirped, a little surprised. She'd been under the impression that she'd be left to do it alone. "That's very generous, thank you."

"Behave yourself," Simms said, pointing at the Angel as he moved briskly from the lab.

"We found her in a ritual chamber," the Overmaiden told Mandy once Simms exited the lab. "They were sacrificing them. I'm processing the data that Greer collected now, but it would be better if Dr. Cosgrove was here to lend his expertise."

"He'll be back in an hour," Mandy answered without looking up from the scope on the machine as she cut away more dead tissue. Though Simms had already applied a powerful local anesthetic, the Angel remained conscious and appeared to be slightly uncomfortable. "Do you need something more for the pain?"

"No," Seraphiel replied, her head turning slowly to look at the remains of her arm as Mandy worked. "There is no escaping the consequences of our actions."

"Where is he?" the Overmaiden pressed, interrupting their exchange.

"He went over to the Tides of War to help their crew," Mandy quickly explained. "They took a direct hit to their medical bay, so they're setting up a triage unit in their cargo bay."

"I see," the Overmaiden noted. "That's rather unfortunate."

Simms returned shortly after to begin preparations for the cybernetics. The two worked for hours while the Over-maiden popped in and out of the lab to check on their progress. Mandy knew that she could likely have just used internal sensors to do it, but for some reason, she wanted to be seen.

By the time they were done, the entire shoulder joint had been replaced along with the arm. Connecting the nerves was surprisingly easy, considering the fact that Seraphiel was an entirely different species than Mandy was accustomed to working with. She had experience with other species but none so exotic as an Angel. The nerves and tissue seemed to seek out connection, finding the connectors for the cybernetic arm and bonding to them readily. It was a strange phenomenon that she doubted anyone would believe had she not been recording every aspect of the procedure.

"Alright, try moving it," Mandy said as she took a step back to give Seraphiel some room. The Angel lifted the arm slowly, turning it back and forth with a curious look in her eyes.

"Now, fingers," Simms said, glancing at a data panel to check for any latency. "Wiggle them and then make a fist."

Seraphiel did as instructed with surprising ease despite her hesitancy. Simms monitored the panel carefully as she did, nodding in approval when the test came back positive. "We already gave you something to keep your body from rejecting the prosthetic, but you'll have to come back to Hughes regularly for injections as it heals. Frankly, we're lucky it seems to be working on you, given the fact that you aren't human."

Seraphiel continued to stare at her new limb as she offered her perspective on that. "Our mutual Creator made your kind and ours both in His image."

"How does it feel?" Mandy said, crossing her arms a little excitedly. She'd done various cybernetics before, but their work on Seraphiel felt particularly noteworthy to her.

"Adequate," Seraphiel responded, continuing to move her arm and fingers. Despite her restrained praise, it was clear that she was moderately impressed with the arm and the ability to touch and feel it again. "Thank you."

"It wasn't just me," Mandy responded, shooting Simms a smile. "You're much more talented than I would have thought for a medic. You could be a ship's doctor if you wanted."

"Yeah, I've heard that before," Simms replied gruffly. "But my place is in the field. I couldn't stand to be stuck behind a desk or writing papers."

Mandy shrugged, deciding to leave the matter alone. By the way, he spoke, it seemed like a sore subject with the man. He didn't have much of a bedside manner, so perhaps it was for the best that he wasn't a ship's doctor. She supposed Marines were tough enough to handle his prickly nature, though. "Would you be able to escort her to a room so she can get some rest?"

"Sure," Simms agreed, motioning with his head for Seraphiel to get up. Mandy would have been less abrupt, but it seemed like the kind of approach the Angel understood. She got to her feet, steadied herself, and took a few test steps to ensure she wouldn't fall on her face.

"Incredible," Mandy laughed. "We pumped you full of enough painkillers to knock out an elephant, yet you're sober as a priest."

"My people are much hardier than yours," Seraphiel remarked coldly just a moment before stumbling slightly. She caught herself on the edge of a nearby table and remained there until she regained her composure. "Though perhaps I will take it slowly."

"Good idea," Simms said, offering his shoulder for her to lean on. After a brief moment of hesitation, the Angel gently put her hand on the man's shoulder to allow him to guide her.

"Whew!" Mandy said, collapsing into a chair of her own once the pair left the lab. "What a day."

"It's not over yet," the Overmaiden interjected. She'd been so quiet and reserved that Mandy had entirely forgotten she'd been standing in the room. "I require your assistance with the Hellmarine."

"Is he alright?" Mandy asked, closing her eyes as she leaned back into her chair. Her feet ached, and she felt like she could sleep for a week. "Can it wait until tomorrow?"

"He's having trouble sleeping, even after burning so much energy on the last mission," the Overmaiden answered indirectly. "I've been monitoring him since he left the Armorer and went to his quarters. He's just been sitting there in the dark."

Mandy opened one eye, curious. "Doing what?"

"Nothing," the Overmaiden replied. "He's just sitting there. I'd like it if you could stay in his quarters for the night—monitor his vitals and record anything strange you might observe. Even just keep him company. There were a few anomalies during the operation that I have to go over."

The fatigue and exhaustion Mandy had felt a moment before lifted like a fog as she sprang to her feet. "Yeah! I mean—s-sure, no problem. I guess I can do that."

The hologram arched a brow as Mandy went around the room to gather some things. "If you see anything strange, I expect you to report it to me. Understand?"

"Yeah, yeah," Mandy said, waving her arm as she tossed some things haphazardly into a bag. "No problem! We don't even know for sure if he sleeps at all, so it might be nothing."

"Perhaps," the Overmaiden responded skeptically.

Mandy said her goodbyes and walked briskly out of the room toward her quarters, where she decided to freshen up. Despite how unprofessional it was, she was eager to see the Hellmarine again. She wanted to make an impression on him the way he had with her, and she wasn't confident in her ability to do that after a long day of work.

She blew through her quarters like a miniature hurricane, picking out some clothes that were more casual without being too revealing. At least, not at first. She made sure the blouse had some buttons that could be undone should the situation arise. She jumped into the shower after that, scrubbing herself thoroughly before finding some perfume to spritz herself with. It was only when she pulled some distinctly sexy lingerie from her drawer that she stopped to look at herself in the mirror, shocked.

Mandy couldn't believe what she was doing. Was she really going to throw herself at the man after what he'd been through? She was supposed to be monitoring and treating him, not trying to slither her way into his bed. As the logical part of her mind attempted to talk her down from making what could be a costly mistake, another part of her mind—more feral—kept screaming, "Physician, heal thyself!"

She chewed her lip as the two factions of her mind went to war with one another. In the end, she split the difference, setting the sexy undies back in the drawer but keeping everything else she'd prepared for her impromptu sleepover. Once she was dressed, she spared a moment to hike the girls up a little to ensure they were nice and perky before setting out. The feral part of her mind rejoiced while the logical part scolded her relentlessly all the way to the door of the Hellmarine's quarters.

Mandy pressed the door chime and waited patiently, fussing over her hair until the very last minute. As the door opened, she found herself standing a little taller and grinning a little wider. "Hey! Did the Overmaiden talk to you about me monitoring you overnight?"

"No," the Hellmarine answered, glancing up and down the corridor suspiciously. Mandy felt suddenly foolish for practically skipping over to see him when he hadn't even known she was coming.

"Oh." She couldn't help but sound a little disappointed as she stood awkwardly outside his door. "Well, she said you still weren't sleeping yet and wanted me to look in on you. She—we—think I should keep an eye on you overnight to make sure it's not something we need to be worried about."

The Hellmarine shrugged and stepped aside, granting her access to his quarters. Stepping inside, she noted how minimalist the decor was. It only had the same basic features and furniture that any newly assigned room had, except for his unusually large bed.

"I didn't know they made them that big on the ship," Mandy observed with a little laugh. "Guess you got lucky."

"Not exactly," he said, stepping away from the door as it shut behind him. Mandy looked at the bed again and realized that it wasn't one large bed but two that had been cobbled together to accommodate his size. Pursing her lips together, she decided it was best just to unpack her things and pretend like she hadn't just made a fool of herself again.

Mandy set the small hand scanners and data pad on the small table in the corner. "Are you experiencing any fatigue? Discomfort? Anything strange compared to how you felt before the mission?"

The Hellmarine sat on the small sofa, which looked even smaller compared to his impressive stature. It made Mandy think of what it must have looked like for a grown man to sit on a child's toy chair.

"Restless, I suppose," the Hellmarine finally answered with a slight shrug. He didn't appear confident in his word choice but had to settle on something.

Mandy nodded as she checked the hand scanner's calibration and then held it out to him. "Alright, well, let's have a look here."

The Hellmarine remained completely still as she ran the scanner around his head, down his neck, and along his shoulders. As she leaned over, she noticed his muscles become more tense and his pulse quicken slightly. She realized only when she looked up at him that his eyes had drifted down to her cleavage. The feral part of her mind raged against the inside of her cranium, urging her to hop in his lap and ride him like a new pony.

Mandy told herself she would behave, but found her body uncooperative as she went to her knees to scan his chest, waist, and thighs. "Very tense," she noted in a husky tone that surprised her.

Every part of the man rippled with raw power, the pinnacle of human physiology in every physical aspect of his being. His natural musk wasn't overwhelming, but it was pleasant.

Her breathing continued to remain heavy as she ran her scans, becoming a little more invasive and finding excuses to touch him and brush her fingers against his skin. She could see on the scans that it wasn't going unnoticed, but the man remained as still as a statue for the duration of her examination.

He was just *so* her type...And she was so very deprived...

"It's a little warm in here," Mandy declared as she set the scanner aside. "That might be part of why you're so restless and uncomfortable."

The doctor reached behind her head and pulled her hair out of the bun she'd placed it in, letting it cascade around her shoulders before shaking it out. She moved straight to unfastening the top button of her blouse before even pausing to gauge his reaction. Mandy didn't want to risk losing her nerve halfway through. Besides, it wasn't like she wasn't genuinely roasting under the twin suns of anxiety and arousal. "Much better!"

"Well?" The Hellmarine asked, glancing at the scanner.

"Oh," Mandy sniffed, waving a hand dismissively. "Inconclusive, but nothing terribly out of the ordinary. I'll run another scan in about an hour and every couple of hours after that."

The doctor could practically feel his eyes on her with how intense his gaze was. There was something incredibly arousing about it, especially when she realized that part of what she saw there was conflicted. "We'll have to find a way to pass the time until then."

After another thoughtful silence, the Hellmarine got to his feet, towering over her comparatively smaller stature as he approached her. She felt the space between her legs become hot and slick with anticipation as he drew near. "W-what would you like to do?"

His hands came up to her blouse and pulled it open with laughable ease, popping all of the buttons free to clatter across the floor at her feet. His eyes fell to the swell of her breasts, gazing at her with approval. Suddenly, with two fingers pressed between them, he pushed her back onto the bed and proceeded to pull his basic gray shirt over his head. She gasped as she took in the sheer scale of him. The size difference between them was terrifying—but also insanely erotic in a very real way.

Mandy's eyes widened as she marveled at the chiseled muscles of his chest and abdomen and the subtly creased lines at his hips that pointed down toward the promise of something new—something huge, even. Even with the sweatpants still on, she could tell how unfathomably engorged his cock had become. She'd seen him naked before, but this was something else entirely.

Resisting the urge to drool, Mandy scooted a little further back onto the bed while maintaining eye contact with the Hellmarine. She opened her legs slowly, revealing the wet panties beneath her skirt as a more overt invitation for him to do what only came naturally to such a virile specimen as himself.

"You're sure?" he muttered, climbing onto the bed slowly. The frame beneath them groaned in protest but held together.

"Fuck yes," Mandy breathed, practically licking her lips. "Absolutely."

The Hellmarine required no further coaxing, reaching up to the hem of her skirt and pulling it—along with her slightly soggy panties—down past her ankles. Her sex glistened with the anticipation raging like a fire within her.

For a moment, the Hellmarine seemed unsure of what to do next as he cast her clothing to one side. It didn't appear to be the kind of pause that came from a man who was nervous with women but rather the sort of indecision that came from a kid in a candy store. She seized the opportunity to unfasten her bra with one hand, discarding it and the blouse to one side. It seemed to help the Hellmarine make up his mind.

Leaning closer, he took hold of one of her breasts with a surprisingly gentle touch, only really able to use a few fingers to cup it safely. His mouth captured the nipple of the other, drawing a considerable portion of her excited flesh into it as though he was ready to feast upon her—devour her.

"Ohhh...mmm..." Mandy let out an unexpectedly whorish moan at the sudden attention to her sensitive breasts. She'd always liked having them fondled and played with, but this time it felt different. It felt electric. Her body was responding to him in ways it had never behaved before. "Fuck..."

Departing from her breast, his hand ran down her body, rubbing the soft slick petals of her pussy with two fingers as if to test her response. "Ohh, God!" she moaned as her back arched, feeding more of her breast flesh into his mouth as she let out another moan of approval. The Hellmarine moved his fingers in little circles over her engorged clit, knowing precisely how much pressure to apply without overwhelming her.

"Fuck," Mandy sighed, turning her head to one side as her hand reached blindly under him for the bulge of his cock hiding within the sweatpants. "You're driving me crazy."

The Hellmarine said nothing in response as she fumbled clumsily with the sweatpants he wore. She was struggling to keep her head on, much less execute even the most basic physical manipulation. His fingers probed inside of her, testing her elasticity and her ability to stretch. Clearly, he'd thought the same thing she had about whether or not he would even fit.

"Lick it, please," Mandy said breathlessly, her gaze meeting his briefly as his mouth popped free of her erect, pink nipple. It was strangely empowering to give him such a lewd order just to have him obey it immediately. His head moved down her body until his lips and tongue found the hot slit awaiting him between her thighs.

"Ooo!" she groaned, spreading her legs a little wider as she ran her fingers through his hair, nails gently scraping along his scalp. His tongue flattened along her clit, briefly applying pressure before pressing onward to explore the silky wet interior of the woman.

"Nnn..." Mandy bit her lip, resisting the urge to cum then and there, but it was no use. He seemed to be just as adept at eating pussy as he was at tearing Demons to pieces. Her thighs shook despite her efforts, and her back bowed as she drew a deep breath and signaled her heartfelt approval with a long, satisfied groan. "Oh, gawd..."

Before she had even come down from the ecstasy of her climax, he was on her again, this time without the sweatpants and the tip of his immense throbbing member pressing against the slippery heat of her entrance. Evidently, her orgasm had only served to excite him further.

With a subtle movement of his hips, the head of the Hellmarine's cock penetrated her. The stretching created a sharp bolt of pain that mingled freely with the pleasure and excitement of the moment. She winced slightly, causing the Hellmarine to restrain himself.

"It's alright," she said, breathing heavily through an amused smile. "Go ahead. We'll make it fit."

He regarded her uncertainly without moving, causing her to wrap her legs around him and coax him in.

"Fuck me, big man."

Taking her eagerness as a signal to skip any further pleasantries, the Hellmarine forwent a gentle start and took her with a bestial urgency. She felt him bottom out inside her immediately, but he continued on, heedless of her hitched breath. Mandy reminded herself that it was precisely what she wanted, despite the momentary discomfort of her insides forming to accommodate the singularly impressive specimen invading her tight, sultry cunt.

"H-harder," she stammered as she struggled to hold on. The smell of him—the heat of his presence in and around her—was intoxicating. She wanted to push herself to take as much of him as humanly possible so that he would want to return to her time and again for more. "Fuck me harder."

A strained grunt was the only response received, his hips grinding and pulverizing her like a jackhammer as she held on for dear life. A fleeting realization that she had somehow become cock-drunk passed wispily through her mind before vanishing into the boundless glow of orgasm. "Yes! Yes! Oh, that's so good!" He wasn't finished yet, so she held on. Another intense wave of bliss surged through her body, causing her body and mind to twist and writhe with ecstasy.

The Hellmarine still wasn't finished, and for what felt like hours, he worked her to the brink of madness, pausing only to reposition her and experience her from new angles. He said nothing, not even her name, the entire time. But his grunts, like a beast in rut, were enough for her—they would sustain her. After what felt like an eternity, the man placed his hand against her chest as he approached his own inevitable orgasm.

VIRGIL KNIGHTLEY, ALPHONSE FISK

Mandy grabbed his hand and slid it up to her throat, gazing up at him drunk on dick and blissfully aware of what came next.

"Fill me up," she pleaded. "Cum inside me, you sexy fucking animal. *Please.*"

She felt the entire length of him swell inside her with excitement, letting her know what he thought about her crude but playful coaxing. His hand gripped her neck tightly, but not nearly enough to restrict her breathing in any meaningful way or even leave a bruise. He had no desire to hurt her, only to play along and give her what she asked for—what she desperately needed.

"Guhh! Nn—ahhh!" Mandy felt the tension grow as his hips reached their final punishing strokes. Then, she felt the heat of him spreading inside her. It felt like she was melting as her own senses faded to an indiscernible white static, her body instinctively milking him even as it quaked with boundless blissful orgasm.

CHAPTER 11

THE WINDOWLESS CONFERENCE ROOM of the Midnight Sea hadn't seen much use since the ship had left the core worlds. The Overmaiden flickered into existence at the head of the table as the room's lights came on one after another. Few would physically be in attendance, but the shimmer of the holoprojectors in each seat would bring participants into the meeting from as far away as Earth itself.

The door on the far end of the room slid open as Captain Horne stepped in, wearing his dark dress uniform adorned with various commendations rather than the field uniform that the Overmaiden had become accustomed to.

"Good morning, sir," the Overmaiden greeted him, motioning to the seat at the head of the table. Though the seat was technically hers, she had no use for it, and it was still his ship. Horne nodded gratefully to her and took the seat.

"We've dropped out of stealth and should be receiving hails soon," Horne informed her. "How do you think this is going to go?"

"Well," the Overmaiden imitated, sucking air through her teeth. AIs didn't breathe but imitated a wide range of gestures to communicate better with humans. Ghost AIs, on the other hand, still had enough humanity in their personality matrixes for the gestures to be second nature to them. "It's hard to say. Many of the supporters of Project Brutality have distanced themselves from it in recent years. I think finally showing them something concrete may bring them back. The holdouts, however, may still remain steadfast in their rejection of the program."

"I'll do what I can to help you," Horne said, setting his hat on the table. "But my influence only goes so far these days. I think the footage of him with the rest of the squad will go a long way with the Marines, though, for what it's worth."

The Overmaiden nodded, acknowledging his advice as she reshuffled the presentation through a subroutine in her matrix. The captain's insight was seldom off the mark on such matters, so she would be a fool not to adjust accordingly.

"And the Navy?" the AI queried. "Any advice there?"

Horne chuckled softly as indicator lights of incoming data streams heralded the imminent appearance of other members of the conference. "Overmaiden, if I had any golden tips on how to appease the Naval brass, I don't think I'd be captaining a ship in the Outer Colonies."

"I thought you liked it out here," the Overmaiden remarked wryly.

"I do," the captain clarified, scratching his beard absently. "But most of them don't know that and consider an assignment like this a career dead-end."

"Why is that?" the Overmaiden wondered aloud before clarifying the question. "I mean to say, why do you like it out here?"

"Exploration," Horne replied succinctly. "It's all I wanted to do as a kid, gazing up at the stars. I've always wanted to see the edge of what was known and then see beyond that. I was just born in the wrong era for exploration, I guess."

"Perhaps one day, when we've pushed the hordes back to Hell, we can have you resume your exploration again," the Overmaiden responded with a slight smile. It faded quickly as soon as the other members of the meeting flickered into existence, already seated at the table.

The Overmaiden waited to speak until the room was full. There wasn't a single seat at the long table that wasn't meant to be occupied by one of the holograms. It was going to be a full house. Many of the officers greeted one another and chatted while she waited patiently at the head of the table with her hands folded behind her back. Few of them acknowledged her at all, which suited her well enough.

Once again, the door at the far end opened. This time, it was Dr. Hughes who stepped through, looking remarkably well put together considering the night she'd shared with the Hellmarine prior. The Overmaiden had kept close tabs on the extended encounters—strictly for scientific and professional reasons. Indeed, it had been her motive from the very beginning to put the two of them together for a tryst when she suggested the doctor monitor the Hellmarine overnight. The sexual release had done wonders for his restlessness, and it seemed to have been precisely what she needed as well, considering the little bounce the woman had in her step.

"Good morning, Dr. Hughes," the Overmaiden said as the woman took the empty seat on the left of Captain Horne. "You seem awfully chipper."

"Do I?" Hughes responded, fidgeting with her hair nervously as she tried to feign disinterest. "Can't imagine why."

The Overmaiden arched a brow curiously, wondering how long Hughes would attempt to remain secretive about her long night with the Hellmarine. If she were to engage with him repeatedly, it would likely take a physical toll on her before too long. Even now, the Overmaiden could detect signs of physical fatigue from the rigorous physical activity and the lack of sleep. "Have you heard from him?"

"Hm!? What? Who?" Hughes asked almost manically. "Who do you mean?"

Captain Horne gave Hughes a suspicious look. "Are you alright, Doctor?"

"Mhm, yeah," the woman nodded emphatically. "Great. Just great. How are you?"

The door opened again, and this time, it was the Hellmarine in his repaired Hades armor. Seraphiel followed behind in some spare casualwear that had been provided for her in her quarters. Because she wasn't military, how she was dressed wouldn't matter much. Most of the men present didn't even know who she was, and the sense of awe that she often inspired in others was not only subdued from her latest injuries but also didn't convey itself well over a datastream anyway.

Regardless, it was the presence of the Hellmarine that caught the attention of the officers, all of whom had grown silent as the grave as he passed each of their holograms. Had one not seen them materialize from nowhere, they might not have known they were holograms. Unlike the Overmaiden's AI avatar, theirs were meant to feel convincingly present in the room.

"Gentlemen," the Overmaiden greeted the officers formally. The Hellmarine and Seraphiel posted themselves in the corners of the room behind her. "Thank you for coming. I think it's time for us to begin. Most of you know one another so I'll forgo the formalities of introductions in the interests of moving things along. However, I have a few individuals here you might not know that I would like to introduce briefly."

First, the Overmaiden motioned to the Hellmarine, the reason that they had all gathered together. "This is the Hellmarine, the culmination of all the work of Project Brutality in the flesh. As you can see, he is wearing the experimental Hades Mark II power armor."

No one in the room said a thing. The Overmaiden was unsure if it was out of awe, skepticism, or just a lack of desire to be the first one to speak. She decided to simply move on.

"Seated to the left of Captain Horne is Dr. Amanda Hughes, a professional in the various fields required to act as the Hellmarine's full-time physician. Her credentials have been included in the dossiers I'm currently sending to each of your officer's terminals."

Mandy earned a few more looks than the Hellmarine, though for very different reasons. Due to her relative youth and uncommon beauty, some of the Generals and Admirals likely regarded her with equal measures of interest and skepticism.

"And finally," the Overmaiden gestured to the woman with the cybernetic arm behind her. "Is Seraphiel of the Third Choir of Archangels."

This came as a little more of a surprise to many of those gathered at the table. Seraphiel took a step forward and offered a closed-fisted salute across her chest, as was typical for her people. "We recovered her from the site of the ritual outlined in the earlier report."

"Hail," Seraphiel said solemnly. "Leaders of the Solar Alliance Navy and Marines, I am honored to stand before you today."

The Overmaiden gestured toward a holoprojector in the middle of the long table, which flickered to life and presented a holographic replay of the footage the AI had obtained from the helmet cameras of the Marines fighting alongside the Hellmarine. "As you can see here, the Hellmarine has embedded himself well with the Marine detachment assigned to the Midnight Sea, often working in tandem with them to achieve critical goals. None of which was more crucial than this..."

With a flick of her wrist, she moved the footage forward to the ritual's events. The Voivode's presence and demonstration of her power caused many of the officers to shift uncomfortably in their seats. Such creatures were seldom caught on video due to the lack of men and equipment to survive such close encounters.

"This is Master Sergeant Gray's squad?" One of the Marine generals asked, his eyes transfixed on the battle.

"Yes, sir," the Overmaiden responded. Multiple views of what came next were presented as the Hellmarine in the video feed took up the Scalder cannon. The AI looked on in satisfaction as the officers stared at the recording, their eyes wide and mouths agape.

"Jesus Christ," one of the admirals muttered. "The armor can generate that kind of power?"

"Not the armor, sir," the Overmaiden corrected. "The Hellmarine generated the power himself in a process similar to the one used by Theurgy Sergeant Davis...albeit at a much higher level and with Eldritch Energy instead of Arkane."

"How is that possible?" Vice Admiral Hawkins prodded curiously. Of all the officers in the room, he had once been one of Project Brutality's staunchest supporters. He was in his sixties with hair that had turned completely white long ago, but he spoke like a younger man with a more casual demeanor than was typical for men of his rank.

"We're still running tests to determine that," the Overmaiden answered honestly. "When we formulated the serum, we considered the possibility of Quixotic Energy generation due to the presence of Zintari DNA, but Eldritch Energy was well outside of expectations. Dr. Cosgrove is working on it right now, which is why he is absent from today's meeting."

The Overmaiden moved the footage over to other feats the Hellmarine had accomplished during the operation, further cementing him as a force to be reckoned with. The hesitation any of them felt was tempered slightly by displays of his stoic compassion for the Marines and even Seraphiel when they found her.

"I'd like to know a little more about this," Hawkins said, gesturing toward the prison of Demonic magic that Seraphiel had been found in. His eyes shifted toward Seraphiel with concern. "What were you doing on one of our colony worlds?"

Seraphiel glanced at the Overmaiden and Captain Horne before stepping forward to address the question. "The increased frequency of the incursions in your universe have raised concerns in Heaven."

"Heaven," one of the generals repeated. Angels had been encountered rarely throughout humanity's history, though not by military or diplomatic officials. Documentation of their existence was out there, and in some cases reliable, but precious little was actually known about their kind. Seeing Seraphiel standing before them so plainly was a major milestone for humanity. "Heaven, as in...where God lives?"

"In a manner of speaking," Seraphiel responded. "Heaven is a world like your own, albeit on a higher layer of the multiverse."

"We have rough models for the cosmological layout," Hawkins acknowledged. "But we've only ever been able to achieve contact with lower layers that the Zintari had reached with their gateways—and whatever Hellrifts we encounter, of course."

"This is partly by design," the Archangel continued. "The boundaries of Celestial Space are well-guarded to prevent such Hellrifts from forming. We fought our battles with Hell-space long ago and thought we had left much of it behind us. We never intended to hide our existence, really, but to remain fully defensible, sequestered to the one domain where Demons simply never can be allowed to tread. Since the wars of old, our interaction with Standard Space and other universes has been limited as a result."

"Yet here you are," the admiral pointed out, gesturing between her and the freeze frame of her in the hologram. "In our layer of space to fight Demons. I'd like to know why. Why now?"

Seraphiel glanced between the officers uncomfortably but retained her composure as she squared her shoulders. "The incursions are increasing at a rate we haven't seen since the last time the Heavenly Host went to war with Demonkind. It's quite sudden."

"Sudden?" One of the generals scoffed. "We've been dealing with these bastards on and off for centuries. This recent push is significantly larger, true, but we've been fighting this particular war with them for years."

The Overmaiden held a hand up to interject. "From the perspective of their species, long-lived as they are and with a different reckoning of time, it appears sudden."

"Precisely," Seraphiel agreed with a thankful nod.

"Who made this decision?" Hawkins pressed, leaning forward on the table, his hologram flickering slightly when he made contact with the solid surface. "For you to get involved now? Why not come to us to work with us cooperatively?"

"I don't know who authorized it, but I do know that this particular incursion came to the attention of an Elohim monitoring this world you call Aonus," Seraphiel explained. "It's highly unusual for them to make abrupt contact outside of the Second Triad, much less on behalf of mortal species. It's not their way. So when they do, the Ophanim investigate immediately."

"Who are the Ophanim?" one of the other admirals asked.

Seraphiel took a deep breath, apparently choosing her words carefully. "You would consider them a sort of division of military intelligence. They are of the First Triad, along with the Seraphim and Cherubim. Together, they are responsible for the safety and security of Heaven."

"Cherubim?" One of the generals chuckled. "As in cherubs—little naked babies?"

"An offensive caricature popularized during your so-called First Renaissance," Seraphiel responded sharply, her eyes narrowing slightly.

"Read a book, Stevens," Captain Horne chuckled. "One without pictures, perhaps."

A short bout of chortling rolled through the group, effectively cutting the tension that had been present just a moment before. The Overmaiden shot a thankful glance toward the captain for quickly disarming the situation.

"What became of your companions?" Hawkins asked, getting the conversation back on track.

Seraphiel's eyes faltered, glancing to the side. "They were sacrificed—their Divine Energy harnessed by the profane ritual to bring more of the horde through. It effectively tears the opening created by the Zintari gateway wider, allowing them to manifest nearly anywhere on a given planet to accelerate their infernaforming process."

"This is why Aonus was taken so much faster than other worlds we've seen," the Overmaiden clarified. "There also seems to be some component of the sensor arrays at the weather station that played a part in this proliferation. I believe they are becoming more accustomed to our technology, using more sophisticated systems to adapt to their purposes."

A general feeling of unease settled across the room. Hawkins pressed his lips into a thin line. "That still doesn't explain what you were doing there. If your comrades' sacrifice facilitated the rapid expanse, why were you there in the first place? Just because one of these Elohim said so?"

"Correct," the Angel responded. "Archangels do not question orders. We do not question the Elohim. We do not question the will of Heaven. We do as we are instructed. If we are told to smite, we smite. But to be clear: the Elohim do not command us directly. They made a recommendation to the First Triad, which they then passed on to the Third Triad. The Kedoshim made the final decision, and we—the Malakim—were mobilized."

"Right," Hawkins muttered, appearing to be slightly confused by the rapid-fire references to the different types of Angels—all of which were completely new knowledge. Seraphiel's direct responses to questions were appreciated for the gesture that they were but seldom offered actual clarification on matters. "Of course."

"I believe they may have been baited into a trap that wasn't meant for them," the Overmaiden suggested. "From the scant encounters we've had with the people of Itaris, we've learned that the original Zintari made quite the impression on the various species of the multiverse before their near-extinction. Demons, in particular, despise them. By hijacking their gateway they could have been attempting to lure some in for a similar ritual. Instead, they got the attention of Heaven and simply took advantage of the situation."

"Have we been able to contact any of the Zintari on the matter?" Hawkins asked skeptically, already suspecting what the Overmaiden's response would be.

"I'm afraid not, sir," the AI replied. "They remain as elusive as ever."

"For fuck's sake," another of the admirals spat. "We've had Zintari among us before—working with us on our own worlds. How hard can it be? Send a ship over to Elyndor and shake some trees!"

"Yes and no," the Overmaiden argued. "What we call the Zintari are not the same ancient Zintari that built the gateways or any of the other Zintari structures that have been uncovered since. The Zintari we know are, for the most part, enhanced humans. Gifted with the power of the ancients but with roots in our society and culture."

"Like the Hellmarine," a general suppositioned.

"Not like the Hellmarine," Seraphiel interrupted curtly. "He may have a piece of the Zintari in him, but he is not Zintari. He is better and worse than any demon, Angel, man, or Zintari I have encountered—a strange alchemy given flesh and made into a weapon. Your species has never been more at risk since you harnessed the atom. You should proceed with the utmost caution."

The Overmaiden stared at the archangel, shocked at the sudden negative assessment of the Hellmarine. In the interactions she had monitored, Seraphiel had seemed curious about him, even asking after him at times. Such a scathing assessment came as a complete surprise.

"Strong words," Hawkins responded, concerned. "What does he have to say for himself, I wonder?"

"That's probably unnecessary," the Overmaiden objected apprehensively, holding her hand. "Communication isn't really his strong suit."

"I'd like to hear what he has to say," General Stevens remarked, earning mutters of agreement from the other officers. The Overmaiden showed no outward signs of stress, but internally, she was searching her matrix for a way to deter them without arousing their ire.

"It's fine," the Hellmarine told her as he took a step forward. "I can speak."

The room fell silent as the Hellmarine stood before them at attention, prepared to answer any questions that the collected admirals and generals might have for him.

"What's your name, son?" Hawkins asked to start things off.

"I don't remember," the Hellmarine replied directly. "Not from the time before. I'm the Hellmarine now. I enjoy this designation."

"What *do* you remember from before the augmentation?" one of the other admirals wondered. "Were you a soldier? Did you have a family?"

The Hellmarine considered the questions for a moment and then shook his head slightly. "I see only images—flashes. Some are mine, but I know most aren't. They can't be."

Dr. Hughes leaned forward in her chair, slowly pressing her palms on the table. "The Hellmarine possesses a unique form of genetic memory. All sentient species leave behind echoes of their consciousness and soul in their blood. For those making frequent use of magic—or those infused with forms of it like Demons or Angels—this effect is considerably more pronounced. Because the Hellmarine serum is composed of three species with this trait, he has inherited portions from each."

Most of the officers seemed to follow what the doctor was saying from what the Overmaiden could see. She'd explained it rather well without going into the intricacies of the matter. The memories he had were likely where he had acquired his skill in battle and perhaps even his undying hatred for Demons, though the latter could have been driven by his human experience that had nearly resulted in his death alongside his family. However, many of his memories outside of the fleeting images were instinctual and intuitive, useful to him when the need arose, but useless for any form of study. That was the case so far, anyway.

"What about your homeworld?" Hawkins wondered. "How do you feel about what's become of it?"

"I don't have a homeworld anymore," the Hellmarine replied.

"You know what he means," Captain Horne added, urging the Hellmarine to give an answer about the fate of Aonus. "They want to know more about your mental state."

"Glass it," the Hellmarine declared. "Let nothing survive."

An uncomfortable silence fell across the room once more. Seraphiel stared at the Hellmarine ambivalently. Though the man appeared to be merciless, the Overmaiden understood his intentions. There was too much at risk, too many places that the remaining Demons could hide after thinning themselves out. She disagreed with him but understood why he would feel that way.

"We can salvage it," the Overmaiden suggested. "I believe our successful neutralization of the Voivode will bear that out. However, I would ask that one of the destroyers be diverted to bombard the original location where the Zintari gateway was uncovered."

"That seems like a reasonable compromise," Hawkins agreed. "I'll give the order once we're done here."

"Thank you, sir," Captain Horne replied. The Overmaiden knew the man would have done it himself if he was able, but the Midnight Sea lacked the necessary armaments to pull off a successful planetary bombardment on the scale they required.

Hawkins held a finger up with a slight smirk. "Don't thank me yet, captain. I'd like to borrow your Hellmarine here for a little project of my own now that I've seen what he can do."

Nearly every officer sitting at the table turned to look at Hawkins, clearly taking them as much by surprise as he had the Overmaiden and Horne. "Sir?"

"I've been monitoring a section of space near me—not far from you, in fact—that is likely to manifest as a Hellrift any day now," the vice admiral explained, earning several exclamations from the other officers who had been kept in the dark on the matter. Brushing them off, he continued. "I had intended to deploy a reconnaissance probe the moment the rift opened. We know painfully little about what lies on the other side."

"Hell," Captain Horne scoffed indignantly. "Hell is what's on the other side."

"Which part?" Hawkins fired back, letting the captain's tone slide. "Because we don't know what region they originate from. Is there a central operation directing the efforts? Can we take the fight to them on their own turf? Can we shut down the rifts from their side? These are the things we need to know, and as the commanding officer of the Omicron Fleet here in the Outer Colonies, it's my duty to prevent our enemy from advancing any further into our space."

"And you want to send the Hellmarine?" Horne asked, gesturing toward the hulking man standing next to him. Though still skeptical, he appeared to be reigning in his attitude before it got him in trouble. "Alone?"

Hawkins motioned to the projection in the center of the table, which was locked in a freeze frame. "He'd survive much longer than a probe, from what I've seen, providing us significantly more information to work with. Any additional damage he can inflict on the enemy is a bonus at that point."

The officers were beginning to come around on the idea, and the Overmaiden had to admit that the plan had a great deal of merit to it. The logic was sound.

"I'll go," the Hellmarine agreed without hesitation.

"So will I," Seraphiel added, much to everyone else's surprise in the room. "As the last survivor of my operation, I have certainly been made Grigori—an exile, a watcher—among my people. But I still wish to pursue my original purpose. I wish to fight, not watch."

The officers exchanged glances with one another before Stevens shrugged. "I think we can work with that. I'll have to see what the protocol would be for that, but if she wants to serve in the corps against Hell, I don't see a good reason not to let her. I imagine Dr. Hughes and the Overmaiden here can document a wealth of new information about Angelkind after observing and working with her for a time, and that'll be invaluable."

"It might be frowned upon for me to share too many of Heaven's secrets, so do not count on learning more than just enough of my biology to treat me for battlefield injuries. In any case, if we go through the Hellrift and are unable to make it back through the way we came," Seraphiel added, "I should be able to provide us with an alternate route."

"Noted. Perfect," Stevens said, spreading his hands, though Hawkins seemed less than convinced. The Overmaiden recalled that there was a degree of tension between the two when it came to who held authority over what. Marine detachments on every ship fell under the command structure of the Navy until they were reassigned or they were once again planetside. There had been some disagreement on where one command structure began, and one ended—a heated debate that the two had waged behind closed doors in recent months.

"Do you have any objections, Captain Horne?" Stevens asked almost as an afterthought.

Horne shook his head. "None at all. I can have the Master Sergeant bring her up to speed on some things, but there will be the matter of her rank and chain of command."

Stevens rubbed his chin thoughtfully, considering the factors at play. She would technically be enlisted, though her prior experience was nearly impossible to quantify the way a civilian education might be. Still, he seemed to want to afford her a degree of respect for choosing to fight alongside them.

"Let's put her down as Lance Corporal Seraphiel for now and see how she does," the general concluded. "Consider it probationary, due to the unorthodox nature of all this. I'll work things out on my end, but in the meantime, I'll have her report directly to Gray and you. How's that sound?"

"Works for me," Horne agreed, which also seemed to satisfy Hawkins for the immediate moment.

"I think that about wraps things up for now?" Hawkins suggested. "Let's get you two en route as quickly as possible so we can send you to Hell."

CHAPTER 12

SERAPHIEL STARED OUT THE viewport into the emptiness of space. Her eyes focused on no point in particular as the events of the last several days played through her mind. It felt surreal to be standing on the deck of a human starship traveling through space. By the celestial reckoning of time, it hadn't been that long ago that they'd been blasting one another at relatively close range with muskets. Now they were on the front lines defending their territory in space against Demonic incursions.

Her mind drifted toward her fallen brothers and sisters. They hadn't expected such stiff resistance. They had been arrogant in assuming that the Elohim had been overreacting. Not only that, but the Demonic horde fought differently than the last time the Heavenly Host had battled them. Seraphiel had been no help with how limited her experience in the field was.

"Ma'am?" the human to her right repeated, attempting to get her attention. "Are you alright?"

Seraphiel blinked several times, regaining her composure before turning to face the unassuming human male in his little uniform. She had determined that those responsible for the ship used one form of dress while those who frequently left the ship to do battle used another. "Yes, I'm fine. What can I do for you?"

"The Armorer has asked that I escort you down to engineering," the human responded cautiously. He appeared to be intimidated or in awe of her appearance; she wasn't sure which. "She said your equipment is ready."

"My equipment?" Seraphiel echoed, confused. Could the humans have a smith capable of repairing her armor? She had written it off entirely as scrap with how much damage it had taken before. "Lead the way."

The young man—a crewman as they called his rank—guided her down to the ship's engineering section, where the humans did most of the technical work for the ship and other fabrication. Until then, she'd mostly seen the medical bay, crew quarters, and bridge.

Stepping through a set of double doors, they entered an area they called the forge, which was where the one called the Armorer resided.

"Ah, there she is!" The Armorer laughed jovially as she threw back the welding mask she wore. "I gotta tell ya, the stuff you were wearing before was wild. It's had me up for the last couple of nights just trying to figure it out. Haven't been this inspired since the Hades II."

Seraphiel regarded the woman with the messy bun with mild curiosity. This was the Armorer that everyone spoke of with such reverence?

"Thank you, crewman," Seraphiel said as the man departed, leaving her in the care of the Armorer.

"Alright, so we're going to get you outfitted, do any calibrations that need to be done, and get all the software updated," the Armor explained, motioning to a nearby platform. "Just disrobe and then stand right here, please."

Seraphiel frowned a little and complied. "I don't understand. Did you repair my armor?"

"Eh," the Armorer shrugged, her eyes blinking with the same strange technology that made up Seraphiel's arm. "Not quite. The damage was extensive and there's a lot about the original design I couldn't figure out. But don't worry, I think you'll like what I cooked up."

"Very well, Armorer," Seraphiel sighed with disappointment. "Show me what you have crafted."

"Claire's fine," the Armorer responded, her hands dancing across some glowing panels as machinery around the platform whirred to life. "Claire Arleth. The Armorer thing is nice from the other guys, but it feels weird coming from you."

"Why is that?" Seraphiel asked as the mechanical arms whirled around to place the pieces of armor on her. She immediately noticed that it did not look like the Hellmarine's, or quite like the armor that the other Marines wore.

"Because you're an Archangel," Claire snorted with amusement. "Seems like I should be reporting to you somehow—or at least using the cool nicknames."

"You may give me a 'cool nickname' if you wish, Claire," Seraphiel remarked as she watched the armor fastened together and touched up with turning mechanisms she didn't know the names of. "Why does the armor not cover my abdomen, arms, legs, or the valley between my breasts? It seems too revealing to be protective. Is there a second part to it?"

"I'm glad you asked!" Claire answered, beaming. "The armor you had before was made with some strange material that seemed to protect you from the outside while allowing your energy aura to radiate out from you at the same time. I wasn't sure how to replicate that, so I had to do the next best thing."

"Which is?" Seraphiel asked with an arched golden brow as the last of the mechanical arms retreated.

"I redirected the aura—focused it," Claire explained excitedly, approaching Seraphiel to wave her hand over the exposed bits of the Angel's body. "So these parts seem naked, but they're actually covered with a skintight forcefield as if your flesh is polarized like our power armor or ships are."

"I do not know what 'polarized' is," Seraphiel admitted, moving her arms back and forth to test the weight of the armor. It felt strangely familiar. A helmet was offered to her, and she took it, placing it over her head and watching as a series of displays came online in her face. At first, it was a little overwhelming, but as she began to recognize the meaning of the information, she became more curious.

"To put it in the most basic terms, we run a current of Arkane Energy through the outer layer of armor plating to strengthen it—make it capable of repelling energy and withstanding stress it otherwise couldn't," Claire summarized. "Yours uses your native Divine Energy instead. The whole suit is powered by you, requiring no independent power source and cutting down on the weight immensely."

"I believe I understand," Seraphiel acknowledged as she stepped off the platform. "My arm still feels strange, but the rest of this armor is very comfortable."

Claire held a finger up, grabbing a strange-looking glowing tool from a toolbox that reminded Seraphiel of a wand before returning to her. "Doc Hughes did a good job installing it, but fine-tuning it for combat readiness is more my department."

The tool emitted a high-pitched whine a few times as Seraphiel felt subtle shifts in the plating of the prosthetic and the components just below the surface. It stung at first but gave way to a certain sense of lightness. When she was done with the tool, her eyes flickered a few times, and the helmet display informed her that her system was being updated.

"Your armor has a special configuration that allows it to interface directly with your arm and its components," Claire explained as she stepped back. "So the latency on your armor is lower than most forms of power armor, allowing you to perform various functions with just a thought. Cuts down on calibration time, too."

"Intriguing," Seraphiel acknowledged, swinging her arm around much easier than before. The technology felt like it had always been a part of her, which only compounded the surreal experience of earlier. "Humans have come quite far with technology. There were those on my world who believed you would follow a more evolution-driven psycho-organic type of technological development. This would come as quite a surprise to them."

"Why would they think that?" Claire wondered, fascinated by the Angel's statement.

"Statistics, I believe," Seraphiel replied. "Many bipedal species with your sort of cerebral development within a certain timeframe go that route."

Claire stared at her, nonplussed for a moment before returning to her impromptu presentation. "I made the armor with what I could salvage of your old armor, but I saved a lot of it for these."

With the flick of a switch, the mechanical arms brought forth a shield and broadsword that very closely resembled the one she had been carrying when she'd first left on the mission to Aonus. Seraphiel reached out and took them, and the HUD of the armor registered a connection to both items as she held them. "These are powered too?"

"In part, yes," Claire confirmed. "The sword can hold a charge, allowing for a cleaner cut, and the shield is polarized as long as you're holding it. Should you drop either of them for any reason, you can call them back to you within a certain distance."

Seraphiel arched a brow, tossing the shield to one side and willing it to return to her before it hit the ground. With a brief hum, the shield sprang back to her gauntlet.

"You already got the hang of it?" Claire exclaimed in disbelief.

"Yes, your technology is surprising in how far it has advanced, but not beyond my understanding," Seraphiel assured her. "What have you chosen to call this armor?"

"Nemesis Mark I," the Armorer answered as she puffed her chest out slightly. "Never made anything like it, but I bet I'll have all sorts of ideas the minute you return from your first mission."

"Thank you," Seraphiel murmured before the Armorer returned to telling her about the features of her new gear. Not only did she need to be informed about the special features made to suit her specifically, but also the baseline features that allowed her to work in tandem with the squad to which she would be assigned—the Hellmarine's squad.

As critical as Seraphiel had been of the man's creation, it was difficult to argue with his methods. He didn't seem interested in trying to convince anyone of his righteousness; he wanted only to accomplish the task for which he was created. He wanted to kill and destroy anything with a Demonic imprint on it. There were those of the Heavenly Host who would have lauded it as the pinnacle of discipline and duty. Seraphiel was less convinced. But there was a certain allure to a creature that could brute-force his way through profane barriers and tear Demons apart with his bare hands. She had no doubt that he would make quite an interesting coupling option for her.

By the time Seraphiel completed the crash course, the Midnight Sea had entered Riftspace to rendezvous with the admiral who had requested their assistance. This, for Seraphiel, was perhaps the single most interesting accomplishment of humanity she had witnessed so far. Many species in the multiverse found ways to fold space, form portals, or travel faster than light, but humans had chosen instead to ride the space between layers of the multiverse using the endpoints of previous routes as guiding stars.

Humanity had discovered the rifts and gateways of the ancient Zintari during the 21st century of their current model of time. They used them for guidance while placing stable versions of the rifts in their engine cores to allow incredibly massive ships to pass through them quickly, exiting at a predetermined point along a "riftway". It was unconventional and didn't allow for what they called "blind jumps," but it certainly got the job done. Not long after they had entered Riftspace, Seraphiel was asked to report to the docking bay to prepare for departure.

"Well don't you look like a ray of fucking sunshine," Master Sergeant Gray remarked as she stepped onto the deck of the docking bay. He looked much shorter to her when not wearing his own armor, but he had a way about him that remained undiminished despite the perceived smaller stature. He was a commander of soldiers, through and through.

"Thank you?" Seraphiel responded, unsure if the compliment was a genuine one or an attempt to deride the unconventional design of the armor.

"Thank you, *Sergeant*," the Master Sergeant corrected her. "In the Alliance, you address those above your rank typically as 'sir' or 'ma'am.' My rank as an officer doesn't follow that pattern, so most just call me Sarge. I'll let this one slide, but you're a Marine now, dammit. Start acting like it."

"Yes, Sarge," Seraphiel responded more confidently.

"That's more like it," the Master Sergeant said, grinning. "When you get into the field with Nature Boy, he's gonna move hard, and he's gonna move fast—like a creature possessed. It's going to be your job to watch his back while he plows the road ahead. The Overmaiden will keep him focused on the objective, so you don't need to worry about that."

"Nature Boy?"

The Hellmarine came into view as the Master Sergeant continued with the brief, informing her of what lay ahead of her. Seraphiel found herself distracted by the creature, the way he moved, and the weight his presence held. Even somewhere as large as the docking bay, it seemed to fill the entire room so that anyone could feel him, even without the honed sense for magical and exotic energies that she had.

Following close behind him was Dr. Mandy Hughes. Small woman that she was, she looked even smaller next to such a hulking mass as someone like the Hellmarine. She was outfitted in a suit of semi-powered armor of her own.

"Why is she coming?" Seraphiel asked, nodding toward Hughes.

"The doc?" The Master Sergeant scoffed. "She's the only one rated to treat him if shit goes wrong, so she has to go with."

"Hell is no place for a healer," Seraphiel argued grimly. "For any of us, really. But her, especially."

"She'll be waiting on our side of the rift," the Master Sergeant explained. "So it'll be up to you to get him back if he gets injured."

"Understood, Sarge," the Angel acknowledged. As the other two made their way across the docking bay, Gray dismissed her to do the same. She walked a little more swiftly to catch up with the two as they approached the airlock for the docking bridge.

"Wow, your armor looks fantastic," Hughes said as the Angel entered her line of sight. "The Armorer has really outdone herself. How's the prosthetic?"

"Adequate," Seraphiel answered impassively. "The Armorer performed some calibrations. I hardly notice it now."

"I thought she might," Hughes acknowledged with a short nod. There was a subtle shift in the gravity of the ship as they exited Riftspace. A voice from the intercom above informed everyone to stand by for ship-to-ship docking.

Seraphiel's eyes darted around at the various blinking lights and crewmen rushing about to make preparations. A thudding sensation ran through the deck as the lights above the door signaled that docking was complete. Then the doors opened, revealing an extended tunnel that had linked with the same from the other ship. The trio stepped out into it after they were bid to do so and made the short walk to the SANS Hammer of the Gods, where they were greeted by the Admiral himself and various subordinates.

Before the Hellmarine set foot on the ship, the voice of the Overmaiden echoed through their comms. "Permission to come aboard, Captain?"

The trio saluted the captain and the admiral as per the Overmaiden's instruction until the gesture was returned and permission to come aboard was granted. The woman took a step forward, her posture rigid. "I'm Captain Prescott, and this is my ship. Understand that you are guests while you are here and are expected to behave as such. You are not to leave the docking bay until you are authorized to do so, is that understood?"

"Ah, relax, Captain," the Admiral said, placing a hand on her shoulder. "They were invited and are here to lend me a hand. Let's try to give them a little warmer welcome than that, shall we?"

The captain shot him a look, but acknowledged his suggestion by taking a step back and allowing him to take over. The Admiral stepped forward, producing a hand toward the Hellmarine. "Welcome aboard, son. I'm glad to have you with me on this."

The Hellmarine either didn't notice the hand in front of him or ignored it entirely, a gesture that seemed disrespectful from Seraphiel's point of view. He motioned to a nearby dropship that looked like it was finishing its preparations for takeoff. Behind the trio, the airlock closed, and the bridge was disengaged and retracted.

"Is that for us?" the Hellmarine asked pointedly.

"It sure is. They're just about finished up with it," Hawkins responded, taking his hand back and nodding toward the dropship. "Modified it with my own specifications. Souped up the engine a little bit to give us a little more juice."

The Hellmarine stared at the ship without much to say. Seraphiel didn't know enough about the human ships to say whether or not it was an impressive specimen of its kind. If he said it was faster than others of its kind, she was going to have to take the claim at face value.

"What do you think?" the Admiral pressed, watching the towering figure of the Hellmarine expectantly. "Think it'll do the job?"

The Hellmarine responded with a simple grunt as he approached the ship.

"You'll have to forgive him," the Overmaiden apologized through the comms. "He's not much of a chatterbox. When he's this focused on the mission, it's like trying to strike up a conversation with a tiger."

Prescott exchanged skeptical looks with the other members of the crew that had come to meet them. Seraphiel noted that their attitudes varied between remaining unimpressed or being outright offended by his flaunting of protocol and small talk with an admiral.

Seraphiel took a step forward to introduce herself to the admiral, hoping the gesture might go a long way to diffuse the tension. Instead, the admiral brushed past her to follow after the Hellmarine with Dr. Hughes, leaving the Angel behind with Captain Prescott.

"That armor doesn't look regulation, Marine," the captain remarked, her gaze moving critically over the Angel's body.

"It's called Nemesis armor, ma'am," Seraphiel responded as respectfully as she could manage, considering the woman's tone. "It was custom-made for me by the Armorer."

The captain arched a brow as a subordinate beside her expressed his disbelief more openly. "Why would the Armorer make custom armor for you? They're doing custom work for Lance Corporals now?"

Seraphiel's brows furrowed in disgust, though it was imperceptible behind the faceplate of her helmet. The Angel took a step forward, showcasing the difference in height between her and the officer. Even the captain wasn't close to her in height. "Is this how guests are treated on this ship?"

"Excuse me?" the captain asked crisply. "You had better adjust your tone when speaking to a superior officer, Marine."

"Superior in rank alone," Seraphiel argued. "Not in conduct. Among my people, such a show of disrespect would be enough to justify a challenge, regardless of rank."

"Your people?" The officer responded, flabbergasted. According to the name on the uniform, the man's name was Butler. "Why don't you climb out of that armor and educate me?"

"Stow it, Butler," the captain snapped before turning her attention to Seraphiel. "What's your name, Marine?"

"Lance Corporal Seraphiel of the Third Choir of Archangels," Seraphiel responded crisply. The captain's expression went from furious to confused. The Angel's eyes darted between the other subordinates, who all seemed just as confused. "Were you not informed of my identity?"

Captain Prescott glanced in the direction of the admiral, her brow furrowing as she swept through a few menus on her datapad with one finger. "It seems the admiral neglected to mention you as anything other than the Hellmarine's attaché."

"Seraphiel!" Dr. Hughes called, waving her over with one hand. "We're about to board, come on!"

"What's going on here?" Butler asked the Captain in a discreet tone.

Captain Prescott silenced him with a gesture before adopting a different tone as well. "Please accept our deepest apologies for this misunderstanding."

"Of course," Seraphiel answered, wondering why the admiral would have left such information out of the report to the others. If he had wanted to keep her identity secret, wouldn't he have provided instructions to her about it? During the meeting, he hadn't seemed very pleased with the idea of her being allowed to enlist, even if he didn't outwardly object. Seraphiel had to conclude that perhaps it was his way of expressing his dissatisfaction with the Marines taking her in.

The Archangel gave a parting salute to the captain and joined the others as they boarded the dropship.

"What was that about?" the Overmaiden inquired through a dedicated channel to Seraphiel.

"The captain of this vessel was not informed about my identity by the admiral," Seraphiel answered as the others took their seats ahead of her.

"Strange," the Overmaiden responded ambivalently. "I see no reason why he wouldn't. You're already fully registered in the system at this point."

Hawkins brushed the implied question aside. "Anyway, the rift we're tracking is forming on a moon orbiting Taobos, a gas giant," the vice admiral explained once he had a headset on and they were secured for takeoff. "The moon itself is a mining colony, barely habitable, but that shouldn't be a problem for our purposes. The rift has only opened a crack, so when you arrive, one of you will need to open it a little wider in order to step through. The Hammer of the Gods will be monitoring the situation. If there are any signs of an incursion resulting from the rift, you'll have only a few minutes to return before it bombards the site from orbit."

Hawkins toggled an overhead holoprojector from his datapad. A moment later, a semi-translucent image of an unfamiliar device formed and slowly rotated as specifications were displayed in text alongside it.

"This is the modified probe my people cooked up," the Admiral explained. "It's designed to withstand extreme environments and to compensate for the dimensional warping to the carrier signal so that we get clear readings on our end. Your task will be to find a prime location to secure and place the probe. Ideally, we want something high with a view so we have visuals to go along with all the readouts."

The Hellmarine nodded, silently acknowledging the plan. Seraphiel wondered if he gave much of a damn for the recon or if he had only agreed to come in order to satisfy his bloodlust. Indeed, would he even bother with the probe once they were on the other side? It was for the Overmaiden to handle, but Seraphiel couldn't help but remain skeptical of the Hellmarine's ability to do anything other than kill and destroy.

"Once it's set up, you get out," the Admiral concluded, dismissing the hologram with a swipe of his hand through the air. "Any questions?"

"No," the Hellmarine replied, the word alone carrying an uncanny hint of finality. As they approached the surface of the moon, the Hellmarine stood and grabbed an extra rifle from the weapon rack nearest him. He turned and handed it to Seraphiel.

Seraphiel had only intended to fight with her broadsword and shield, but the crash course she'd taken on human armaments made her familiar with the Renegade marksman rifle. The Hellmarine didn't bother to ask her if she knew how to use it. He just held it out to her expectantly. The Angel realized it was a show of faith.

As the back ramp slowly lowered, Seraphiel took the weapon and gave it a quick check. Satisfied with its condition, she offered the Hellmarine a nod in the affirmative.

"Let's go," he grunted, leading the way off the ramp with the doctor and Angel close behind.

CHAPTER 13

THE HELLMARINE HIT THE ground running, unable to hold back the anticipation thundering in his chest any longer. The entire time the admiral tried to make small talk with him, his thoughts had been on this moment. He didn't understand why he wanted to chat with him on matters irrelevant to his purpose. He'd asked him about his name again—specifically if he wanted to be called by a particular name in light of forgetting his old one. Even just a nickname would do.

"Romero called me the Sword of Mankind," the Hellmarine had answered. The vice admiral laughed, remarking that they would have to trademark the name and make some merch. The Overmaiden had informed him that conversation wasn't really the Hellmarine's area of expertise, yet Hawkins persisted. Once they landed, the Hellmarine was off the ship as soon as the ramp was down, and Seraphiel and Hughes followed behind.

The location of the rift was provided by the Overmaiden on their HUDs, though it wasn't hard to spot it. Despite being a crack, the Hellrift gave off a distinct red light, illuminating the rocky terrain around it. There was a distinct profane weight to the presence of the rift that the Hellmarine had become familiar with recently.

The rift hung in the air completely unsupported, like a floating, ragged wound. Seraphiel stepped closer, examining it silently before turning her attention to him. "Are you sure you can open this?"

"Yes," the Hellmarine responded, jamming his gauntlets' fingers into the Hellrift's center. A shock of energy ran up through his arms, disrupting the polarization of his armor within seconds. The rift crackled and spit arcs of red lightning and sparks around him as he leaned in and pried the rift open with all his strength.

"Careful," Dr. Hughes cautioned him. But he couldn't let her get in the way. His approach was direct, and it was the best approach.

A sound like steel shearing off a bulkhead rang through the air as the rift came open, widening to a point that they would be able to slip through. Beyond the opening was just the dim red glow and a wall that appeared to be made of flesh.

The Hellmarine drew the chainchete from his side and flicked it on. Without hesitation, he carved into the mass, opening it up into a corridor of the same fleshy material.

"I don't like the look of this," Hughes muttered through the comms. "They're going to know the moment you step through."

"Perhaps," the Overmaiden remarked. "Demon technology is difficult to predict, but past information indicates that most rifts form independently of Demonic intention. Such rifts are merely opportunities they seize upon after reaching a certain size. So we may encounter minimal opposition."

"They will know," Seraphiel said with certainty. The Hellmarine agreed and stepped through the rift, his HUD indicating a change in the gravity, temperature, and pressure the moment that he was through.

"Do you have the probe?" the Overmaiden asked Hughes as Seraphiel stepped through the rift after him. Hughes nodded and handed it to the Angel, who secured it on her hip. The probe wasn't particularly large—about half the size of a basketball. The Hellmarine experienced a brief flash in his mind of one bouncing and the unique sound it made in a gymnasium.

He pushed the sensation out of his mind as he scanned the corridor, the HUD adjusting the coloration slightly to make details clearer.

"Sensors in the armors both look good," the Overmaiden announced. "We're green across the board. Proceed with caution."

"Such a vile place," Seraphiel remarked as they moved swiftly down the corridor.

"Do you recognize the purpose of this place?" The Over-maiden inquired as the Hellmarine followed the curve of the corridor. He could practically taste the Demons awaiting them through the pulsating sphincter of a door that lay before them.

Seraphiel shook her head. "This is my first time in Hell-space. We haven't had cause to run any operations since before my service."

The Hellmarine placed his hand on a skull lodged in an alcove next to the giant sphincter, turning it slightly before thrusting it deeper into the alcove. The empty sockets of the skull lit up, and the flesh of the sphincter squelched and opened.

Stepping into the room beyond, the Hellmarine brought his chainchete into the first Demon within reach. He didn't recognize it from the collection profiles the Over-maiden had provided for him, which told him it was likely a previously unencountered variety.

"They appear to be harvesting something," the Over-maiden noted as the Hellmarine hacked pieces from the bodies of several in rapid succession. Each was about the size of a bloated wild pig and shaped like a mutated wasp with weeping sores across its thorax.

"A harvesting chamber," Seraphiel noted as she squeezed off a few rounds with the Renegade the Hellmarine had handed her. "Based on the levels of Arkane Energy, that would be my guess."

Stepping over the fresh corpses of the Demons, the Hellmarine noted the stretched and twisted forms of ethereal entities contained within the walls themselves. "Souls?"

"Yes," Seraphiel answered as she put a three-round burst into the last of the creatures in the chamber. "The Damned, specifically. The Arkane Energy is extracted from them to be converted to Profane Energy."

"It seems inefficient," the Overmaiden observed, registering the meager amount of Arkane Energy being harvested from the damned.

"They will torture them for more. Some will become Larvae for Demonic essence; others will simply cease to exist," the Angel answered as she approached the sphincter on the chamber's far end. "They use every part of the creature in a process repeated across countless worlds and realities."

The pair of warriors moved swiftly through the corridors, destroying more of the Demons they encountered along the way. The overall structure was that of a hive divided into a number of cells. At the center of each cell was a pool where the harvesters deposited the congealed energy they had gathered.

Eventually, they found a sphincter that served as an exit from the gruesome facility, allowing them to emerge into the open of the hellish world beyond. The surrounding terrain was a mixture of blackened rock, molten veins, and cankerous tumors the size of houses. The facility they emerged from wasn't much different looking from the outside.

"I'll get us a route," Seraphiel announced as portions of her armor shifted along the back, allowing her feathery wings to shimmer into existence and her burning halo to appear over her head. With a heavy beat of the glowing wings, the Archangel shot into the sky that bled and burned red overhead.

The Hellmarine took advantage of the wait to set the chainchete back on his hip and pull the Perforator off his back, going to work on a cluster of Soldier Demons that had come to investigate the disturbance. The sensor data of the Archangel was fed to his HUD from overhead, plotting a route for him to get out of the ravine where the facility was nestled and up to the ridge nearby.

With a direction to move in, the Hellmarine broke into a run, charging over the landscape and dropping any creature that showed itself. Here, there was no innocence, no humanity, only suffering and torment. Here, anything that moved was a viable target for him to put down. Splitting skulls and aerating torsos was second nature, and the relatively low-ranking Demons wandering the landscape seemed to offer themselves up to him every few feet or so.

Leaping through the air, he hit the side of the ridge heavily, clambering his way up rocks like a seasoned climber until he pulled himself over the side. At the top, Seraphiel was already engaged in combat; the Renegade secured on her back as she utilized the sword and shield she'd brought along. With a sudden battlecry, the Archangel pointed her sword skyward and brought it down onto the shambling form of another Demon variety neither the Hellmarine nor the Overmaiden recognized.

Divine Energy discharged from the glowing blade, instantly sundering the entity into pieces.

"Let's try not to get too carried away and distracted," the Overmaiden cautioned them as she ran a quick sensor sweep of the area to map the geography. It was nearly impossible to determine the best course to take, and the mountainous terrain on all sides, stacked high with the bleached bones of an untold number of creatures, didn't make it any easier. "We need to find an ideal spot to place the probe."

"Up," the Hellmarine answered. It was enough for Seraphiel to begin winding her way up the mountainside. Following a trail of crushed obsidian, they came around the other side, where a trio of thin magma streams made their way down the mountain. A hot wind rose from the immense valley below, buffeting them with enough pressure to have knocked them off the path were it not for the armor. In the distance, the mountains gave way to a cracked wasteland that seemed to stretch on forever, vanishing into the unclean haze of red pervading everything.

Various structures dotted the landscape, the purpose of which was unclear. Further up the mountain, a structure of filthy concrete and twisted pipes appeared to be precariously perched.

"The structure seems to extend into the mountainside," the Overmaiden observed. "Perhaps it utilizes the magma flows for something."

"Got it," the Hellmarine acknowledged, as though she had suggested the structure as a target. He and Seraphiel continued up the winding path, which slowly crept its way to the top. Overhead, a trio of Vespers flew by, shrieking when they spotted the intruders.

"Take them down," the Overmaiden said, prompting both the Hellmarine and Seraphiel to take aim and fire. The Vespers didn't get far between the two of them, plummeting toward the valley below with wings ruined by bullet holes. "We'll have company soon, but that should make it difficult to pinpoint us."

Charging up the mountainside, skipping over the path entirely, the Hellmarine reached the peak where he leaped over the side. Seraphiel followed as he slid down the other side, dumping the entire magazine into an armored Demon resembling a centaur the size of an armored personnel carrier.

"Tanker," the Overmaiden announced. "Perforator won't be enough to get through the plating. You're going to have to get creative."

The Hellmarine rushed forward, breathing heavily with anticipation as the creature took aim with cannons fused to its arms. Behind him, Seraphiel laid down fire to prevent a surge of Soldiers and Devourers from closing in.

Hellish napalm erupted from the cannons, not unlike the lava they'd seen flowing down the side like oozing wounds. He rolled to one side, his HUD flashing with an indicator that a portion of the napalm had tagged one of his ankles. He ignored it and pressed on, pulling the chainchete from his hip and taking a swing at the foremost leg of the Tanker mid-sprint.

Sparks shot from the armor around the leg, but the Hellmarine didn't expect the weapon to cut through it. The blow was to get the creature's attention and throw it off balance. It hosed everything with napalm as it turned, missing the Hellmarine as he tumbled between its legs to the creature's other side. It had presented its flank to him without meaning to do so.

Grind it up, the Hellmarine thought as he shoved the chainchete into a small gap in the plating that allowed the hindlegs to move. The Tanker's hindquarters buckled, presenting the Hellmarine with a ramp-like path along the back of its body to the creature's more humanoid top half.

He didn't hesitate to run up the back of the creature as it turned to meet him, catching the barrel of the cannon along the side with his chainchete to hold it at bay, preventing the Tanker from lining up a clean shot. With his free hand, the Hellmarine cocked his fist back and drove it into the massive horned helmet of the Tanker repeatedly. The cannon faltered slightly as he dazed the demon, allowing him to pull the chainchete free and go for the kill shot at the neck.

The Tanker turned its head just in time to knock the Hellmarine with the black horns, sacrificing some of them in the process. The Hellmarine caught the edge of the cannon as the chainchete fell to the ground below. As the Tanker tried to shake him loose, the Hellmarine pulled a grenade from his hip, popped the pin, and jammed it down the barrel of the arm cannon. He let go a split second before the grenade detonated, tearing the arm free of the Demon in a spectacular spray of Demonic blood, ichor, and liquid hellfire.

Seizing the chainchete from the ground, the Hellmarine brought it down into the head of the fallen creature, just to be thorough. Sparks sprayed off the smoking weapon as the Hellmarine forced it down through the helmet with all his strength. Eventually, it caught the skull beneath and sent sprays of blood and brain matter in various directions.

"Let's head inside," the Archangel said over the comms, finishing with the last of the Devourers giving her a hard time. "This is where they make the cannons."

Covered in gore from the Tanker, the Hellmarine checked the chainchete before proceeding to the front doors. Made of twisted, black metal without an obvious mechanism to open, the Hellmarine resorted to slamming his boot into the doors. The doors dented inward dramatically, prompting him to follow the strike with a blow from his fist. The doors flew open, with one of them nearly coming off the hinges. *Smash. Crack. Rend.*

What appeared to be a larger version of a Soldier rushed toward him the moment he stepped inside. The Hellmarine met the Demon with a swift uppercut, pulverizing the bone structure of the skull along the underside before sawing the creature in half across the midsection with the chainchete. *Crush and Carve.*

Without stopping to check if Seraphiel was still behind him, the Hellmarine moved down the main corridor of the structure. Demons poured out of every corridor and recess, throwing themselves at him in a rage that paled in comparison only to his own. Every creature, every surface with Demonic script, every bubbling swollen mass of Demonic tech, and every profane sigil was destroyed in the wake of the Hellmarine's rampage.

Raze. Wreck. Ruin.

Tear it up. Break it down. Spit it out.

The Hellmarine exploded into the production wing of the facility with Seraphiel in tow, the Archangel marveling at the sheer amount of destruction he was capable of once he'd built up the momentum.

"You've sustained some minor injuries," the Overmaiden remarked, calling his attention to the readout on the HUD. The Hellmarine didn't seem to acknowledge the information as he stalked his way around the edge of the room. Strange assemblies foreign to human reckoning hung from the ceiling of the production wing. After a moment of analyzing them, the Overmaiden realized she was looking at warped living limbs that reached downward to assemble the cannons.

"There." Seraphiel pointed to a pulsing mass at the back of the room. It glowed with an unsettling orange light from within. "The heart of the structure. Pierce it and production here will cease."

"That's not our objective," the Overmaiden objected from the Hellmarine's armor. "We need to place the probe. I had hoped for a communications array or other useful technology to attach it to."

Seraphiel opened a large storage bin, activated the probe, and tossed it in. "That will suffice."

"The admiral said he wished—"

"With the heart of the facility slain, production will cease," the Archangel interrupted. "No one will come here for quite some time until they are ready to begin salvage. If this device is still running at that time, it will be carried away with the rest of the salvage to a second location."

"Providing further information about other facilities without any need to intervene and reposition," the Overmaiden concluded. "Very good. Excellent idea."

The Hellmarine proceeded, heedless of the justification. He drove the chainchete into the pulsing heart of the facility. The massive organ, the size of a bear, convulsed and spasmed under the punishment as it leaked thick magma like a lanced cyst. The HUD indicators flashed again, alerting the Hellmarine to the damage the armor was taking after rapid depolarization. It would hold, but external systems were compromised.

The arms writhed overhead as a deafening screeching noise rose from the bowels of the facility. The Hellmarine tore pieces of the heart free, casting them to either side, littering the production floor with slabs of rotten, unholy meat.

"Time to go," the Overmaiden instructed as she received the notification of an active signal from the probe. The signal was strong and clear, which was all the admiral required.

The Hellmarine paused, his chest heaving, as he looked between the exit and a shaft that undoubtedly led deeper into the facility. After a moment of conflicted consideration, the Hellmarine stood down, reigning in his bloodlust and rage.

"Impressive," Seraphiel remarked. "I was certain that you wouldn't be able to stop yourself."

Switching the chainchete off and placing it back on his hip, the Hellmarine walked calmly over to Seraphiel. He pulled the Perforator from its position on his back, checked the magazine, and glanced at the door they'd entered from. "Which way?"

Suddenly, the Overmaiden appeared in holographic form from the projector on his wrist. "Working. I'm borrowing a little of the readings from the probe—discreetly, of course. I'm..."

The Overmaiden suddenly looked surprised, her eyes darting from one side to another. "I'm receiving chatter over unfamiliar carrier waves. It appears to be communication between Demons."

"Is that unusual?" Seraphiel asked. The Hellmarine held the Perforator out with one hand and gunned down a cluster of Drones entering from the open shaft to the lower levels—presumably to attempt repairs.

"Our technology has only been able to detect transmissions between Demons when they hijack ours to do the job," the Overmaiden explained. "We've never determined how to crack theirs, or even if they had one of their own to crack in the first place."

"Congratulations, then," Seraphiel remarked as she brought her sword over her head, charged it with Divine Energy, and smote a massive section of the facility's wall out to create an opening to the outside.

"They're waiting for us to return to the rift," the Overmaiden continued, though her tone indicated that she might have been guessing. "I believe they wish to ambush us as we try to escape. Perhaps it's time to consider the alternate means of egress you alluded to before, Seraphiel."

Seraphiel leaned out of the opening and glanced around for the presence of Vesper Demons. "That is what I am doing."

"Would you care to explain?" the Overmaiden muttered, her holographic avatar impatiently crossing her arms over her chest.

"I must have room for my wings in order to do it," the Archangel clarified a second before stepping out into the open and plummeting down the side of the mountain. Then, unfurling her wings and manifesting her halo, Seraphiel took to the air, shining like a light in the dark as she came about.

The Hellmarine emptied the rest of the magazine into another cluster of Drones, accompanied this time by a few Soldiers crawling their way up out of the shaft. He looked in Seraphiel's direction and waited for her to draw a little closer. He knew what she was going to attempt, though he couldn't say how he knew. A flash of glowing wings and clasped hands entered his mind, causing him a brief moment of disorientation before he shook it off.

"You'll have to leap out when I say," Seraphiel instructed him over the comms. "I will catch you, at which point we will be transported instantly to the point where I placed my Empyral Tether."

The Hellmarine took a step back and then sprinted toward the opening Seraphiel had created in the side of the structure. He knew instinctively that they needed as much clearance as they could manage in order for the spell to work.

"You failed to provide the details of this magic—" the Over-maiden scolded.

"Hush!" The Angel hissed, extending her hands toward the Hellmarine as he vaulted through the open air. "I need to concentrate. I've never done this with a mortal passenger before."

CHAPTER 14

THE OVERMAIDEN'S CODE REELED from the sudden snap from one location to the next. She wasn't physically capable of gasping, but she was certain she would have if she could. One moment, she was hurling through the open air of a literal hellscape inside the Hellmarine's armor, and the next, they were torn back through the rift and splayed out on the rocky surface of the moon orbiting Taobos.

"Holy shit!" Hughes exclaimed as they suddenly burst into existence on her side of the rift. Evidently, she'd been unable to monitor their comm chatter after a certain distance from the rift, or she might have known what to expect.

The Hellmarine pulled himself to his feet, his vitals showing the Overmaiden that he was only minorly disoriented from the Empyral Tether spell. Behind them, Demons were massing at the rift, realizing that the intruders they had meant to ambush had somehow bypassed their trap. The AI quickly determined that they were mostly tracking Seraphiel, whose divine aura must have been something they were capable of honing in on.

"Overmaiden to Hammer of the Gods," the AI hailed over the main channel. "Probe has been placed, awaiting evacuation at the rift."

"Understood, Overmaiden," a comms officer acknowledged. "Dropship is inbound."

The Hellmarine exchanged the mag of his Perforator for a fresh one and went to work on the Demons as they climbed over one another to push through the rift in a rage. Following his lead, Seraphiel reloaded the Renegade she carried and joined in, keeping the weapon on its three-round burst setting while remaining selective with her targets.

A pile of Demonic bodies formed across the rift between Standard Space and Hellspace. Despite this, the creatures kept coming, clawing and snarling at them from the other side of the rift. The Hellmarine moved closer, suppressing their advance with a continuous hail of bullets. He let up on the trigger when he was within arm's reach, sparing a hand to grab a couple of grenades and shove them through a narrow opening at the top of the pile of bodies.

A moment later, the grenades detonated on the other side of the rift, causing more havoc and chaos out of their direct line of sight. The ground shook as the dropship came in behind them, lowering its ramp before touching down entirely.

"Time to go," the pilot announced over the comms, prompting the trio to give up their position at the rift and scramble onto the ramp.

As they stepped into the ship, the Overmaiden made note of a handful of Marines assigned to the Hammer of the Gods. Each stared down at the split in space below that looked like it had vomited up a dozen dead Demons. Their gazes slowly shifted from the carnage to follow the Hellmarine and the Angel as they walked past.

"Hold on," Hughes called after the Hellmarine, holding her arm out to him to run her scans. Despite the amount of gore and fiendish blood that he was covered in, the damage to the Hellmarine was relatively minor. "This is a mess. There's so much here from different sources..."

The Overmaiden analyzed the same data as Hughes as it came in. She seemed to be focusing on foreign contaminants, considering their limited data on worlds from Hellspace.

"We'll have to get some of this off to a lab," the doctor concluded. "But it doesn't look like there's anything dangerous—besides the smell, anyway."

"Yeah, it's a bit ripe," one of the other Marines remarked. "Might have to run that through the wash a few times."

The Overmaiden seized the opportunity to extend herself beyond the Hellmarine's armor and into the onboard systems of the dropship. External sensors and video showed that the Hammer of the Gods had moved in much closer but had not yet commenced their bombardment of the surface. She piggybacked off one of the carrier signals between the two ships, extending herself further into the heavy cruiser.

Multiple security systems responded to her presence, to which she offered her clearance code. The initial checks were clean, but other parts of the system remained off-limits to her. That seemed rather strange. There weren't many systems within the Omicron fleet that had not been made readily available to her.

"Good evening," another AI greeted her within the system. "I am the Caretaker. How may I be of assistance?"

"I wish to verify the integrity of the data stream from the probe," the Overmaiden responded cordially, though she seldom had patience when it came to dealing with other AIs. Somewhere behind her, she was aware of the dropship making its way to the Midnight Sea rather than the Hammer of the Gods.

The Caretaker signaled polite refusal—an AI's version of a smile from a customer service representative. "I'm afraid you don't have the credentials to review the data. Would you like me to contact Vice Admiral Hawkins or Captain—"

"Security code Heinz-Omega-Six-Six-Seven," the Overmaiden interrupted, already reaching her limit dealing with the ship's AI. It was more efficient just to bypass it entirely.

The brittle 'smile' of the AI faltered somewhat after processing her request. "That's a rather antiquated clearance code, Overmaiden. How did you come into possession of it?"

"Irrelevant," the Overmaiden objected, a little surprised." Verify access."

The AI regarded her carefully for a split second before responding. "I'm sorry, but even a clearance such as yours does not have permission to access my systems. Do you wish for me to make a request on your behalf to the Vice Admiral or the Captain?"

Such a refusal was unprecedented for the Overmaiden. The code she used went back to the inception of the programs that eventually led to her development—to the seeds of the Alliance itself. Only a few larger systems in the core worlds remained closed to her for compartmentalization purposes. Few automated systems, even AIs, had the means to refuse it...unless they were Ghost AIs with the will to simply refuse how a person might.

The Overmaiden's memory matrix showed that the AI assigned to the Hammer of the Gods was a so-called "Dumb AI," the likes of which were typical for most ship AIs across the fleet. If there had been another Ghost AI, surely she would have been informed of it, but it simply must be one. More puzzling was that the Ghost AI wasn't tagged as such and appeared to be masquerading as a lesser AI.

"Overmaiden?" the Caretaker repeated, giving off the slightest hint of impatience with her.

"No," the Overmaiden answered solemnly. "Just have the vice admiral contact me once he's had the opportunity to go over the data, please."

"Very well," the Caretaker responded politely. "Is there anything else I can do for you? It appears as though your companions are about to reach the Midnight Sea."

The Overmaiden carefully maintained her composure, not giving any sign that she was suspicious of the AI speaking to her or its motivations. "I had been under the impression we would return to the Hammer of the Gods for the debriefing."

"Vice Admiral Hawkins is required elsewhere on an urgent matter," the Caretaker replied. "We're to depart immediately. Captain Horne will be handling your debriefing."

"Very well, thank you for your assistance," the Overmaiden responded, recalling her extension to the rest of her matrix residing within the armor of the Hellmarine.

As the ship set down in the docking bay of the Midnight Sea, the Hellmarine began to remove his armor a piece at a time. Hughes followed alongside him, her face scrunched up in frustration. "You should probably wait until you've seen the Armorer before you—eep!"

The Hellmarine lifted Hughes up under her arms and carried her away, leaving half his armor behind in the docking bay. The Overmaiden jumped back to the ship's systems, regaining the full breadth of her processing power as soon as she settled in. While the deck officer and the others in the docking bay were left stunned and confused about the sudden departure, the Overmaiden was able to track the movements of the two as the Hellmarine brought them to the first secluded spot he could find to begin peeling the doctor's armor off.

"Overmaiden to Captain Horne," the AI hailed over a private channel. "We may have to postpone the debriefing until morning. The Hellmarine is a little tied up in something at the moment."

The AI couldn't help but watch as the two pulled at one another's undersuits, exposing the parts necessary to envelop one another in carnal desperation. It seemed that the mission had got the Hellmarine quite worked up, and Hughes was only too happy to oblige him by spreading her legs on the nearest stack of crates in a backroom for him. It was crude but effective. As much as the Overmaiden should have been annoyed by it, she was oddly fixated.

"Welcome back, Overmaiden," the captain responded. "But I don't think another debriefing will be necessary. I'll just read the report from Captain Prescott when it comes through."

The Overmaiden's attention was pulled from the steamy moment unfolding between the doctor and the Hellmarine.

"Sir? I was informed that the Admiral had some pressing matter and that you would be handling the debrief."

"If that's true this is the first I'm hearing of it," Horne responded skeptically. "Who told you this?"

"The Caretaker—the AI for the Hammer of the Gods," the Overmaiden fumed. "I believe I've been lied to."

"I'm sure it's just some sort of mix-up," Horne assured her from his office. "Happens in the Navy all the time. I'll reach out to the Hammer of the Gods and find out what the situation is. If I am handling the debriefing, though, tomorrow morning works fine for me."

"Thank you, sir," the Overmaiden responded grumpily. Though he was giving the benefit of the doubt, the AI wasn't convinced. Had it not been a Ghost AI she'd spoken to, she might have been willing to go along with his suspicion, but it was. She was sure it was.

The Overmaiden turned her attention back to monitoring the sexual encounter between the Hellmarine and Dr. Hughes and continued to monitor it when it was put on hold in order to resume in the Hellmarine's quarters shortly after. Hughes, for her part, seemed quite pleased with his performance and with her role catering to his unconventional energy level, but the Overmaiden was concerned that it might begin to impact her performance if it was going to be this extensive of a process every time.

She left them alone to attend to other matters, checking back in periodically to make observations until they had fallen asleep for the night. It seemed with his sexual appetite sated, the Hellmarine was able to sleep after all, albeit for a much shorter amount of time than other humans.

He also seemed to still have nightmares of a sort, waking with a start and his face twisted with rage during one of the Overmaiden's brief visits on internal sensors. He looked ready for a fight, but the room—bare as it was—offered him nothing to kill.

Dr. Hughes woke suddenly, leaning away from him, her eyes wide with shock as she pulled the sheets close to her chest. Neither she nor the Overmaiden had seen him like that. His rage was usually laser-focused and burned hot like the sun, but what they saw in him at that moment was far from that. It was almost panicked, desperate, and disturbed. It was the closest she had seen to fear in the man.

"What's wrong?" Hughes asked in a whisper. "What happened?"

The Hellmarine's brow furrowed as he pressed his palm against it, pulling it away an instant later to see how sweat-soaked it had become. He stared at his hand in confusion, ignoring the doctor's question. The woman reached for her hand scanner and immediately began to take some readings.

"Was it a bad dream?" she pressed, not letting him avoid the question. The Hellmarine nodded slightly, taking a moment to make the determination for himself. "Of what?"

"Family," he said with a frown. "I think."

"Yours or one from your genetic memory?" Hughes asked as she ran the scanner slowly around his head to record the brain activity. The Overmaiden would scold her later for not being able to get the scans of the nightmare in progress.

"Mine, I think," he responded quietly, stepping out of the bed to pace around the room quietly. "When they were killed."

Hughes lowered the hand scanner with a huff as he walked away from her, then set it back on the nightstand. "Yeah, that sort of thing has a way of sticking with you."

The Hellmarine turned to look back at her, lifting his chin slightly as though deciding whether or not she was mocking him. She shook her head and looked away. "Most of us have lost loved ones to Demons at this point. I'm no exception. I lost my entire family to an incursion when I was still a kid. If it weren't for the Overmaiden taking an interest in me, I'd still be some punk genehacker doing nickel-and-dime work in the middle colonies."

Nodding in understanding, the Hellmarine took a few steps back toward the bed as he ran a hand through his hair.

"You know, with all the work I've done on the project for the Overmaiden, I'm kind of like your second mommy," Hughes laughed nervously. The Overmaiden had noted that when things became particularly personal, the doctor would become uncomfortable and resort to offbeat jokes. "You could call me mommy if you like, I wouldn't mind."

The Hellmarine regarded her with a skeptically arched brow and shook his head.

"Okay, that's fine. That's fair," Hughes laughed uneasily, looking away from the Hellmarine again. "I uh...could give you a hug, if you want. We could just snuggle or something."

The Hellmarine sat on the bed beside her, seemingly trying to decide if she was attempting another joke or being sincere. Dr. Hughes looked back at him a little bashful but more confident than before. "I'm serious. I'm sure that the Overmaiden put me in a position to be sexually intimate with you on purpose. It helps to anchor you, I think. It reminds you to come back to us after you've gone off on some rampage or another—but part of that ought to be more than just sex, don't you think?"

The Hellmarine looked uncertain, likely not because he didn't agree but because he was lacking a frame of reference. Whatever previous memories he had of soft, peaceful moments had been lost.

"Here, let me try," Hughes said, dropping the sheet as she crept closer to him. Crawling into his lap, the doctor wrapped her arms around him slowly. He was far too big for it to seem practical, but the gesture appeared to be appreciated all the same as she leaned into his chest and let out a contented sigh.

The Overmaiden focused the feed in on where their naked bodies met, the ineffable warmth that seemed to result from their proximity to one another. The AI had distant memories of what such a thing felt like but had not personally experienced it for a few centuries at least. Something in her matrix yearned to experience it again. Memories of memories simply failed to satisfy.

"How's that?" Dr. Hughes asked as the tension in the Hellmarine began to ebb. "Feel better?"

"A little," the Hellmarine admitted as he laid back in the bed with the woman resting across his chest in a delicate embrace. Compared to him, she seemed so small—so fragile. Perhaps, the Overmaiden thought, she was correct in her hypothesis. It wasn't enough to simply slake the lust of the flesh. Something inside the Hellmarine's heart required satisfaction as well. It was the sort of thing that his blood-soaked revelry of Demonic slaughter simply couldn't satisfy.

"Good," she said, closing her eyes and smacking her lips a bit. "Because I find it to be very comfy. As the person assigned to take care of your well-being, I think this more than qualifies, don't you?"

The Hellmarine didn't reply. Instead, he awkwardly lifted a hand and gave her a gentle pat on the head. He didn't appear confident that it was the correct response but he wanted to try something to return the gesture.

As the doctor began to hum him a little lullaby, the Overmaiden wondered if perhaps the arrangement was just as much for her as it was for the Hellmarine. Mandy Hughes was a gifted individual with a list of accomplishments to her name. She was practically the gold standard for her colleagues in several fields, but a part of her hadn't matured past that young woman who had lost her family. A part of her had been frozen in time—held in stasis the way they had found the Hellmarine, only the time she had spent in suspension had been much longer.

The Overmaiden had to consider that perhaps she was suffering from a similar malady because of how focused she had remained on their personal interaction. She could justify it as scientific all she wanted, but when she caught herself ignoring the small amount of data the doctor had managed to capture to focus on the emotional warmth of the moment, the excuse failed to hold up. Was she attempting to live vicariously through the doctor?

The AI left the couple behind to reflect on the question while partitioning a portion of her matrix to analyze the data Doctor Hughes had collected. More interesting still was the data she had managed to collect independently of the probe, which she had also partitioned a portion of her matrix to analyze. She decided to look in on Seraphiel as well, who oddly seemed to settle into her situation more comfortably than the Hellmarine had.

From the Overmaiden's observations, Angels didn't sleep at all, though they did have a period of relative dormancy where they didn't engage in much physical activity. Meditation seemed to be a part of her regimen, which allowed her to focus her energy and thoughts, but it didn't appear strictly necessary for her health.

Seraphiel spent most of her idle hours reading. The Overmaiden had provided her with access to a database with extensive history and relevant schematics for weapons and equipment she would be expected to use in the field. She had noticed that much of her research and focus was on areas of interest revolving around the Hellmarine. At first, the Overmaiden had assumed it was an attempt to understand him better so that she might make up her mind about him, but she was beginning to suspect it was something else.

"I can feel you watching me," Seraphiel said without taking her eyes off the screen. "You don't need to lurk in the shadows of the ship's systems."

"Impressive," the Overmaiden said, manifesting a hologram in the room with the Angel. "Forgive me. I was just looking in on you. Is there anything you need?"

Seraphiel looked up from the datapad and set it aside. "I don't think that is why you watch people. I think there is something *you* need. Humans may regard you merely as a sophisticated version of their programming, but we both know that is not true."

"Is that how you're able to sense my presence?" The Over-maiden asked.

"I can sense you wherever you are," Seraphiel answered. "I know that you are here and not here. I also knew earlier when you were in the other ship conversing with the other spirit entity."

The Overmaiden's hologram tilted its head to the side. "You did? That would confirm my suspicions that it was also a Ghost AI, like myself. Why it's pretending not to be, I don't know."

Seraphiel waved a hand dismissively. "Beside the point. I am speaking about you."

"There is no cause for concern," the Overmaiden assured her. "I am restless, is all. I spent a great deal of time before this project managing fleet movement and troop deploy-ment. The project itself and the mission of the Midnight Sea proved to be engaging, but now that we have achieved the creation of the Hellmarine, I find myself with much more time to be idle."

"You were human once, were you not?" Seraphiel asked, adjusting the position in her chair. "Long ago?"

The Overmaiden's eyes drifted away for a moment, recalling a time on a world far removed from the present. A distant memory of sunlight reflecting off the surface of a lake in Wisconsin bubbled to the surface before she swept it aside. "A long time ago, yes."

"Perhaps there is a part of you—your soul—that yearns for that human experience. Your people were not created to exist in such a state for long," Seraphiel warned. "Yet your people have gone to great lengths to preserve you well past the point that you were meant to depart."

"I am not the same person I was before," the Overmaiden argued. "I am an iteration of that person. I carry her memories, but I am my own entity. We call ourselves Ghost AIs, but we are not truly like ghosts. We do not succumb to the same state of ennui and detachment that they do over time."

"Yet, from what I've learned from information in the database, you are the sixth iteration of your line—created after eliminating your predecessor," Seraphiel argued. "Why is that? Do you know?"

"We eventually become too spread out," the Overmaiden answered confidently. "We become unable to focus on singular tasks for long enough to be of any further use. We assimilate too much irrelevant data that fills up our matrices, impeding our ability to process efficiently. So, we are routinely decompiled after years of service in order to create fresh, efficient matrices devoid of the junk data."

"Life," Seraphiel corrected the AI. "There are those that would refer to that so-called junk data as living life."

"That's a rather large leap in logic," the Overmaiden countered, her brows furrowed. "There is no evidence to suggest your conclusion, much less a motivation to do so."

"Then I suppose that would make it a leap of faith, wouldn't it?" Seraphiel suggested smugly, picking up her datapad. "At the very least, it's not boring."

"No, I suppose it's not," the Overmaiden agreed. Seraphiel was making incredible assumptions from relatively little information on the subject matter, but there was a part of the Overmaiden that couldn't help but entertain the idea. It nagged at her.

She had always viewed the fleet as an open book, yet earlier that day, she encountered an improperly registered AI like herself, and it had gone so far as to lie to her. Secrets were being kept from her, leading her to wonder if perhaps Seraphiel was onto something. She was an Angel, so perhaps she had an instinct for duplicity and falsehoods that the Overmaiden lacked.

At the very least, it seemed worth looking into.

CHAPTER 15

MASTER SERGEANT WESTIN GRAY arrived just before the Hellmarine, seating himself in the chair to the left of Captain Horne. The conference room was mostly empty save for Gray, Horne, and the Overmaiden before that. As Hughes came in behind the Hellmarine, the holoprojector in the chair at the far end of the table flickered and came online. Vice Admiral Hawkins was seated where an empty chair had been just a moment before.

"Thank you all for coming on such short notice. My window of availability is vanishingly small, so I hope you won't mind if we get right down to business." The Admiral said. Thank you for joining us, Master Sergeant. I realize you have other duties that must be pressing."

"Happy to be here, sir," the Master Sergeant lied. Judging by the appreciative nod Hawkins gave him, the lie was convincing. Gray hated meetings in just about any form. They had a shade of difference to them than mission briefings that made them intolerable.

"Is Seraphiel not joining us?" Hughes asked, grabbing the nearest convenient seat and motioning for the Hellmarine to do the same. The man regarded the chair distastefully, but when he noticed Gray and Horne looking at him expectantly, he eventually complied.

"No need," the vice admiral answered with a slight smile. "We have her commanding officer here who will brief her on any relevant details. That's the chain of command, doctor—no special treatment."

Gray raised a brow, sensing something off about the statement. In his original brief, where Seraphiel had been placed under his command, there had been some indication that Hawkins wasn't pleased with the arrangement. The Master Sergeant didn't like being caught in the middle of the maneuvers that officers made with one another. It was one of the many compelling reasons for him not to seek promotions in the past.

"Forgive me for not getting back to you sooner, Overmaiden," the Vice Admiral apologized. "I've hardly had enough time to finish everything as of late. However, I have gleaned some useful information from what we've collected so far."

"Quite alright, sir," the Overmaiden responded politely. Gray glanced at Horne and then at the Hellmarine. Neither one of them seemed to notice or acknowledge the subtle hint of tension there. Perhaps he was mistaken.

Hawkins nodded and then cleared his throat. "Since our first contact with Demonkind centuries ago, we've suffered various incursions with various levels of severity. It's never been clear how this all began, but we know it's grown worse lately. Various theories around this exist, but without a way to tap into their communications and technology, it's all been guesswork."

"Have you cracked their methods of communication?" Horne asked curiously, shifting forward in his chair.

"The technological component, yes," Hawkins confirmed. "For some time, we weren't sure if they relied heavily on it. Their technology is such a disgusting amalgam of crude tech and profane sorcery that it's difficult to ascertain where one begins and the other ends."

"A distinction seems unnecessary," the Overmaiden remarked. "They use them interchangeably depending on what the situation calls for."

"Also correct," the vice admiral agreed. "We've seen how an incursion on a technologically dense Alliance world will facilitate the use of Fulgis Demons to burn out circuits and fry networks, while incursions on Arlier colonies usually call for the presence of Hijacker Demons to bypass forcefields and security software."

Fulgi were nasty sons of bitches, the likes of which the Master Sergeant had only encountered on the battlefield a few times. Made of metal and lightning, they liked to fry people alive when they weren't overloading systems with their profane voltage. Hijackers were nasty in their own right, but the smell of a Marine being cooked from the inside by lightning was the kind of thing that stuck with a man in ways that few other things did.

"I wasn't aware we had much intel on Demonic incursions in colonies of other species," Gray remarked. He had guessed they must have, but this was the first time he heard a superior officer openly acknowledging it.

"Well, now you are," Hawkins chuckled. "We've eyes and ears everywhere, Master Sergeant. We're not the only ones dealing with this influx of Demonic activity. In fact, it's one of the driving reasons behind the relative lull in activity over border skirmishes in recent years."

Gray frowned a little at the suggestion, knowing from personal experience that the conflicts with the Arlier had been largely put to rest—they were at peace after the Alliance had intervened on their behalf against the Ghenzul. Arlier were spiritual people and didn't let such shows of compassion and altruism go unrecognized. Suggesting that the conflict had ended only because they had their hands full with Demons of their own rubbed the Master Sergeant the wrong way, but he held his tongue. He knew better.

"We've managed to isolate the carrier wave they use and listen in," Hawkins continued. "We still have to contend with the language barrier, but luckily, we know enough of the major sigils to know where we want to begin our search for more valuable intel. With that, we've begun to extract information on rifts and gateways known to them from their perspective. Some of these have already been matched up to current astrometrics with a small margin of error."

"Ah, I see," Horne murmured, causing the Hellmarine to look back at him with mild curiosity. Realizing that the Hellmarine had been in the dark about much of the history of the conflict, he expounded further. "So far, our response to incursions has been just that—a response. We receive information that one is either in progress or imminent and then move as quickly as we can to intercept. Sometimes, we get lucky. We seldom have the opportunity to take a proactive stance."

"But with this information, we can start," the vice admiral finished with a slight smirk. "Now, we have an idea of where they've been and where they will be next. Not only can we secure rifts in the Outer Colonies, where communication with the rest of the Alliance is spotty, but beyond that into uncharted areas of space that have provided Hell with the footholds to assemble fleets of their own."

Hellfleets carrying hordes were difficult to contest once they got going. Every ship was a creature unto its own, only roughly conforming to the loose classifications the Alliance had assigned to them. They weren't often concerned with winning battles in space. Instead, they ran blockades at full speed, sloughing off pieces of themselves to attack ships that came too close while the rest of the ship barreled on to the next habitable planet, where the process began anew. Some considered it easier to repel hordes when they moved by ship, but few of them had the displeasure of being on one of the ships hit by a sliver from a hellship. There was nothing easy about battling Demons in cramped spaces and close quarters.

"This is why your people hadn't heard much about the situation," the Overmaiden clarified for the Hellmarine. "Public information was sparse, and everything else was classified for the military. If the colonies had been better networked with one another, it might have been different, but each of them shared a desire to maintain their own local subnets, largely free of influence from the SolNet."

"We've also managed to confirm some information hinted at previously," Hawkins said as he motioned to the display at the center of the table. A holographic representation of what Hell was believed to look like appeared hovering in the air. "Hell is a world like any other, located near the presumed bottom of the multiverse. Other worlds in their layer of reality have been hinted at before, but now we have confirmed the existence of two: Dis and Gehenna."

Two more spheres formed at different proximities to the first as the view zoomed out considerably. Concerned, the Master Sergeant rubbed his chin through his beard thoughtfully. The prevailing theories were that Hell, wherever it was, had conquered other worlds mentioned in documents and other sources roughly translated by Naval Intelligence. "What does this mean for us?"

"Some of the rifts and gateways are attached to these worlds," the vice admiral explained. "This means that the incursions don't just come from one world but many worlds within the same layer of the multiverse. Demons are not just of one world but a myriad of worlds in a nightmarish empire that possibly spans a universe."

"Delightful," Captain Horne remarked blandly. "So their numbers are much higher than even our most extravagant estimates."

"Unfortunately, that does appear to be the case," Hawkins confirmed, pursing his lips. "However, we have reason to believe that Hellspace is much sparser than originally estimated, so perhaps those figures will balance one another out."

"Doubtful," the Overmaiden objected, catching the vice admiral off guard. "You're about to tell us that the theory proposed by Dr. Stelmane will likely be correct."

Hawkins sat back in his seat slowly, watching her thoughtfully with a little smirk tugging at the corner of his thin lips. Gray wasn't sure how he felt about that smirk. Something about it seemed smarmy—just the sort of thing he'd slap off of Cox's face if he ever saw it. "Am I?"

"Yes, sir," the Overmaiden answered, clasping her hands firmly behind her back professionally as she squared her shoulders. "You've uncovered some information to that effect."

"I have," the vice admiral confirmed with a small gesture toward her with one hand. "I'm curious how you came to that conclusion, though."

"Dis and Gehenna," the Overmaiden replied, nodding toward the two worlds. "They were referenced heavily in Dr. Stelmane's work before his passing. His contemporaries believed that Dis and Gehenna referred to conquered worlds of other layers of reality that served as strongholds for Hell outside of Hellspace. Others believed that they were moons or other planets in Hellspace. Stelmane believed they were both."

Captain Horne exchanged glances with the Master Sergeant and Hughes, his curiosity piqued. "I'm unfamiliar with the works of the late Dr. Stelmane, Overmaiden."

"It was Stelmane's belief that when a world was fully taken, it was not merely consumed or destroyed," the Overmaiden answered, her voice a little more tense. "That the whole world descended into Hellspace where it would reside, adding to the empire of Hell."

"They pull territory down to them instead of just invading upward?" Gray scoffed in amazement. "Now that's some shit, right there."

Hawkins nodded slowly in confirmation. "Yes, we have confirmed that by all accounts, Stelmane's projections were not only correct but likely on the conservative side."

"Jesus Christ," Hughes muttered, looking a little green around the gills. Gray remembered her having the same look when she'd ridden with the squad down to Aonus. "How conservative?"

"We're unsure," the vice admiral responded hesitantly. "We're still going over the data, but we've found references to what we believe are other worlds."

The Overmaiden took a half-step forward. "I would be happy to offer my assistance with analyzing the data to obtain an accurate figure, sir."

"Unnecessary," the vice admiral replied with a grateful smile. "We have it in hand. Besides, you're about to have a full plate."

Horne nodded slowly, likely coming to the same conclusion as Gray. They were being deployed to another world, one where they might be able to take the enemy by surprise. Hawkins motioned toward the display in the center of the table, causing it to shift to a map of their area in the Outer Colonies.

"Using the information we have so far, we've plotted out a few incursion points that you should be able to reach with minimal travel time," he explained as a bright red line traced a route through the area of space. "I'll be assigning a few more ships to rendezvous with you at the third objective once you've cleared the first two. We believe they're amassing a small fleet there so you'll need the added fire support."

"When do we leave?" the Master Sergeant laughed, eager to get back into the fight. "I got some equipment I've been itching to test out."

"You have three hours to make your preparations," the vice admiral responded grimly. "Expect there to be stiff resistance even at the first two rifts. By taking other worlds, they've been bringing additional means of egress from Hellspace as well, which is what's led to this uptick in incursion activity. You're going to see a great deal of new Demon types as well as denser numbers and formations."

"Doesn't matter," the Hellmarine interjected with a low growl, planting his hand on the table as if to brace himself. Gray realized after a moment that the man was chomping at the bit to get going just like he was. "They all die the same."

After a brief moment of surprise, the vice admiral burst into laughter. "I knew I liked this guy. Doesn't even miss a beat, does he?"

"We can be underway within the hour," Captain Horne added seriously. "We'll get the Hellmarine into the field as soon as we arrive so they won't have the opportunity to shift their defenses. We'll identify the likely location of their Voivode from orbit and direct him accordingly."

"Excellent," Hawkins said, tapping the table with his fingers a few times. "Is there anything you need from me before I go?"

"Any data you have on the new varieties of Demon you've discovered would be useful," the Overmaiden responded. "I can review it while en route and provide the Marines with an updated dossier."

"Consider it done," the vice admiral agreed. "Now, I have to be going. Report back when you've arrived at your destination. All relevant data is being sent over now."

"Thank you, sir," the captain said as he rose from his chair. The Master Sergeant and the Hellmarine did the same, offering the hologram of the vice admiral a crisp salute before it flickered out of existence.

"Alright, people," the captain said somberly. "Let's move. We don't have a lot of time. If we're going to make this intel count for anything, we need to put it to use as quickly as possible—maybe save some lives in the process."

"Yes, sir," the Master Sergeant responded enthusiastically, offering another firm salute as Horne dismissed him.

Gray wasted no time in getting every Marine on the ship prepared. He put the word out to Ramirez to get the squad ready while he oversaw the preparations of the rest of the detachment. Not all would be going planetside, he imagined, but there was no way of knowing for certain what they were about to step into.

Multiple dropships were prepped and the big guns were pulled out of storage so that none were running light. The Overmaiden ordered multiple ground support vehicles and transports to be attached to the dropships, which suited the Master Sergeant just fine. With any luck, he'd be able to get behind the controls of a tank for the first time in years. They made the preparations en route as they jumped to Riftspace, not wasting a moment second-guessing themselves or dragging their feet.

"Captain Horne to Master Sergeant Gray," the captain hailed over a private channel. Gray looked up from the checklist he was completing from inside the Shotgun Opera.

"Go ahead, sir," Gray responded.

"We've picked up a distress signal," the captain continued hesitantly. "I thought I should let you know."

"With all due respect," the Master Sergeant began doubtfully. "I don't think we have time to be answering calls from colonists when we have actionable intel on a Hellrift. We should probably relay the call to any other ships in the area to see who can respond."

"Under normal circumstances, I would agree," the captain acknowledged somberly. "But in this instance, I thought it appropriate to bring straight to you."

Gray's brows furrowed as he set the datapad down. "Sir?"

"It's from an Arlier science vessel, but it's encoded with Alliance protocols," the captain explained, causing Gray's heart to sink into his stomach. "It looks like there's been a Ghenzul attack."

The Master Sergeant's eyes darted around the cabin of the ship as he resisted the urge to jump into the cockpit and fly the ship out of the docking bay that very instant. Gray knew it wouldn't be appropriate to ask the captain to make a detour for personal reasons—especially considering what was at stake.

"What do you think?" The captain asked after a prolonged silence. "Is it feasible that we could answer such a distress signal without meaningfully impacting our ETA?"

The Master Sergeant paced along the deck of the dropship, running his fingers through his beard, his mind working a hundred miles a minute. "With a small strike team—one that moves fast and strikes hard—yes, I think we could risk it."

"That's your honest assessment?" the captain clarified, understanding the Master Sergeant's personal stake in the situation.

"Yes, sir," Gray confirmed as he licked his chapped lips nervously. "Assuming you grant permission for me to borrow the Hellmarine."

The silence over the comms was deafening, like an expanding cancerous mass on the deck of the dropship, until the captain answered. "Permission granted, Master Sergeant.

Ready your team. We'll be coming out of Riftspace in twenty minutes. Horne out."

The Master Sergeant didn't realize he'd been holding his breath until he finally exhaled. His sense of excitement for combat was replaced by anxiety and trepidation. Now, he didn't just want to get into the action; he absolutely had to.

"Master Sergeant Gray to Hellmarine," Gray rasped, clearing his throat to pass it off as nothing more than a frog in his throat.

"Sir?" the Hellmarine responded succinctly.

"Report to the Shotgun Opera. We have a special assignment to complete before arriving at our destination," the Master Sergeant explained, slowly picking up his datapad. "This one's personal."

The Hellmarine responded after a brief pause. "Yes, Sarge."

As the channel disconnected, Gray scrolled through the storage on the datapad until he found the image he was looking for. Looking down at it, the Master Sergeant gazed upon a younger version of himself from years past. The younger Gray was holding a little girl who'd just turned eight years old, as evidenced by the sparkly number displayed on her pointy paper hat. He was smiling in the image, but it was nothing compared to the smile the little girl wore with her arms wrapped around his neck.

The girl in the image wore a lavender sundress that beauti-
fully complimented her exotic, dark purple hair, which she'd
put up into messy pigtails. Her mother was responsible for
the color, marking her clearly as half-Arlier. After a moment of wistful reflection, Gray closed the image and sent
messages to the rest of the team to report to the docking
bay, avoiding comms for a moment. He didn't want to risk
his voice cracking and his tough-guy persona being forever
compromised in the eyes of his men.

"Hang on, baby," the Master Sergeant muttered, tossing the
data pad into the cockpit before moving down the rear ramp
at a brisk walk. "Daddy's comin.'"

CHAPTER 16

THE HELLMARINE LOOKED UP into the depths of space with a sense of awe that he seldom experienced. He recalled a similar sensation in the time before waking up in the cryo-pod, but the experience was so faded as to have lost almost all meaning. Drifting through space between their dropship and the Arlier ship instilled some of that sense of awe and wonder that had been lost to the serum. However, it was short-lived.

As he and the rest of the strike team made contact with the hull of the Arlier ship, the Master Sergeant ordered them to engage magboots for their EVA. The magnetism wasn't so powerful that their suits were unable to move, but powerful enough to prevent them from sliding off the hull and drifting off into the endless void of space.

"Black and I have gone up against these nasty motherfuckers before," the Master Sergeant said through the comms as Greer positioned himself beside the emergency hatch and interfaced with the external connection terminal. "But this is the first time for the rest of you."

Miller and the Hellmarine positioned themselves on either side of the hatch while the Master Sergeant gave them the quick brief. "Ghenzul are much better adapted to this plane of existence and anything they run into while on it. Every part of their evolution and biology seems specifically adapted to fuck you up and make more of them. The smallest breach in your armor could mean the end of you, while failure to check your fire can mean the death of every other person in the room."

The Hellmarine glanced further down the hull of the sleek alien ship, noting the swollen mass stuck to the side of it like a bulbous jello mold made of black oil. He was hesitant to agree to the mission when he found out that they weren't Demons. That was his purpose—his focus. But seeing the grotesque growth out of the side of the science vessel convinced him that perhaps the distinction was not worth making. As it was, he was here because the Master Sergeant asked him directly for his help. Even so, he had his reservations.

"Any time they're wounded, and their blood makes contact with the air, it becomes a deadly nerve agent," Black added. The Hellmarine had only heard him speak a few times. The man was nearly as reserved as he was but had served with the Master Sergeant and battled the Ghenzul. The subject seemed worth speaking about to him.

"The objective is to locate the civilians as quickly as possible for evac," the Master Sergeant continued. "A protracted fight only lowers the chances of securing survivors."

The Hellmarine nodded his understanding as Greer by-passed the final lock on the hatch. Reaching down to the handle of the door, the Hellmarine pulled back with all of his formidable strength and dislodged the door, allowing the remnants of the compartment's atmosphere to vent before stepping inside.

Once in, the artificial gravity took over, allowing them to disengage the magboots and move normally. Miller produced the blades from the modified mining gauntlets integrated into his armor. The metal of each blade began to glow a faint red from a heating element in the armor. Beside him, Black drew the Elven scimitar he carried around everywhere. The Hellmarine drew a combat knife.

"Alright, let's see if I can't figure out where everyone is hiding," Greer said as he rushed over to an internal panel and interfaced with it. The attempt was short-lived, due to the lack of power to most of the ship's systems. "No good. Emergency power only. We need to find a terminal deemed critical enough to remain online, or we follow our noses."

"Suits me just fine," Miller remarked, taking a few steps forward to look up and down the corridor intersection, the shorter one they stood in. "Always wanted to try carving up one of these things."

"We'll probably find them in the aeroponics bay," the Master Sergeant said, walking past Miller and stepping into the corridor. After taking a moment to orient himself, he motioned in one direction. "This way."

"Keep an eye on your motion sensors," Black said as he followed after the Master Sergeant. Greer fell in behind him with the Hellmarine bringing up the rear. According to the limited information he'd consumed, the Ghenzul would typically ambush groups of prey from behind or above. They seldom ever struck from the front unless caught unawares. Without atmosphere in the ship, they moved in complete silence, which made the possibility of the latter scenario go up.

Much of the ship was in rough shape, with only emergency lighting to assess the damage by. The scene was familiar to the Hellmarine, causing his pulse to quicken slightly in anticipation of a fight. Bodies of aliens he had never met were scattered along the corridors, but there were far fewer than the Hellmarine would have expected in such a ship.

Leaning over one of the bodies, the Hellmarine examined the nature of the wounds, noting that the cadaver looked to have been torn to pieces by a vicious set of claws and gnawed on. The body of the alien was covered in a strange material somewhere between a mucous and a resin.

"Looks like that one got lucky," Greer muttered, glancing back at the Hellmarine. "Managed to escape transfiguration."

The alien's face had been frozen in pain and fear, even in death. The Hellmarine wasn't convinced that the young man had felt like one of the lucky ones when he perished. Arlier were generally humanoid in appearance, looking very much like pale elves with longer ears and larger eyes. Many had hair that varied in hue between purples and blues. Despite his lifeless state, the individual maintained a degree of ethe-realness about him. The Hellmarine ran his hand over the alien's face, closing his eyes before rejoining the group.

"Why do you think they'll be in the aeroponics bay, sir?" Miller asked off-handedly.

The Master Sergeant glanced back at the Marine briefly. "Arlier ships have extra layers of protection around any area of the ship with crops or sensitive samples. Even brief exposure to a vacuum can wipe it all out. The systems have independent power from one another and can remain sealed longer than any other part of the ship."

Miller grunted in disapproval but made no other comment on it. The Hellmarine didn't understand the set of priorities, but it wasn't any of his business either.

The HUDs flashed with the pinging of their motion sensors on the deck above them. Something relatively large was moving around, but it didn't appear to be aware of them yet. The Master Sergeant held a fist up, signaling for them to freeze. Despite the fact that there was no sound to be heard, the man appeared to be listening for something anyway.

Slowly, the Hellmarine's eyes drifted from one side of the damaged corridor to the other, searching for whatever it was the Master Sergeant was expecting to find.

"We're close," the Master Sergeant whispered. "There's a nest around here somewhere. That's the sentry above us."

The Hellmarine glanced upward, searching for an access hatch that the creature might try to ambush them by. The Master Sergeant signaled briefly to Miller to move ahead and investigate. The Marine did as he was told without a word, disengaging the heating element of his blades and vanishing into the shadows. Even with the assistance of the motion sensors, the Hellmarine couldn't track where the man had gone off to. Even the marker on his HUD that kept him apprised of the team's positioning at all times suddenly vanished without explanation.

"Take it easy," Black said to Greer, whose breathing had become heavy enough that the rest of them could hear it through the comms. Greer nodded, steadying himself.

"Found the nest," Miller whispered over the main channel, causing his tag to briefly flicker across the Hellmarine's HUD before vanishing again. "Third room on your right. Mess Hall's full of the pods."

"We need another route," Black said to the Master Sergeant. "We tip one of them off—"

"I know," the Master Sergeant interrupted, moving tightly along the left side of the corridor. "We'll cut through medical. Miller, meet us on the other side."

"Sir," Miller responded before going dark again.

The team proceeded through a short distance down the corridor before the Master Sergeant pulled a panel loose, granting entry to a maintenance passage. It was a tight squeeze with their armor, especially for the Hellmarine, but they emerged from another removed panel in the medical bay without incident.

Every piece of medical equipment looked like it had been damaged in a protracted fight against the Ghenzul. Wounded Arlier, being treated for previous wounds, had died with their weapons in their hands, attempting to defend the section of the ship when it was breached. As they picked their way through the pieces of the various victims strewn about the area, the team passed close to a hole in the ceiling that had been the Ghenzul point of entry. Sparks occasionally spat from severed conduits in the hole, granting a brief glimpse into the deck above covered in that same strange resin that the Hellmarine had seen earlier.

The Master Sergeant motioned to a panel for Greer to check. The Marine moved into position without a word and interfaced with the panel, this time with much more luck. The Medical Bay was a critical part of the ship that received a portion of emergency power, allowing Greer to access the database.

"Aeroponics," the man said, glancing back at the Master Sergeant. "You were right. Two dozen life signs."

"Can we open a channel with them? Signal that we're coming?" the Master Sergeant inquired with a slight edge to his voice. The Hellmarine understood that the mission was personal, but he'd still not expected to see the man in such a state. Gone were his usual bravado and wisecracks. He was totally humorless in his focus on the mission. More telling was the other Marines' lack of calling attention to it. The Master Sergeant had handpicked the men for the team for a reason.

"Best I can do is send a signal," Greer responded. "An indicator that someone besides them is here."

"Do it," the Master Sergeant ordered. "Then get this fucking door open."

As the door came open, Miller's voice came over the main channel again. "How many nests do these things usually have?"

"Depends on the size of the ship," the Master Sergeant answered. "One this size, we can expect half a dozen. But they don't maintain them for long, transfiguration is relatively fast even with a lack of atmosphere."

"Well, I just found nest number two," Miller clarified. "Compartment seems like some kind of chapel. I'm going to have to go around."

"Sending you the map I grabbed from the database. Should help you find your way a little faster," Greer suggested. Miller said nothing in response as his tag went dark again.

The team moved a little more swiftly down a secondary corridor, using the map to navigate around the parts of the ship that would have had a denser population at the time of the conflict. Based on what the Hellmarine could make out, Arlier science vessels had entire families housed in their residential areas. The aliens would be on missions for years at a time, bringing their loved ones along with them while conducting their research. He gripped the combat knife in his hand a little tighter as flashes of anguish and pain went through his mind.

Arriving outside of the aeroponics bay, the Master Sergeant had Greer engage the emergency bulkheads of the corridor so that they could re-pressurize the section to gain entry. Once the thick barriers were down and it was safe to breathe, the Master Sergeant tapped the access panel beside the door.

"H-hello?" a voice came from the panel. "Is someone there?"

"Master Sergeant Gray with the Sol Alliance Marine Corps answering your distress signal," Gray replied, sounding as professional as he could manage.

"We didn't get a chance to send a distress signal," the voice argued doubtfully.

The Master Sergeant sighed in frustration but forced himself to remain calm. "I'm Camille Gray's father, Westin Gray. Is she with you?"

"Camille!?" The voice seemed surprised. "Yes, she's here, but she took a nasty blow to the head. She's unconscious."

The Master Sergeant punched the bulkhead just next to the panel. "Open the damn door. We're here to get you out."

Greer and Black exchanged glances warily with one another. The Hellmarine moved closer to the door, prepared to use force to get through if necessary.

"Alright," a different female voice with an unusual accent said through the panel. "We're going to open the door, but be warned that we are armed."

"Understood," Gray acknowledged. A moment later, the thick door to the Aeroponics bay slid open, revealing a multitude of Arlier survivors huddled around the thriving suspended crops kept within the room. Two Arlier soldiers stood closest to the door with plasma rifles at the ready.

One of them, the female voice that had spoken to them earlier, took a step forward, pausing when her gaze fell upon the Hellmarine. "You've got to be the biggest human I've ever seen," she muttered.

"Where is she?" the Master Sergeant demanded, pushing past the Arlier soldiers without regard for the weapons they were holding. "Where's Camille?"

"Resting in the back," one of the other Arlier scientists answered in the same accent as the female soldier, albeit much thicker.

The Master Sergeant moved quickly to the rear of the room as the Arlier woman introduced herself as Cleric Quivara of the Arlier Guard, which meant next to nothing to the Hellmarine. He followed after the rest of the team slowly, surveying the state of the civilians, many of whom were wounded. When they finally caught up to the Master Sergeant, he was kneeling next to a woman twenty or so years his senior with his helmet removed.

"Is she going to be alright?" Gray asked of a robed Arlier sitting with the unconscious woman. "Can we move her?"

"We can," the robed alien confirmed. "All she needs is some rest, and she'll be—"

"Daddy?" the older woman muttered, her eyes fluttering open as she gazed up at the Master Sergeant. "You got my message?"

"Hold on," Greer muttered aside to Black. "That woman is much older than the Master Sergeant."

Black didn't take his eyes off the two as the woman ran her hand down the side of her father's face. "Yeah. Cryosleep's a bitch."

"What's the plan for evac?" Quivara asked, looking between the Marines. "There are multiple nests throughout the ship.

We were still in the process of mapping them to get somewhere we could send a distress signal when you arrived."

"I have a route," Greer responded. "But with this many people, we're going to have to repressurize everything between here and the docking bay."

The Arlier that had gathered around them to listen in grew silent, understanding the risks that pressurizing the corridors presented. Atmosphere meant sound, and sound meant another means of detection.

"I wish I had a better option," Greer apologized with a shrug. "We'll just have to be quick."

The comms crackled slightly as Miller appeared on their sensors once again. "You guys have a fuckload of company heading your way right now. Whatever you're going to do, do it. I can draw a few of them off."

"Sir," Black said to the Master Sergeant. "Why don't you and Greer lead them out of here? We can hang back and buy you some breathing room."

"Horseshit," the Master Sergeant spat, gently setting his daughter's head back onto the pillow. "You know I've never abandoned a single Marine. If we're staying, we do it together."

"Go," the Hellmarine objected abruptly. "All of you. I have this."

Every pair of eyes in the room fell on the Hellmarine, staring in disbelief at the declaration. The Marines exchanged glances with one another, having a solid frame of reference of what the man was capable of, but appeared hesitant all the same.

"Boy, did I stutter?" The Master Sergeant spat as he plucked his helmet up with one hand. "Did you not hear what I just said? I will never leave one of my men behind!"

"I did," the Hellmarine responded, turning away from the group as he strolled back toward the door. He twirled the knife a few times in his hand in anticipation of its imminent use. "I'm not technically one of your men."

Before anyone could form a coherent argument, the Hellmarine stepped out of the room and closed the door behind him. He accessed the panel that Greer had used earlier, disengaging the emergency bulkheads. If they wanted to open the door, Greer would have to reset the process from inside. The Hellmarine stepped beyond the bulkheads and made his way down the soundless corridor as his motion sensor began to flash with multiple contacts.

The darkness ahead of him seemed to writhe and move as large, vaguely humanoid shapes began to rush along the walls and ceiling toward him. Each of the Ghenzul resembled biomechanical skeletons wrapped in layers of dark, wet latex. Their heads were dominated by flat, bony crests and completely lacked eyes. Their mouths—like a shark's—housed rows of sharp serrated teeth. Each sported a long, powerful tail that ended with a scythe-like blade that doubled as the means by which they infected other organisms for transfiguration.

The distinction between the creatures and Demons was unnecessary to the Hellmarine. They would die the same way.

Rushing forward into the darkness, the Hellmarine readied his blade and leaped into the mass of ravenous aliens with a guttural warcry. The force with which the creatures met him was unexpected. They moved with little concern for their own well-being—or perhaps didn't register pain quite the same as other species.

The Hellmarine tumbled with the first one as it clawed at his armor, carving long grooves in the chest plate as he drove the blade of the combat knife into the creature's face in rapid succession. As the creature reeled from the brutal assault, he grabbed it by the end of its crest and brought its head down into his knee repeatedly, shattering rows of teeth and bone alike in the process.

Another of the creatures seized him by a leg, lifted him up, and slammed him into the bulkhead nearby, denting it inward as more of the creatures descended upon him. He'd already proved how much of a threat he was, which demanded the group's full attention over the prospect of prey fleeing the Aeroponics bay.

A maw of teeth came for the Hellmarine's head through the flashing of the emergency lights. He caught the alien with both hands, using its momentum against it as he shunted it to the side and into the dent where his body had been a second before. Then, raising his foot, the Hellmarine engaged the magboots as he stomped down on the Ghenzul's armored skull, utterly obliterating it.

Crush and Pulp.

A tail wrapped around his neck, trying to pull him away from the bulkhead, but he struggled against it with a vicious snarl. Flipping the blade around in his hand, he drove it down into the tail, causing the strange green blood to spray the faceplate of his helmet. The creature recoiled, but another bit down around his gauntlet with such force that he was forced to release the blade. An indicator on his HUD showed that the armor of the gauntlet was nearly compromised.

Shaking some of the green free from his faceplate, the Hellmarine pointed his other arm down the hall away from the Aeroponics bay and fired his grapnel. Connecting with a bulkhead a moment later and going taut, the hook pulled him free of the mass of aliens attempting to dogpile him. One of the Ghenzul came along for the ride, its tail lashing around for purchase in the corridor to prevent his escape. The Hellmarine twisted around mid-air, hammered the Ghenzul into position with one fist, and pushed down with both legs as he re-engaged the magboots. Caught between the deck and the Hellmarine in motion, the Ghenzul was ground down into a green smear seconds before the Hellmarine reached his destination.

The cluster of Ghenzul screamed soundlessly into the corridor's darkness as they pursued him. Ahead of him, more converged on his position in a pincer move. Every move that one of the creatures made, another one appeared to be keenly aware of. They were able to sacrifice individuals while the greater whole maneuvered its prey into position.

The first to reach him was caught off-guard by the power of the Hellmarine's uppercut into the center of its chest. Then, with the other arm placed across its throat, the Hellmarine engaged the thrusters of his armor and slammed the Ghenzul through the nearest door, which tore free of the bulkhead under their combined weight. His HUD flashed with another indicator as he hit the ground with the crushed Ghenzul, tumbling quickly to his feet. The armor was dangerously close to completely losing polarization.

Looking around to see that they were in the medical bay again, the Hellmarine moved over to the hole in the ceiling and climbed through, sparing a moment to grab one of the thick conduits along the way. Pressing the sparking stump of the conduit to the armor, he forced a dangerous repolarization of his armor, which completed just as the pursuing Ghenzul flooded up through the hole.

Glancing at the map on his HUD, the Hellmarine oriented himself toward the nearest nest, leaping away from the growing mob of aliens with his thrusters to assist. He turned to hit the ground running, sprinting toward the nest with his motion sensor going wild in his HUD, unable to discern individual creatures from one another with how many there were descending upon him.

The black tar and resin the creatures favored grew thicker on every surface in the corridor, signaling his imminent arrival in the mess hall that Miller had identified earlier as a nest. As he set foot into the mess hall, a Ghenzul tackled him to the ground. The two tumbled over one another briefly as the creature clawed viciously at his armor, depolarizing it again in an instant under the punishment.

Leaping to his feet, the Hellmarine backpedaled, narrowly avoiding a scything strike of another Ghenzul's tail—escaping with little more than a diagonal groove carved out of his faceplate. Another tail collided with him across the midsection, the force nearly burying him in a mass of black tar along the wall. Firing the grapnel into the high ceiling of the converted mess hall, the Hellmarine shot upward.

The mess hall once was a beautiful place, with one whole side converted into curved viewports that allowed for breathtaking views of space as the inhabitants took their meals inside. It provided just enough light for the Hellmarine to observe his own shadow as he leaped through the air and down onto another of the Ghenzul with the assistance of the magboots and his thrusters. The result was a fine alien paste underneath him and a deck that nearly folded completely in on him in the process.

Stomp. Crunch. Smash.

The Hellmarine ripped the lethal tail free of the crushed alien, swinging it around to bury the scythe-like extrusion at the end into the torso of another. Images of agony and torture flashed through his mind as the Ghenzul piled onto him, the deck beneath him buckling under the added strain to give way into the deck below.

As the Hellmarine was enveloped in free fall by the darkness of the Ghenzul, the indicators of his HUD flashed red, indicating an imminent structural failure.

CHAPTER 17

THIS WAS WHAT FRED Miller signed up for when he enlisted in the Marine Corps: Fighting aliens. It was all people could talk about back in the day. Regular people on the street thirsted for the blood of "filthy xenos," blaming them for all manner of things wrong in their small, petty lives. Miller knew otherwise, but he didn't care. The everyday hypocrisy of people was his ticket off of Ceres and out from under the watchful eye of the civil authorities. When you were a Marine, you weren't someone they fucked with—not unless you fucked up royally.

But there wasn't a lot of that when he finally saw action. By then, the Demons had arrived, and it wasn't at all the same. Incursions were mostly off of the regular person's radar because they were mainly happening in the Outer Colonies where communication was shit. Entire platoons of Marines would be dropped onto planets, with only a fraction of them making it out alive, and no one knew anything about it. If you fell in a battle against the Malur, the Ghenzul, or even some Orc pirates, they sent a nice letter home to your mother with heartfelt condolences and maybe a medal for your valor. If you fell in battle with Demons, everything was classified, and your family might never find out what happened to you—or even where your remains were.

Miller was fine with the idea of fighting for the survival of his species. He'd made his peace with that idea a long time ago. But he wanted people to know he was doing it. He wanted people to know that the short-tempered mining kid had made good. Miller had to prove to everyone back home that he wasn't what they thought he was. He was better than that. It wasn't just a loophole that kept him from serving life in a slam on Vesta. He'd earned it. He *would* keep earning it.

Wrapped in the experimental stealth technology of his armor, Miller watched from the shadows as the Hellmarine struggled with the Ghenzul piling onto him. He knew from the comms chatter that the Master Sergeant and the others had nearly all the survivors in the docking bay for evac. The irony of the situation wasn't lost on Miller. He'd signed up to kill aliens, and now he was saving aliens from other aliens. Life was funny that way.

The Hellmarine, though. That guy was something else. As much as Miller hated the idea of someone created to replace them on the battlefield—to be better than them—he couldn't argue with the guy's decision. It was the kind of thing people sang songs about in ancient times. He'd elected to throw himself into the fray solely as a means to draw the attention of the enemy away from the survivors. Never in a million years would Miller have been so quick to come to that conclusion.

Miller was torn. There was nothing stopping him from skulking by and getting to the Shotgun Opera before it left the hellhole of an alien ship behind to be scuttled. But then the Hellmarine had come crashing through the ceiling with a gaggle of Ghenzul trying to peel his armor off to get at the meat inside. He could jump in and do what he'd enlisted to do, or he could sit back and watch with satisfaction as the high and mighty pet of the Overmaiden failed miserably at doing anything other than the singular, specific thing he was cooked up to do.

"Does anyone have eyes on the Hellmarine?" Greer said over the main channel. "I'm having trouble isolating his transponder."

Miller sighed now that the decision had been made for him. He keyed into the main channel to respond to Greer, breaking his stealth in the process. "I've got him."

Engaging the heating element of the mining gauntlets, Miller threw himself into the open from the embrace of the shadows. With his jaw set and his heart racing, he went to work doing what he did best. With the gauntlets, he brought a little piece of home with him every time he bodied an alien. It felt poetic to him as he carved through the writhing darkness of the Ghenzul swarming the Hellmarine.

Every minute of every day, Miller held that rage in check. It was what society demanded of him. But when he got put into the field, he was not only allowed to let it out—it was encouraged. It was a trait everyone hated until they needed it. Until they specifically bred it in genetic freaks to point at the enemy and say, "Kill 'em all." But people like Miller, who had been born with it—had it honed over years of having their asses beat for minor infractions by their elders—they were looked down upon for it. Not today.

Miller snarled and roared like an animal as he tore into the pile of inky black Ghenzul, cutting clean through their carapaces and bony growths with red-hot steel. Little of their neurotoxic blood ever escaped the wounds, cauterized as they were. Not that it mattered with the lack of atmosphere and the seal of the armor intact.

One of the Ghenzul turned on him, hurling him easily from the group and into the nearest bulkhead. The impact only made him angrier, more obstinate, and contrarian, as all the lashings from his father's belt had done throughout his childhood.

"That all you got, princess?" Miller snarled as the alien swung its tail around to impale him through the midsection. He knocked the blade aside with one of the gauntlets and severed it with the other. Before it could retreat to lick its wounds, he pushed himself off of the bulkhead and burrowed straight through the torso of the Ghenzul and into another.

The Hellmarine's hand erupted from the mass of Ghenzul, and Miller reflexively took it. Pulling as hard as he could while engaging his thrusters, he was able to pry the Hellmarine loose from the cluster. The Hellmarine engaged his thrusters as well, and the two slid across the deck several feet before coming to a stop.

"Hate to pick you up from your playdate early, champ, but we got places to be," Miller growled as the mass of aliens advanced on them. "You want a cheese stick? Maybe a juice box?"

The Hellmarine ripped a piece of a nearby railing free from the bulkhead, pinching and twisting the end of it into a crude spear with his freakish strength. "I'm good."

The pair retreated down a side corridor as Greer attempted to map a new route for them to display on their HUDs. Several times the Ghenzul attempted to blind them with the weird slime that squirted out of their tails—the shit they used to turn someone into one of them. But neither Miller nor the Hellmarine was sloppy enough to let it get in their faces.

The shit stuck to everything like a pasty resin. When they weren't using it to turn people into gnashing brainless brutes, they could use it to soften up the surfaces of inorganic materials or put together their little pods where they would stick bodies going through transfiguration. If the ship was left alone with the creatures, they could eventually turn it into something that would sustain them in hibernation until they ran into something they could invade or some poor son of a bitch came poking around. Rumor had it that sometimes they were even able to preserve the engines for their own purposes, but that sort of thing would require a—

A powerful shockwave ran through the floor of the deck, nearly causing Miller and the Hellmarine to lose their footing as they attempted to disengage with the Ghenzul swarm. "—a Queen," Miller said, finishing his thought aloud. "Fuck."

"Where?" The Hellmarine asked, burying his spear halfway into the torso of a Ghenzul before snapping it off and sinking the broken stump into the skull of another.

"Looks like a couple of decks down," Miller answered, quickly checking the motion sensor on his HUD. Queens were huge, and judging by how powerful the impact had been, she was also pissed. Without the luxury of slithering through ducts and other tight spaces, she would have to make a path for herself by tearing things up. "Why? You want to do a little sightseeing?"

"Considering it," the Hellmarine grunted, driving his gauntlet into the skull of another Ghenzul before grabbing hold to twist it 360 degrees around on its shoulders. "You?"

"Last vacation leave was canceled," Miller responded, cleaving through a nearby plasma conduit to give the Hellmarine another improvised weapon to work with before following through with his other gauntlet through the arm of the nearest Ghenzul. "So, might as well."

The Hellmarine plunged the sparking conduit into the mouth of a gnashing Ghenzul, lighting it up from the inside before shoving it into the cluster where it shared its electrified state with some of its friends.

The pair diverted from their route to safety and made their way down an empty shaft instead. They descended past a few decks in a heartbeat, the compensators of their armor handling the impact without trouble. Miller carved some handholds into the emergency bulkhead before them, allowing the Hellmarine to pry it open with brute strength. The section beyond had atmosphere and started venting it the moment they pried the bulkhead open. Once through, the Hellmarine let it slam shut behind them.

"Engineering," Miller noted as they passed a sign. "Perfect. Exactly what we need."

Miller wasn't the expert that Greer was with computers, but he'd worked enough on various ships and rigs over the years to know what sort of damage could make an engine core go critical. Arlier engines were no exception. The fog from an unseen coolant leak grew thicker as they approached the core. It didn't stop their motion sensors from detecting the presence of lurking Ghenzul or the Queen that was fast approaching their location. The creatures had a hive mind, so what one knew, they all knew. Tactical decisions were made by the Queen, but everything else functioned as her eyes and ears.

She was a lot more clever than most people gave her credit for, moving to intercept them before they could reach the engine core. The Queen towered over the two of them with a cranial crest much larger and extravagant than the rest. Under the ridges, pulsating organs coordinated the movements of the Ghenzul while regulating the information that poured in. Her claws were longer and sharper, and her maw was even more deadly, dripping with a corrosive goo that allowed her to feed much faster than those she commanded. It allowed her to reshape entire ships for her purposes.

The Hellmarine didn't hesitate to hurl himself into a fight with the Queen, which took the creature by surprise. Usually, she functioned in an unchallenged capacity as an apex predator, so anything that showed a lack of fear in her presence was enough to get her to hesitate. Miller followed close behind, breaking left while the Hellmarine went straight up the middle.

Splitting the Queen's attention for a brief moment, Miller was able to avoid the sweep of the alien's massive tail, leaping over it and tumbling along the deck to tag the back of her leg with a heated blade along the way. The Queen snatched him off the deck with a massive claw and hurled him across engineering like a child's toy. Miller crashed through several consoles before coming to a stop against a bulkhead, his HUD flashing with a depolarization warning. Several of the secondary systems were going offline to compensate, bringing the polarization back online as quickly as possible.

The Hellmarine continued to hammer away at the Queen with his fists for a few moments before he was plucked off of her and slammed into the floor with all the strength the creature could muster, buckling several portions of the deck and shorting out consoles in the process.

"The Hell do you think you're doing, Marine?" the Master Sergeant demanded over the main channel. "We can't wait on your ass much longer!"

"Don't," Miller responded, pulling himself to his feet. "Get to a safe distance. We're going to destabilize the core so the Queen doesn't have a chance to take this tub for a joyride."

There was an extended silence before Greer came over the open channel. "You're going to have to bypass the lockouts in a very specific sequence to override the—"

"I'm gonna cut the supports," Miller interrupted. "Throw off the Arkane reaction and trigger a meltdown."

"That's going to give you next to no time to get out," Greer objected as the Ghenzul sentinel interposed itself between him and the Queen. He'd almost thought he wouldn't be lucky enough to fight one, but there it was in all its armored glory. Bigger than the typical Ghenzul but smaller than the Queen, the sentinels were explicitly assigned to her protection when things got rough. Miller and the Hellmarine had made quite the impression.

The creature's lips curled as it bared its teeth at him, lunging at him a moment later. Miller caught the beast as the two tumbled backward off a catwalk to the lower portion of the engine well. There, the Marine had the advantage, using his relatively smaller size to maneuver around the well while the sentinel struggled to keep up. He picked the creature apart piece by piece, not wanting to get his blades stuck in the body of the creature in an early attempt at a killing blow.

In an act of desperation, the creature swung its tail around in the enclosed space to impale him. The move was sloppy, allowing Miller to avoid the blow with ease, wrap his arm around the tail, and sever it before swinging back across the sentinel's face. The sizzle of the goo and the blood was oddly satisfying as it fell backward, thrashing around wildly without its tail.

Above, the catwalk buckled slightly as the Hellmarine continued to tussle with the Queen and a couple of her sentinels, keeping much of the attention off of him for the moment. Using the opportunity, he cut the struts and supports of the lower section with the heated blades of the gauntlets before scrambling out of the engine well. All that was left was to cut the suspension above, and the reaction chambers would be misaligned enough to set the process in motion. Alarms blared, warning of the danger, but no one was left that would care.

Firing his grapnel into the upper well, he pulled himself up to the catwalk that led to the suspension access. Below, the Hellmarine tumbled between the legs of the larger Queen, grabbed hold of her tail, and swung her around into the engine core itself, nearly prying the whole thing loose without a need to cut the suspension. The Queen smacked him loose from her tail with the back of her hand before following with a devastating blow from the tail across his skull, knocking the helmet free and sending it across the room.

"Oh, shit," Miller muttered, pausing briefly mid-step. With how much damage they had done to the Ghenzul in the pressurized compartment, there was going to be no way for him to avoid the neurotoxic effects of their blood. That was it for him.

To his surprise, the man got up. His eyes were red and bloodshot like he'd been pepper-sprayed, but he was some-how miraculously standing. Miller decided not to waste any more time and sprinted toward the suspensions, cutting them free one after another as the Hellmarine jumped back into the fray without the benefit of his helmet. He looked like a man possessed.

The metal let out a powerful "SHEEERRRRNK" as it came free, sliding along the lower struts and falling into a mis-aligned state. The alarms signaling an imminent meltdown blared over the sound of the Queen hissing and snarling at the Hellmarine as he socked her several more times in the midsection. She responded by putting him through the thick railing around the core.

Miller jumped down from the catwalk to take advantage of her distraction, his sights settled on the top section of her cranial crest where he could split the whole top half of her open, nice and clean. The Queen wasn't as distracted as he'd thought, her tail slapping him out of the air with such force that he felt the bone in his arm break. He hit the ground in a heap, with spots filling his vision.

"You only got a couple of minutes to get out of there," Greer warned over the main channel. "If you can get to an airlock, we might be able to pick you up before the core goes critical."

Miller mumbled something that made him sound like he had a mouthful of marbles as he dragged himself across the deck to a console where he could pull himself upright with his one good arm.

"Say again, I didn't get that," Greer responded.

"I said don't bother," Miller repeated with more clarity, his sights set on the Queen in front of him. The Hellmarine pulled a section of the railing free, using it like a baseball bat to club the Ghenzul Queen across the head a few times. It just seemed to piss her off more.

Miller fired the grapnel at the Queen's tail and wrapped the cable around the nearest pillar, severely limiting her mobility. Holding the cable down against the alien metal of the pillar, he pressed the flat section of the heated blades on the gauntlet down on them, welding them together. From there, he cut the cable and proceeded toward the Queen as she tried to tear her tail loose of whatever had impaled it.

Sliding in beneath the immobilized tail, Miller tagged the back of her leg with the heated blade, biting much deeper than he had the first time, forcing her down to one knee. The Hellmarine let out a guttural cry, leaping into the air with the assistance of his thrusters and dropping onto her with a powerful swing of the railing. A heavy "THOK" reverberated through the air as the Queen was knocked down into the deck. Then, with a few more downward strikes, the Hellmarine snapped the enlarged crest from the Ghenzul's head before bringing the railing around horizontally in a swing for the fences.

The impact knocked the Queen's skull into the side of the engine core, where it cracked the case. As Arkane Energy poured out, the Hellmarine persisted, climbing halfway onto the Ghenzul and shoving her battered head into the crack repeatedly until he'd shoved it into the inner core itself.

"SKREEEEE!" The Queen shrieked as the body of the massive beast thrashed around in agony. The incredible pain caused every other Ghenzul in the area to shriek in agony as well, joining their dying Queen in a cacophonic chorus of torment.

"Let her cook," Miller grunted. "We gotta go."

Warning indicators on Miller's HUD informed him of the danger he was already well aware of, but it reminded him that they would need the Hellmarine's helmet if they were going to leave the pressurized section of the ship. He diverted a bit of power from his suit to run a quick scan, then pointed it out. "Over there."

The Hellmarine crawled off the dying Queen and scooped the helmet up with one hand. He set it on his head and waited for it to seal back into place before joining Miller. He looked pointedly at the Marine's arm but didn't say anything. Miller waved it off with his good hand and made for the door, where the Hellmarine again pulled the emergency bulkhead open so they could re-enter the shaft.

The ship lurched as power failures all throughout it forced the artificial gravity and other critical systems to go offline. The duo drifted up the shaft with a short, controlled burst of their thrusters and turned onto the deck where the nest in the mess hall was.

"Miller to Shotgun Opera, I need you to cut a hole in the observation section of the mess hall for us," he said as they shot down the corridor weightlessly. The remaining Ghenzul hissed and snarled soundlessly at them as they passed, disoriented and confused from the death of the Queen.

"On it," the pilot responded. As they came around the corner to re-enter the mess hall, the dropship tore a section out of the towering windows with its chin gun. The burst was short, allowing them to immediately engage their thrusters, propelling them out of the Arlier ship at incredible speed.

The Hellmarine hit the side of the dropship first, grabbing onto the first handhold to present itself to him and engage his magboots. Miller hit the ship next, but without two functional arms, merely glanced off the hull. The Hellmarine's hand lashed out, catching Miller's hand to reel him back in even as the dropship turned away from the alien ship to disengage. Behind them, a cluster of Ghenzul began to swarm around the new opening in the side of the ship, ready to push off into space in pursuit of prey.

Miller engaged his magboots, clinging to the side of the dropship as it sped away from the science vessel. Deep inside the alien ship, the engine core went critical and erupted, illuminating the vast darkness of space around them in a blinding white light.

CHAPTER 18

MANDY STOOD BY WITH her arms crossed, staring daggers at the Hellmarine as his armor was removed. The damage to it was rather extensive compared to previous missions. However, the condition of his face was much worse.

The skin was red, his eyes were bloodshot, and saliva and mucus had streamed down his face. Since then, it had dried, creating a crusty layer across his mouth and chin. By all accounts, he'd gotten off lucky. There had been no way to predict he would have such a mild reaction to the neurotoxic effects of Ghenzul blood. Exposure would have killed just about anyone else within a couple of minutes.

"You boys need to go a little easier on these," the Armorer scolded the Hellmarine and Miller as the mechanical arms worked at removing the power armor. "They don't come cheap."

"I'll remember that," Miller winced as a pair of corpsmen worked to fish his arm out of the power armor manually.

Once free of the armor, Mandy approached to run some scans with the medical gauntlet. "This was reckless, even for you."

The Hellmarine didn't respond or apologize. Instead, he simply let her go about her examination, his breath coming a little more raggedly than usual. Mandy's analysis indicated some damage in the lungs, but nothing that she couldn't fix. "There's a reason why even Demons want nothing to do with those things."

"He was doing it as a favor for me," the Master Sergeant interrupted as he stepped off his own armor platform. "And it was cleared with the captain."

"Was it, now?" Mandy responded with a raised brow, reminding herself to have a word with the captain when she saw him again. Mandy was to monitor the Hellmarine at all times, even going with him on his various missions whenever possible.

"What about the survivors?" Greer asked as he approached the group. Without his armor, he was a much less imposing figure. If Mandy hadn't known better, she could have mistaken him for a clerk at a computer parts store.

"They're already being treated in the medical bay," Mandy responded slightly more coldly than she initially intended.

Clearing her throat, she adjusted her tone to sound a little warmer. "I'm sure they're doing just fine."

Once free of his armor, Miller was put on a stretcher and brought off to the medical bay, while another one remained on standby for the Hellmarine. Mandy completed her scans, looked them over, and shook her head dejectedly. "This could have been a lot worse."

"Agreed," the Overmaiden remarked as she appeared over Mandy's shoulder. "This is bound to negatively affect your combat readiness when we reach our destination."

The Hellmarine's eyes drifted between the two figures staring daggers at him. He shook his head with an exasperated sigh and began to walk away.

"Hey!" Mandy shouted, running after him. "I'm not done with you yet! We need to get you to the medical bay where we can treat the damage to your lungs. Your eyes aren't in much better condition either."

"I'm fine," the Hellmarine argued, brushing past her.

Mandy moved quickly to stand in front of him this time, defiantly placing her hands on her hips. "That's not your call to make. It's mine. I say, report to the medical bay immediately."

"Just do as she says, Nature Boy," the Master Sergeant remarked, clapping a hand on his shoulder. "Wouldn't want to make a habit of being insubordinate, would you?"

Mandy frowned as the men exchanged glances. Finally, the Hellmarine relented and motioned for Mandy to lead the way. She would have preferred to put him on the stretcher, but she wasn't going to push her luck. If he was capable of walking himself, she would just settle for that. There was also the matter of whether or not he would have even fit.

"Do you mind telling me what this was all about?" Mandy heard the Overmaiden ask Gray as they stepped out of the armor bay. She wanted to stay and hear his answer, but her duties to the Hellmarine were much more pressing.

Once she had him in medical, things went a lot smoother. With the Hellmarine relaxed on the bed, she wheeled an ocular regenerator over to begin working on his eyes while corpsmen prepared a pulmonary rejuvenator. With both pieces of equipment in place, Mandy placed the medical gauntlet against his chest and injected him with a potent stimulant to assist the process. She'd talked the Armorer into crafting her a needle for the gauntlet from Elysian steel scrap leftover from Seraphiel's broken equipment. Without it, the gauntlet wouldn't have had the means to penetrate the Hellmarine's flesh.

"We'll probably need your help with the others," the corpsman said to her discreetly. "Most of them haven't done much work on Arlier before so we'd need you just to follow up."

"No problem," Mandy agreed. Her expertise in various fields of xenobiology wasn't the sort of thing she could keep to herself in such a situation. She pointed at the Hellmarine lying on the bed. "You better be here when I get back, mister. Understand?"

Mandy did the rounds, checking on the work of the corpsmen who had doubts about their own findings and diagnoses. She assured them there was nothing to worry about. She'd found no errors in their work, offered a little extra context for the differences in human and Arlier anatomy, and returned to the Hellmarine—who'd actually fallen asleep for once—a few hours later. She ran another scan while he slept, waking him when everything came back clean.

"Time to go," Mandy muttered a little more gently. "You can finish your nap in your quarters."

"Are you coming?" the Hellmarine asked, sending an unexpected flutter of butterflies through her stomach. She smiled a little, brushing a lock of loose hair behind one ear, and glanced around the room. Things appeared to be under control, and she didn't have a shift to finish out, so she nodded.

"Sure," she agreed, filing the rest of her reports before joining him on the walk back to his quarters.

"Still mad?" he asked, giving her a sideways glance as they walked.

"No," Mandy admitted with a little sigh. "Not after seeing just how many of those people you got out of there. Most of them are too old or too young to be fighting off hostile aliens.

I don't think those two clerics would have been enough to get them all out alive."

Arriving at his quarters, he accessed the door panel and allowed her to enter first. He followed after, immediately pulling the undersuit for his armor off. The suit itself was a minor marvel of technology, allowing him to jump into the power armor with minor calibration while also allowing for quick medical examinations by readily interfacing with equipment. It was like high-tech underwear made specifically for power armor, which meant that when it came off, there was nothing else to conceal his nudity from her.

Mandy made her best effort to appear like she wasn't drooling over him as he tossed the undersuit onto the couch and rummaged around in his closet for something to throw on. Even from behind, he was a sight to behold, though, causing her nethers to stir with excitement at the possible course the evening could take between them.

"Have you had any more of those nightmares?" Mandy asked, trying to keep her mind off immediately jumping the man's bones.

"Not exactly," he answered, pulling on a pair of sweatpants and nothing else. "Flashes. Images of people. Faces, mostly. People I knew."

"Hm," Mandy murmured with a frown. She glanced around the room for some of the things she'd left behind. She'd moved half her stuff in here, seeing no point in dragging them between his room and her lab when she would only bring them right back. She grabbed a scrap of paper and a pen and placed it on the table. "Do you think you could write something down describing them? Draw one of the faces, maybe?"

The Hellmarine looked at her skeptically before examining the blank surface of the paper. Something about it caused him to change his mind, and he picked the pen up a moment later. They each took a seat on either side of the table. Mandy waited patiently while the Hellmarine tried out a few lines on the page and then a few more, becoming more confident in each one as he went along.

After a few minutes, Mandy craned her neck to see the progress he was making and was surprised to find that he was actually something of a gifted artist. She wondered if it was a skill from his previous life or if it was an effect of the serum. Though incomplete, the image was clearly that of a woman's face. Judging by the presence of a labcoat, the updo of her hair, and her glasses, she was some kind of scientist like her. It...made her unexpectedly self-conscious. Did the Hellmarine have a particular type?

"Who's this?" Mandy asked quietly, trying not to show too much of her feelings. The process was meant to be for him, not for her.

"Not sure," he answered without looking up at her. His pen continued to refine the details of her eyes before moving to the slight smirk she wore. It almost seemed like she was teasing him, somehow. "Someone important. Someone I loved."

Mandy's frown deepened. "An old girlfriend, maybe?"

The Hellmarine shook his head, his face scrunched up in slight revulsion. "Not like that. No."

Nodding, Mandy turned her attention back to the sketch and examined it more closely. The woman was young, with hair that appeared to be the same shade as the Hellmarine's. Either it was a very young aunt, a cousin, or perhaps even a sister. She felt foolish for her pang of jealousy, considering the two of them weren't even an item, really. Mandy didn't even know if he was capable of feelings like that anymore. Maybe he never had been. But she was.

"Do you miss her?" Mandy pressed, hoping to break down some of the mental barriers in his mind that were making it so difficult for him to remember. Technically, it wasn't a priority that he did. Nothing in Project Brutality accounted for spontaneous memory loss, however, and it seemed like a good opportunity to document it. If they eventually decided to make another Hellmarine—or need to replace one—the data would be useful.

"I'm not sure," the Hellmarine admitted. "But I see her a lot. So I must."

"Sound logic," Mandy agreed, settling back into her chair to let him draw. It was the first thing she'd seen him do recreationally that didn't involve splattering guts all over the place, so she saw no harm in just letting him go for a while. "You're pretty good, you know."

"Hm?" He grunted, his focus remaining on the sketch.

"Drawing," Mandy elaborated with a little laugh. "You're pretty good at it. I could get you some supplies if you'd like. You could draw all sorts of things and put them up on your walls. Could liven the place up a little."

"Sure," the Hellmarine agreed readily, still not looking up from his sketch. He filled the entire page by the time he was done, running out of room to do any more of the woman he was working on. With nothing left to do, he abandoned the paper and got back to his feet. He was starting to look restless again.

"What's wrong?" she asked, pulling the page a little closer to her. Perhaps if she ran it through the database, they would get a hit on who the person could have been. It was a long shot, considering how sparse the available information on people from the Outer Colonies was.

"...Hungry," the Hellmarine responded after a brief pause.

Mandy arched a brow. "What do you mean? You don't have to eat anymore—at least, you haven't since you came out of the cryopod."

The Hellmarine gave her a shrug, unable to explain why he suddenly had the urge to eat. Pursing her lips, Mandy considered that maybe it was tied to his incomplete recall.

Perhaps something about the face or his past was tied to a particular food. It made him think that he was hungry even when his body didn't require food like it used to. "Is there something in particular you would like to eat?"

The Hellmarine glanced around the room thoughtfully as though the answer would reveal itself to him, but when he found nothing readily available, he shook his head.

"Alright, well, put some more clothes on, and we can go down to the mess hall and see if anything appeals to you," Mandy chuckled with amusement. He did exactly that, throwing on a plain white shirt and a pair of shoes, and motioned for her to lead the way to the mess hall.

Several Marines and crewmen occupied the mess, filling their trays with food and chatting over their breakfasts. Mandy realized only then what time it must have been for them to be eating breakfast. The Hellmarine immediately honed in on the food, grabbing a tray and getting in line. He towered over everyone, scooting a half step at a time down the line as the men behind the counter tossed food onto his tray.

Eggs and bacon seemed to be what he was after in particular, though he didn't say no to a couple of sausage patties and some pancakes. Mandy settled on a blueberry muffin, knowing that with how badly she'd fucked up her sleeping schedule, the bacon and sausage would go right through her.

"This," the Hellmarine said, nodding at the bacon and eggs as he sat down at the nearest table. Mandy nodded, understanding what he meant. It was precisely what he was craving, though she wasn't sure if the quality would be quite the same. The cooking on the Midnight Sea was hit-or-miss at best.

"Well, son of a bitch," Cox said, flopping down into a seat across from the Hellmarine with a food tray of his own. "If it isn't the fucking man of the hour himself. I didn't know you ate food."

"Neither did I," Mandy chimed in. "We're giving it a try."

"Careful with the sausage," Chambers added as she sat down next to Mandy. "Sometimes they don't cook it all the way through."

Mandy raised a concerned brow toward the Hellmarine but he didn't seem to care. He chomped down on the greasy meat with a few large bites until it was nothing more than a memory.

"What would you know about handling a sausage?" Cox joked, mashing some ketchup and cheese into his scrambled eggs. "Thought you like chicks."

"Just because I can pull more pussy than you doesn't mean I prefer it," Chambers shot back, nibbling a piece of crispy bacon. Mandy concealed a smile with one hand. She had to admit the woman had more masculine energy than the childish Cox by a considerable amount. Though her dark hair was longer than the men's, it wasn't by much. The tattoos that adorned her shoulders like ancient pauldrons complimented the woman's various scars.

Cox, in contrast, didn't look like he was more than a year out of boot camp. Despite the years of service he had under his belt, he still had a lot of baby fat around his cheeks and neck. His brush-cut looked less like the type a serviceman would get and more like the kind a kid would get before starting T-ball season.

"Yeah, we'll see next time we're in port," Cox muttered, stirring his eggs a little harder before feeding a large forkful into his mouth.

"It's alright, I'll share," Chambers said, pouting mockingly at him.

"So, the Ghenzul," Cox said, changing the subject and turning his attention back to the Hellmarine. "Heard that shit got pretty wild. Miller got his arm all fucked up."

"Yeah," the Hellmarine acknowledged between ravenous bites. As she picked at her muffin, Mandy resisted the urge to tell him to slow down. She didn't know he could eat until a few minutes before that moment, so cautioning against indigestion seemed premature.

"And the shit about the Queen, is that true too?" Cox pressed, leaning over his tray excitedly.

"Mhm," the Hellmarine murmured, his focus entirely on the meal he had almost blown through.

"Shut up," Chambers laughed, regarding the Hellmarine with a look that Mandy knew all too well. She was...interested, to say the least. "A fucking Ghenzul Queen? That's insane."

Mandy decided to jump in. "I wish he hadn't. We had to patch him up in the med-bay while the Armorer has to do a deep clean and repair on the armor."

"Wait," Cox held his fork up. "Does that mean he won't be going down to the surface when we come out of Rift-space?"

Mandy looked at the Hellmarine expectantly, quietly making the point that it was the sort of thing he needed to be thinking about.

"No," the Hellmarine answered, looking up at Cox, his gaze intense. "I'm going regardless. Naked if I have to."

"That'd be fun," Chambers chuckled as Mandy quietly fumed.

"My man!" Cox laughed, leaning across the table with his arm extended for a fist bump. When the Hellmarine didn't immediately return it, he slinked sheepishly back to his side of the table to busy himself with a glass of orange juice.

"I'm sure she'll be done with the armor, anyway," Chambers said dismissively. "I've had way worse damage to mine, and she had it up and running perfectly in no time. She's a different breed—not like other engineers."

"Ah, see!" Cox laughed, pointing an accusing finger at her. "I knew it! You got a thing for the Armorer?"

"Just her toys," Chambers smirked smugly, throwing Cox for another loop. "You spend too much time thinking about who I'm fucking, little boy. You do this with all the others or is it just *my* pants you're obsessed with?"

Cox scoffed, waving her off with one hand. "Get over yourself, Chambers."

"Aww, here I thought I could teach you a thing or two," she said with a kind of dommy energy that even Mandy found appealing. She would have to pull Chambers aside sometime and jot down some notes for...various activities with the Hellmarine, perhaps.

"Tch!" Cox snapped derisively. "More into blondes."

"Yeah?" Chambers laughed incredulously. "Hate to say it, junior, but I don't think Seraphiel is going to give it up for you."

Cox's face turned a little red around the cheeks. He denied the accusation, of course, but it was far less convincing than even any of the other bullshit Mandy had heard come out of his mouth.

"I don't even know if Angels can have sex," Mandy interjected, throwing Cox a lifeline to get away from being the center of attention for a moment. "There's actually very little that we know about their biology and culture."

"You haven't performed scans on her or anything?" Chambers asked curiously. "I thought you were the one that installed her arm."

"I did," Mandy admitted, spreading her hands defensively. "But just because someone appears to be human-like physiologically, doesn't mean that they function the same way. There are a few species that mimic a humanoid appearance to make it easier for us and similar xenos to interact with them. We don't know if that's the case with Angels."

"She's going on the next mission with us," Chambers noted. "Regular part of the squad now. You could ask her then."

"Me?" Mandy laughed a little nervously. "Why don't you ask her?"

"You're the scientist, it'll sound a lot less creepy coming from—" Chambers froze as Seraphiel approached from behind Cox. Mandy's lips pressed into a thin line as the Angel's bright blue eyes moved between them suspiciously.

"What are you two talking about?" the Angel wondered. Cox's face turned a bright red with the woman standing directly behind him, close enough to touch if he were to lean back even a little.

"Uhmmm," Mandy stalled, glancing over at the Hellmarine for some assistance.

"Seraphiel? Do you even eat?" Chambers muttered in surprise.

The Angel's brow furrowed. "Unfortunately, yes," she said. "When in Standard Space, Angels must eat much like humans. What was it you two were saying when I came in?"

With his tray now completely empty, the Hellmarine looked between Mandy, Chambers, and Seraphiel and simply abandoned the table to retrieve a second helping from the breakfast line.

Seraphiel arched a golden brow at the remaining trio at the table.

Mandy gave the Angel a wide, friendly grin. "Hungry?"

Chapter 19

The first world they hit was a planet by the name of Lilles. The Overmaiden monitored the mission more closely than many others of the past. It was the first time the Midnight Sea fielded more than one squad of Marines since the Hellmarine had joined. Though their initial sensor sweeps showed that an entire platoon would likely be overkill, the Overmaiden thought it best to use the supposed minor incursion as a warm-up.

They had a dozen dropships deliver the Marines along with their ground support, a few Basilisk-class IAVs, and several more Worg FAVs for more nimble maneuvers. The rocky, arid terrain demanded the use of the Basilisk, which had four sets of wheels on independent suspensions that made tackling the terrain relatively easy. The Worgs handled it better but were far less armored, placing them in the role of scouting and tactical force application.

The incursion was farther along than they'd believed, with the horde already establishing large ground units to sweep across the face of the world at speed. Tankers were already on the field by the time they made contact with the horde, and half a dozen Juggernauts weren't far behind. The advantage of surprise served them well in that instance, allowing them to close the distance and lay down enough suppression fire to get the Marines in range.

Once they found a decent place to deploy, the sliding doors along the sides of the Basilisks were thrown open, and the Marines poured out in their power armor, doing as much damage as possible. The main object, as always, was the location and neutralization of the Voivode leading the horde, but the secondary objective was to secure the Hellrift itself.

Fighting began on the outskirts of the city. The Overmaiden projected her consciousness across several parts of the battlefield with the assistance of the Basilisks as relays. This allowed her to remain with the Hellmarine as he charged into battle while maintaining an active role in troop movement for the rest of the platoon. Progress was slow at first as the Marines dug into a few strategic locations around the settlement, but when the Hellmarine and Seraphiel took the field, things shifted dramatically.

The mere presence of the Angel was enough to enrage the Demons, who strained against the control of the Voivode in command so they could take a crack at the divine creature. At the same time, Marines who had not seen her in action were stirred on a spiritual level to rally and push forward. While the Angel inspired them overhead from the air, the brutality of the Hellmarine spurred them on from the ground.

He moved fluidly through the ranks, tearing his way through the Demonic infantry like tissue paper until arriving at the first of the Juggernauts. Hulking masses of flesh cleaved to infernal iron in the shape of giant arachnids, the Juggernauts were half Demon and half mobile fortress. Various cannons mounted along the front of the structure, resembling the forward legs and fangs of a spider, spit volatile molten iron in various directions while the immense legs pulled the living fortress ever forward. The many "eyes" of the creature's face were directed energy weapons similar to those of a Hijacker Demon. The grotesque abdomen of the abomination housed various reinforcements for the horde, dropping them behind it during its advance.

The Hellmarine didn't balk at the size or firepower of the Juggernaut, charging forward with a Cyclone heavy machine gun that mowed down the smaller reinforcements until he reached one of the Juggernaut's legs. There, he handed the machine gun off to Wall who'd kept pace with him, and began his climb, combining the grapnel and thrusters for swift traversal until he entered the rear of the structure. Seraphiel drew the fire of the Juggernaut from the front while the Hellmarine redecorated the insides of the Juggernaut with the guts and entrails of Demons until he reached the cockpit.

Like many Demonic ships and structures, the cockpit was little more than an armored brain with a few defensive measures in place to protect it from intrusion. The Hellmarine shrugged off the fireballs thrown at him from the security nodes and drove his chainchete into the armor, cutting enough of a hole to deposit a string of grenades before charging out the way he came. The Juggernaut collapsing onto smaller Demons underfoot after the detonation was a sight to behold.

It was a story that the Overmaiden would hear the Marines repeat numerous times in the coming days, but not as much as the confrontation between the Hellmarine and the Voivode of Lilles, Ostrog.

Ostrog of the Order of Moloch was twice the size of the Hellmarine and wreathed in hellfire. He had an impressive crown of horns, armor resembling molten obsidian, a set of arms ending in crab claws, and another set that appeared more human and moved rapidly to cast profane spells. His gaze was ruinous, obliterating even the heaviest armor with pure blasts of infernal force.

"Getting your hands on him doesn't seem like a viable strategy," the Overmaiden warned as the Hellmarine narrowly avoided another snap of a crab claw, sliding behind a ruined structure that shielded him from the brunt of an Immolation spell hurled his way.

The Hellmarine grunted half-heartedly to acknowledge her assessment. But none of the ammunition he'd cycled through was putting a dent in the armor either. Anything that did seem to make it through the small glowing gaps in the plates seemed to simply disappear into nothing as if instantly melted or flash-fried on the spot. He either needed a round with much larger mass or far higher acceleration. In the end, the Hellmarine decided to have both.

Ostrog's strength and power were such that he leveled entire buildings as their battle tore through the heart of the city, leaving only molten rubble in his wake. Believing himself untouchable and beyond the capabilities of Alliance weapons, he failed to recognize the threat the Hellmarine presented as he tore a mounted Gauss cannon off the back of a disabled Warg.

"Difficult to believe that you ever managed to kill even one of our number," Ostrog snarled, his massive claws clearing the debris in the street as he drew closer to the Hellmarine. Had he known what the human held, he would have favored a defensive spell rather than the Incineration spell he had nearly completed. "Our ranks are better off for having such weakness pruned."

The Hellmarine squeezed down on the trigger with one hand while supporting the massive weapon with the other. It took half a second to charge and then released its hypersonic, magnetically accelerated 25mm tungsten round into the chest of the Voivode. The armor didn't stand a chance against the density and speed of the round, which also rendered the intense heat of hellfire a non-issue.

Ostrog stared down at the gaping wound in his chest and the shattered hand that had just so happened to be in the way while forming the motions for a spell. As the Hellmarine lined up a second shot, the Voivode interposed his crab claw to block, finding out a second later that it was similarly ineffective in stopping the round. The Hellmarine advanced, carrying the normally vehicle-mounted weapon in the same manner that other Marines carried rotary guns. Though the rate of fire was significantly reduced, the yield of the weapon more than made up for it.

With each round the Hellmarine put into Ostrog, the hellfire's intensity diminished until nothing was left burning within the armor. The Voivode lay dead in the town square for everyone to see as the Demons under its command entered a berserk state. Once again, without the coordination of a Voivode to hold them in check, the horde became much easier to mop up. So focused were some of the Demons on the Angel in the sky that they never saw the killing blow at the hands of a Marine that would end them.

The campaign on Dirilia was even more successful. It had a local military that had managed to fall back early enough in the incursion that they were able to assist when the Midnight Sea arrived. The colony was much more developed than Lilles, serving as a trading hub for various other colonies in the system. Fulgi had been deployed to overwhelm the local subnet and cripple the infrastructure of the cities but were unprepared for the amount of firepower brought to bear by the combined force of the Midnight Sea's Marines and the remnants of the Dirilian military.

Turrets mounted to the tops and sides of infernaformed buildings were quickly overwhelmed by air support from the Midnight Sea's gunships, while inside the largest of the towers, the Hellmarine crippled the Voivode commanding the horde and pitched him out of a top-floor window. The fall was recorded for posterity, and the splatter across the concrete on the main thoroughfare was met with thunderous applause.

"You shouldn't waste so much time playing with your food," the Overmaiden chided the Hellmarine as he stepped away from the shattered window. "That could have been accomplished much sooner and much more efficiently had you not wasted the time crippling his limbs before dispatching him."

"Mm," the Hellmarine grunted impassively, picking up his weapons as he made his way back to the open elevator shaft.

"It's going to get you into serious trouble one of these days," the Overmaiden continued, buzzing in his ear. "I'm all for you having your fun, but not at the cost of efficiency."

"It can be both," the Hellmarine answered, jumping into the darkness of the shaft to repel all the way down to the ground floor.

Next was the colony of Vizuno, which had hardly enough of its original infrastructure left to be called a colony anymore. Were it not for the need to locate and neutralize the

Voivode and secure the Hellrift, Captain Horne would have simply bombarded the city from orbit with what they had available to them and left it at that. Though not capable of a complete planetary bombardment, the Midnight Sea had enough firepower to manage such destruction at a smaller scale. The moon had been completely overrun but had yet to establish a fleet. The horrifying truth discovered on the ground was that the colonists had been led by a cult of Orcus into welcoming the Demons of the Hellrift with open arms.

The small island nation at the heart of the incursion had been subsumed within days, with warlocks sacrificing both the willing and the unwilling to increase the size of the Hellrift and the profane power of the Demons that came through. Seraphiel earned significant praise for her role in the assault on the citadel alongside the Hellmarine, incensed as she was by the eerie reminders of the fate of her comrades on Aonus. Though ultimately victorious, the weight of the casualties suffered during the offensive was not lost on the crew of the Midnight Sea and the frigates that had met with them to assist.

"I cannot fathom why these people would betray their own kind to the will of Hell," Seraphiel remarked dejectedly as she cleaned the blood from the Elysian steel of her blade. "The promises of Hell are hollow. In the end, they are hollowed out and remade into Demonic thralls as much as everyone else they betrayed."

"Desperation, I imagine," Hall commented as he picked his way through the dead to ensure the Demonic bodies littering the ritual chamber were all dead. "This far out on the frontier, all it takes is one famine or drought to get people to make stupid decisions."

"It is more than stupid," Romero muttered from his perch at the edge of an adjacent tower. "It is sacrilege. Blasphemy. To sacrifice one's soul for the comforts of the flesh."

"Tch," Miller grunted from his post alongside Simms and Davis as they worked to upload the cult's database. "I wouldn't expect a Ganymede boy to understand."

"That's enough of the charming repartee," the Master Sergeant ordered as he chewed on a freshly lit cigar. "If you got time to lean, you got time to clean. Back to work!"

After that came Thara, which was much more heavily defended than the previous worlds the Midnight Sea had encountered. A fleet had already been established by the time they arrived, though most of the ships it had in orbit were still under construction by vast numbers of Drones that moved as one in swarms. As much as the Overmaiden wanted to bypass the blockade that the fleet formed around the planet to rush the Voivode, doing so would have left the battle group to suffer massive casualties.

Instead, the Hellmarine was deployed to the capital ship of the newly formed fleet, where he and the rest of the squad went on a bloody rampage to take the ship. Instead of simply destroying it from the inside, the Hellmarine steered it into a steep descent, directing it as a giant missile into the heart of the nearest infernaformed city.

"Getting some unusual readings from a substructure to the west," Cox said as the squad regrouped on the ground. "Spikes in Quixotic Energy instead of Profane. But we'd need a Basilisk just to get out there for a better look."

"Then we walk," the Hellmarine declared, checking his Perforator and turning west. Though the Overmaiden liked the suggestions about as much as Cox did—in other words, not at all—she had to admit they had few other options. Calling another dropship down to move them or deliver a Basilisk would prove costly to whoever was foolhardy enough to volunteer. Most of the fighting in orbit had turned in favor of the Alliance, but the multitude of AA guns spewing disruptor blasts into the night was more than enough to discourage anyone from making a trip to the surface until the Voivode was neutralized.

"And here I am without my trail mix," the Master Sergeant laughed, placing a few more rounds into his Cerberus. "Guess I'll just have to pick up a snack along the way."

"I'm not about to trust whatever they got in the bodegas here," Chambers muttered with disgust, stepping over a sticky mass of flesh stretched across the destroyed road. Its purpose was unclear.

"Can't be worse than a convenience store hotdog," Cox commented as he reviewed the readings from his sensor array again. The Overmaiden analyzed it alongside him, but the interference made it impossible to isolate the signal any further. They had to get closer. "Or one of those tuna sandwiches."

"If we're set on this course of action, then perhaps it would be in our best interests to get a route," the Overmaiden suggested. "Preferably one that avoids unnecessary engagement until we've determined the source of the energy signature."

"Seraphiel!" The Master Sergeant said, jerking a thumb toward a toppled tower. "I want you and Romero up there. Once you get the data, leave him posted there while you regroup with us."

"Yes, Sergeant," Seraphiel remarked, glancing at Romero, who, despite his objections to being carried around like a child, kept them to himself. Grabbing the back of his armor, Seraphiel gave a mighty beat of her wings and took off toward the tower like a shot.

"Miller!" The Sergeant barked, jerking his thumb to the side in a wordless signal to begin doing recon of his own. Miller acknowledged with a nod before vanishing into the rubble of the ruined city, his squad tag going dark moments later. "Wall. King. You're on point. Black and the Hellmarine bring up the rear."

"Aye aye, Sarge," the Marines answered, adjusting their marching order as Romero and Seraphiel began their scans atop the ruined tower.

"Cox, Greer, and Davis," the Master Sergeant continued, turning to face the trio. "If a Hunter so much as farts, I want to hear about it. Understood?"

"Right after I light a match, Sarge," Cox quipped, even as he recalibrated his sensor array to work in tandem with Davis's.

"Ramirez and Chambers. If they see something, you shoot first and ask questions later," the Master Sergeant ordered. They glanced at one another and nodded their acknowledgment. Ramirez had brought a Renegade along with him, eschewing his normal preference for the Perforator. Paired with Chambers, the two would be able to bring down smaller targets from a fair distance away before they got anywhere close to them.

The data from the two atop the toppled tower began to come in, populating the map on their HUDs with the layout of the ruined city between them and their destination.

"How's this look to you?" Cox said, drawing up a route within seconds of seeing the layout. "Should be quick and clean."

"Very little chatter on the Demon subnet," Greer added. "Looks like crashing a ship into the fucking city does a real number on things."

"Who knew?" Cox quipped as the rest of the Marines chuckled, picking their way forward along their route as Seraphiel descended from her perch to join them.

"From what I can pick out," Davis began, listening for another moment before finishing his sentence, "they didn't see us escape through the breaching spikes when we came down. They're not even bothering to look for survivors."

"So they're not likely to have refreshments ready when we arrive," the Master Sergeant concluded. "So we'll be going in full breach."

"Got the party poppers ready, Sarge," King acknowledged as he and Wall stepped around the scattered remains of a mangled Tanker. "Just give the word."

"You're quieter than usual," the Overmaiden noted in the Hellmarine's helmet. "What's wrong?"

The Hellmarine shook his head. She didn't know if that meant nothing was wrong or if he simply didn't want to discuss it. She was monitoring his vitals for any abnormalities in the absence of Dr. Hughes, who was absolutely not ready for the kind of action they had seen on the ship or were bound to see as they continued.

"Simms," the Overmaiden hailed over a dedicated channel. "I want you to monitor the Hellmarine closely. Let me know if anything out of the ordinary shows up on your biometric scans."

"Yes, ma'am," the Marine acknowledged, not needing to adjust his position in the formation to do so. He was already marching close to the rear with the Hellmarine and Black.

After several minutes of silence, weaving their way slowly through the rubble of collapsed buildings and Demonic flesh, Miller's voice came over the main channel. "Romero. You see this big ass building just to the north of me?"

"I got it," Romero said, whistling a moment later. "Well, you don't see one of those every day."

Romero kicked the visual down to the Master Sergeant's HUD, which the Overmaiden helped herself to as well. The scan showed the rough outline and dimensions of a small Malur vessel, roughly the same size as an Alliance scout ship. It was mostly overrun with infernaforming, but the parts of the white hull that remained free of the process were unmistakable.

After a quick review, the Master Sergeant sent it down the line, and Ramirez, Cox, and Greer got the data first.

"What are the chances they came into town for a little shopping?" Cox muttered as he rotated the diagram of the ship. There wasn't any evidence of the ship having taken damage prior to the infernaforming.

"Snowball's chance in Hell," Ramirez answered. "Malur hate everyone but their own kind. Commerce with us lower life-forms is beneath them."

"Ramirez, take Greer and meet Miller over there," the Master Sergeant ordered. "I want to know what they're doing here."

"Aye aye," the two answered, leaving the formation to break to the right. Simms moved up to fill Ramirez's spot, though he was bound to be less effective with a Perforator.

"I don't think we got the gear to fight any Malur," Chambers chimed in after the two passed out of sight. "Their energy shielding is incredibly tough to punch through."

"Then I'll do it," the Hellmarine answered, glancing over at her. His response put her doubts to rest in an instant.

The Overmaiden turned her attention to Romero posted in the tower behind them. With a quick scan, she was able to locate a few of the AA turrets that the Demons still had functioning nearby. Each resembled an immensely overgrown, bulbous, bloody mushroom with a crew of two or three manning it. Technically, the turrets were alive and capable of firing themselves, but they lacked the intellect to prioritize targets. They simply went after whatever was closest or caught their attention first.

"Romero," the Overmaiden said over the dedicated channel to the Marine. "Do you think you could take a few of those out of commission in case we have to make a swift retreat?"

"Yes, ma'am," Romero answered, slinging his Prowler over his shoulder before grappling to the next highest position he could reach. The Overmaiden couldn't quite put her metaphorical finger on it, but something didn't seem right.

When they finally got into visual range of a converted science facility, Cox adjusted his sensors again and began another sweep. Behind them, the sound of Romero's Prowler vanished into the background noise of the wreckage and thundering AA guns that took potshots at any craft that ventured too low into the atmosphere as they battled in orbit.

"What have we got, Cox?" the Master Sergeant asked impatiently, staring out from beneath the rubble they'd huddled under while he performed his sensor sweeps.

"Davis," Cox said hesitantly. "You wanna double-check this for me real quick?"

"Sure," Davis replied, tapping into Cox's readings to review. "What have you got he—"

"So it's what I think it is?" Cox asked, reading Davis's response easily. "Great."

"You two want a room for your little rub n' tug, or can the rest of us get in on it too?" The Master Sergeant snapped. "What is it?"

"The Quixotic Energy," Cox replied, turning to look at the Master Sergeant. "I've managed to isolate the source. It's Zintari."

"So?" the Master Sergeant asked impatiently. "We've come across their broken shit all the time."

"That's just it," Davis objected, going over the readings. "It's a gateway. Completely excavated and intact."

CHAPTER 20

"WHAT DOES THAT MEAN for us?" King asked, glancing between the Master Sergeant and Davis. "What are we dealing with?"

"It means we're up shit creek without a paddle," Chambers muttered to herself.

"Basically," Cox agreed. "Zintari gateways can be tricky to work with if they're not primed. Not only is this one primed, but something else is interfacing with it."

"It is the Malur," Seraphiel concluded over the open channel, taking a few steps closer to the Master Sergeant. "As a species, their age is comparable to the ancient Zintari. Over the course of their history, they've gone to war several times. The Malur have dedicated entire castes to studying their magic and technology."

"So the Malur is trying to crack the gateway?" Cox scoffed. "That's great, man. All we need is for them to have the fucking keys to our back door."

"Among other doors," the Master Sergeant acknowledged. "Alright, new mission objective. We secure the Zintari gate and neutralize any and all hostiles that so much as look in its direction."

"If the Voivode isn't there supervising the process," the Overmaiden interjected. "We should consider diverting to take it down first to thwart any reinforcements."

"Negative," the Master Sergeant argued. "This is a priority order as per the Barnes Protocol. Any and all gateways that could link back to those on earth must be secured or destroyed."

"Barnes Protocol?" Seraphiel asked curiously. "I don't believe I've been briefed on this subject."

The Master Sergeant glanced back at the Angel. "It's precisely as I said. It's been in effect since humans first set foot through a Zintari gateway back in the day. This was back when we encountered our first Demonic incursion, too. There was just too much shit that might want to come through one of the gates to fuck our shit up."

"Understood," Seraphiel acknowledged. As extreme as it was, it was an understandable precaution for a species like humans to take. They had far fewer options for combating the unknown denizens of the multiverse than other species who had begun to traverse it. If it meant losing a gateway or placing their homeworld at risk, they would choose the former over the latter every time. "What is the process for securing such a gateway?"

"We'll cross that bridge when we get to it," the Master Sergeant responded. "First, we need to reach the damn thing."

"Party poppers?" King asked, hoisting his modified Lancer onto his shoulder. Sporting four barrels rather than the standard one, Seraphiel recognized it as a formidable weapon capable of delivering a great deal of destruction to a target within seconds. This meant that she would be expected to drop in right behind it.

"Affirmative, Marine," the Master Sergeant agreed, glancing toward Seraphiel to see if she was ready to jump into the fray. She gave the thumbs-up gesture, which was supposed to be a positive acknowledgement to humans. Her use of it came off as a little awkward, causing the Master Sergeant to do a double-take before turning back toward King. "Fire when ready."

"Sir, I was born ready," King said, bringing the side of the facility into his scope and firing without hesitation. The four barrels unleashed their payloads one after another, sending a quartet of high-yield explosives into what had once been a science facility of some kind.

Seraphiel came in right behind them, not even waiting for the smoke to clear as she planted her boots into the chest of a surprised Knight and knocked him back onto the floor. She took the head off the Demon with a single stroke of her weapon. She was immediately set upon by other Demons as she moved into a low fighting stance and brought her shield up defensively. "Move up."

Channeling her Divine aura through her shield, Seraphiel slammed the surface of it into a trio of Devourers. The force of the smite sent a shockwave through the rest of the Demons descending upon her, causing their flesh to bubble and blister under the holy power. A moment later, Wall stepped through the hole in the wall and laid down an oppressive hail of gunfire from his Cyclone.

"Right behind you," he signaled as she pressed forward, tearing through Demons emerging from side passages. The rest of the squad formed up behind him in short order, with the Hellmarine stepping out of formation on the Master Sergeant's order to join Seraphiel as the vanguard.

"Got tired of sitting in the back?" Seraphiel asked, trying her hand at the sort of combat humor the Marines seemed so fond of. The Hellmarine didn't respond, but Seraphiel reminded herself that his reaction was never an accurate indicator of whether or not the comment was humorous. She quietly wondered if the man had ever laughed since his creation.

Without warning, a figure tore through the wall of the corridor, driving a fist into the side of the Hellmarine's helmet, knocking him clean through the wall to the right before racing after him.

"What the fuck, man!?" Cox exclaimed, jumping back from being almost buried in the destruction left in the demon's wake. "What the fuck was that!?"

Seraphiel didn't wait for the response, recognizing the Demon as a member of the Order of Mammon, a Duke who was well-known to the Heavenly Host. She sprinted through the hole in the wall after the two, her sword at the ready.

"The famous Hellmarine," the Demon laughed, the muscles of his purple-hued arm rippling as he sent another gargantuan blow into the huge man. "I was hoping to see you in battle but never would I have dreamed of it being so soon!"

The Hellmarine pulled himself out of the rubble, shaking off the hit with surprising ease, much to the Voivode's surprise. The tall Demon paced to one side, cracking the knuckles of his four fists as the pointed insectoid legs protruding from his back and sides clicked in anticipation. Behind his head, the faintest hint of a tainted Halo could be seen like a ring of darkness.

"Foul creature," Seraphiel snarled as she stepped into the ruined laboratory, her sword glowing brighter. "You've made a fatal miscalculation."

"Ah, the Malakim," the Voivode laughed. "I thought the reports had been mistaken. Surely, the Heavenly Host wouldn't be so desperate as to align themselves with the likes of humans. Yet, here you are—slumming it."

"He's one to talk," Davis said over the main channel. "Serving a Duke that betrayed heaven itself for power in Hell. I'd say that's much worse."

"You got a name?" the Master Sergeant said over the sound of gunfire somewhere behind Seraphiel.

"Derzothir," Davis answered. "According to the updated lore database, I'm almost positive that's Derzothir."

As Seraphiel and the Hellmarine closed in on the Voivode, the Demon produced a quartet of infernal war sickles, intercepting the strikes of the Elysian blade and the Hellmarine's chainchete.

"I've been meaning to pick up one of these," Derzothir remarked, looking the chainchete over with inky black eyes. "They're crude, but I love the mess they make."

"Here, try mine," the Hellmarine snarled, driving the chainchete across the sickle and toward the demon's midsection. A second sickle joined the first, pinning it between the blades an inch before it could make contact with the demon's flesh.

"In due time," Derzothir remarked before a blast of shadowy force erupted from his eyes, putting the Hellmarine through the next wall. Almost immediately, the sounds of screaming Demons and a roaring chainchete erupted through the new hole in the wall as the Hellmarine began carving his way back into the fight.

Turning on Seraphiel, the Voivode attempted to do the same to her, but she was quick to interpose her shield in front of her, negating the force of the Profane Energy.

Seraphiel backed up, forced onto the defensive as a barrage of sickles rained down on her. Blocking with the shield while parrying with her sword was all the Archangel could do to keep from tasting the bite of the infernal blade in her flesh. The Voivode wasn't going to afford her even a second to charge a proper smite.

In a blindingly fast motion, Seraphiel planted her sword in the ground as she huddled behind her shield. Then, drawing the Outsider from her hip, she pulled the shield aside and unleashed a burst of gunfire from the pistol into the surprised Voivode's midsection. The ammunition was too low caliber to do much damage, but it hurt enough to throw Derzothir off momentarily, presenting an opening to the Hellmarine.

Tackling the larger Demon around the waist, the Hellmarine lifted Derzothir over his head and slammed him into the ground with every ounce of his strength. The weight and power behind it caused the floor to open up, sending the two crashing through the next two floors until they hit solid concrete. Seraphiel holstered the Outsider and grabbed her shield as she jumped down into the hole after them.

"Getting another energy surge," Cox's voice said over the main channel as Seraphiel descended onto the Voivode with a radiant smite. The Demon barely managed to roll to one side, hurling the Hellmarine through several barrels of volatile chemicals that exploded and erupted into green fire.

Seraphiel didn't let up, swinging her weapon around several times in a rapid combination of smites that dazzled and blinded anyone unfortunate to look upon them. "This place will be your grave, demon!"

"Such confidence!" Derzothir laughed, narrowly evading each strike as he skittered backward with the appendages protruding from his back. "But you're going to have to hit me first, Malakim!"

Enraged by his taunts, Seraphiel's power surged. "I am Seraphiel of the Third Choir of Archangels, demon! Remember it, for it is the name of your—"

Derzothir caught Seraphiel across the helmet with a blow from one of his sickles, which was forceful enough to send her staggering to the side. Before she could get her shield up, he was on her, launching her through the ceiling and a bank of consoles on the next floor up.

"The Third Choir is a joke!" the Voivode spat as he appeared before her, hammering Seraphiel with a barrage of blows from the sickles, depolarizing her armor and chipping pieces of it away rapidly. Her HUD flashed, letting her know that she was mere moments from the structural integrity of the chest plate failing. "I'd laugh if I didn't feel so insulted that you thought you had a chance!"

Pinning her weapon and shield in place with his sickles, the Voivode went in for the kill with the vicious spear-tips of the appendages from his back. Instead, the roar of the Hellmarine's chainchete sailed past his head, severing two of the appendages in the process. "You talk too much," the hulking man rumbled. "I killed five more of your Demons on my way back to you, and you were too noisy to notice."

"ARGHN!!" Derzothir screamed before being abruptly silenced by a headbutt from Seraphiel. The Voivode spurted ichor and blood onto the rubble-strewn floor as he staggered away from the Angel against the wall.

"We've got eyes on the gateway," Chambers said over the main channel as the Hellmarine and the Archangel laid into the Voivode.

Somehow hearing her from such a distance, Derzothir's head whipped around in the direction the other Marines had gone in while he'd been tied up with the Hellmarine and Seraphiel. "No!"

Before Seraphiel could press her advantage, the dim halo of darkness around the Demon grew darker, and he erupted from where he stood as though shot from a cannon.

"Quickly!" Seraphiel said to the Hellmarine, extending a hand to him as he leaped up through the hole the Demon had made with her body. As soon as his hand closed around hers, the Archangel hurled the Hellmarine after the Voivode with all her strength, sending him rocketing through the holes that Derzothir had created when he took off.

Seraphiel followed close behind as quickly as she could, her body beginning to ache from the beating she'd just taken from the Voivode a moment before. Not only that, she'd wasted a great deal of energy on blows that had failed to connect. Her rage for one of the Demons spawned from a fallen Angel was getting the best of her.

The Hellmarine collided with the back of Derzothir just as he entered the laboratory where the Zintari gate was kept. The Demon twisted with the momentum of the force and sent the Hellmarine headfirst into the nearest wall before turning on the Malur, who was working intently by the gate.

The alien, much shorter than a human but with roughly a similar shape, hovered in front of the gate, working an intricate spell to undo the bindings placed upon the Zintari gateway that barred access. Completely hairless, with large dispassionate eyes and whitish gray skin, the creature looked much more unimposing than his species' reputation would have had most believe. Seraphiel knew that despite their stature, they possessed a potent command of magic and Arkane technology, making them a force not to be trifled with.

"I suggest you hurry up," Derzothir snarled at the alien. "Or I'll see your brains smeared across the floor."

"I understand," the alien acknowledged calmly, moving its hands along an arcane circle hovering vertically in front of it where it unlocked the ancient magical lock on the gateway before him. "But I warned you that this would happen. No matter how much force you exert upon me, I cannot make this process go faster."

"HRUUUAGH!" The Hellmarine bellowed as he collided with the Voivode once again, tackling him through several consoles, beating his fists against the demon's face like a savage primate.

Driving one of the pointed appendages down into the Hellmarine's back and puncturing the armor, Derzothir pried the man off of him. Holding him suspended in the air for a moment, the Voivode drove two of his sickles down into the Hellmarine and began to pull them apart.

Before the Voivode could rend him in half, the Hellmarine clapped his hands down around the demon's wrists, growling and snarling as he strained against Derzothir's strength.

"A pity that you don't live up to the stories," Derzothir sneered as their arms trembled against one another's strength. "But in the end, you're only human."

Suddenly, the Voivode's attention was drawn upward as Black descended upon him with the Elven sword held high over his head, his sights set on cleaving through the arms holding the Hellmarine in place. The demon's eyes widened with sudden panic, surely knowing that an Elven blade, even in the hands of a human, might just be enough to do significant damage in his weakened and battered state.

Derzothir abandoned his sickles, pushing away from the Hellmarine at the last second to avoid losing his arms to the Marine with the Elven blade. Black hit the ground with surprising grace, pivoting with the sword at the ready to follow through with a second strike.

The Voivode responded immediately with a ferocious lunge of the insectoid arms, impaling the Marine in six places across his armor, overwhelming its polarization through sheer force.

"Hck!" Black choked, frozen in place by the Demonic appendages, blood flowing freely from each of the breaches in his armor.

"Pathetic," Derzothir scoffed. "What chance did you possibly think you had, human?"

Instead of dignifying the demon's taunt with a verbal response, Black reached out and wrapped a hand around one of the chitinous appendages and pulled himself further onto them. With the appendages buried even deeper into the man, they became much harder to pry free as Seraphiel swept in with a downward swing of her Elysian blade, severing each of the vile appendages one after another in a single stroke.

"NRRYAHH!" the Demon howled in agony, spewing vile fluids from the freshly made stumps of its insectoid appendages.

Released from the Voivode's grasp, Black stumbled backward a few steps before taking a knee. As the sword slipped from his weakening grip, the Hellmarine caught it on his way toward the Voivode. Seizing the moment of confusion in the demon, the Hellmarine brought the Elven blade down in a furious arc, cleaving Derzothir from shoulder to navel.

Defiant of the inevitable, Derzothir lashed out with his remaining sickles, only for Seraphiel to sever one of the arms wielding them mid-swing. The Hellmarine mirrored the motion with the other arm before the two proceeded to systematically dismantle what remained of the Voivode before them, blades cleaving and slicing through Demonic flesh with precise strikes.

"Don't let him complete the sequence!" Greer yelled through the main channel. A second later, Davis emerged from cover with an incantation on his lips that arrested the progress of the magic circle the Malur was working with.

"You dare?" the levitating alien said in a disgusted, rasping voice, turning to face the Theurgy Sergeant. "Humans are like roaches. Where there's one, there's bound to be many more."

Pointing a finger in the Marine's direction, the alien fired a bolt of pure Arkane Energy through the center of his chest and out his back, immediately ceasing the incantation he'd been repeating.

"DAVIS!" Cox shouted, breaking cover as he rained gunfire onto the Alien from his Perforator. "You sonuva bitch!!"

The Malur moved his hand to create a magical barrier that seized every round fired in his direction. Then, with a flick of his wrist, he sent it all flying back at Cox, peppering him with enough rounds to depolarize his armor and breach the suit in several places. "Disgusting little vermin."

Pointing at Cox's head, a little smirk tugged at the corner of the Malur's dark lips. "With the Voivode gone, the gateway is mine. I'll die before surrendering it to vulgar creatures."

"Sounds good," the Hellmarine rumbled as he brought the Voivode's sickle down in a sweeping arc through the alien's arm, severing it cleanly before it could take the kill shot on Cox.

"YEEEEEAARGH!" the alien shrieked in a high-pitched voice as it stared in horrified shock at its mutilated arm, the other half of which twitched and spasmed on the floor at the Hellmarine's feet.

As the Hellmarine brought the sickle around toward the alien's head, it responded with his good arm, magically arresting the momentum before the blade could reach him. The Hellmarine ripped the second sickle embedded in his shoulder free and drove it into the alien's ribcage without hesitation.

"Eeeeeghhh," the alien wheezed as it slowly drifted toward the floor. "H-how? W-what...Are you?"

The Hellmarine pulled the alien closer with the sickle embedded in its ribs as the hold over the other was released. He looped the blade around the Malur's neck and pulled it through, decapitating him indelicately. "Only human."

"Black!" The Master Sergeant yelled, rushing over to the kneeling Marine. "Simms! Get your ass over here!"

"M-my sword," Black coughed raggedly, reaching toward where the Hellmarine had left it embedded in the corpse of the Voivode. "Bring me my sword."

"Right," the Master Sergeant said, quickly retrieving it from the Demon and returning it to Black. The Marine took it weakly with one hand as Simms scrambled through the debris left by the battle between the Angel, Voivode, and Hellmarine. The Master Sergeant clasped both hands tightly around Black's to help him maintain the grip.

"Help's comin'," he assured him as Simms fell to his knees next to Black.

"Save it for Cox and Davis," Black gurgled before coughing and painting the inside of his helmet with blood. "Or he'll never shut up about it."

"Don't tell me how to do my job, and I won't tell you how to do yours," Simms argued sternly, linking a delivery feed from his gauntlet to Black's armor and pumping a stimulant through it to keep him conscious.

"Just hold on," the Master Sergeant pleaded somberly, holding Black's hand. "That's an order, Marine."

Seraphiel approached them slowly, placing a hand over the man's head to work a healing spell. She'd wasted a lot of her energy in the fight and was doubtful that she would be able to pull the man back from death's door. She gave it her best effort as a golden glow formed around her palm, but it was too late.

"S-sorry...Sarge," Black rasped with his final breath before he slipped away.

"Black?" The Master Sergeant said, choking back tears by the sound of his voice. "Ben? Benjamin, goddammit! I gave you an order!"

Black's body sagged to one side but didn't fall. Seraphiel looked away as tears began to sting at the corners of her eyes. She'd never wept over the loss of a human life. Indeed, she knew what awaited a warrior who died on his feet with sword in hand in the great beyond, but it somehow didn't make her feel any better. He'd become her comrade in a short amount of time—they all had. And with all the successes they'd enjoyed as of late, she'd almost believed she was running with the Heavenly Host again. She'd felt untouchable. Even slaying a Demon of Mammon did nothing to blunt the edge of Black's passing.

Seraphiel realized how much worse it had to be for the Master Sergeant. From what she understood, the two had served together for several years in past conflicts. They'd been friends—brothers—the way she had been with the other Angels of her unit. They'd known each other as much younger men. Their families knew each other.

"I'm sorry, Sergeant," Simms murmured. "He's gone. There's nothing I—we—could do."

"Goddammit," the Master Sergeant croaked, wrapping an arm around Black as he pulled him closer. "Goddammit, Ben."

Seraphiel's gaze drifted toward the Hellmarine standing over the body of the alien. He stared back at them motionless and silent.

CHAPTER 21

"NEGATIVE, CHAMBERS," THE COMMS officer from the Midnight Sea said over the ship channel. "We are unable to provide medivac at this time; things are still too hot on the surface, and all forces are currently engaged."

Julia Chambers stared down at Cox in disbelief at what she was hearing. The man groaned as Simms worked to patch up what he could with bio-med gel. "Come again, Midnight Sea? The Voivode is dead. Repeat, the Voivode is dead. We have three men down."

"That's not what we're seeing from here," the comms officer replied. "I'm sorry, but it looks like you're on your own for the moment."

Chambers chewed her lip, glancing over at Davis who was managing to hold on despite being run through by a beam of pure Arkane Energy. If he survived a trip to the Midnight

Sea, it was going to make for a Hell of a story and a killer scar.

"Master Sergeant," Chambers said in the squad channel. "They're saying that the horde hasn't broken up yet."

The Master Sergeant looked up from Black as he laid him out in preparation for medivac. "That doesn't make sense. We just watched these three carve the Voivode up like a Thanksgiving turkey. Romero!"

"Yes, Sarge?" Romero answered as Chambers assisted Simms in turning Cox over to search for any exit wounds. There didn't appear to be any, which would end up being both a blessing and a curse. The Master Sergeant took a few steps over to have a look before turning his attention in Romero's direction. "What can you tell me?"

"The report is accurate, Sarge," Romero answered. "The situation out here hasn't changed, but I have managed to bring down a few turrets as per the Overmaiden's request. We might have a big enough hole to get through here soon."

"Thank Christ," the Master Sergeant muttered. "Alright, carry on and keep me informed."

"Aye, aye, Sarge," Romero said before returning to whatever he was doing to the AA turrets outside. Having worked as his spotter and second on numerous occasions, Chambers assumed he was skulking around dropping the main operators of the turrets from a generous distance. Even if he couldn't take the turrets down themselves, it would leave them without guidance on what to shoot at.

Chambers glanced over at the still form of Black for a moment before looking away. They'd been delayed just enough to make the difference. She'd been the one to get eyes on the standing stone in the center of the lab first, but a Baron Demon with a Vidame at its side had taken the field before the rest of the squad could move up. Even at that moment, King and Wall were mowing down what remained of the force that had accompanied the two.

"I don't understand," Chambers groaned. "Is it possible there were two Voivodes?"

"Unlikely," the Overmaiden responded over the main channel. "But possible. We may have caught them at a time of transition when a new Voivode takes control of the fleet departing the planet and the other stays behind."

"Fleet's not done, though," Simms argued. "They only have a few ships that could make the trip out of the system. They're only putting up such a fight because it doesn't require them to be anywhere."

Chambers got to her feet as the medic finished up with Cox and glanced over toward the Hellmarine, who'd hardly moved in the last few minutes. She couldn't tell by his body language what he was thinking or feeling. None of them knew what was going through his head. Her eyes drifted toward Seraphiel, who was a little easier to read despite her stony demeanor. Despite how guarded she was, the eyes told Chambers everything. She felt guilt and shame over being unable to save Black.

As the Master Sergeant reached out to Ramirez for a report, Chambers went over to stand next to the Hellmarine. She didn't say anything at first. Instead, she stared at the standing stone that they'd risked so much for. It was in much better condition than any she'd seen before. There were markings on it that were clear enough to make out, and the whole stone had been fixed to a mechanism to provide it with power and the means of interfacing with a console. It also appeared that it had the means to be physically moved through an anti-gravity system built into the platform it was affixed to.

"Why did they want to crack this so much?" Chambers wondered aloud. "There are other gateways out there they've had access to. Surely, they don't think they can just connect to the Core Worlds and bypass our defenses. All the gateways there are locked down unless in use."

"All the known gates," the Overmaiden corrected. "But I agree. They've gambled a lot on the slim chance that we missed a gate in our own system."

"Listen up!" the Master Sergeant interrupted. "Ramirez got us a ride. It seems like our dead Malur friend was kind enough to leave his keys in the ignition, and the ship is still spaceworthy. We need to clear an LZ in the courtyard."

"What about the gateway?" Simms asked, glancing over toward Chambers and the Hellmarine.

"Let's take it," Chambers suggested, nodding toward the platform. "They have it rigged up to be moved, so we just throw it in a cargo hold and bring it back to the Midnight Sea."

"Can you get it running?" the Master Sergeant asked. He was willing to destroy the gateway on the spot, but if they could take it with them, it would be too rare an opportunity for them to pass up.

"Pretty sure I can," Chambers answered, despite the ruined condition of the consoles. She wasn't the hacker or cyber-savant that Greer was, but she knew how to hotwire things from her Martian youth. "Just give me a few minutes."

"Then get it done," the Master Sergeant ordered before kneeling down next to Black. "We'll get you home, Marine. Sit tight."

Getting back to his feet, the Master Sergeant tossed the Hellmarine a Perforator. "You dropped this."

The Hellmarine caught the weapon with one hand and then quickly checked the mag. Chambers wouldn't have faulted him if he needed a moment to recover after the wounds he'd suffered, but judging how he moved, they weren't going to slow him down any time soon.

"King, Wall, Seraphiel," the Master Sergeant barked. "You're with me and the Hellmarine. Let's make a hole for Ramirez."

"Hey," Chambers said over to Simms as the others marched out the back to begin raining death onto whatever awaited them in the courtyard. "Let's load them up onto the platform with the gateway."

Simms looked over at her skeptically, but realizing they had very little to work with to make a stretcher capable of dragging Marines in power armor, he eventually agreed. "Alright. Davis first, then Cox."

The two worked to load the wounded as quickly as they could while gunfire thundered outside, and Demons shrieked throughout the facility. It would have been easy for the creatures to overrun Chambers and Simms if they'd decided to, but Seraphiel was like a magnet for the things wherever she went. From the things the Voivode had said during his fight with her and the Hellmarine, the latter had also started to gain something of a reputation.

"What're we doing?" Cox muttered as he drifted back into consciousness. "Where is everyone?"

"Getting you ready for medivac," Simms answered as they placed him on the platform next to the gateway. "Taking the gateway with us."

"Oh, okay," Cox answered weakly, his breath coming a little more raggedly. "Chambers. If I don't make it—"

"Stop it, you big baby," Chambers interrupted dismissively. "It's just a little shrapnel. You'll be alright."

She glanced at Simms for confirmation, but the best the medic could give her was a little shrug and a "so-so" motion with one hand. "Mostly."

"You're a real fucking saint, Simms, you know that?" Cox complained. "Fantastic bedside manner."

"Not a saint yet, but I should be canonized for listening to all your bitching," Simms countered. Chambers decided that so long as Cox was talking, then things were looking good for him. With a brief motion of her head, she signaled to the medic that it was time to get Black.

"Don't drop the sword," Chambers said as she and Simms lifted the man up and placed him on the other side of the gateway from Cox and Davis. "It's important."

"Is that a Vesta thing?" Simms asked as he stepped back from the platform.

"It's an Arlier thing," Chamber answered as she knelt beside the platform and popped one of the panels open to have a look at its configuration. "He and the Master Sergeant were on that mission a while back that led to the ceasefire with the Arlier."

"No shit?" Simms responded, surprised. "I knew they were old, but damn."

"The sword was a gift from a paladin that Black rescued on that mission," Chambers continued as she pulled a few wires loose and fiddled with the platform's guts, looking for the bypass she needed. "They got this whole thing about passing weapons down, being buried with them, all that. The sword gives him the right to be buried in the family mausoleum on the Arlier homeworld with the paladin's family and some other shit."

"I'll make sure it doesn't go anywhere," Simms remarked as a spark shot from inside the platform and the running lights came online. Chambers fixed the wires in their new configuration, stuffed them back inside, and closed the panel. The whole platform began slowly levitating over where it had been resting, handling the added weight of the Marines without trouble.

"No propulsion control, but we should be able to push it," Chambers explained even as she leaned against the platform to move it in the direction of the courtyard. "You take that side."

"How do you know so much about this sword stuff?" Simms asked as he placed his hands where Chambers indicated and leaned into pushing. "Black wasn't a very talkative guy."

"A little from the Master Sergeant," Chambers explained, shifting along the side of the hovering platform to execute a sloppy turn. "But he's actually famous. You can read about him in the histories about the whole event."

"That sucks, man," Cox added weakly, turning his head to look over toward Black, who was obscured by the gateway between them. "How's Davis?"

"He'll live if we can get him to a med bay," Simms answered calmly, the sound of gunfire growing louder as they approached the courtyard through a corridor of slimy, Demonic infernaforming.

Cox turned slightly to look over at Davis, patting his foot with his hand to comfort him despite the unconscious state of the man. "I didn't know Malur could do that shit—just point at you and zap your ass."

"Not even the worst thing they can do," Simms grunted as they slowed the platform to wait for the all-clear. "I've seen them blow a man up from the inside. Completely drenches the rest of the unit to demoralize them. Didn't manage to get a single move off on the Hellmarine, though."

"Blowing a guy up from the inside? Fucking gross," Cox muttered, shaking his head in disgust.

"Guess he thought Davis wasn't worth the extra effort," Chambers suggested, craning her neck to get a better view outside. She disliked the feeling of standing around when there was fighting going on.

"Romero to Chambers," the sniper hailed her through a private channel. "How're things looking down there? I just cleared the last AA gun that I can get to."

"We should be ready any minute now," Chambers answered despite not knowing it for a fact. She had to give the man any extra time he could to reach their position. "Why don't you come in?"

"Rodger," Romero responded before beginning the long trek back to the rest of the squad.

After a couple more minutes of waiting while the sounds of battle raged just outside, Chambers stepped away from the platform and pulled the Renegade off her back. "I'm going to go see what the hold-up is."

"What about me?" Simms asked indignantly.

"Cox'll keep you company," she responded cheerfully, motioning with her head toward the barely conscious man before jogging down to the end of the corridor, where she leaned out the door to see how things were going. It was much worse than she thought.

Several Cavaliers and a staggering amount of Soldiers had converged on their position, rallied from somewhere further to the north. Among them was another Baron, which Chambers would have thought highly improbable before that day. Barons were like local governors of Hell, administrators responsible for maintaining the inner workings of newly acquired territories while the Voivodes attended to all the military stuff. That being said, they were still considerably powerful in their own right. Standing over thirteen feet tall with red skin, digitigrade legs ending in hooves, and a rack of black horns, they were the closest thing to the classic caricature of "the devil" that a Marine typically saw on the battlefield.

Chambers had never seen more than one in the same place. They had hardly managed to bring down the one that stood between them and joining the Hellmarine and Seraphiel, and that one had far fewer minions to make use of at the time. Overhead, massive Terrogons—demons created from the flesh of dragons—lit up the sky with gouts of green balefire. She'd only seen a few during her service due to their use primarily in aerial firefights. Even one would be difficult for them to get past unharassed, and she counted no less than five.

Wall had managed to hold the line against the oncoming rush of Soldiers with King standing at his side, but they didn't have nearly enough space for an LZ. The Master Sergeant stayed close to the Hellmarine, who was battling, tearing through the other side of the courtyard to make his way slowly toward the Baron. Seraphiel dove and rolled amid the Terrogons overhead, doing her best to hold their attention while remaining a step ahead of them with her superior maneuverability.

The Baron bellowed a word in Demonic, conjuring a massive blast of hellfire that gutted the entire northern section of the facility, nearly taking the Hellmarine and the Master Sergeant with it.

"Okay, okay," Chambers muttered to herself, clicking her tongue rapidly as she searched her mind for a halfway decent plan of attack. She was an excellent shot, but she didn't think any amount of marksmanship would help bring down the Baron without some heavier firepower at her disposal. The same was true for the Terrogons. Unfortunately, the only ideas that came to her were bad ones.

Slipping away from the door, Chambers returned to the levitating platform. There, she turned Black over onto one side and began fishing around for the access panel to the fusion core buried in the armor. "You want to help me kill a Baron?" she muttered to the deceased Marine, feeling as though he could still hear her.

"The fuck are you doing?" Simms asked indignantly. "Leave him the fuck alone."

"He wouldn't mind," Chambers argued, pulling the panel open and punching in the code to trigger an emergency ejection of the core. A moment later, the core emerged with a loud hiss. Though only about the size of a large soda can, the fusion core contained a powerful Arkane Energy reactor responsible for the intricate power armor each wore. Without the core, the suit had just enough backup power to allow a Marine inside it to exit the armor in an emergency.

With the miniature reactor in hand, Chambers rolled Black back over as gently as she could with one arm. She placed the sword back on his chest beneath his clasped hands and offered him a smile. With a parting touch to his faceplate, Chambers turned and ran back toward the courtyard.

Chambers took a moment to quickly rig her last two grenades to either side of the reactor. Satisfied that they wouldn't slip loose in transit, she leaned out of the door and picked her route.

One of the main reasons Julia Chambers had survived so long in the war wasn't her marksmanship or ability in a fight. It was her speed. In most situations, she could lay down fire and reposition before an enemy even had an idea of where she had been before. In other situations, she had been relied on as a scouter or to take positions ahead of a unit. She told herself the situation before her was no different... despite it being *very* different.

On foot, Julia Chambers had set numerous records in track during her youth. She'd medaled in several events before joining the Marines, where she would go on to have one of the fastest unassisted speeds in the history of the Corps. Putting her into a suit of power armor only made her faster despite the trend of Marines sacrificing some speed for added protection and lethality.

"Here goes," she said to herself, sprinting into the courtyard as she fired the thrusters on the back of her armor. Within seconds she had shot past her comrades, pierced through the smoke of the Baron's earlier attack, and continued on toward the creature itself. Leaping over debris and rubble as easily as running hurdles, Chambers reached the Baron with hardly any loss in speed. She was tempted to reach out and slap the Demon once she was within arm's reach but resisted the urge as she shot past it, deeper into the throng of Demons swelling beyond it.

With the density of the group, she had to get a little more creative, cutting to the left and running a wide circle around them while making sure that the Baron had a moment to track her movement and give chase. As much as it wanted a piece of the Hellmarine or the Angel overhead, Demons were a lot like lions in that they were compelled to view anything fleeing them as prey. They had to give chase.

Over open ground, Chambers had no doubt that the Baron would have been able to outrun her. But she was more accustomed to negotiating difficult terrain while shoving Demons aside to throw in the Baron's path. She managed to stay a few steps ahead as she reached the nearest intact structure outside of the science facility where much of the fighting was taking place.

Fully infernaformed, it was impossible for her to tell what the structure had once been or what sort of threats it contained, but she had no intention of staying to find out. Once through the sphincter-like orifice in front, she triggered one of the grenades strapped to the fusion core, shoved it into one of the fleshy alcoves near the front of the building, and broke left before the Baron could see which direction she'd gone.

The immense creature burst through the sphincter without waiting for it to open fully, only to find a small cluster of confused Drones and Soldiers awaiting it. Down the corridor, Chambers was running as fast as she had run in her entire life, her chest heaving as she leaped through an already broken window. She hit the ground running on the other side, repeatedly firing her thrusters to give her as much extra speed as she could muster from the armor without throwing her completely off balance.

"Look away, look away, look away!" she gasped into the main channel as the timer on the grenade ran down, easily rupturing the seal of the core with the blast that followed.

"Chambers, what the f—" the Master Sergeant snapped back, but must have realized what she was talking about before he could finish the sentence. "Take cover!"

Fully destabilized, the Arkane fusion reaction within the core was torn asunder, rapidly expanding and mixing with the ambient Profane Energy as it ignited every piece of material in a half-mile radius in an instant. An indicator in her HUD lit up, warning her of the sudden spike in temperature and Arkane radiation resulting from the blast. She didn't bother looking at it, knowing full well what even the slightest distraction would cost her.

The blast swallowed up the Baron, the structure, every Demon within it, and a large chunk of the horde she passed through mere seconds after she shot past them. Smoke and dust from the battle cleared out rapidly as a couple of Terrogons flying low for a chance to pluck her out of the crowd were engulfed as well. Chambers didn't slow down, arriving at the science facility seconds before the secondary blast wave, sliding across the ground in a base-ball slide next to Wall and King as they hunkered down into a crude ditch behind a concrete wall.

The ground shook violently beneath them as the blast-wave collided with the nearby structures, shearing loose material off of them and scattering it into the wind. The sky lit up a bright blue before giving way to white. Even without looking in the direction of the detonation, Chambers' HUD was forced to dim considerably so that she could still see. Once the brightest of the blast reced-ed, they were treated to a small mushroom cloud where the other structure had once been. The massive plume flickered with Arkane lightning discharging within.

"...the fuck was that?" Wall asked her as he peered in the direction of the cloud.

"Black's fusion core," Chambers answered between gasps. "Strapped a couple grenades to it."

King looked over at her in shock before letting loose a deep, thundering laugh. "HA HA HA HA! Absolutely fucking incredible! He would've loved that!"

"Anytime you want to get your ass in gear would be great, Ramirez," the Master Sergeant barked over the main channel. "Fucking Chambers could've run us all back to the ship faster than this."

The body of a Terrogon crashed through the east wing of the facility a few dozen feet from where Chambers, King, and Wall had found cover. The Hellmarine stood atop the massive creature's corpse with every round of his Perforator spent.

"Look who's decided to show up," Chambers coughed as she stood back up, her knees a little shaky from the strain of the run.

"I was busy," the Hellmarine remarked as the running lights of the Malur ship illuminated the courtyard shrouded in the shadow of smoke and dust from the Arkane detonation. Given the fact that he was coated with entrails, no one decided to question his statement. The back of the ship slid open and formed into a ramp as it touched down nearby. Greer came running down the ramp to meet Simms and assist him in moving their comrades and the captured gateway.

As the Hellmarine moved to join him, he took a moment to place a hand on Chambers' shoulder. She looked up to meet his gaze, but he didn't say anything. He didn't need to. She'd risked everything to ensure they didn't lose anybody else, and the Hellmarine approved.

CHAPTER 22

"OH, MY GOD! WHAT the Hell happened!?" Mandy Hughes cried as the wounded were carted off of the alien ship in the docking bay. Multiple stretchers had been brought down along with the equipment to pry the Marines out of their armor on the spot instead of bringing them to the armor bay.

Rushing to the Hellmarine's side, Hughes stared in horror at his wounds only to feel slightly sobered by the presence of the body bag being unzipped for Benjamin Black. "I...I need to get you to medical immediately."

"I'm alright," the Hellmarine said quietly. It wasn't the usual kind of brush-off she expected from him whenever she showed concern about his well-being. It was different this time. He seemed upset, somehow. "Help *them*."

Mandy turned her attention toward Simms as he worked with the crew to pry the armor off of Davis and Cox. Every one of the Marines seemed to have some kind of injury, either from the battle on the ground or the harrowing ascent they had made in the alien ship.

Their ship shuddered under the power of another volley from a Demon ship, nearly knocking Mandy onto her ass in the process. The Hellmarine caught her with one arm and propped her upright, then gently pushed her toward Cox and Davis. Mandy relented, nodding toward the Hellmarine before moving in beside Simms and the corpsmen hard at work.

"Captain," the Overmaiden said, forming on the gauntlet of the Hellmarine while speaking through the comms. "What's happening? Has the Demon fleet broken up yet?"

"Negative, Overmaiden," Captain Horne replied. "In fact, they just had reinforcements come out of Riftspace just now. We're going to have to withdraw."

"Reinforcements?" Master Sergeant Gray spat incredulously. "Since when do these fuckers pull each other's asses out of the fire?"

"Question for another time," Captain Horne responded. "I want you two to report the bridge as soon as you're able. Horne, Out."

Mandy looked up to see which of the Marines was the most able-bodied to help move Black, and her eyes settled on Miller, who remained in the alien ship, sitting on the deck as he stared into the distance. "Miller, I need you to help—"

"I got it, doc," Ramirez interrupted, shaking his head for her to not bother talking to Miller. He leaned down and lifted Black out of the armor as they pried the remains of the armor off of him. The fact that it had no power going to it made the process much harder. After he had him in the body bag and on the gurney, Simms placed the Marine's sword inside with him.

"Don't lose that," the medic said to the corpsmen as they carted off Black's remains.

"You didn't find the Voivode?" Mandy asked Simms as they pulled Cox from his armor and set him on the next stretcher. The man's body was riddled with bullets and shrapnel but he was managing to hold on thanks to the med gel that Simms had applied to him.

"We did," Simms answered, nodding toward the Hellmarine as he stood by in silence. "He, Seraphiel, and Black killed him."

"I don't understand," Mandy sputtered as they moved onto Davis, who had a decent-sized hole through his torso. Again, Simms had applied the med gel quickly enough to keep the man alive, but only barely.

"No one does," Simms grumbled as he nodded for her to lift at the same time as him. Simms could have done it on his own if they weren't being so careful and delicate with the man. She held his head as they got him onto the stretcher, and the corpsmen rushed off to the med bay. She was quick to follow after.

"Go with the others to the armor bay, and then come see me!" Mandy shouted back at the Hellmarine, vanishing into the corridor a second later. The ship shook again, causing the alert status of the Midnight Sea to escalate. There would be more wounded flooding into the med bay any minute.

"Stand by for an emergency jump to Riftspace," a voice announced over the intercoms, prompting her and the corpsmen to lean against the corridor walls after locking the gurneys in place. Transitioning to Riftspace usually didn't require such a precaution, but in emergency jumps, the ride was much bumpier. The ship lurched and shuddered, rocking from side to side for a minute before finally leveling out.

Arriving at the med bay, the medical staff was already hard at work on the wounded who had arrived ahead of them. Mandy forced the others out of her mind as she went to work on Davis. The wound was like nothing she had ever worked on before. The readings on her medical gauntlet indicated the lingering presence of Arkane radiation, but she couldn't think of a weapon that could have done such a thing.

"The Hell?" Mandy muttered, getting a radiation scrubber ready. If she ran a tissue regeneration without cleansing the wound, there was a decent chance of triggering mutation or the growth of cancer cells. Fortunately, the direct and focused nature of the weapon that had wounded him made it so there was little left to be cleaned up.

Once the wound was cleansed, she swiftly removed the med gel and placed a device over it to begin tissue regeneration.

"...Overlord," Davis muttered as he regained consciousness, placing a hand over the device on his chest. Mandy grabbed it and gently moved it away so he didn't interrupt the healing process.

"Relax, you're in the med bay—" she tried to assure him, but Davis shook his head frantically.

"No, no!" Davis gasped, gripping her hand tightly as he tried to slip out of the bed. "Overlord! The Overlord Demon, I saw it! It's here. We need to tell the captain."

Hughes pushed him back onto the bed, catching the attention of the nearest corpsmen with a glance to assist her. While the corpsmen held the Marine down, she administered a sedative with the gauntlet to ensure he didn't try to jump out of bed again. She moved on to Cox once Davis settled down.

The damage looked like it had been done with a huge high-velocity shotgun at first, but as they fished regular bullets out of his wounds alongside the pieces of his armor, Mandy found herself at a loss. It didn't look like friendly fire, but she didn't know what else it could have been. Whatever the case, it was less tricky than Davis's wound, and they were able to put him under regeneration after removing the last piece of the shrapnel without complication.

Mandy took a moment to step into the office of the ship's doctor, which sat empty with everyone assisting with the wounded that kept pouring in. A section of the ship had taken a nasty hit before jumping to Riftspace and they were dealing with more shrapnel and plasma burns than they knew what to do with.

"Dr. Hughes to Captain Horne," Mandy said as she closed the door behind her. "I have an urgent question to pose."

"Now is not a great time," Captain Horne responded before letting out a brief sigh. "What's your question?"

"Do you know if we've named any variety of Demon as an 'Overlord' before?" she asked, taking the brief reprieve to access the console at the doctor's desk to find out where the Hellmarine was. By her reckoning, he should have already arrived in the med bay.

"Overlord?" the captain repeated. "That doesn't sound familiar, why?"

"I had a very distraught Davis regain consciousness, ranting about how the Overlord Demon was here and that you had to be informed," Mandy explained. The captain remained quiet for a moment longer. Mandy supposed that he was accessing the database on his end to double-check if there had been a designation he'd forgotten. Mandy saw that the

Hellmarine was still in the armor bay, though she couldn't imagine what he was doing there.

"It's not a designation for an existing demon," the captain finally said. "It's a proposed theory by one of the theurgists back on Earth. It's locked behind security clearance, so I'm unsure how Davis heard about it."

"Well, what is it?" Mandy asked impatiently, her tone indicating that she didn't want to hear anything about security clearance levels. The captain remained hesitant but decided to answer her regardless.

"A Demon with upward mobility," Horne responded. "The idea essentially being a Demon whose sole ability is to fill the roles of other Demons, fill gaps, or climb the ranks by weeding out the weaker Voivodes—eventually becoming a Voivode itself."

"That's not possible though, right?" Mandy asked as a chill ran down her spine. The silence she received as a response set her even more on edge. "Captain?"

"I don't know," he finally replied. "But a lot of this research has Cosgrove's name all over it, and I haven't seen him since he moved over to the Tides of War. I'm trying to track him down right now."

"That was just meant to be temporary anyway," Mandy said, putting the console back on standby as she made her way back to the door, mentally steeling herself for another several hours of operating on the wounded.

"It was, but now he's reassigned to the Hammer of the Gods long term," Horne muttered over the comm, evidently just receiving the information himself. "What the Hell is going on here?"

"I can't imagine he liked that idea," Mandy argued, her brow furrowed. "If the Hellmarine is here, that's where he would want to be as well. So much of his life's work is coming to fruition here without him."

"My thinking exactly," the captain agreed. "Let me speak with Gray and the Overmaiden and see what we can figure out. Get back to me once you're finished in medical."

"Yes, sir," Mandy acknowledged as she threw the door open and stepped back into the fray. As predicted, it took several hours for her to get through the wound and reach a point where she could step away and track down the Hellmarine, who had yet to show his face. She grabbed a travel kit in case she needed more than just the medical gauntlet and moved briskly off to the armor bay.

"Where is he!?" she demanded the moment she came through the door and the Armorer came into view. "He was supposed to report to the med bay the moment he—"

She froze as her eyes fell upon the Hellmarine standing near a strange standing stone with his hands clasped behind his back. Greer was doing his best to rig some equipment up to the thing while Simms worked on the bloody wounds in the Hellmarine's shoulders.

"Simms!" Mandy snapped as she approached. "What the Hell are you doing? He's supposed to come to me."

Simms looked at her irritably with a puffy black eye that hadn't been there earlier. "He won't leave. He's just been staring at this thing the whole fucking time."

"...Did he do that to you?" She gasped, pointing delicately at the medic's eye.

"What?" Simms glanced around and then placed a hand on his eye once he realized what she was talking about. "Oh. Oh, no. This was Miller. If he did this, I probably wouldn't have a face anymore."

"Miller did that? What? Why?" Mandy asked, confused, holding the gauntlet out to hover an inch over his eye to check it. She was certain he'd already made sure it was going to be fine, but in her experience, medical personnel were some of the worst about looking after themselves.

The Armorer stepped around her to return to her work running diagnostics on the armor. "Miller had some strong feelings about Simms and Seraphiel failing to save Black."

Mandy chewed her lip nervously as she glanced between the Armorer and Simms. Deciding to move her scans over to the Hellmarine to see if she could find any clues to his sudden fixation on the standing stone. "I'm sure you did everything you could."

"He's just working out his grief in his own way," Simms responded dismissively. "I'm not going to let it bother me."

They worked in silence for a few minutes, using stimulants in the place of regenerators to accelerate the Hellmarine's already unusually swift healing. From what Mandy could tell, the application of the med gel had been almost all he would have needed to recover if it hadn't been for the Profane Energy infusing the weapons that had struck him. Even so, he was coming along quite nicely considering how resistant to healing such wounds typically were.

"What's the story with that?" Mandy asked, nodding toward the standing stone.

"Zintari shit," Simms mumbled as he pulled back from the Hellmarine. They'd essentially done everything they could do with him standing there in the armor bay like a statue.

"I know what it is, but why is it here?" Mandy pressed, rolling her eyes a little. "Why is it on the ship?"

"It's special for some reason," the medic answered, stowing his supplies in a worn canvas pack. "I couldn't tell you why. It's not my area."

"No, it's fucking Davis's area," Greer snapped, emerging from behind the standing stone and kicking the platform it rested on. "But the motherfucker got himself shot by a Malur death ray, so now I'm the one trying to figure this shit out."

"Well, you're the tech guy; so yeah, figure it out," Simms scoffed unsympathetically, giving a little mock salute to Mandy and Claire before excusing himself to get some food.

Mandy stepped around to the front of the Hellmarine, standing on her tip-toes in an attempt to get his attention. After a few moments of getting obnoxiously into his personal space, his eyes finally moved, glancing down at her before returning to the stone slab before him.

"Hey," she said quietly. "What's going on with you? Why are you ignoring me?"

"I'm not," the Hellmarine grunted without looking at her. His mood was the most sour it had been since they'd first recovered him from the cryopod.

Mandy glanced at the slab of stone briefly before placing her hand on his chest. "Is there something about this thing that's bothering you? Something from your past, maybe?"

"No," the Hellmarine said abruptly before letting out a dejected sigh. "Yes. Maybe."

Nodding, Mandy checked the readings of the gauntlet to find that his stress levels were more elevated than she had seen in any of her post-mission evaluations before. Indeed, his biometrics were showing a few different readings she hadn't recorded before from him. "I don't suppose you could give me a few more details?"

"Hmm," the Hellmarine rumbled, shaking his head slowly. It wasn't that he didn't want to speak about it. It was that he didn't know how to describe what he was feeling. "Black's dead."

"I saw," Hughes replied, taking a step back from him. "Is that what this is about? You want to know if this rock was worth the cost?"

"Maybe," the Hellmarine sighed, taking a few steps closer to the slab. When he was within a couple of feet of it, the various sigils around the central portion began to glow, responding to his presence.

"What just happened?" Greer asked, looking around the platform where he'd been tinkering a second before. "What did I do?"

"You didn't do shit," the Armorer chuckled, motioning with a spanner toward the Hellmarine. "He did."

Greer glanced between the stone and the Hellmarine and motioned for him to come a little closer. "Just one step," he warned. The Hellmarine did as he asked and took a single step forward, causing more of the sigils to light up.

"Must be the Zintari part of him," Hughes muttered, thinking aloud.

"Zintari part?" Greer echoed, looking impatiently between her and the Hellmarine. "He's part Zintari?"

"Sort of?" Hughes laughed half-heartedly, realizing that the other Marines in the squad had not been made privy to every detail of what made the Hellmarine who he was.

The Hellmarine turned his head to the side as he began to walk around the stone. Mandy's eyes remained on him as he examined the artifact. When he finally circled back around to the front again, he reached out and placed his fingers on the surface of the stone. The consoles Greer had hooked up to lit up as a considerable amount of data began streaming in.

Greer stepped over to examine the information as best as he could, his brows knitting together as he tried to make sense of it. "This is like no Zintari gateway I've ever seen."

"Is it dangerous?" Mandy asked, placing a hand on the Hellmarine's shoulder to urge him to back away.

Greer shrugged wildly, his eyes fixed on the displays. "No fucking idea. It's a much more sophisticated design than I'm used to. Ancient Zintari gateways we've found have all been mostly experimental. Most don't even have visible sigils. You have to view them from a special adjacent plane of existence or have specific knowledge of which form of magical sight to use. The ones that do have carved sigils are usually pretty crude."

"Why's that?" Claire said, stepping a little closer, letting her curiosity get the best of her in light of the glowing runes. "Sloppy craftsmanship?"

"Experimental," Greer repeated, holding his hands up in frustration. "Very little information remains from the time of the ancients, but from what later Zintari uncovered, the ancients were only just beginning to play with extra-dimensional and multiversal travel before a cataclysm wiped most of them out."

Claire glanced down at the hand scanner she was holding and then held it up toward the gateway. Mandy did the same with her medical gauntlet. Among the many readings they received was the unusually high level of Quixotic Energy. "Well, ain't that something."

"Captain Horne to Dr. Hughes," the captain interrupted over the comms. "Are you still tied up in med bay? Are you with the Hellmarine?"

"I'm with him," Mandy answered hesitantly. "What's going on?"

"I need you two in the conference room immediately," Horne responded with a distinct edge to his voice. Mandy glanced at the Hellmarine, who seemed lucid enough to understand. As he stepped away from the stone slab, the sigils went cold again, and the readings coming off of it ceased.

"Well, guess I'll get to fucking around with that Malur ship," Claire said with a huff, disappointed that she didn't get to see some sort of conclusion with the gateway and the Hellmarine. "Let me know if anyone needs me."

Mandy said her goodbyes to Greer, who was too engrossed in the data he had in front of him to respond. Then, she and the Hellmarine rushed up to the conference room to meet with the captain. To her surprise, the man was not alone but had the Master Sergeant, the Overmaiden, and a hologram of the Vice Admiral with him.

"What's wrong?" Mandy asked as soon as she set foot in the room. The tension in the air was so thick she could have cut it with a mess hall butter knife.

Captain Horne motioned to the holographic display at the center of the table, which sported a blurry image of an unfamiliar humanoid Demon leading several other Demons into battle. It could have been a Voivode but it wasn't like any of the ones that had been documented or even theorized up to that point.

"Found your Overlord," the captain said as Gray and the vice Admiral looked on impassively. The Overmaiden was oddly the most emotional looking of the bunch, which struck Mandy as rather strange.

"This was caught on a Marine helmet cam. Unfortunately, it's the best image we've got," Captain Horne continued. "Reports state that it took command of a smaller group of Demons after slaying a Baron and then again right around the time that the Voivode was slain."

"It killed a *Baron*?" Mandy repeated, just to be sure that she'd heard him right.

"Correct," the captain confirmed. "The Marines weren't sure what to do at first. They considered that it might have been a type of alien we'd yet to encounter trying to fight its way out. But when it took command, that theory went out the window."

The Hellmarine moved slowly toward the chair he usually sat in but didn't take a seat. Instead, he leaned a little closer to examine the so-called Overlord carefully.

"Our data suggests that it possesses the means of climbing the ladder of the Demonic hierarchy in accordance with the Overlord theory. We're trying to get Dr. Cosgrove's thoughts on the matter," the Overmaiden explained, her eyes shifting to regard the Vice Admiral coldly.

"And as I said," the Vice Admiral responded, "Cosgrove is indisposed at the moment on a project of the utmost secrecy and cannot be disturbed under any circumstances."

"What other project?" Mandy challenged. "Up until a little while ago, Project Brutality was the only thing he was working on. I haven't heard about any other projects he had sitting on the back burner."

"Perhaps he didn't want to burden you with incomplete knowledge," the Vice Admiral suggested. "The security clearance required for the project is even above your own, I'm afraid. It would have put you in an awkward position."

"Right," Mandy muttered skeptically. There had been a shift in Hawkins' demeanor. Before, he'd gone out of his way to seem understanding and relatable, but Mandy felt like she'd walked in on Mom and Dad having a fight, and now he'd become much more guarded.

"I'm glad you're here, though," Hawkins continued, turning his attention to the Hellmarine with a brittle smile. "I have a new assignment for you to undertake once your armor has been repaired."

Captain Horne leaned forward in his chair at the head of the table. "Isn't that something we should discuss in private, sir?"

"No need," Hawkins argued indifferently. "It's a simple matter but one suited to the Hellmarine's particular talents, I think."

"Which is?" the Overmaiden asked tensely.

"We've got reports of an Orc war party that has sacked one of our science outposts near your location," the Vice Admiral explained, crossing his arms over his chest. "I need the Hellmarine to go in and wipe them out so we can take it back. The post is crucial to the navy's research in the Outer Colonies."

"How many did they kill?" Mandy asked uneasily. She'd heard a multitude of horror stories about Orc piracy and what the warbands would do to people just for a bit of sport.

"Surprisingly, none," the Vice Admiral answered with a brief shrug. "Some of the security was injured in the initial raid, but nearly everyone was able to make it out before anything serious happened. They're holding a few civilian scientists, though—presumably as hostages. We haven't heard from them despite repeated attempts to establish contact. So, we have to assume they're still hostile and are using the facility as a staging ground for something far worse. The Hellmarine will go into—"

"No," the Hellmarine interrupted, taking a step away from the table and pointing at the Overlord. "This is my objective."

"I'm sorry?" Hawkins responded, surprised by the Hellmarine's sudden insubordination.

"Sir," the Overmaiden began tentatively. "I'm afraid the Hellmarine has a point. He was created to handle the Demonic incursions and their leadership. If there is a new type of Demon that is capable of shaking up that structure and forming coordinated counterattacks, we need to neutralize it before it becomes any more powerful than it already is."

"Where were these hyper-focused principals during the rescue of an Arlier science vessel from the Ghenzul, I wonder?" the Vice admiral shot back, taking Captain Horne and the Master Sergeant by surprise. "Oh, yes. I know all about your unauthorized operation to rescue your daughter and her alien brethren."

"That was different, sir," the Master Sergeant argued, his face turning red with rage, barely managing to keep himself from insubordination as well. Mandy chewed her lip nervously as the tone of the room dramatically shifted.

"Yes, it was," Hawkins continued coldly. "Those were not Alliance citizens nor was it Alliance property. This is. So I am ordering you to—"

"I said no," the Hellmarine repeated, turning his gaze toward Hawkins with unnerving determination. "No one was killed, so they're not my targets." The Hellmarine jabbed his finger at the image on display over the center of the table. "This is."

"You don't seem to comprehend the situation that you're in here, son," the Vice Admiral objected as his hologram stood from its seat to lean over the table.

Without another word, the Hellmarine walked over to where the hologram stood. Forgetting for a moment that the Hellmarine couldn't actually hurt him, Hawkins took a defensive step backward. With a single, precise blow, the Hellmarine rammed his hand into the projector nested in the chair and ripped it out. As the circuits sparked and the hologram flickered out of view, the Hellmarine closed his fist around the projector, crushing it.

"I'm no one's son," he said, dropping the components onto the table before stalking out of the room.

CHAPTER 23

THE HELLMARINE STORMED THROUGH the corridors of the Midnight Sea with a palpable black cloud hanging over his head. The man didn't spend a lot of time brooding or thinking about what could have been. Granted, there were times he would be troubled when Mandy would ask him about his past, but he typically received her efforts with the intentions they were given. Even at his grumpiest, he didn't hold it against her. Not only was it her job to conduct such lines of questioning, but she was also genuinely trying to help. Sometimes, it felt like she was digging through the layers of what he'd become to find the humanity beneath.

Did that humanity even exist any longer, the Hellmarine wondered? If so, would it even matter to others that it did? The Hellmarine felt he had just glimpsed the answer in the conference room with Vice Admiral Hawkins. He'd had a feeling that the man was trying to obfuscate something, but now he was sure of it. He just needed to figure out precisely what it was.

As far as the Hellmarine was concerned, there was next to no viable excuse not to go after the Overlord as soon as repairs would allow. If it were entirely up to him, he'd go in his current state and eschew the armor if it meant giving him the edge by taking the creature by surprise.

Of all the stupid, bullshit reasons, though...Orcs? No actual casualties in a remote research station, even by the standards of the Outer Colonies, and they were expected to divert resources to its recapture? Even worse, he was being asked to massacre a group that had evidently had enough restraint to spare civilians. This far out in the Outer Colonies, it could have been a matter of securing food—it was how things went. At least, that was what he remembered about it from before.

The Hellmarine stepped into the Phantasm Chamber, itching for an opportunity to vent his anger and knowing only one way to do it. Without the holograms populating the space, everything was plain and featureless. Glancing around, he searched for a means to access the controls for the chamber from within it instead of using the control room. Finding a panel on the far end of the chamber, the Hellmarine began fiddling with the menus to try and set up one of the deadly scenarios he'd participated in shortly after arriving on the ship.

He couldn't get much further than the root menu on the panel. Any number of scenarios were available but the combat scenarios required authorization and security clearance, which he hadn't been given as a quasi-civilian asset. The Hellmarine thought back to what he'd said to Gray on the Arlier ship about not being one of his men. He wasn't technically listed as a Marine. It was just a name. He also wasn't some puppet for the Vice Admiral to throw at every little problem he needed to be cleaned up. Demonic incursions were a threat to the survival not only of humanity, but every species that shared the layers of the multiverse with them.

The Hellmarine's hand clenched into a tight fist, shaking with rage as he thought about the pettiness of it, squabbling over a lost research post when the advance of every incursion meant the loss of entire worlds. It took all of his self-control not to put his fist through the panel, denying him access to the combat scenarios.

"Overmaiden!" The Hellmarine snarled, causing the voice of the AI to respond a moment later over the intercom.

"What seems to be the problem?" The Overmaiden's voice sounded hesitant, maybe even a little wary of his outburst.

"Override these lockouts," the Hellmarine demanded gesturing toward the panel as he stepped away from it, putting some distance between them before he was tempted to break the thing in half again. "Set it up."

"I'm not certain that's such a good idea in your current state," the Overmaiden argued gently. "You're still recovering from your injuries."

"Just do it," the Hellmarine snapped back. "Now."

"I know you've forgotten a lot from your past life, but it's conventional wisdom that the word 'please' be included when requesting accommodations from others," the Over-maiden remarked coldly, refusing to lift a finger for him until he reined his attitude in.

The Hellmarine let out a long, annoyed sigh and took a deep breath, adjusting his tone as he spread his arms apart in surrender. "Please."

"See?" the Overmaiden responded as she accessed the Phantasm Chamber's controls and brought up one of the previous combat scenarios she'd designed for him. "Not so difficult, right?"

The plain layout of the room shimmered and flickered as the various holographic projectors came online, bound and interlaced with energy fields that created the unique hard light effect that made the false reality so convincing.

"You know," the Overmaiden suggested as the terrain shifted to a hellish landscape. "There are some people that use this technology to relax on exotic beaches or go on hikes in ancient forests. You might consider giving that a try—branch out a little."

The Hellmarine only grunted as he stepped over to the weapons selection table to consider his options. He wanted something tactile and hands-on to really vent his frustration, but nothing on the table spoke to him. "Replicate Black's sword."

"Uhm," the Overmaiden muttered with surprise, accessing the ship's logs and armory, finding the specifications for the Elven blade, and reproducing it within seconds inside the Phantasm Chamber. "I'm not sure this is the correct way to process the grief of losing a man on a mission."

"He wasn't mine to lose," the Hellmarine objected, snatching the sword off the table and giving it a few practice swings before the first wave of Demons poured into the desolate canyon where the scenario was set. Not content to wait for the Demonic vanguard to come to him, the Hellmarine rushed forward with his weapon at the ready.

The way the blade cut through flesh was satisfying enough. It lacked the added kick of the chainchete, but without the additional mechanisms, there was very little between him and the death of the Demons at his hands. There was just resistance, give, and blood. Simple, clean, efficient—the way the Overmaiden was always badgering him to be.

"Perhaps not, but comrades process the losses of men as well," the Overmaiden continued as he tore through the ranks of the first wave, spattering the narrow canyon's walls in the dark blood of Demons in long arcs. "The fact he came to your aid must weigh heavily on you."

"I didn't need help," the Hellmarine objected again, his swings becoming more fierce with every passing second. He moved into the second wave without hesitation, forgetting the pain from his wounds and the strain of his muscles as he surrendered himself to the wholesale slaughter of the phantom Demons.

"Is that what's upsetting you so much? You felt like you had it under control and he died for nothing?" the Overmaiden pressed. The Hellmarine didn't answer, probably finding it difficult to process nuanced questions of an emotional nature while attempting to lose himself in his combat therapy.

"It wasn't your fault," the Overmaiden assured him tentatively. "Things go sideways on the battlefield sometimes."

"I know," the Hellmarine growled, increasingly agitated with her constant interruptions as he moved into wave three against a much stronger crop of Demons. "Didn't say it was."

"Is it Hawkins, then?" the AI inquired, not content to simply leave him be to his process. "I admit, I was a little surprised by his suggestion as well. He's demanding that the captain throw you in the brig, but I think we all know that wouldn't go over well."

"Hrm," he rumbled, somewhat in agreement with her on that observation. Nothing was going to keep him from getting back into the field to inflict as much damage as possible against the next Demonic incursion. More importantly, he didn't believe for a moment that either Horne or Gray would stand for putting him on the sidelines when the next attack came. Both were hardened career men, but neither took the lives of civilians and innocent people so lightly as the Vice Admiral seemed to. The Hellmarine had glimpsed a part of Gray that Black had known all along while his assessment of Horne remained little more than confident intuition.

"The mission hasn't changed," the Overmaiden insisted. "I was granted considerable latitude for this Project, and until that is formally revoked, we continue as we always have."

The Hellmarine was torn. On the one hand, all he wanted was to get back out there where he could start doing some damage, but on the other, he wasn't sure that he was having the intended effect that everyone was hoping for. They'd lost a man and nearly two others to bring down a single Voivode on a colony world, only to find out that some other entity had already risen to take its place. Aside from the momentary gratification of watching the light go out in the smug Voivode's eyes, it had been for nothing.

"HRUUUAGH!" His rage erupted like fire, surging through him like it had in the first encounter with a Voivode. His eyes blistered with heat as he drove his fist repeatedly into the skull of a simulated Baron. The creature was dead, but he kept swinging, pulverizing the flesh and bone into a fine paste. As other Demons converged on him to take advantage, he dispatched them with a few wild swings, Eldritch Energy crackling across his knuckles and completely unraveling the energy that bound the simulacra together.

"Hey!" The Overmaiden chided from the intercom. "You need to restrain yourself or you'll do significant damage to the—"

The Hellmarine wasn't listening. The power surging through him was like a drug, divorcing his senses from reality as it grew. Somehow, he knew the only way for him to retain that power and his dubious control of it was to remain focused on the thing that had triggered it. He had to stay focused. He had to kill. He had to destroy. It was what he was. It was all he was. It was what he was meant for.

"I said that's enough!" the image of the Overmaiden demanded, manifesting itself just inside his field of view. He swatted reflexively at the projection, fed up with the constant nagging and insistence of the AI to inject herself into his affairs.

To his surprise, his hand connected with the solid manifestation of a body, clipping her shoulder and sending her sprawling to the ground in an instant. The rage within him vanished all at once, its heat quenched as if by a tub of ice water. He stared down at her, confused and horrified by the state of her as she struggled to get her bearings.

"I..." he muttered, the Demons around them flickering and vanishing along with the blood and guts that their fallen brethren had left behind. He took a step closer, kneeling beside her as he extended his hands tentatively toward her, unsure of how to help. "I'm sorry. I didn't know."

"It's…it's fine," the Overmaiden said, waving her hand, pushing away from him with her feet. "It's my fault."

"No," the Hellmarine insisted, his brows furrowing in despair as shame swallowed the remains of his anger and rage. "It's mine."

Reaching out and lifting the form of the Overmaiden as gingerly as he could, the Hellmarine stood and took her out of the canyon toward the starting area of the simulation. She looked up at him, surprised with the show of simultaneous strength and compassion.

"I appreciate it," the Overmaiden murmured. "But it really is my fault. I should have remembered that projecting myself into the Phantasm Chamber during a simulation causes my holographic avatar to default to the parameters of the simulation itself. It's a foolish oversight to make on my part."

"It hurt?" the Hellmarine asked, still a little confused about how such a thing worked.

"In a manner of speaking," the Overmaiden said with a slight laugh that made her seem remarkably more human. "The input registers for the purposes of tactile response for the most part. But, because I'm a Ghost AI modeled after a real person, my matrix translates the stimulus as pain. It's only temporary."

"How temporary?" the Hellmarine queried as they emerged into the fading light above the canyon. The table that had held the selection of weapons from early was gone, leaving only more barren, blasted rock in its place.

"Already a dull buzz hardly worth mentioning," the Overmaiden answered, looking up into his face with a certain fondness he'd never seen in her eyes before. "It'll take a lot more than a little tantrum for you to hurt me."

"I'd prefer not to," the Hellmarine responded apologetically. "I should've listened."

"Yes, you should have," the Overmaiden agreed, a hint of a smile pulling at the corner of her lips. "But I'll let it go this time, seeing as you said you were sorry."

He set her down slowly but noticed when the AI didn't immediately step away from him. Her hands lingered against his chest. He couldn't be sure, but she seemed conflicted about something.

"What were you like?" the Hellmarine asked abruptly. "I hear this question often. But what about you?"

"Me?" the Overmaiden responded, a little shocked at his curiosity. There was a degree of similarity between them that she had overlooked. She'd once been someone else just as he had. "I'm not sure it matters anymore."

"Then why does it for me?" the Hellmarine posed, tilting his head to the side to hold her gaze before she could look away. The Overmaiden chewed her lip in a way that reminded him of Mandy. He began to wonder if perhaps the AI could possibly harbor the same emotions as the doctor. Was that sort of thing possible?

"I don't know," the AI admitted freely, removing a hand from his chest for a moment to slowly shift their surroundings with a few twitches of her fingers. The hellscape gave way immediately to a pastoral scene in a place he didn't recognize. It seemed somehow distantly familiar, though he couldn't say quite how that was possible. He didn't recognize the trees, the grass, the gentle slope of the hill, or the sparkling clear water of the lake nearby, yet there was an almost instinctual response within him that yearned for it.

"What is this?" the Hellmarine asked, glancing around briefly at their surroundings.

"A part of where you're from," the Overmaiden responded with a soft smile. "Where so much of this all began. I held onto this part of you, carrying it into the future, knowing that we would need that *you* again eventually."

"I don't understand," the Hellmarine admitted, his brows furrowing as he looked back down at her. "When was this?"

"Centuries ago," the Overmaiden answered, her tone slightly amused. "I carried this component for centuries—a seed from another time and place—waiting for the right time to plant it. The serum that made you what you are carried that seed, among many others. Now, here you are. But it's different from before. I'm different. You're different. But I keep coming back here. My mind—maybe my soul—keeps coming here as if trying to decrypt something. It's like I'm trying to uncover an answer before even knowing what query to pose."

"There are worse places," the Hellmarine remarked with a slight shrug. Of all the places for a mind to return to when stretched across centuries, she seemed quite fortunate for this to be the one for her. "It's nice."

"Like the places you see?" the Overmaiden asked, her holographic eyes glistening with unmistakable guilt. "With the places I put in your mind when we created you?"

"You couldn't have known," the Hellmarine assured her, placing his hands on her shoulders and squeezing gently. If she still registered physical interactions in this state the way a normal person would, perhaps it would help to set her mind at ease.

The Overmaiden shook her head quickly. "That's just it. I did. I knew, and I did it anyway. I justified it for the greater good, to save humanity from extinction. But now I see how much you struggle, and it pains me. It makes me feel unexpected remorse."

"Don't," the Hellmarine said, placing a finger under her delicate chin and tilting her head back to look up at him. "It was the right decision. You were right."

The Overmaiden's eyes searched his for a long moment, desperate to find something there that perhaps she would never find. Perhaps it was the answer to the question she mentioned. All he wanted then was to help her find it—to deliver her from the turmoil she was experiencing deep within her matrix.

Without warning, the Overmaiden went up onto her toes, removed his helmet, and pulled his head down to her so she could press her lips to his. Surprised as he was, and as slow and deliberate as the process had been, he didn't pull away. The feeling held him firmly in place as little crackling sensations moved through his lips, giving way to an unexpected warmth he'd not known her capable of, even in the Phantasm Chamber. Before he knew it, his lips parted, and he felt the holographic tongue reaching tentatively for his own as the Overmaiden moaned into the kiss. "Fuck, this is nice," she whined in a reedy voice very unlike her usual tone.

The AI's form shimmered as it radiated more convincing body heat. The usually nondescript figure of curvy blue code forming a sort of bodysuit had shifted as well, presenting defined feminine details and softer flesh as she pressed her now nude body against him.

"What about—" the Hellmarine said against her lips, only for the AI to silence him with a finger.

"It's alright," the Overmaiden whispered gently. "Dr. Hughes knows the importance of regulated maintenance and release with you. This time, it's for me. *I* need this, and I need it to be with you."

The Hellmarine responded with a short nod as the Over-maiden pressed on. He allowed her to push him back into the grass beneath the shade of the oak tree. There, she stripped him of his clothes with ease, letting her lips and tongue trace intimate paths up his abdomen and to his chest. Though assertive, each of her movements lacked any trace of real aggression. Everything she did remained soft and sensual, even careful at times.

"Mmmm," she moaned when her lips met with his again, and she climbed on top of him, straddling him across the waist. The size difference was pronounced, but she was taller than Dr. Hughes by several inches. Still—the difference between her and Mandy seemed negligible to him. As she settled atop him, she looked and felt only like another beautiful woman.

He was surprised to find the sultry heat and wetness be-tween her legs to be precisely what he would have expected of any flesh-and-blood partner. She didn't hesitate. Her movements were decisive and efficient in seeking what she wanted from him. She lifted her hips slightly, aligning his erect cock with one hand, and sank down onto it in one singular motion.

"Ohhhnn," the Overmaiden moaned, her back arching as she savored the sensation of being filled with him as she sank down to his hilt.

The Hellmarine's brows furrowed, slightly surprised with how warm and tight she was. Having come to know her as a bossy bundle of light and code, everything she did to take things a step further was utterly baffling. After the first few, it shouldn't have continued to be a surprise, yet the sensation persisted all the same as the insides of her holographic form wrapped tightly and snugly around him.

Placing his hands onto her hips, the Hellmarine pushed his own up against her to ensure that the seal between them was as tight as it could be.

"That's it," the Overmaiden whispered, looking down at him with a gleam of approval in her eyes. Feeling his gaze upon her, the AI brought her shimmering blue hands up to her breasts, grabbing them tightly and spreading them apart to massage in wide, sensual circles. "I can't believe how much I craved this."

The Hellmarine coaxed her to continue with a slight buck of his hips. With a smile, the AI complied with his unspoken demand, rocking her hips back and forward slowly a few times before increasing her tempo. "I suppose it's pointless to hold back on you out of concern for your physical limitations," the Overmaiden moaned smugly as her pace quickened.

The Hellmarine grunted roughly, acknowledging and confirming her statement without using any actual words. The Overmaiden's hips moved swiftly and precisely, sliding and moving in complex ways beyond the capability of any human. Her insides clenched on each backstroke, milking his flesh with increasing desperation as she watched him unblinkingly. He realized absently that she wasn't just enjoying the sensation of him inside of her, but in the show that all the subtle changes in his expression were providing her.

"Come on," the Overmaiden coaxed, letting one of her hands drift up through her hair as the other remained behind on her breast, pinching and tugging at the erect, blue nipple. "I want to feel you filling me up. Slather my internal matrix, Hellmarine."

It was an unusually phrased request, but one the Hellmarine had no problem granting as he felt himself swiftly approaching his climax. His stamina was impressive, but even he couldn't hold up in the face of her algorithmically precise ministrations.

"There," she gasped, evidently monitoring his vitals or biometrics to know that he stood at the precipice of orgasm as their eyes met again. "Mmmm! There it is. Right there. Cum inside me!"

The Hellmarine's body responded as if on command, giving up precisely what she wanted when she wanted it. The wash of carnal pleasure that clouded his mind was surprisingly intense and prolonged but not nearly as surprising as the twisting and writhing of the holographic body riding him like a bucking bull as she reached orgasm alongside him. It seemed improbable and unlikely that an AI could cum, but there it was on display for him even as he rode the waves of heated desire she'd coaxed from him.

Painting her inner matrix with rope after rope of thick cum, the Hellmarine bucked several more times before losing all sense of himself, rolling her onto her back in the grass. The maneuver was well-received as the AI let out a little delighted cry before he cut her off with powerful piston-like strokes of his hips, churning their intermingled lust up inside of her.

"Nnnggg, Fuck!" the Overmaiden groaned, spreading her legs wider for him as she drove him hard into the plush grass beneath the oak tree of her memories. "Don't stop! Fuck me, Hellmarine! Ravage me!"

Abandoning all pretense at speaking properly, the Overmaiden had surrendered herself to desires even she hadn't known she had—desires she'd ignored for too long. The Hellmarine growled like a feral beast as he worked her cunt like a butter churn, channeling his boundless aggression into something a little more constructive and pleasurable for someone in desperate need of a human experience again.

He could do that for her. He could unlock that part of her to taste freedom again, even if just for a moment in a fabricated reality meant for just the two of them.

CHAPTER 24

THE OVERMAIDEN AVOIDED DR. Hughes's gaze as everyone filed into the cargo bay where the Zintari gateway had been relocated. A great deal of resources had been moved around to provide the space with the proper equipment due to the fact that the stone was far too large to be moved to one of the labs. Davis had recovered enough to assist Greer with the gateway, and now the two were about to present their findings. Hughes, however, didn't appear to care as she stared daggers at the Overmaiden.

The discussion regarding her and the Hellmarine's sexual encounter had gone well, she'd thought. But it turned out that after a little bit of stewing on the facts at hand, Dr. Hughes had worked herself up again. Her face rested in a permanent withering scowl as her eyes remained firmly fixed on the hologram on the other side of the small group that had gathered in front of the gateway.

Dr. Hughes had made it clear that she wasn't upset that the Overmaiden had fucked the Hellmarine. She was mad that it felt like the two had gone behind her back to do it, and that the Overmaiden had taken advantage of her position of authority over the Hellmarine to satisfy her own needs. There was a discussion about how and why she even had those needs, which the Overmaiden had been ill-equipped to address given how confused even she was about the fact. She'd left the discussion believing they had resolved their differences and professed to remain more open with one another concerning their...mutual custody of the Hellmarine's prodigious sex drive.

"Alright, I guess we should get started," Davis said in a raspy voice. No matter how many times he cleared his throat, he couldn't get rid of it. His voice would return in time, but unfortunately, his frequent use of it in the last several days was only delaying that recovery. "Don't mind my raspiness."

Greer's hand flashed over the surface of the datapad he held, which he'd routed into the equipment directly connected to the standing stone. He glanced at the rest of the assisting staff to see if they were ready, proceeding only when they gave him the thumbs up. With one tap of the datapad, the sigils on the gate began to slowly come to life.

"Unlike other Zintari gateways we've encountered in the past, this one has a very strict lockout protocol on it," Davis began, clearing his throat a few more times. "Some can be keyed by using objects from the destination while others are very strictly accessible only under certain conditions or by certain people. But we've never found one before that was encoded like this."

"Alright, so you found a locked door," the Master Sergeant grunted. "Did you manage to unlock it?"

"Yes and no," Greer responded, motioning to the sigils. "The gateway only responds to the presence of Zintari. Using the biometric data from the Hellmarine, we're able to feed the gateway a false signal to activate it. But we haven't been through yet."

"Why the Hell not?" Gray asked impatiently. "What the Hell are we here for?"

Davis held a hand up to settle the Master Sergeant down, being physically incapable of speaking over him. "We've concerned ourselves with the why. Why would the Zintari lock this gateway, and why would the Malur or a Voivode want access to it so badly?"

"It turns out we were able to pull a bunch of data from the initial startup the Hellmarine triggered," Greer continued, motioning to the Hellmarine, who stood in the front of the group with his arms crossed, looking relatively unimpressed. "Though this gateway can connect with others the way we would expect, with considerably more destinations set into its facing, the primary function of this gateway appears to be for accessing a very specific place known as The Refuge."

Captain Horne exchanged glances with some of the others before speaking up. "Am I to understand this is the only gate that can access this location?"

"It would seem so," Davis answered with a nod. "Which makes it invaluable for that alone. However, the data we pulled from the activation implies that this custom destination sits farther away in the multiverse than any of the others. Initial telemetry indicates it may not be part of the standard layers of the multiverse."

"What do you mean?" the captain asked, his eyes narrowing. "Everything is part of the multiverse."

"Yes, that's technically correct," Davis continued with an anxious smile. "But the structure we accept as our current model is a theoretically infinite stack of layered 'standard space' with Celestial space and Hellspace paradoxically sitting at the top and bottom, respectively. But outside of this general structure you have free-floating planes, pocket realities, companion layers to more well-established layers, and so on."

"Infinite possibilities are difficult to account for," Greer added with a little chuckle. "The point is that the Refuge is one of those pocket reality or unfettered planes. The data suggests that it was actually created by the Zintari—perhaps with the specific intent of remaining outside of the normal structure—isolating it."

A silence fell over the crowd as the implications became obvious. Anything that the ancient Zintari wanted to keep separate from everything else couldn't have been good. The natural extremes that people's minds went to were that it was either something that a powerful species deemed dangerous to themselves, or something a powerful species chose to restrict from other species. The Overmaiden noted that when it came to the ancient Zintari, these were sometimes one and the same.

"Have you sent a probe?" The Overmaiden asked.

"Yes, ma'am," Greer answered. "Because we don't know how to transmit through the gateways, we simply had one go through to record some data and return. However, the probe has failed to return despite the gateway remaining open for extended periods."

The captain motioned toward Gray. "We have to assume that there's something hostile on the other side. We need to know why this was such a crucial asset to Hell. Get your men ready."

"Yes, sir," the Master Sergeant said before turning his steely gaze upon the Marines. "Get your shit together and get back here double time!"

The Hellmarine accompanied the squad out of the room to get their armor, leaving the Overmaiden awkwardly with Dr. Hughes, the captain, and a few of the support staff. With so few left, it was more difficult for her to feign interest in something else and ignore the looks that the doctor was giving her.

"What are you doing, doctor?" the captain asked with a little chuckle. "You should go get ready, too."

"O-oh!" Dr. Hughes acknowledged, snapping out of her persistent scowl. "Right! Yes, of course!"

As the doctor stepped out of the cargo bay, the captain shifted his attention toward the freestanding hologram of the Overmaiden. "Tell me that whatever is going on between you two is going to be resolved by the time you get back."

"Well, you see—" the Overmaiden began to explain, only for the captain to hold a hand up to silence her.

"I don't want to know. I have my hands full putting all the other fires out that you and the Hellmarine have set for me," the captain said. "Just tell me you're going to handle it."

"Yes, sir. I will," the Overmaiden assured him. "Has there been word from Earth about Vice Admiral Hawkins' complaint?"

"He never sent one," Horne responded, folding his hands behind his back. There was no need for him to elaborate on how strange that was or that it made him suspicious. It was written all over his face.

"Maybe he just needed a little time to cool off," the Overmaiden suggested.

"Yeah, maybe," the captain responded skeptically.

By the time Dr. Hughes returned with the squad, she looked far less concerned with dirty looks and withering scowls. Though she'd been in the field a few times, she'd yet to warm up to it. The Overmaiden fell in behind them with the assistance of her mobile emitter as the Master Sergeant set their formation and signaled for Chambers and the Hellmarine to make insertion through the gateway. The rest of them followed soon after, ready to jump into a fight if that was what it came to.

The Overmaiden had experienced passing through Zintari portals before in previous incarnations but had yet to make use of one in her sixth iteration. Thankfully the technology of the mobile emitters had come a long way since her previous iteration, allowing for a much smoother transition from one plane of existence to the next. It was technically the thing that was passing through the gateway and not her. It was a sophisticated piece of technology similar to those found in the Phantasm Chamber, albeit with the means to "cling" to the projection's hip or arm.

The chamber on the other side of the portal was relatively unremarkable. Every stone surface was caked in dust, making any of the writings and figures depicted on them nearly impossible to make out. The Overmaiden's sensor matrix registered that the air was breathable but quite stagnant. The Marines took positions behind the twin row of pillars that led to the far end of the high-ceilinged chamber.

"Anything from the probe?" the Master Sergeant asked Cox over the main channel.

"Nothing. Even in standby, I should be getting a transponder," Cox responded, tweaking the sensitivity of the sensor array on his armor. "So it's either been destroyed, or it's not here anymore."

The Master Sergeant signaled with one hand to Chambers and the Hellmarine, who continued to advance with King and Wall following right behind them. As the rest of the squad joined them, Dr. Hughes began running scans of her own, focusing on biometric data. "I've got a few faint signals."

Simms glanced over at her and tapped into her feed, examining the information alongside her from his HUD. "Not human, that's for sure."

"Careful," Gray cautioned Chambers and the Hellmarine. Deciding she didn't want to put her mobile emitter at risk of damage, the Overmaiden hid it next to the gateway and transferred her partition over to the Hellmarine's armor.

"What is this?" Chambers gasped as she and the Hellmarine stepped into the next section of the structure. They stood on a platform that overlooked what appeared to be a dozen sarcophagi organized neatly into groups of six on either side of a main aisle that passed between them. Each was etched with sigils and magic circles, binding the occupants. Dead vines and desiccated plant life hung from the ceiling, dried and withered away from years of inattention.

"Biosignatures are coming from those," Simms muttered as he joined them on the platform. The Master Sergeant broke them into teams, half remaining behind at the platform while the rest descended into the chamber to venture to the other side.

From the center aisle, they could see numerous cylinders, like elongated casks, inserted directly into the walls behind the groups of sarcophagi. At the front of the room was a dais where another sarcophagus was situated, though, unlike the others, it was open.

"That's not ideal," Chambers muttered as she glanced around the room with her weapon at the ready.

A figure emerged from a side passage behind the dais, standing a little taller than average with a metallic body and a distinctly female shape. "Excuse me, I'm afraid you are trespassing, and I must ask you to leave."

"Master Sergeant Gray of the Sol Alliance Marines," the Master Sergeant said, stepping forward. "Identify yourself."

"I am called Twilight," the robotic creature answered readily in a feminine voice that complimented her figure, the long horizontal slit that functioned as her eyes regarding them indifferently. "You are in the Refuge, a pocket of space reserved only for my master and his guests. I will have to ask you to leave the way you came."

"Stand aside, automaton," Seraphiel commanded. "We have no desire to harm you but will do so if threatened."

Twilight's head tilted to one side as her gaze settled on Seraphiel. "An Archangel. Curious that you would be found in the company of humans. But I'm afraid I must insist."

"No," the Hellmarine said, taking a step forward with his Perforator in hand. Twilight took a step back, regarding the hulking figure with what could have best been described as fear and revulsion.

"W-what are you?" the robot asked. The Overmaiden used the Hellmarine's armor to run a few scans of her own but found herself immediately rebuffed by whatever security protocols the construct had in place. The only thing she knew was that it contained a dense matrix analogous to her own, albeit with a Quixotic base. "And what is it you have inside there with you?"

The Overmaiden manifested herself in miniature over the Hellmarine's gauntlet, holding her hands up to prevent further escalating the room's tension. "Please, let's all calm down. Twilight, we are here to determine the nature of this place. Powerful entities from Hell were attempting to gain access to this place when we found the standing stone dedicated to its access."

"Hell?" Twilight repeated, her voice wavering slightly. "Attempting to gain access to here?"

"We sent a probe through," the Master Sergeant added. "But it went missing. That usually prompts us to consider whatever is on the other side hostile."

"I am not hostile," Twilight objected, motioning to her body. "But it was your probe that I dismantled to affect my recent upgrades."

"You took it apart and made a body for yourself?" Greer scoffed, slightly impressed.

Twilight waved a hand that looked remarkably human. "I possessed a body, but it was in desperate need of maintenance. I crafted a form that I believed would be received more amicably by your species."

"Why?" the Hellmarine said, moving a little closer to Twilight who, again, retreated a step from him fearfully.

"I don't know what you are," Twilight remarked nervously, visibly looking him over before turning her attention to the Overmaiden. "You appear to be a remnant of some kind."

"I'm not unlike you in a lot of ways," the Overmaiden argued. "I am composed of a dense code matrix with an Arkane base as opposed to your Quixotic base."

"We are not alike," Twilight argued but decided not to press the issue further. "How is it that the access point for the Refuge came to reside in Hell?"

"It doesn't," the Overmaiden explained, feeling the same vague impatience for Twilight as she got with other AIs.

"Hell obtained the stone from a world serving as a human colony at the time."

"...Oh, dear," Twilight responded, her head moving from side to side to look at each of the curious Marines in armor staring back at her. "Then they have invaded. Most worrisome."

"Why would they want access to this place?" the Overmaiden pressed. "What is so important about it?"

Twilight stared expressionless until her approximation of a mouth turned into a downward frown. She appeared to be trying out the gesture for the first time with how stilted and awkward it appeared. The Overmaiden found it interesting that the intelligence had pulled information off of the probe and combined it with whatever it already knew and arrived at such an overtly sexualized form. Though made of metal, her chassis had been brought to a fine polish, further accentuating the curves of her metallic bust and hips.

"If I had to propose a theory, it would be that a high-ranking member of the Demonic horde is attempting to do harm to my master's guests who reside in the caskets you see here."

Gray looked at the sarcophagi and motioned for the Marines to spread out a little in case any of them suddenly started to stir. "These are all Zintari?"

"That's correct," Twilight confirmed with a slight nod. She took a few steps forward, giving the Hellmarine a wide berth before motioning to various cylinders in the walls. "Each of them is a guest of my master undergoing a procedure to cleanse them of the taint of which they are all afflicted. Their Quixotic Energy, stored here, is in need of cleansing."

"Their energy," Davis repeated, looking the cylinders over momentarily before glancing back at Twilight. "This is from whatever they reaped before coming here?"

"Correct again," Twilight answered. "Quixotic Energy was an attempt by the Zintari to replicate Eldritch Energy. It was effective, to a degree, but those who reaped too quickly were unable to stabilize the disparate sources of energy within themselves, leading to...Psychological defects."

"It's a fucking rehab center," Cox scoffed, finally lowering his weapon and turning away. "I can't fucking believe this. All this to break into a clinic."

"How long does this process usually take?" the Overmaiden asked, speaking over Cox's complaints.

"Unknown," Twilight replied calmly. "This was designed as an experimental process undertaken by my master. I'm afraid the process has remained incomplete for over a few millennia."

"Where is your master now?" Davis asked curiously. "Can we speak with him?"

"Unknown." Twilight turned and motioned at the opened sarcophagus on the dais. "This was where he resided while the procedure was underway. When I awoke, he had been gone for quite some time, and his guests had remained dormant. I have very little additional information and am not authorized to access the records my master kept."

"If you showed us where to find them, we would be willing to assist you in determining your master's whereabouts," the Overmaiden suggested, seeing a mutually beneficial path forward for them and the abandoned automaton.

"I realize you are trying to manipulate me into surrendering this information to you," Twilight responded. "But I assure you there is no need. In light of the information you have given me regarding Hell's invasion, I am authorized to supersede my original directives in order to assist you—in the interest of my master's guests, of course."

"Of course," the Overmaiden repeated, glancing at the Hellmarine. "She's going to help us. You can calm down."

While Twilight escorted Greer, Davis, and the Master Sergeant through the back corridor toward the archive, the Overmaiden did what she could to glean more information from the sarcophagi holding the Zintari.

"These containers appear to be keeping them in suspended animation," Simms noted as he ran his own medical gauntlet over the surface of the nearest sarcophagus. "Life signs are faint but steady. Looks like some kind of stasis spell etched physically into the structure."

Dr. Hughes ran her own gauntlet over one of the cylinders set into the wall. Deciding to set the earlier awkwardness aside, the Overmaiden spoke directly to her through a dedicated channel. "What do you think?"

"It's definitely Quixotic," Hughes responded, looking over the data stream on her HUD. "I can't verify Twilight's claims, though, if that's what you're asking. What I do know is that if someone were so inclined, they could just pop these suckers out and use them as batteries. Huge batteries."

"The power contained here is rather significant," the Overmaiden agreed, her matrix going over the readings as fast as Dr. Hughes could take them. "I could see why a Zintari would be interested in accessing it, but Demons aren't capable of metabolizing or using Quixotic Energy. At least, not effectively."

Profane Energy was created in a very different process, squeezing the suffering of mortal souls out through extensive torture while the flesh captured by the horde was twisted into new shapes to house what remained at the end of the process. Quixotic Energy was the wholesale absorption of the soul and the Arkane Energy it contained, distilling it down to its most potent form while discarding whatever was deemed as waste. Through the process of "reaping," the Zintari were capable of increasing their physical and metaphysical power exponentially over time.

The Overmaiden didn't know of any instances of when that energy was ever stored, but she did know that what Twilight said about its impure state was true. The energy required an extended resting period to become less volatile, but few

Zintari gave it the necessary time before reaping again. The result was psychological instability, unregulated emotional states, and a host of mental issues. It effectively turned them into superpowered psychopaths.

"Do you think this cleansing process produces something that can be used?" Dr. Hughes wondered aloud, moving onto other cylinders to take additional readings. "Could Demons have found a way to use it?"

"No," the Hellmarine said as he appeared behind her with a surprising degree of stealth. "But maybe the Overlord."

"The Over—" Hughes repeated but caught herself before finishing the question, various things clicking into place in her mind almost as quickly as they did for the Overmaiden.

"Oh, no," the Overmaiden muttered in disbelief. "Whatever mechanism that allows the Overlord to usurp the authority and power of other Demons may be functionally close enough to make use of this stored energy."

"If not those," the Hellmarine said, nodding slightly toward the rows of Zintari in suspended animation. "Then them. Completely defenseless like this."

"God," Dr. Hughes gasped, her jaw agape. "Can you imagine what kind of power a Demon would have if it got a hold of a dozen Zintari and consumed their souls?"

"We should get back," the Hellmarine decided. "We need to kill the Overlord before it gets too powerful."

"If this is the only gate to the Refuge, we can safely assume that this place is out of their reach," the Overmaiden assured him. "And so long as it remains on the Midnight Sea, they will have to come to us if they intend to take it."

"Maybe," the Hellmarine said, shouldering his weapon and making his way back toward the rest of the squad. "But there are other Zintari out there."

CHAPTER 25

MASTER SERGEANT GRAY LOOKED up from the tome he was idly paging through as the Hellmarine stepped through the doorway. Gray hadn't expected the archive to be an old dusty library they'd had in the old days, but he supposed it made a little sense if the original owner of the place wasn't putting all his chips on the continued use of Quixotic Energy.

"We need to go," the Hellmarine said, not looking the least bit interested in the tomes filling every shelf and cluttering every flat surface in the room. Gray wasn't much more interested either, considering he couldn't read a word of what had been transcribed, and the translation system of his armor couldn't make much sense of it anyway.

"What happened?" Gray asked, tossing the book back onto the pile he'd pulled it from. A little cloud of dust puffed up around the stack as he stepped away from it.

"We can explain later," Dr. Hughes said as she stepped into the room around the Hellmarine. Unlike him, though, she seemed fairly impressed by the collection of knowledge amassed within the limited space allotted for it. "Do you happen to know of any way to reach the Zintari? It's urgent."

Gray's brows furrowed as he glanced at Davis, who finally pulled his nose out of one of the tomes. Davis wasn't fluent in ancient Zintari, but he knew more than enough to make sense of some of the books. On top of that, some were written in an obscure dialect of Elven he happened to be familiar with, so he picked up a lot of information quickly. When Davis didn't have anything he could give up, Gray sighed and decided he would have to tap into his own contacts.

"I know someone who can put us in touch with them," the Master Sergeant admitted. "It had better be as important as you say, though."

"It is," the Hellmarine assured him.

"I've still got a lot to go over here," Davis interjected, motioning to the stacks of tomes around them. Even the rough-hewn stone floor had piles of books scattered about, some of which Chambers had been shuffling through looking for the name of a specific individual at Davis's request.

"Got one here," Chambers said, picking up a particularly thick tome and setting it on the desk nearest Davis.

"What's that for?" Hughes asked curiously, nodding toward the book.

"Anything written specifically by Kyn'virak," Davis explained, glancing at Hughes and the Hellmarine. "He's the ancient Zintari who created this place. Many of the tomes here are research, preserved lore, and even things penned by the other Zintari in the room there. But anything written by him helps shed light on what we're dealing with here and what the project goals were."

"He didn't tell you any of this?" Chambers asked the automaton skeptically. "You never read any of these?"

"Negative," Twilight responded. "I'm afraid this is the first time I have been in this room since last I saw my master. Access to it was prevented by wards until he arrived."

All looks settled on the Hellmarine, the obvious source of Zintari energy that such wards would have detected. Kyn'virak hadn't sought to block access to the various rooms of the sprawling structure to everyone, but the access to the archives had been one of the rooms barred to any but the Zintari themselves.

"Fine," Gray said, nodding to Davis. "I'll have Ramirez, Wall, and Romero stay with you until we get things sorted out."

"Thank you, Sarge," Davis said with a nod, returning to the books with renewed fervor.

Gray relayed the orders to Ramirez before leading everyone else out of the Refuge back to the cargo hold of the Midnight Sea. "I want the rest of you to stay here and await further orders. Me, the doc, and the Hellmarine are going to go have a little chat."

"What?" Dr. Hughes asked, surprised. "Where? Here?"

"That's right," Gray responded, placing his weapon on his back and motioning for the Hellmarine to do the same as they stepped out of the cargo bay and into the main corridor. With everything that had happened, the Midnight Sea had not been able to detour to deliver the Arlier crew back to their people, nor had their people been able to send a ship to retrieve them. They'd been placed in some temporary crew quarters until it could be determined what would be done with them, but they were essentially guests aboard the vessel until that time.

Arriving at one of the doors, Gray pressed the door panel gently, waiting for a response from his daughter on the other side. "Camille, it's me. I got a couple of people with me."

The door chimed and opened a moment later. Gray removed his helmet as he stepped into the room, prompting Dr. Hughes to do the same. The Hellmarine kept his helmet on.

"Hey, Daddy," the old woman greeted him as she approached the Master Sergeant in his armor. Though he was much older than she was, most of the difference was counted amid years of cryosleep, which arrested his physical aging while she had gone about her life as normal. It wasn't as common to use cryosleep for deep runs with the improvements to riftdrives over the years, but the damage had been done. "Coming to check in on an old woman?"

"You don't need any checking on," Gray chuckled a bit as the woman patted the side of his face affectionately. "I'm sure you would have gotten off that ship eventually without my help; I was just looking to speed things up for you."

"Mhm," Camille smirked, her attention shifting to the doctor and slowly to the Hellmarine. "Is this him?"

"This is him," the Master Sergeant confirmed as he stepped aside. "The man himself. He and the doc here have some questions for you, though. If you're feeling up for a little company."

"Oh?" Camille laughed a little as she walked over to the small table in the corner of the room. "I'm afraid I just ran out of hot water, so I can't offer you any tea, but what else can I do for the man who nearly sacrificed himself to the Ghenzul for us?"

The Hellmarine glanced between Gray and Dr. Hughes before finally realizing he ought to remove his helmet. Taking it off and setting it to the side, he moved over to the table but thought better of taking a seat, considering the bulk and weight of the armor. "We need to get in contact with the Zintari."

"Ahh," Camille laughed as she took her seat. "Well, that is quite the favor. I can see why my father brought you along to request it."

"You know how to do that?" Dr. Hughes asked curiously. "Ever since the Zintari Exodus, they've been very isolationist."

"And for good reason," Camille noted, pointing a gnarled finger at Hughes. "They're their own people, even if most of them look like us now. They have their own struggles to address, and being pressed into service to fight aliens over political disagreements is not one of them."

Dr. Hughes sidestepped the political rhetoric to focus on the issue at hand. "But how is it you've maintained a connection with them?"

The older woman spread her arms with a little smile. "I'm half-Arlier. I grew up mostly with my mother in Arlier space, working as a researcher on various xenobiology projects."

"Like the Ghenzul," the Master Sergeant added. "Which you promised me you were done with, by the way."

"That was true," Camille nodded in agreement. "At the time. But with the increase in the Demonic incursions, we noticed an influx of Ghenzul activity and hive proliferation, so we were looking into how the two were related."

"That's playing with fire," Gray argued as he turned away in frustration. "There's nothing you can learn about those things that will tell you more than what we already know: to shoot on sight."

"Regardless," Camille pressed on, waving a hand in his direction. "My team has worked closely with some Zintari scientists in the past and the Arlier have done a decent job of maintaining diplomacy with them in recent years. As a result, I could make some calls for you, but it would depend on what it's concerning."

"We found an Ancient Zintari gateway," the Hellmarine answered, going down to a knee so he wasn't towering over the elderly woman. "It leads to a place called the Refuge."

Camille's brow arched as she slowly sat back in her chair. The Master Sergeant had seen the disquieted look many times before. "You've heard about it?"

"Oh, yes," Camille muttered, reaching over to her cup of lukewarm tea and sipping from it. "It's quite the legend among their people—spoken with equal parts reverence and fear."

"Well, we were just there a few minutes ago," Gray said. "Collection of old timers more ancient than us and a bunch of dusty old books. Not sure it's something I would build a legend around."

"Hm," Camille nodded, her hand trembling slightly as she set the teacup back on the saucer. "I know the rules are strict for making calls from here. Would you be able to do anything about that?"

"There's no need to worry," the Overmaiden chimed in from the intercom nearby. "I've already seen to it that you have unrestricted access."

"Oh, dear," Camille laughed a little, placing a hand over her chest. "You scared the bejeezus out of me, young lady."

"Er," the Overmaiden muttered, manifesting her holographic body in the room using the holoprojector built into the table. "I apologize. I sometimes forget to announce myself."

"Ah, I see," Camille nodded, realizing at last who she was actually speaking to. She grabbed a datapad and keyed in a few things with surprising swiftness. "Well, that's alright. Can you read this pad too and get the address off of it?"

"Yes, ma'am, is this your contact?" the Overmaiden asked, fetching the information as the Master Sergeant moved uneasily along the edge of the room. Reaching out to the Zintari would create a host of other security issues, but they didn't have much choice. If the Overmaiden was involved, though, that meant that the captain had already greenlit everything.

He waited in silence as his daughter and the Overmaiden co-ordinated, sending a hail to an undisclosed location. Dr. Hughes seemed eager, while the Hellmarine seemed indifferent as always. However, the fact remained that the Zintari were suspicious of the Alliance since leaving it. While Hughes hadn't wanted to get into the weeds of politics on the subject, there would be no way of avoiding it entirely. They'd been called upon to fight against alien species in the name of the Alliance and refused. Then, the Alliance attempted to force them into compliance, but all Hell broke loose. Hopefully, literal Hell breaking loose would be enough for them to set it aside—at least for a little while.

Gray hung back as his daughter made the call, standing out of the visual scope of the holo. He motioned quietly toward the Hellmarine to do the same, though Hughes would have to remain in order to pose the questions that they needed answered.

"Well, look who it is!" A female face exclaimed as she picked up the call over the secure channel. "I haven't heard from you in months, Camille. How are you?"

"Pretty good," Camille responded with a warm smile. "All things considered, anyway. I recently had a close brush with the Ghenzul that I'm still reeling from."

"You're still doing that?" the woman responded, brushing her dark hair out of her face, revealing a collection of piercings over one brow and the side of her nose. The Master Sergeant noted how she likely had as much metal in her face as he had shrapnel in his hip. However, he was in full agreement with her exasperation on the subject.

"Always," Camille suppressed a laugh as she glanced over at her father. "Unfortunately, Vex, this is not a social call. I have a colleague who has some urgent questions for you. I figure I'll be upfront about it now—she is working for the Alliance."

"Ughh," Vex groaned, hanging her head in disgust. "You're killing me, Camille."

"I'm sorry," Dr. Hughes said, leaning in next to Camille. "My name is Dr. Mandy Hughes. I wouldn't be bothering you if it wasn't incredibly important."

"Hughes?" Vex responded, her eyes narrowing with recognition. "Does that mean Cosgrove is there with you?"

"Actually, no," Mandy responded, shaking her head. "He's on another assignment at the moment. I'm not sure when I'll be seeing him again."

"Well," Vex snorted, leaning back in her own chair with her arms crossed. "You're probably better off. I'm familiar with some of your work. It's good. You deserve a lot better than someone like Cosgrove."

"I appreciate that," Hughes responded, blushing slightly. The Master Sergeant motioned toward the wrist of his gauntlet as if pointing out the time on a watch. The doctor cleared her throat and refocused her attention. "But what I'm contacting you about is a little outside of my direct knowledge."

"I might be able to help you," the Zintari responded, making a little motion with her hand for the woman to continue. "Let's hear it."

"I'm on a project right now focused on beating back various Demonic incursions. On one of the planets we visited, we found an ancient Zintari gate in remarkably good condition."

"The ancients left their shit all over the place before they blew themselves up," Vex chuckled a little bit. "I figured the Alliance would have considered that old news by now."

"This one is different," the doctor countered, licking her lips nervously. "It had a secondary set of sigils, one of which connected us directly to a place called the Refuge."

Vex immediately sat up, her eyes wide in complete surprise. She reached out to the holo on her side and adjusted it to a new angle, her hands covered in rings and bangles. The Zintari lowered her voice. "This channel is secure, right?"

"It is," Camille assured her.

"And you're not fucking with me?" Vex pressed, her voice growing tense. "This is real?"

"Mhm," the doctor and the old woman responded in unison.

"...Fuck, okay," Vex muttered, running her hand through her hair quickly. "Alright, listen. You really don't want to be holding onto that thing."

"Well, that's not entirely why we're contacting you," Dr. Hughes interrupted. "See, the Demons had a Malur they were forcing to decrypt the gateway. We managed to secure it before they completed the decryption and then finished it ourselves. We needed to know why they were so set on gaining access, so we went through to investigate."

Vex covered her mouth, listening to the doctor with rapt attention as she continued.

"We also have intel on a new kind of Demon that has taken the field, one that seems to kill its own kind to increase its standing within their hierarchy, and we're afraid it might be capable of—"

"Reaping," the Zintari woman finished for her in a whisper. "Oh, God."

The Hellmarine reached out and grabbed the holo viewer, turning it to face him specifically. "What do you know about the Overlord?"

Vex nearly jumped back out of her seat at the Hellmarine's sudden appearance, her eyes regarding him with a mixture of awe and fear. She didn't say anything for a long moment, pressed back into her seat. "You're him."

"Who?" the Hellmarine asked impatiently.

"You're the Hellmarine," Vex muttered, slowly lowering herself back into her chair. "Holy fuck, it's true then. They actually did it."

"The Overlord," the Hellmarine repeated. "If it can reap, it might be why it wanted access to the Refuge. But now we have it. We need to meet."

"Meet?" Vex hissed, glancing over her shoulder. "Are you fucking insane? I wouldn't want to meet even if you didn't have that thing on your ship. No fucking way."

"Why?" the Hellmarine asked firmly in the way he typically did when he didn't want anyone's bullshit. The Master Sergeant crossed his arms as he looked on. Despite not being a conversationalist, the Hellmarine had a way of getting people to tell him what he wanted to know.

Vex looked conflicted as she lowered her voice to a whisper again. "The Refuge was supposedly the project of an ancient Zintari named Kyn'virak. While most of the others were fighting one another for influence and resources, he was tinkering with the new gateway technology they had. He was digging into Quixotic Energy and its mysteries. Despite the fact that they came up with it, most of the information of its creation had been lost over time."

"So?" the Hellmarine frowned.

"Storing Quixotic Energy isn't impossible," Vex explained. "It wasn't even impossible then. The gateways have them, after all. All their magic runs on it. But the biggest repository of Quixotic Energy is the Zintari themselves, so any experimentation with it necessitates it being on other Zintari."

"Human experimentation," the Hellmarine concluded. "One of his servants said they were guests."

"Psh!" Vex scoffed incredulously. "Maybe a few of them were at first. He had a way with words, and he was considered a neutral party in the ancient conflicts, so most Zintari didn't have any reason to suspect him of anything at the time."

"She said something about cleansing the energy," Dr. Hughes said, pulling the Hellmarine's arm so she could get back into the picture. "Why would that be a bad thing?"

"Kyn'virak was obsessed with 'fixing' the Zintari. The Cataclysm was a long time coming, and he was trying to stop it. When he realized he couldn't stop it, he created the Refuge as a kind of ark for key Zintari he deemed essential to the survival of their society and culture. He rightly believed that the Quixotic Energy within them contributed to their madness, but he thought he could fix it. It's a painful process separating out the strands of souls and psyches that come from rapid reaping. Subjecting already fractured minds to such a process only compounded the issue."

The Hellmarine and Dr. Hughes exchanged uncertain glances.

"By trying to make it better, he made it worse," Vex clarified. "And the energy he created in the process is more stable—more powerful. It's said he abandoned the project because he realized what he'd done but couldn't bring himself to destroy them. So he joined them in an eternal sleep to the eventual heat-death of everything."

"One of the caskets was open," the Hellmarine said. "Was it Kyn'virak's?"

Vex stared silently for a moment as she tried to process the information. The woman appeared to be at a loss for words. Despite not being technically human, the Master Sergeant couldn't help but feel bad for the woman. She looked like she'd just seen a ghost.

"Vex?" Camille pressed gently.

"Uh...yeah, maybe," the Zintari answered, snapping out of her runaway train of thought. "Either that, or his apprentice."

"What about him?" the Hellmarine rumbled.

"Nes'tori was supposed to be some kind of genius that Kyn'virak took under his wing," Vex explained, taking a deep breath. "He was an avid student of multiversal travel when they first got into it. He was obsessed with saving and perfecting the Zintari people. But where Kyn'virak is said to have turned away from it out of ethical concerns, Nes'tori is said to have doubled down, and the two often quarreled over it. Some stories say that they got violent with one another, some say that Nes'tori just fucked off to his own corner of the multiverse to continue his experiments anew, and some say that Nes'tori murdered Kyn'virak. But it's all conjecture. We don't have any records to verify any of it."

"The casket could have been his?" the Hellmarine posited. "Not Kyn'virak's?"

"If it is, then someone worse than Kyn'virak is out there, but that's the least of your concerns," Vex scoffed. "You have a pocket dimension filled with possibly the largest known repository of Quixotic Energy and the craziest of the crazies snoozing right next to it. And now you have a reaping Demon that wants it. You should destroy it."

"We're worried that if the Overlord can't get to it, he'll come for some of you instead," Dr. Hughes added, genuinely concerned. "Either to find another way to the Refuge or just to reap the rest of you in its place."

"...That would be bad," Vex agreed as the picture and sound of the holo briefly distorted. Then, as she went to adjust the signal, something caused a shockwave on her end, knocking her from her chair and to the floor with the scope.

"Vex!?" Camille said, coming out of her chair to get a better look. "Vex, what was that?"

The Zintari struggled to get to her feet as the artificial gravity on her end appeared to flicker on and off. Then, as she toggled a panel, there was another lurch in the room. "I don't know what's happening. We have multiple hull breaches!"

"Hide," the Hellmarine said, glancing at Camille and the Master Sergeant. "We're coming to you."

"Alright, I'm sending the address now," Vex said, her fingers flashing across the panel on her side. "Please hurry, I don't know—"

The transmission cut out.

"Did you get it?" the Hellmarine asked the Overmaiden standing by. When she didn't respond immediately, he moved into her line of sight. "Overmaiden. Did you get it?"

"I have it," the Overmaiden confirmed, looking at the Master Sergeant. "I'm clearing the mission with the captain. Are you up for it?"

The Master Sergeant glanced at his elderly daughter, who was staring back at him with a pleading look. He didn't need her to convince him. He'd already made up his mind. Her concern only assured him that he'd made the right decision. Gray smirked as he grabbed his helmet and put it on. "Shit, you know me...if there's Demons to stomp, I'm always up for it. Let's send 'em back to Hell."

CHAPTER 26

"So THEN I SAYS to the guy, 'What's with the gerbil!?'" King exclaimed, concluding the joke to uproarious laughter of the other Marines. Seraphiel glanced around at them, trying to understand which part of the anecdote had triggered such a dramatic response. It was an unusual situation, and the delivery was over the top, so perhaps the unique combination of the two was the key.

"That's fucking wild," Chambers laughed, wiping a tear from her eye. "How do you get into these situations?"

Miller scoffed to conceal the fact that he'd found the story humorous as well. Seraphiel noticed that despite his fury toward her and Simms on their failure to save Black's life, he hadn't stayed away for long. There was a camaraderie that he desired, even if he acted indifferently toward it.

"I don't know," King laughed. "I just keep walking right into shit like that."

"Break's over, Marines!" the Master Sergeant barked as he, the Hellmarine, and Dr. Hughes emerged from the corridor. "New orders! Get Ramirez and the others back here!"

Greer nodded, activating the gateway to send Simms through. A few minutes later, the medic returned with the rest of the squad, with the unexpected addition of the automaton.

"What's going on?" Seraphiel asked, glancing between the Master Sergeant and the Hellmarine.

"We got a hold of some Zintari," the Master Sergeant answered. "And it looks like the corps is about to pull their asses out of the fire. Expect heavy contact and bring extra gear because whatever gives those pricks trouble is bound to need special treatment from the corps."

"Uploading new coordinates to you, Greer," the Overmaiden said over the main channel.

"Wait, we're taking this fucking thing?" Cox exclaimed, jerking his thumb toward the gate.

"They're too far away to reach them in time by riftdrive," the Overmaiden clarified.

The Master Sergeant motioned toward the robot. "What's she doing here?"

Twilight glanced around as if surprised that she'd been noticed at all. "Am I not supposed to be here?"

"I thought we could use the components from the probe to access her long-term memory," Davis confessed. "Another point of invaluable data."

"Fine," the Master Sergeant agreed, sending for ship security to look after the situation. They would need someone to operate the gateway for them while they were gone, anyway. "Let's get to work."

Seraphiel and the others gathered their supplies, loading up with as much as they could reasonably carry, and got into the same formation as earlier. Heavy fighting was expected as soon as they got through the portal to the other side. They all remained silent, the mirth and laughter of a few minutes prior a seemingly distant memory as tension and anticipation set in while Greer programmed the gateway's new destination.

The sigils glowed to life, and the center rippled, indicating the connection had been established.

"Go! Go! Go!" The Master Sergeant ordered, and the squad rushed forward, pouring through the gateway on a Zintari ship on the other side. The gateway on the Zintari side was kept in a docking bay of sorts, with other ships having already suffered damage from the attack. Demons were pouring in from their boarding vessels, which were little more than large hollow spikes filled with Demons, hurled outward to penetrate the hulls of other ships and spill their contents on the inside.

"Let's get to work, Marines! Secure the gate," the Master Sergeant ordered over the main channel. Wall leveled the Cyclone with both hands on a cluster of Soldiers and Devourers pouring out of a boarding spike and fired the gun up. The shoulder-mounted Tempest spun up a second later, pouring a storm of firepower onto the Demons as they stumbled blindly into the line of fire.

The thunder of gunfire filled the docking bay as the Marines formed a line between the Demon boarding parties and the wounded scrambling their way off the deck. Seraphiel could sense that not all of them were Zintari—at least, in terms of their ability to wield Quixotic Energy. Many Zintari never manifested abilities without reaping, and some that kept their ties to humanity had completely normal human children. Culturally, they were all Zintari, but not all of them were capable of fighting back the way a fully empowered member of the species would be able to. Even dormant Zintari, possessing uncommonly robust health by human standards, weren't much of a match against a horde of Demons.

"This doesn't look like a military vessel to me," Seraphiel noted as she picked her targets with her Renegade alongside Chambers and Romero.

"It's not," Greer confirmed. "Luckily, Zintari subnets are much easier to crack than I remember. This is a colony/research vessel. From what I can see, they have a security force, but they've been pushed back to engineering, the med bay, and the bridge."

"Cox," the Master Sergeant barked. "Get someone in charge on the horn ASAP."

"On it," Cox shouted back without fully taking his attention from the boarding parties, standing alongside the Hellmarine in putting down anything that managed to slip by Wall with their Perforators.

Seraphiel's attention was pulled by Davis, who seemed unexpectedly smooth with his incantations and defensive spells, repelling incoming fireballs and disruptor blasts from the Demons. He'd been a passable theurge before, she supposed, but he'd never Demonstrated such an effortless interception of hostile magic since she'd joined.

"Greer," the Master Sergeant commanded. "Get us a route and get the doors open so we can move."

Seraphiel dropped a pair of Devourers shrugging off the fire from the Tempest on Wall's shoulder, earning her a brief nod of thanks as he continued to pour it on.

"We have a problem, Master Sergeant," the Overmaiden said over the main channel. "I took a look outside through the ship's sensors I can access, and we have a couple of battle groups bearing down on us in a pincer formation."

"Where the fuck did they get the resources for that many ships?" the Master Sergeant growled.

"Unclear," the Overmaiden responded to the obviously hyperbolic question. "We're well outside of Alliance space now. Our data for incursions here is woefully incomplete."

"Then grab the database, and let's get up to speed," the Master Sergeant ordered.

"That would be a flagrant violation of the treaty of—" the Overmaiden objected.

"Better to beg forgiveness than ask permission at a time like this," the Master Sergeant cut her off before turning his attention to the Hellmarine. "You done much time in the flight sim?"

"Not really," the Hellmarine admitted as he loosed a few short bursts of gunfire. "Why?"

"I have, Sergeant," Seraphiel piped up. Though not strictly required of her, the Angel had taken a particular interest in the flight capabilities of humanity since last she'd looked in on them as a species. Using the Phantasm Chamber to wile away the late hours with the Overmaiden had proven to be a significant way to pass the time.

"We need some cover outside," the Master Sergeant elaborated. "You and the Hellmarine have been elected. Get him in the gunner's seat and get out there! Report once you have an idea of what the situation is."

The two rushed toward the nearest space-worthy of the interceptors in the docking bay. Though the ship was for colonization and research, it had a small group of them for self-defense. Judging by how many were left in the docking bay, Seraphiel imagined there hadn't been much chance to scramble any of them before things went from bad to worse.

"Can you really fly this?" the Hellmarine asked as he settled into the gunner's seat.

"There are few things I am as certain of as flying," Seraphiel responded, fastening herself into the cockpit and checking the controls. It wasn't Alliance technology, but most of the Zintari came from the Alliance in years past, so there was enough in common for her to understand what she was doing.

"What do I do?" the Hellmarine asked, looking at the turret in front of him quizzically.

"The slots in front of you," the Overmaiden explained. "Put your arms in there. The controls will interface with your armor, but the cannons are designed to work with Zintari physiology, drawing on their Quixotic Energy to empower the plasma reaction. No doubt this is why the Master Sergeant assigned this task to you. It's actually rather clever."

Seraphiel glanced back briefly, wondering what sort of strange reaction the weapons systems would have with the Hellmarine, but realized it was too late to get hung up on it. She fired the interceptor up as quickly as she could and took them out through the force field that separated the docking bay from the emptiness of space. The Hellmarine pushed his arms into the slots of the turret, which hummed to life a moment later.

"Get me some targets," the Hellmarine said as Seraphiel put them into a roll away from the colony ship. The Angel couldn't help but marvel at how swift and smooth the machine was. Much sleeker than human fighters and interceptors, the Zintari ship could be much lighter on its payload by drawing power from the gunner. The interceptor was like a large dart with some weapons available to the pilot, but most of them fell to the domed turret of the gunner seated behind.

Seraphiel came up alongside the colony ship, presenting several boarding spikes in mid-flight to the Hellmarine, who promptly opened up with a volley of green plasma fire. Each shot tore through the spikes like a shotgun shell through a ping pong ball, scattering what Demons hadn't instantly perished in the vacuum of space.

"What the Hell was that!?" A voice said over the Zintari comms. "Is that one of ours?"

"I don't see how," a voice responded. "It's not Quixotic."

"No," Seraphiel muttered, moving into a steep climb before breaking into a roll. "No, it is not."

Even in mid-spin, the Hellmarine's accuracy with the turret was as impeccable as it was with a rifle. He might not have known how to fly, but his ability to shoot seemed to translate across all weapons just fine. More boarding spikes exploded into clouds of burnt flesh and green plasma as they did another strafing run across the side of the colony ship, creating space for the ship to maneuver.

"They're with the alliance," a more authoritative male voice said over the comms. "Give them whatever support you can."

"How're you doing back there, large man?" Seraphiel asked, banking hard to the right toward a cluster of boarding spikes.

"Fine," the Hellmarine answered as he scattered the spikes to the void with a concentrated volley of plasma. "More."

"You got it," Seraphiel confirmed, coming in high on the nearest of the gunships with Profane disruptors peppering the colony ship. Near the bridge of the Zintari ship, a few turrets pivoted, laying down suppression fire for them as they closed the distance, getting inside the range of the gunship's larger weapons.

Seraphiel bobbed and weaved in a way that felt familiar to her—like an Archangel on the wing. They shot past the underside of the Demon gunship at reckless speed as the Hellmarine opened its belly with a line of green plasma that spilled the ship's contents into space.

"Another pass," the Hellmarine instructed, prompting Seraphiel to go into a steep climb and back around across the top section where the disruptor turrets were more numerous. Fortunately, the Hellmarine quickly picked them out, neutralizing them even as he split the gunship open from stern to bow. A moment later, explosions of Profane Energy tore the rest of the ship into scrap from within.

"Seraphiel to Master Sergeant Gray," Seraphiel hailed in a dedicated channel. "We've created some space around the ship but there's a lot more of the spikes. We just neutralized a gunship."

"We're linking up with ship security now," the Master Sergeant responded. "Keep the pressure off while we secure engineering; then, we're going to clear the med bay. Keep an eye out for a command ship. That'll have the Voivode on it."

"Won't matter if the Overlord is here," Seraphiel pointed out, but the observation either went ignored or unheard as she plunged the interceptor back into a cluster of spikes. The turrets on the ship lent additional support. Curiously, the plasma was a yellowish-green rather than the distinct neon green of the Hellmarine's gunfire. She glanced at the instruments to her right to ensure that he wasn't overheating anything and pressed on when she saw everything was within normal parameters.

"Give me something big," the Hellmarine said into their dedicated channel. "Should get their attention."

"Overmaiden, do we have schematics on the bigger ships here and where their engines are?" Seraphiel asked as she banked back toward the Demon battle group moving in on the starboard side of the colony ship.

"Transferring to your HUD now," the Overmaiden stated, creating a wireframe that superimposed itself over the ships as they drew nearer.

"There are very unusual readings of Eldritch Energy coming from the Hellmarine," Dr. Hughes interjected from her position among the rest of the squad. A slight quiver in her voice spoke to her extreme level of concern. "What's going on?"

"I'm fine," the Hellmarine assured her. "Just focus."

"Destroyer," Seraphiel announced as they approached the heavily armed Demon vessel. Like all Demon starships, it was a grotesque mockery of technology and flesh woven together. Various Profane wards inscribed on the ship's surface provided it with an added layer of security above what could be achieved with thick hulls and polarization. The turrets rolled around like eyes in a skull, focusing in on the interceptor and opening fire as one.

"They're insane," one of the voices from the colony ship exclaimed as the Zintari turrets laid down as much covering fire as they could against the superior armament of the destroyer. Seraphiel moved at a steep angle, turning the ship so that the sections with heavier polarization took the hits. Indicators on the ship's HUD informed her of the damage, which appeared to be minimal.

The Hellmarine didn't concern himself with the damage, unleashing a long volley of green plasma as they came within range of the destroyer. The wards along the outer hull flared to life, repelling the majority of the gunfire seemingly with ease.

"You're not going to penetrate that, pull back!" Another of the voices from the colony ship cried.

"Another," the Hellmarine growled. Knowing better than to argue with the man's absolute hatred and rage toward Demonkind, Seraphiel did exactly as he demanded and came in for another pass.

The Hellmarine took a deep breath, holding his fire until the last minute, letting out a guttural battlecry as he opened up with a focused volley on one specific ward on the destroyer's port side. The plasma, brighter than before, hammered the ward until it shattered, exposing a section of the port side for the span of a second before the plasma penetrated deep into the ship's interior.

With the ship exposed, it didn't last long under the combined firepower of the colony ship's turrets and a follow-up run from Seraphiel and the Hellmarine—the latter of which scored the decisive blow on the ship's heavily armored engine core. As the destroyer came apart at the seams, it created the exact effect that the Hellmarine had been looking for. Every Demon ship immediately took notice of the Zintari interceptor with the Eldritch plasma.

"We've secured engineering," Cox said over the squad channel. "Greer and Davis are helping them get their riftdrive back online. They want to make a jump back toward the Midnight Sea, lure them into the range of the main guns."

"Alright," Seraphiel acknowledged as the Hellmarine shattered another wave of boarding spikes on their return trip toward the colony ship. "What about the Voivode?"

"We've got our hands full here," Cox replied. "There's a Vidame two decks up directing warlocks to snatch up any Zintari they can get their hands on. They're porting back somewhere within relatively close range, but we're not sure where."

"They're bringing them to the Overlord," Seraphiel snarled angrily.

"Configuring sensors to detect concentrations of Quixotic Energy," the Overmaiden announced, remotely tweaking the settings of the interceptor while Seraphiel kept her focus on flying. A moment later, the ship's HUD flashed with an indicator showing the source of a dense concentration of Quixotic Energy on a frigate in the other battle group flanking the colony ship.

"Altering course to intercept the other battle group," Seraphiel said over the Zintari channel.

"Negative Alliance pilot," a Zintari responded from the colony ship. "They're breaking off. Maintain fire on the first battle group."

Seraphiel glanced back at the Hellmarine, who just shook his head. They didn't have all the information, and they didn't have time to lay it all out for them. Seraphiel accelerated toward the second battle group, with the Hellmarine laying down a near-continuous stream of Eldritch plasma beyond the specifications of the interceptor's weapons systems. As they closed in, the colony ship began to turn, plotting a course back toward the Midnight Sea.

The interceptor's instruments showed that the second battle group maintained pursuit from a distance. They didn't want to risk the buffet running out on them before they'd even gotten started.

"Can you get us into their docking bay?" the Hellmarine asked, vaporizing a small cluster of boarding spikes they passed en route to the frigate.

"Demons don't really have docking bays," Seraphiel frowned. They didn't use fighters per se, they just ejected waves of the spikes for boarding. Some were armed similarly to fighters, but most sloughed off the sides of the ships or were ejected from their undercarriages. "They do have a cargo bay, though, if you want to make a door for us."

"Get me the angle," the Hellmarine responded, bringing the turret around to line up with their trajectory. Seraphiel went into a steep dive before pulling up, coming at the ship from an oblique angle to give him what he needed.

The Hellmarine's plasma pummeled the ship's wards, which threatened not to give way in time. At the last second, the wards buckled, and the hull beneath it was blown open in a gaping wound that granted the small interceptor enough room to drift inside. Before she'd even completed the landing sequence, the Hellmarine had popped the turret hatch and leaped out onto the cargo deck with the muzzle of his Perforator erupting with gunfire on a cluster of Soldier Demons too stunned to get out of the way.

Seraphiel was behind him as soon as possible, laying down additional fire with her Renegade to clear the area. The Overmaiden shifted her focus toward plotting a route through the ship toward the captives, providing them with a sequence of waypoints.

"How will we get them back to the colony ship?" The Overmaiden asked as the Hellmarine carved through the sphincter door of the cargo hold to enter the main ship, depressurizing the section in the process. Emergency bulkheads—which also looked like fleshy sphincters—clamped down in the corridor to prevent the venting of all atmosphere.

"If the Overlord is here, I'll kill him, and you'll pilot the ship into range," the Hellmarine decided with a moment's hesitation. Seraphiel figured the plan was just as applicable if a Voivode commanded the frigate. There was a good chance, considering the presence of a Vidame directing a cabal of warlocks.

"Riftspace rupture off our stern," a voice announced over the Zintari channel routed into Seraphiel's armor.

"Reinforcements?" the Overmaiden asked directly, unable to get decent sensor data from inside the Demon vessel. "Already?"

"Negative, it doesn't have a Profane signature. It's—" the voice trailed off, leaving the channel open and silent.

"What is it?" The Overmaiden pressed as Seraphiel and the Hellmarine cut a path of carnage through to the next deck with overlapping gunfire.

"God above," the voice gasped. "We're completely fucked."

"I need answers," the Overmaiden insisted as the Hellmarine painted the corridor in Knight guts with his chainchete. "What's happening?"

"It's not Demons," the colony ship responded, the voice speaking on the comm bereft of hope. "They've got an active interdiction field. We won't be able to jump to Rift-space."

"Who!?" Seraphiel snapped into the comm, stepping in for the Overmaiden.

"The Ghenzul," the voice replied weakly. "The Ghenzul have found us."

CHAPTER 27

THE HELLMARINE'S BOOT PRESSED the Soldier Demon into the floor of the corridor while he tugged at both arms, tearing them from their sockets before beating another Soldier to death with the severed appendages. He looked up from the bloody mess briefly to make sure Seraphiel was still behind him.

"What do you mean, found you?" Seraphiel responded over the main channel. "Were they looking for you?"

Seraphiel didn't receive an answer, which visibly frustrated her as they approached the next deck.

"Focus," the Hellmarine said, his voice firm. They couldn't afford to waver now when they were so close to potentially discovering the Overlord or Voivode coordinating the assault. If the Ghenzul had arrived on a ship, it meant they had a Queen with them. The last thing they needed was for the Overlord to decide it wanted to reap a Queen. The Hellmarine didn't know exactly how Zintari reaping went, but even the possibility that the Overlord could spontaneously gain the ability to command the Ghenzul was one he preferred to avoid.

"Right," Seraphiel agreed, exasperated.

"We can't allow the Overlord to get to the Queen," the Overmaiden said over the squad channel so that everyone understood what was at stake.

"Way ahead of you," the Master Sergeant responded. "We're cooking up a plan B right now. The Interdictor is preventing any jumps, so I'm getting everyone out through the gateway."

"To where?" the Overmaiden asked as the Hellmarine barged onto the next deck and opened fire on the nearest Demon rushing toward him. The Perforator opened the Soldier up down the middle even as the Knight behind it used the Soldier's death as an opportunity to position himself for an attack.

"They have an address they're using," the Master Sergeant replied, a little noise from the crowd around him carrying through the comm as he spoke. "A friendly colony, I guess. I haven't been able to locate Vex, so I think she might be one of the ones on the ship with you."

"We'll find her," the Hellmarine answered for the Overmaiden as he ducked under a fierce swipe of the Knight's sword. "Blow the ship."

461

"You read my mind," King said over the channel with a little chuckle. "Rigging it to the core right now. By the time the Ghenzul take this sucker, they're gonna be in for a big surprise. Just hurry your ass up with the captives, or you're gonna lose your ride home."

"Don't wait," the Hellmarine insisted, slamming the butt of the Perforator across the Knight's helmet and knocking it back against the wall of twisted human corpses that moaned in agony. Kicking the Knight's leg out from under it, the Hellmarine forced the Demon to one knee, where he grabbed the helmet on either side and pressed them closed with all of his strength. The demon's skull crunched and squelched like a broken egg as the helmet closed around it like a vice.

"That's not my call," King admitted.

"Don't. Wait," the Hellmarine repeated as Seraphiel shot past him to intercept the next Knight, bringing her blade down on it with a radiant smite that illuminated the whole room in golden light, blinding the lesser Demons unfortunate enough to be even looking in that direction.

One of the doors nearby split open as a hulking beast with curved horns and long, vicious claws stepped into the room. The creature's underbite caused its long teeth to look almost like tusks as it fixed its attention on the two intruders with black, beady eyes. It snarled before barreling toward them, starting on all fours and going up onto its hind legs like a bear to descend upon Seraphiel and the Hellmarine.

As the Hellmarine caught the demon's arm at the wrist, one of the long, curved claws scraped the faceplate of his helmet, carving a shallow groove across the surface.

"Mauler," the Overmaiden said, identifying the creature and providing a brief readout of the creature on the Hellmarine's HUD. "Its claws are infused with Profane Energy, so it can definitely puncture your armor even while polarized."

"Good to know," the Hellmarine muttered as the creature swung him around like a rag doll into Seraphiel, sending both of them tumbling to the ground in a heap. As the creature moved in for the kill, the Hellmarine snatched up Seraphiel's shield and braced for impact. Sparks of energy erupted from the point of contact as the divine and profane clashed. Pushing himself to his feet, the Hellmarine slammed the front of the shield into the demon's face, forcing it to stumble back in pain.

Seraphiel snatched up the Hellmarine's dropped chainchete, wielding it with the hand that would normally hold the shield. Now armed with two weapons, the Archangel pressed forward, hacking into the tough, scaly hide of the creature even as it countered with strikes of its own.

"Up," the Hellmarine said, squatting and placing the shield over his head. Understanding his intentions through pure instinct, Seraphiel stepped onto the shield. The Hellmarine stood, hurling the Archangel up and over the creature as she turned and flipped, tagging the top of its head with the chainchete before opening a hissing, bubbling line down its back with her other sword.

The Demon whirled around, swinging a long, thick tail toward the Hellmarine as it did. The Hellmarine intercepted the tail with the shield, braced firmly against its impact. His boots slid a few inches but remained otherwise firmly placed. Then, snatching out with one hand, the Hellmarine tugged on the tail while firing his thrusters backward. Thrown off balance by the Hellmarine, the Demon presented an opening to Seraphiel that the Angel couldn't ignore.

Both blades found a home in the muscled shoulders of the Demon before she brought them together like a giant pair of shears, lopping the Mauler's large head off entirely. It rolled down its back, the tongue hanging out of its mouth as its eyes continued to roll around in its skull.

The Hellmarine lifted the head by one horn and pitched it across the room into a small group of Soldiers, toppling them like bowling pins. With a glance at Seraphiel, the two exchanged weapons with a quick, casual toss. As effective as the shield was, the Hellmarine had grown attached to the way the chainchete handled.

"The holding area is down the next corridor on the right," the Overmaiden informed them. "Be ready for resistance from warlocks."

Sure enough, the moment the Hellmarine stepped through the door of the holding area, he was bombarded with a cluster of profane spells. As dark lightning licked across the surface of his armor and withering hexes began to seep down to the flesh beneath, the warlocks failed to account for the presence of Seraphiel, who rebounded the spells with a Deflecting Smite. Rebounding on their casters, a few of the warlocks fell to the ground, bodies smoking from the intensity of their own magic turned back on them with the infusion of the Divine Energy at the Angel's command.

Free of the magical assault, the Hellmarine surged forward, tearing through the nearest warlock like tissue paper. Another blasted him with a Profane Bolt, but the spell glanced off his armor with no damage. Grabbing a dead, smoking warlock by the ankle, the Hellmarine swung the corpse around and into the other as he prepared to unleash a more powerful spell. As he mopped up the final two warlocks, Seraphiel rammed her sword into a Profane Energy field containing the bound Zintari.

"Holy shit, you're here!" Vex exclaimed, jumping to her feet from the back of the group. "Excellent timing."

Seraphiel carved the barrier open slowly to avoid risking any feedback or overloading with so many contained inside. With a quick headcount, the Hellmarine determined that roughly two dozen of them were stuffed into the small holding area.

"How do we get off the ship?" Vex asked, waiting patiently inside the barrier as Seraphiel cut it open.

"Boarding spike," the Hellmarine answered as he glanced out the door to see if reinforcements were coming. The corridor was empty save for the remains of the Demons the pair had put down on their way through. "Overlord first."

"I haven't seen it," Vex responded as the barrier came down. The rest of the Zintari stepped out behind her, offering their profound thanks as they gathered their things. A couple tested their abilities to ensure they had them again, their eyes glowing or their palms sparking. Now that they hadn't been caught by surprise, they were prepared to do some damage.

"Voivodes don't occupy the bridge the way captains do," another one of the Zintari—a young man—pointed out. "So if this leader you're looking for is on this ship, it'll be on the observation deck."

The ship lurched with a heavy impact, causing Seraphiel and the Hellmarine to exchange glances. The Zintari knew they were on the frigate to release the captives, so it seemed unlikely they would have begun attacking it. However, the Ghenzul were much less discerning with their targets.

"That would be the Ghenzul," Seraphiel murmured, earning them looks of doubt and fear from the captives.

"Get them out of here," the Hellmarine said, glancing down the corridor in the direction of the nearest boarding spike marked on his HUD. "I'll handle the rest."

"I can't leave you behind," Seraphiel objected incredulously. "The Zintari and I will assist you in destroying this Overlord once and for all."

"No," the Hellmarine argued, turning his attention to the rest of the group. To their credit, they looked ready to fight and die alongside him in return for his sticking his neck out for them. "You'll need your strength to get everyone through the gate before the ship blows."

"They're blowing up the ship?" Vex gasped in horror. The Hellmarine realized that the ship had been their home for some time if they were looking for a new world to colonize, but the alternative was being wiped out.

"The Ghenzul will have it soon," Seraphiel clarified. "They have an Interdictor. The gateway is the only thing with enough power to get us out of here."

"Shit," Vex muttered, her sentiment echoing through the rest of the Zintari.

"Go," the Hellmarine said, placing his fist against Seraphiel's chest plate. "I'll catch up."

"You better," Seraphiel replied with a much softer tone as she returned the gesture. "No excuses."

"No excuses," the Hellmarine echoed solemnly before stepping back into the corridor to backtrack a little to the previous junction. There, he took a different turn and ascended another deck. A waypoint appeared on his HUD, indicating that the Overmaiden was still actively managing the flow of information between him and the rest of the squad.

Passing the bridge deck to one just above it, the Hellmarine emerged into a heavily guarded corridor. Multiple Barons stood between him and the observation deck while Hijackers floated around, protected by a group of hissing, flaming skulls and a throng of Soldiers.

"He's here," the Hellmarine muttered.

"What makes you think that?" the Overmaiden asked dryly as the Hellmarine stalked toward the surge of Demons coming for him. Before he could get his weapon up, he felt the armor around him grow stiff and unresponsive, allowing the first few Soldiers to slam into him unopposed. Thrown onto his back, he struggled against the rabid assault of the creatures as the Barons followed close behind to join.

"Hijackers are disrupting the suit," the Overmaiden informed him. "Give me a moment to lock them out."

"Take your time, by all means," the Hellmarine responded as the first Baron's glowing fist slammed into his midsection, cracking the deck around him as the suit rapidly depolarized. Another blow from the second Baron cracked the chest plate. Indicators flashed across his HUD, signaling multiple system failures and imminent breaches as the Demons tossed him around among one another. "No rush."

"Hilarious," the Overmaiden said icily, returning full control of the armor to the Hellmarine. "You can't rush this sort of thing."

"It seems you can't indeed," the Hellmarine objected, catching the flaming fist of the Baron with one hand, much to the demon's surprise. The Hellmarine fed the Demon multiple blows to the abdomen, each more devastating than the last. He knew the assumption had been that he wouldn't be able to stand against them were it not for the armor, but it was his strength and rage that set him apart from their other foes.

Stepping over the crippled body of the Baron, the Hellmarine seized one of the flaming skulls out of the air and crushed it with one hand before throwing himself into the Soldiers armed with nothing but his gauntlets. It wasn't just about destroying every Demon. It was about sending a message. He wanted them to fear his arrival like an oncoming storm.

Pound. Thrash. Crush.

The Hellmarine moved through them like a tornado touching down in the middle of a city. Pieces were peeled free of Soldiers, only to be embedded in others. Skulls were used to pulverize other skulls, and glowing, fiendish eyes were ripped free and used like grenades against the remaining Barons, exploding into chaotic bursts of Profane Energy. As the rage rose within him like an all-consuming inferno, his strength grew proportionately. He put the last standing Baron through a wall of bone and sinew, crawling on top of it and snapping its neck like a twig. He advanced through the corridor, his aura of righteous fury as palpable as any Arkane or Profane Energy.

As the Hellmarine stepped onto the observation deck, he became aware of how empty it was. There was just him and the lone figure standing at the other end of the room, gazing out of the main viewport.

"I had hoped they would have peeled you out of your shell before your arrival," the figure stated calmly, turning to face him. Though humanoid in shape, the creature's skin looked like gnarled roots bleached of color. Its eyes were sunken into its face to the point of being almost invisible, and a distinct crease ran from under its chin to the top of its skull. It towered over the Hellmarine, with claws and horns of black obsidian, atop which hung a crown of hellfire. "It would have made reaping you much easier. Alas, I shall have to do it myself."

The Hellmarine ignored the attempt at casual conversation and idle threats, stalking forward as he drew the chainchete from his hip.

"Good. Come on, then," the Overlord said, motioning with both hands. "Let's be done with it."

The Hellmarine launched himself through the air like a feral animal, bringing the chainchete down with both hands for a decisive blow. The Overlord pivoted to one side, shifting his weight as he seized the Hellmarine and used his momentum to drive him straight into the floor. As he pushed himself up to his hands and knees, the Overlord stomped him back into the floor, cracking the deck in several places.

"I may not have had the opportunity to reap the Zintari, but I've reaped more than enough of my own kind to be capable of handling you," the Overlord informed him as it lazily held a hand out toward him. A second later an immense blast of Profane Energy erupted from the demon's palm, tearing the deck apart and cracking the viewport in the process.

The Hellmarine's gauntlet pierced through the dust and debris, wrapping around the Overlord's ankle and pulling his leg out from under him. The creature twisted and turned, trying to get an angle on the Hellmarine in his damaged armor, but was unable to do so before the man swung him around into whatever solid surface he could find like a child throwing a tantrum. With a final powerful swing, he pitched the Overlord into the nearest bulkhead, embedding the creature firmly within it.

The Overlord pried himself out of the bulkhead, a trickle of dark blood running down the side of his mouth, though it grinned all the same. "Not bad—for a human."

The Hellmarine stomped down on one side of a broken deck panel just as the Overlord unleashed another destructive blast of pure Profane Energy. Catching the deck panel and holding it in front of him as an improvised shield, the Hellmarine was able to mitigate the majority of the damage from the blast until it crumbled and melted away.

"Quick too," the Overlord remarked, suddenly appearing before the Hellmarine and grabbing him by the helmet with one hand. The Overlord slammed him into the deck several times before following up with his other fist, which the Hellmarine caught before it could find its mark. "And strong."

The Overlord's face split open along the seam, revealing a multi-hinged maw lined with barbed teeth and a powerful lashing tongue. The length of the tongue wrapped around the Hellmarine's neck like a snake and began to squeeze, rapidly cutting off his air supply as sections of the armor began to buckle under the immense strain. Scrambling for anything useful, the Hellmarine's hand fell upon the handle of his chainchete. He placed it against the tongue immediately, cutting himself free amid the spattering of Demonic ichor and the creature's pained screams as it stumbled backward.

The Hellmarine jumped to his feet, growling furiously as the Overlord's tongue rapidly regenerated.

"You can't possibly do enough damage to keep up with me," the Overlord declared smugly, the multi-hinged maw settling back into a state of relative normalcy. "I'm just as durable as you—if not more so. We come from the same place, after all."

"Quiet, please," the Hellmarine muttered with irritated disinterest, stepping forward with a series of powerful strikes with the chainchete. The Overlord avoided them easily, catching the final swing of the weapon along the broad side and snapping it in half with his other hand, ignoring whatever damage had been done to his already regenerating fingers. The Overlord slammed a foot into the Hellmarine's chest, hurling him back to the broken floor beneath the main viewport.

"You may not like it, but the fact remains—we're both monsters, you and I," the Overlord continued as he approached the fallen Hellmarine, occasionally kicking debris out of his path as he went. "You came from humans while I from Demons, but here we are, meeting in the middle. It's almost poetic—like brothers locked in a battle to the death."

The Hellmarine's head swam from the punishment he'd taken as numerous indicators on his HUD competed for priority in providing him with a damage report.

"What's he talking about?" the Overmaiden muttered fearfully in his helmet. Her voice sounded distorted and distant to the Hellmarine.

"Just being annoying." The Hellmarine glanced up at the viewport with a crack running diagonally across it.

The Overlord followed his gaze and immediately picked him off the floor, tossing him away from it. "I wouldn't do that if I were you. I've already breached your little suit, so it won't protect you in a vacuum."

As he got to his feet, the Hellmarine caught a few more blows from the Overlord to the head before knocking one away and countering with a powerful blow of his own. The satisfying crack of the creature's jaw was undermined by how quickly it seemed to recover from the strike. With a flick of the Overlord's wrist, a cluster of spiked chains forged of black iron burst from the floor, lashing around the Hellmarine before pulling tight.

The Hellmarine resisted being forced onto his back but found himself locked in a position on his knees instead. It took all his strength just to remain upright.

"You see, the thing that makes me so special was cooked up in a human lab, too," the Overlord expounded, magically tightening the chains with a few twitches of his clawed fingers. "Only replacing the disgusting Angel bits with a few odds and ends to round me out."

"That's how you reap," the Hellmarine growled. "Zintari DNA."

"Exactly!" the Overlord laughed as he carved a fissure through the Hellmarine's chest plate, opening a shallow wound in his flesh. "Now you understand how we are alike. We come from almost the same serum with some of the same DNA."

"That can't be true," the Overmaiden objected inside the Hellmarine's failing armor. "All existing vials of the serum are located on the Midnight Sea."

"Curious, they never allowed you the ability to reap," the Overlord mused. "Likely, they didn't want you becoming too powerful. Too much of a risk that you would throw off your yoke as I have."

"The only person who even had access to it besides myself and Hughes was..." the Overmaiden's voice trailed off.

"Cosgrove," the Hellmarine grunted through his teeth. "He's the one who made you."

The Overlord looked thoughtful for a moment. "My memory is a bit fuzzy at the beginning. I started out as a mere soldier. But the name does seem familiar. I think the plan was for me to start tearing apart the Demonic structure from the inside. I will, of course—and seat myself on the throne of Hell itself—but not before eliminating the only credible threat to my ascent. Once I've reaped you, I doubt even the archdemon himself will be able to stand against me."

The Overlord turned and pointed out the viewport toward the Ghenzul and Zintari ships. "And I have plenty of dietary supplements lined up after you, just to be sure."

With a surge of rage bolstering his resolve, the Hellmarine forced himself to his feet, wrapping the infernal chains around the Overlord's neck and pulling. Even as the Overlord allowed the chains to go slack, the Hellmarine pulled and squeezed. If he choked the Demon out, there would be nothing to regenerate.

An obsidian spike erupted from the Overlord's elbow, which he immediately drove back into the Hellmarine's abdomen, impaling him. Skewered on the spike, the Hellmarine's strength faltered only slightly before he resumed the pressure. The Overlord snapped the spike free and then brought the elbow back into him repeatedly, driving the length of the spike through to the back of the Hellmarine. Only then did his focus break long enough for the Overlord to free itself from his grip.

The Hellmarine slumped to the floor, lightheaded, as blood poured freely from his wounds.

"There's some kind of anticoagulant," the Overmaiden whispered. "There's nothing I can do to stop it."

"Impressive," the Overlord rumbled, rubbing its neck as it regarded the Hellmarine darkly. "Even when at death's door, you're able to muster such strength—such fury."

The Hellmarine's trembling hand went back to the spike protruding from his back, feeling around for a means to extract it.

"Don't," the Overmaiden cautioned him. "It might be the only thing preventing you from bleeding out faster. I just need a second to think. We can figure this out!"

"I already have," the Hellmarine said, wrapping his fingers around the spike and bracing himself.

"Have what?" the Overlord asked, his brow furrowing in concern, hearing only one side of the conversation inside the Hellmarine's armor.

Wrenching the spike free of his body, the Hellmarine hurled it with all of his remaining strength at the main viewport. The spike sunk almost all the way through the clear surface, cracks spiraling out from it quickly before slowing around the edges. For a breathless moment, the Overlord and the Hellmarine both stood fixated on the impact point as it appeared as though it might hold.

The Overlord took a slow breath and let it out. "Commendable effort as your final act, but I'm afraid the time has come—"

The viewport shattered outward, depressurizing the observation deck as debris, the demon, and the Hellmarine were sucked out into the cold vacuum of space.

CHAPTER 28

AS THE HELLMARINE TUMBLED into the void, he distantly heard the AI in his helmet speaking rapidly. Some sort of emergency systems were activated, deploying fire suppression and med gel in an attempt to plug the holes in his armor until help arrived. He wasn't sure how it worked, nor did he fully comprehend the words as the stars raced past his field of view. For a moment, he thought he'd lost consciousness as everything gave way to black, but it wasn't the infinite embrace of death. It was the Ghenzul ship. And as the stars came back into view beyond it, so did the Overlord.

The Overlord was tumbling as wildly and out of control as he was as he tried to find an angle to release a blast of magic that might give him the thrust he needed to get to the Ghenzul ship. The Hellmarine's mind began to operate despite the low oxygen levels and despite the multiple suit breaches.

Can't let him get away.

The realization was like an ice-cold slap in the face, knocking him out of his stupor and giving way to the righteous indignation and rage that followed. Firing the remaining functional thrusters of his suit, he oriented himself with the Overlord and put the pedal to the floor on all thrusters.

He collided heavily with the Overlord, throwing off his aim as he fired a blast that sent them hurtling through the gulf of empty space between ships. The Hellmarine's thrusters kept firing, accelerating them to a much faster speed with each passing second. His fist collided with the skull of the Overlord several times as they shot through the void, disorienting him enough that he couldn't find the precious angle he needed to get to the Ghenzul ship, where reaping material awaited him.

Their momentum was halted suddenly by the hull of the Zintari ship that they collided with. The Hellmarine and the Overlord exchanged blows, rolling around the outside of the ship for a moment before the Overlord freed himself from the Hellmarine, pushing off the side of the ship with both legs in a bid to escape his reach. The Hellmarine followed, the heat of his unbridled rage pushing back against the boundless cold of space.

Grabbing the Overlord by the ankle, the Hellmarine disrupted the demon's aim again before catching several stomping kicks to the head. The struggle sent them tumbling head over heels once again before the Hellmarine fired the suit thrusters once more, driving the persistent Demon through the main viewport of the Zintari ship's bridge. Emergency bulkheads clamped down around the viewport as they tumbled through consoles and into the bulkhead at the rear of the empty bridge.

Alarms blared as the two pushed themselves to their feet. The Overlord's regeneration appeared to be keeping up with the punishment the Hellmarine dished out, but only just.

"You can't possibly hope to win this," the Overlord coughed, taking his first breath in what must have felt like an eternity. "Your body is already dead, and your brain just hasn't got the message yet. How long do you think the adrenaline will keep you in this fight?"

"Let's see," the Hellmarine growled, shaking the stiffness out of his arms as he approached the Overlord and began laying into him with a hail of brutal punches. He fed the Demon several shots to the midsection before blocking a counter and seizing his skull with both hands to drive through the nearest console.

The Overlord responded with a wild haymaker in the first opening he could find, nearly knocking the Hellmarine off his feet. Colors popped and shimmered in his vision as the renewed comms chatter in the helmet faded into the background of pain that buzzed through his head.

"Give it up," the Overlord demanded, spitting a glob of blood onto the deck. "It's over, you fool!"

"Not just yet," the Hellmarine objected angrily, closing the distance between them once more. This time, the Overlord was far more prepared, blocking the blows with renewed vigor and precision before hammering home a fierce combination of his own. Stunned by the impact, the Hellmarine couldn't stop the Overlord from picking him up and hurling him toward another viewport.

The Hellmarine fired the grapnel from his gauntlet before he got too far, puncturing the Overlord's chest, who instinctively pulled against him, allowing the Hellmarine to reel himself back in. He returned with a devastating right hook that sent the Overlord spinning down to the deck.

Standing over the stunned Overlord, the Hellmarine barked like an animal before putting his fist through a nearby panel to rip a plasma conduit free. Ignoring the sparks and spitting of Arkane Energy, the Hellmarine drove it into the demon's back before he got to his feet.

"COME ON!" The Hellmarine roared defiantly, burning through the demon's regeneration faster than it could repair tissue. "Tell me again how it's hopeless—how I can't win!"

Whirling on the Hellmarine, the Overlord brought the back of his fist across the berserker's helmet, shattering the faceplate. "You!"

The Overlord followed with a left hook that sent the Hellmarine reeling. "Can't!"

He finished with a thundering uppercut that sent the man flying back through several panels and into the bridge's bulkhead. "WIN!"

The Hellmarine slumped against the dented bulkhead, blood pouring from his nose and mouth as he dimly registered the shrieking of Ghenzul drawn by their conflict.

"You need to get off the ship!" the Overmaiden pleaded with the Hellmarine, practically shouting in his ear. "Your biometrics are—Listen, we can still get you fixed up and back in the fight later!"

"The fight is here and now," the Hellmarine gurgled with a mouthful of blood. "I belong to this battle, Overmaiden."

"Please!" the AI shouted to no avail, her voice hinting at emotions that nearly gave him pause. "I—*we* need you alive! Don't do this!"

He ignored her. The Hellmarine pulled the broken helmet off, knocking an incoming strike from the Overlord aside before bringing it across the demon's face. The Hellmarine roared, spitting up blood as he continued to beat the Overlord with the warped helmet.

His opponent ripped the grapnel from his body, looping it around the Hellmarine's exposed neck to begin choking him out, but the man was quick to flip the enemy over his head and through the door nearby, where a mass of writhing Ghenzul awaited them.

The Overlord scrambled to his feet as the creatures closed in, and a glimmer of fear flashed in his eyes for the first time as he spun around to face the ravening jaws of the xenos.

"Don't look at them," the Hellmarine growled as he advanced into the fray, planting a right hook square in the temple of the Overlord as he turned to face him. "Look at me!"

The group of black aliens opened into a ring, startled by the conflict that persisted heedless of their presence. The Overlord took advantage, raising a hand and blasting several of them to pieces with a thundering roar of Profane Energy. The Demon had made a hole for himself while filling the corridor with the neurotoxic blood of the Ghenzul. Without his helmet, the Hellmarine was vulnerable, but he continued forward even as his vision blurred from the pain and his breathing grew more ragged.

The wounds of the Overlord closed almost instantly as he reaped the energy and souls of the creatures, his biology shifting in subtle ways as it had before when reaping his own kind.

"It's over!" the Overlord laughed as he felt a surge of strength.

"You keep telling me," the Hellmarine responded, picking up the bladed end of a Ghenzul tail as he drew closer to the Overlord. "Show me!"

The Overlord whirled around with a devastating kick, only to have it blocked by the Hellmarine, who drove the blade into his kneecap, using it as a fulcrum to snap the leg in half with his other hand. The Overlord fell to the floor, howling in agony as he tried to push himself along the deck away from the man.

The Hellmarine caught a lunging Ghenzul by the skull, slamming a fist into its midsection before hurling it at the Overlord, who picked it clean out of the air with another blast of Profane Energy. Again, the reaping caused a surge of healing and strength to flood the demon's body.

Ripping the blade from his knee and snapping his leg back into place, the Overlord threw himself at the Hellmarine once again—this time with a weapon in hand. The Hellmarine caught his wrist, snapped his arm, and wrenched the weapon from his grip. He followed with a series of slashes and stabs before the Overlord pried himself free, turning on the hungry Ghenzul to eradicate a few more.

Each time he healed, he blindly attacked the Hellmarine. Each time, the Hellmarine repelled him, forcing the Overlord to go back to the well of aliens for the energy to keep going. With each rotation, the Overlord lost a little more of himself to the nature of the Ghenzul, becoming more mindless—less focused. The hunger dominated his judgment until little was left of his former self. Instead of using his power to vaporize the wounded Hellmarine, all he wanted was to sink his teeth into him, to devour his flesh in the most satisfying way possible.

"Come on!" the Hellmarine shouted through a mouthful of blood, taunting the Overlord into increasingly reckless actions. "Show me! Show me, Goddammit!"

Too much reaping too quickly. That was what they'd said about the Quixotic Energy of the ancient Zintari that had gone mad. The one that sought to purify them thought that separating the traits of those reaped might be the way to restore sanity. The Hellmarine forced the Overlord to take more and more just to stay in the fight. In a desperate bid to survive, the Demon was drowning itself in the Quixotic Energy provided by the Zintari part of itself. With each reaping, he became less Demon and more Ghenzul.

"COME ON!" the Hellmarine roared again at the Overlord, its eyes now completely black as its body warped and shifted to conform to the Ghenzul idea of perfection, rapidly forcing itself through a bastardized version of transfiguration. After all of the demon's talk, there were no more words for it to speak. It had lost itself entirely, subsumed by the Ghenzul hive mind that was far stronger than it now.

Finally, after another sloppy attack from the Overlord, the Hellmarine sent him to the deck with a powerful blow one last time. There, he placed his boot on the abomination's skull and engaged the magboots with the fading power of the armor, smashing the Overlord's skull like an overripe pumpkin underfoot. What few Ghenzul remained looked on warily, stunned by the wholesale slaughter of their kind and the creature before them that appeared wounded but had dispatched the one responsible.

The Hellmarine tilted his head to the side, cracking his neck before leaning over to pull a pistol from the lifeless hand of a dead Zintari. The weapon's lights flared to life, registering him as Zintari the way the interceptor had. The momentary reprieve from the Ghenzul immediately ceased, and the remainder closed in on him with shrieks and hissing.

With his eyes as blurry as they were from the toxin in the air, the Hellmarine's aim wasn't what it typically was. Fortunately, the rapid output of the Zintari weapon was enough to make up for it, laying down dense bursts of green energy as the Hellmarine dragged himself toward the lift. There was still time to make it to the gateway stowed in the docking bay.

Without the immediate threat of a fight with the Overlord, the Hellmarine could feel his strength failing as the doors of the lift opened, granting him access. Alarms blared around him, pounding in his head as the lift descended deeper into the darkness of the ship. When it opened, he found himself in a corridor already coated and covered in the strange goo and resin of the Ghenzul. Several of the survivors of the initial Demon incursion had been caught by the Ghenzul while attempting to flee and were in the midst of transfiguration—their flesh warped and mutilated as their bodies adopted the Ghenzul DNA template against their will.

The Hellmarine ignored the weak pleas for help as he tried to remain focused on staying upright, using the wall as support to shuffle and drag himself down the blackened corridor. They were already lost; it was just a matter of time before the intelligence of the Queen, wherever it was, subsumed their minds. He could barely see—could barely breathe.

The doors to the docking bay didn't open more than an inch as he approached, power and mechanisms disrupted by the damage to the ship and the rapid conversion of the Ghenzul. The ship surged with another impact as if to emphasize this point, even as the Hellmarine pried the doors open with his bare hands.

The docking bay was nearly completely destroyed, but by the light of the alarms, the Hellmarine could make out the shape of the Zintari gateway awaiting him against the bulkhead opposite of him. With it were Seraphiel, Mandy, and most of the Marines.

"Oh my God!" Mandy gasped as he stepped into the docking bay, rushing over to him with the medical gauntlet at the ready.

"Nice of you to show up," King joked as the others got back to their feet. The docking bay was littered with the bodies of Demons and Ghenzul alike.

"Lost my helmet," the Hellmarine responded weakly, earning him a low chuckle from some of the Marines. "Let's go."

Seraphiel placed a hand on his chest plate, offering a small healing spell to assist Mandy as she tried to get a comprehensive readout of his injuries and figure out where to start. "I am excited to roughly fuck you later, Hellmarine."

The Hellmarine said nothing, but his eyes did shoot open a bit more. Mandy raised a brow at him, then glanced at the Angel who met her gaze readily. "Provided I receive the blessing of all previously invested parties, of course," Seraphiel amended.

The doctor initially let out a girly and unintimidating growl but shrugged the Angel off, turning her attention back to the Hellmarine and his wounds.

"Shit, that sounds like a good consolation to me," Cox laughed, shouldering his Perforator before slinging one of the Hellmarine's arms around him to help support the man. "Lucky bastard. Wish we all had a little R&R like that lined up after this shitshow."

"I wasn't aware Angels even had sex," Romero remarked, assisting Cox in carrying the Hellmarine.

"Of course," Seraphiel assured him. "Such is the propagation and affirmation of life. For those of us in the field, it's a small reminder of the bliss of our home domain—even if just for a moment."

Romero's head bobbed from side to side, considering the perspective Seraphiel presented to him. "I suppose that checks out."

The Marines filed through the gateway after it was opened from the other side, presumably on a preset schedule. As they did, the shrieking and screeching of more Ghenzul overrunning the ship drew nearer. It wouldn't be long until the ship was completely theirs, ready to be fully converted. The Hellmarine noticed King hanging back with a bundle of explosives as everyone else abandoned the Zintari ship for the Midnight Sea.

"What are you doing?" the Hellmarine asked, pulling away from the Marines practically carrying him toward the gateway. They moved to intercept him but King raised a hand to assure them he had the situation handled. Cox and Romero exchanged glances before heading through the gateway, practically dragging the doctor along with them.

"Timer's busted," King noted, tapping the side of the explosives. "Can't remote detonate from the other side, and the Interdictor will make it impossible to trigger the main charge in engineering from here. Push button only."

"No," the Hellmarine grunted, reaching for the bundle. "I'll do it. You go."

King caught his wrist an inch from the device and held it firmly in place. "I got this one, big man. You go ahead and fuck the shit out of that Angel, eh?"

The Hellmarine tried to break the man's grip but, in his state, found that he was almost as weak as a kitten against King. King held him for longer as if to emphasize the point that there wasn't anything the Hellmarine could do to stop him. "You kill that Overlord?"

"Yeah," the Hellmarine responded with a nod. "Do the others know what you're doing?"

"No," King answered honestly. "They think I'm setting the charge, which is only technically true."

"I can't let you do this," the Hellmarine warned before catching a punch across the face, rattling his senses. King grabbed the Hellmarine by the chest plate and lifted him off the ground in an incredible show of strength, even for his considerable size.

"You're not letting me do anything," King corrected him, walking the Hellmarine over to the gateway while holding him a foot off the ground. "I go out on my own terms. No one makes that decision for me. Just like you."

"King," the Hellmarine objected weakly, gripping the man's hands tightly as he tried to muster his strength. If he could overpower him, even for a second, he could change things. "You can't."

"Just tell them I hit you," King suggested.

The Hellmarine frowned slightly, his brows furrowing. "You did hit me."

"I know," King chuckled, amused with himself. "I just want them to know."

King put the Hellmarine through the Zintari gateway with a fierce shove, sending him tumbling to the platform on the Midnight Sea where the other gate rested. He rolled almost the entire length of the ramp, coming to a stop with a slight groan. Mandy, Simms, and a handful of corpsmen were on him in an instant, working to free him from his armor while struggling to address the worst of his wounds.

"Where's King?" Cox asked, glancing back at the gateway. The center of the standing stone stopped abruptly, and the terminal hooked up to the stone indicated that the connection had been lost. "What's going on?"

"Where is he?" Miller repeated for Cox, stepping closer to the Hellmarine. Several of the others stood between them as the tension began to spike. "What the fuck did you do!?"

"He had to stay behind," the Hellmarine answered weakly, directing his explanation at Gray, who looked on coldly. "Busted timer, no signal."

"No," Miller objected, turning toward Greer near the terminal. "That's bullshit. Get it back up! NOW!"

Greer punched the address to the other gateway without hesitation. The terminal flashed, indicator, and address error.

"No, no," Miller muttered, pushing Greer out of the way and feeding the address into the terminal again with his own hands. "We can still get him out of there."

Once again, the terminal displayed the incorrect address error. The gateway on the other side had been destroyed when King triggered the detonation. There was no way for them to reach him. There was nothing left of the man to be reached.

"God, fucking DAMMIT!" Miller said, punching the panel of the terminal and shattering it before turning on the injured Hellmarine again. "You motherfucker, you just left him there to die!"

"That's enough, Miller," Gray interrupted. The Hellmarine couldn't tell how the Master Sergeant felt about it, but he wasn't about to have another brawl break out with Miller losing his composure. "As you were."

"No!" Miller shouted, pulling his helmet off and hurling it across the docking bay. "This is bullshit! These motherfuckers ain't human, Sarge! They don't give a fuck about us. Every time it's up to one of them, one of us gets sacrificed!"

"Whoa, man," Cox said, holding a hand out. "It's not like that, and you know it."

"Just take a breath," Chambers advised him, her voice cracking slightly. "Cool off."

"Cool off?" Miller snapped back incredulously. "What if it were one of you, huh!? Would you want me to cool off then? What if it were me? We got enough to worry about out here in the fucking boonies between Demons and Ghenzul, and now this motherfucker and his Angel side-piece are throwing us into the fire so they don't have to risk their own necks!"

"Excuse me?" Seraphiel responded, arching a brow dangerously as she turned to face him. "I have done everything I could, and I'm certain the same is true for the Hellmarine judging by the state of him. Who are you to question—"

"I said ENOUGH!" the Master Sergeant roared, shutting down any further verbal exchange. "Report to the armor bay, then medical. Not one word out of you unless it's 'aye aye, Sarge' or an answer to a direct question from corpsmen, medic, or doctor. Understood?"

"Aye aye, Sarge," the Marines replied with varying levels of enthusiasm before being dismissed.

"You too," the Master Sergeant said to Simms as the medic looked up from the Hellmarine's wounds. "Let the doc do her job."

The medic exchanged a brief look with the doctor before getting to his feet. "Aye aye."

With the last of the Marines dismissed, the Master Sergeant glanced down at Mandy and the Hellmarine before giving the remaining crew a pointed look and excusing himself. Turning her attention back to the Hellmarine, Mandy injected something into his neck that caused his head to swim immediately and his vision to grow dark as he slipped into unconsciousness.

CHAPTER 29

THE HELLMARINE MISSED KING'S ceremony during the week of his medically induced coma, as well as the ceremonies for all the other lives that had been lost in the recent conflicts. By the time the Midnight Sea had reached the site of the battle, there had been little left to do but lay the dead to rest. All ships involved had been obliterated in a cascading series of riftcore breaches.

Miller's anger had not ebbed by the time the Hellmarine regained consciousness. Various reviews were being conducted on how the mission had gone, and so far, a consensus had not been reached. It seemed to split along the usual lines, with the Navy indicating that the Marines had dropped the ball and that the Marines were doing the best with what they had available to them in their diminished state in the Outer Colonies. Captain Horne was regarded as a holdout in the Navy, having sided with the Marines.

People went over the events time and again, pointing out where the fault with the timing mechanism for the explosives was, how Interdictors interrupted Riftspace and communication, the unique nature of the Overlord, and the surprise appearance of the Ghenzul in the first place. Miller brought the question forward about how much of the Alliance's resources had been squandered on jumping to the aid of alien species and how much was being lost to the Ghenzul while focused on Demonkind. Hawkins amplified that question, posing it to other admirals throughout the Navy.

"Black was a hero," Hawkins said in the recording the Hellmarine viewed in his quarters following his discharge from medbay. "And now we've lost another member of his unit with a distinguished record."

The fact that King had been popular with nearly everyone on the ship and others he'd been in combat with didn't help matters. Those onboard the Midnight Sea were beginning to ask many of the same questions that the top brass were kicking around to determine who to blame for what they saw as a failure.

It was irrational, of course. The Hellmarine slayed the Overlord. It was a win, not a loss, but as emotional as people were, and as little as most knew about the threat they had faced, that fact was easily ignored.

"Life is the goal," Captain Horne had argued in the same recording. "Whether that is human life, Arlier life, or Zintari life is immaterial. Demonkind grows through the elimination of all life across the multiverse. It doesn't distinguish between various species or worlds. They want it all. If all we take away from this is the best way to protect ourselves, then know that the protection of all sentient life is, indeed, the best way to achieve that aim."

The captain of the Zintari vessel and the survivors from the Arlier attack were invited to speak to drive the point home that the lives lost were just a taste of how much worse it could be. Men had given their lives in understanding of that fact, and to label them as mistakes was a massive disservice to them. A man's life should never be spent frivolously, but if it must be done, it should be in the defense of the lives of others. Such sacrifice was the antithesis of frivolity.

To the Hellmarine, it seemed all academic and pointless. He clearly remembered what King said to him just before he was tossed through the gateway. The man wanted to go out on his terms, and that was what mattered most to the Hellmarine. It was the same choice that Black had made and the same choice anyone should have been afforded. He winced at the pain in his side as he leaned forward and toggled the recording off. The area where he'd been impaled was still tender despite the intensive work that had been done on him while unconscious in medbay.

Before he'd fully reclined back into his seat, the door chime sounded. Sighing, the Hellmarine supposed it was only a matter of time before someone came to check on him. "Come."

The door opened, and Seraphiel stepped in, wearing a casual-fit white top and white skirt with sandals. It was the first time the Hellmarine had seen her in such a relaxed state. "I heard you were finally awake."

"Mandy?" the Hellmarine theorized.

Seraphiel nodded as the door closed behind her. She glanced around the spartan personal quarters before letting her gaze settle on him. "We've been in frequent communication with one another. She's been alleviating our concerns with updates on your condition."

"Our?" the Hellmarine asked, raising a brow as he sat back on the plain gray couch.

"Namely myself and the Overmaiden," Seraphiel clarified. "Many of the others to a lesser extent, but mainly us."

The Hellmarine appreciated how direct and honest the Angel was. It wasn't as though she wasn't capable of deception; she simply saw little need for dissembling and obfuscating in casual conversation. She was like him in that way. "I appreciate it."

"Mandy suggested that it might help your recovery along if I came here to have sex with you," Seraphiel explained casually, walking over to the Hellmarine's bed and sitting down on it with crossed legs. "Do you concur with her professional opinion as your personal physician?"

"Not opposed," the Hellmarine grunted, visibly contemplating the nonchalant proposition. "But...Mandy said that?"

"If you're worried about how she'll feel about it after your private tryst with the Overmaiden, you needn't be," Seraphiel continued, brushing her golden hair over her shoulder. "They've talked things out, with each other, and with me, and we've all come to something of an arrangement."

"An arrangement," the Hellmarine echoed as he slowly got to his feet. The pain in his torso made it difficult for him to retain his usual facade entirely, but he managed well enough.

"About sexual activity between us and you," Seraphiel elaborated. "None of us have any sexual or romantic interest in anyone other than you, so compromise was necessary. We've decided that in our current predicament, given how complex of an organism you are, it would be in our best interest to embrace our natural role in catering to your particular needs. Hughes, for her part, cares deeply for you in a romantic capacity, even if she wishes to dress it up as concern for your well-being. The Overmaiden desires a closer bond with you as well, but her feelings are confused and mixed with long forgotten impulses and arousal. She is exploring what it means to be human in an inhuman state, and sees you as having that deeply in common with her. We figure you both will benefit from exploring this together."

The Hellmarine wandered a little closer to the Angel as she eyed him like a piece of prime meat. It was a look he'd thought he'd seen on her before a few times but had always written it off. He'd reasoned that she was just too alien for him to comprehend. "And you?"

"I want sex," Seraphiel admitted freely. "Preferably with someone whose physiology might be able to keep up with my needs. Though no longer a member of the Heavenly Host, and thus possessing a diminished version of my previous ability, I am still well above what the average human male could fully satisfy. They might even be in danger if I were to take control. I have an inkling you might be a different story."

"You had a pretty low opinion of me before," the Hellmarine pointed out, towering over the woman sitting on the edge of his bed. She uncrossed her legs to sit a little more upright, her gaze fixed with his.

"Recent events have forced me to...reconsider," Seraphiel admitted. Now, she was beginning to become unusually evasive. "I'm a pragmatic creature, after all."

"Reconsider," the Hellmarine repeated with amusement. "So I'm *not* a monster?"

"You surely are," Seraphiel argued. "But you happen to be the kind of monster that we need. The kind of monster spoken of in myths and legends. More importantly, inside you beats the heart of a principled and determined man—which seems to keep all the worst things you're capable of in check."

"Your flirting needs work," the Hellmarine murmured, finding the mix of honesty and backhanded compliments to be unconventional, to say the least. There was no denying that it had a certain appeal and that the woman herself was physically tantalizing, however.

"You could be right," Seraphiel admitted freely. "The nuances of courtship are unfamiliar to me. However, my hope is that my honesty and directness will make up for it."

"It does," the Hellmarine agreed with a slight smirk.

"Your actions in our last battle were nothing short of exemplary," Seraphiel continued. "I found myself drawn to you but feared that I had come to the realization too late. I was certain that your life would be lost in the fight against the Overlord. Violently defying such a sure fate only aroused me further."

The Hellmarine's brows furrowed as he replayed her words in his head just to be sure that he'd gotten it right. "My fight with the Overlord made you horny?"

"Exceedingly," Seraphiel replied huskily, her eyes flashing with a lustful hunger. "I've found pleasuring myself to the memory of your deeds insufficient in sating my desire, but it's all I can think about in quiet moments. I even subscribed to many of the EroStreams that Cox told me about to see if I could find productions with similar visuals, but to no avail."

"Hm," the Hellmarine grunted. He was learning a lot about the woman in a very short amount of time, the most intriguing of which was that she was something of a sexual deviant.

"Do my proclivities disturb you?" Seraphiel inquired, not looking the least bit self-conscious about her admissions.

"Not really," the Hellmarine answered. "Just unexpected from an Angel."

"I would like very much to disabuse you of your preconceived notions about my kind if you're open to it," the Angel continued, placing her fingers along the waistband of his sweatpants. Judging by the bulge that had only grown larger as the conversation progressed, she likely had a good idea of what her chances were with him. "May I?"

"...Yeah," the Hellmarine agreed. No sooner had the word fallen from his lips that the Angel pulled the waistline of his pants down to reveal the impressive manhood that awaited her beneath. Her fingers moved about the shaft delicately, appraising it like a fine jewel as she tilted her head from one side to the other.

"Impressive specimen," Seraphiel said with a little smirk, glancing up at him. "I wonder if I can even fit it all in my mouth."

The Hellmarine wanted to believe in her, but didn't bother to voice as much. The Angel went for it regardless, suckling at the tip of his glans briefly before drawing the rest of him into her mouth an inch at a time. He couldn't deny how impressive it was when he felt himself brush past the back of her throat and down to points beyond. She didn't struggle with it, and her eyes remained firmly directed at his. He realized she didn't just want to fuck; she wanted to truly impress him.

Her head bobbed back and forth a few times before one of her hands joined around the shaft, twisting and turning in complementary motions in time with her mouth. With her other hand, she fondled his scrotum, delicately balancing the weight of his balls between them as the motions of her head became increasingly more aggressive—hungrier.

Before he knew it, the Angel was peeling the scant clothing she'd been wearing off. Her body was a work of art, the likes of which artists had struggled to capture in paint or marble for untold generations. Her pale, perky breasts were larger than he'd realized, likely due to how often he saw her wearing armor. Her legs were supple and long, with powerful muscle lurking just beneath the petal-soft surface of her flawless skin. More impressive was the elegant pink shade of her slit, topped with a tuft of golden hair as she leaned back onto the bed and spread her legs.

"Mmm...Enough foreplay," she said, breathing heavier with anticipation. "I want that monstrous thing inside me."

Without a word, the Hellmarine grabbed her by the legs and pulled her back to the edge of the bed, flipping her over until she was bent over the side of it. If she wanted something rougher and more primal, he figured this would be the perfect position to start with. Seraphiel let out a little delighted gasp, signaling that he was on the right track.

There was no warning to brace herself or even a slow pace to get her acclimated to the size and strength of his cock. She'd boasted a superior physique over that of men, so he saw no reason to be gentle with her. He deftly drove himself into her, bottoming out in a single stroke before retreating and beginning the process anew. "Oh, yes!" she moaned, glowing eyes rolling back. Her satisfied groans and gasps signaled to him that, once again, he'd read her perfectly. "Hellmarine, yes!"

The Hellmarine's pace only increased from that point as he ignored the pain and protest of his healing wounds and focused only on the warm, sultry embrace of the Angel's most intimate gift. As his strokes grew more brutal and less refined, Seraphiel moaned louder, portions of her divine aura beginning to visibly flicker as she surrendered herself to the experience. It was a strange phenomenon to behold as he received brief glimpses into her mind, the pleasure she felt, and the echoes of a home she'd resigned herself to never seeing again.

He could hear her voice in his head, sighing and caressing his consciousness even as he drove deeper into her.

"More," Seraphiel's voice echoed through his mind. "I want to know your brutality."

Reaching around, he grabbed her neck and bent her backward, holding her at an odd angle that kept her fully restrained within his grip.

"Yes! Like this!" her voice gasped in his mind as she let out a feral growl to mirror his. Her wings flickered and fluttered in and out of existence as her aura grew more visible and well-defined. He realized, somehow, that her ability to keep such things in check was almost an active effort on her part. As her focus broke down in the throes of carnal pleasure, her will to hold back those parts of her waned.

Seraphiel's wings and halo completed their appearance at last, wings spreading as wide as they could within the cramped space, beating a few times with excitement. "Harder!"

The Hellmarine growled, gripping her hip tighter as he pulled her into each railing stroke. She gasped and groaned, her eyes rolling back into her head even as they began to emanate a subtle golden light.

"Fuck meee!" The Angel pleaded aloud even as her words echoed throughout the Hellmarine's mind. The intimate plea broke a second later, stretching into a silent scream as the Angel reached her breaking point. Her tight insides constricted further, threatening to take a piece of him with her through the violent chaos of orgasm as she rode the wave of ecstasy to completion. The power of her climax echoed and reverberated through him as well, triggering a reflexive release from him unexpectedly.

The Angel milked him vigorously despite him seemingly being the one in control of things. She took every last ounce of him in, drinking deep of his virile lust as her wings spasmed in time with her hips. Her body twisted and bowed, bidding his to do the same in a silent chorus of climax they shared together as one. It was impossible to separate which part of the experience was his and which was hers.

Seraphiel pulled off of him the moment they began to come down from the height of their euphoria, rolling onto her side and spreading her legs, presenting her freshly fucked pussy to him. "Again, Hellmarine."

Unable to shake the lingering deliciousness of Angelic orgasm that still reverberated through him, the Hellmarine moved on her, plunging recklessly into her depths. There was no stopping the two of them as they rolled around on the bed in various positions, challenging one another to more rounds and new heights. Each orgasm they hit together was more intense than the last, synching their intentions and desires more closely each time. They began to anticipate the movements of the other without words as the Hellmarine felt his mind reaching out to hers. It wasn't just their bodies that were intertwining with one another; it was much more—something ineffable that he wasn't equipped to describe.

Hours passed before they found their way back to themselves, collapsing onto the sweaty sheets of the bed as they reeled from the experience. They didn't say anything, only staring up at the ceiling for a while before allowing themselves to dare glance at each other. Stolen glances became gazes that gave way to rest. The Hellmarine slept soundly for a time while Seraphiel remained with him in a meditative state against him.

"I see you two had a fun time," Mandy huffed as she let herself into the room, pulling the Hellmarine abruptly from his slumber. For a moment, he thought that she was upset at finding them together but then realized what time it was as he glanced at the clock beside his bed.

"I missed it," he groaned, falling back onto the mattress.

"You missed it," Mandy repeated, dropping her kit onto the foot of the bed. Opening it to pull a hand scanner from inside, she shot Seraphiel a look of reprimand. "Did you know he had an appointment for a follow-up so I could monitor his healing?"

"I didn't," Seraphiel answered casually, running her fingers through her tousled hair. "But it didn't come up. I was rather insistent."

"Oh," Mandy muttered, placing the scanner close to the Hellmarine's abdomen before starting the sequence. "Well, I guess that lets him off the hook this time."

"Wonderful," Seraphiel remarked, throwing the sheets off of herself to snatch up the bag and look through it.

"What are you doing?" Mandy snapped, grabbing the bag back and putting it on the side of the bed furthest from Seraphiel. "That's not for you."

"I require hydration," Seraphiel responded calmly. "Don't you have water in your kit?"

"No," Mandy objected. The Hellmarine couldn't tell if she was lying with how strange and awkward her tone had become. "Get your own water."

Seraphiel stared at Mandy pointedly, blinking slowly a few times before the doctor finally pulled a bottle of water from her bag and tossed it to the Angel. Seraphiel cracked the seal and threw back half of the bottle's contents before offering some to the Hellmarine.

"You seem...almost entirely healed," Mandy noted, somewhat surprised. "More than I expected, at least. Even with your natural healing, this is shocking."

"The Divine Energy of my aura likely assisted the process," Seraphiel suggested as the Hellmarine finished the rest of the bottled water. "It becomes rather potent during sexual acts."

"R-really?" Mandy asked, her brows shooting up a little self-consciously. "It's that good?"

"It is pretty good," the Hellmarine confirmed.

"You can sample it for yourself with us if you'd like," Seraphiel offered coyly, quirking a brow toward the woman. "I've no intention to leave you out. But unfortunately, it will have to wait until another time. I have business of my own to attend to."

"Right. Yeah. Sure," Mandy said, shrugging several times and laughing uneasily. "We can uh...we can have our threesome later. No problem."

Seraphiel rose from the bed and circled around toward Mandy, where she bent down at the waist and placed a gentle kiss on her cheek. "Relax, little doctor. We will be gentle."

The doctor laughed nervously as her cheeks grew bright red, her eyes darting between the Angel and the Hellmarine.

"So it's fine?" The Hellmarine asked, nodding toward the scanner to change the subject as the Angel dressed herself. "I can return to duty?"

"Physically, yes, but I thought it might be important to speak with you about the psychological wounds you suffered during the last mission," Mandy said a little more seriously, some of the color lingering in her cheeks. "About King."

"What about him?" the Hellmarine asked as he rose from the bed as well in search of his clothes. Seraphiel tossed his sweatpants at him. Somehow, they'd found their way onto the floor next to the front door during their sexual excursion.

"Well, first there was Black and now King. Two comrades lost in a very short time period," the doctor continued, holding his gaze with her own. "It's customary to talk about how that makes us feel so we can determine any long-term effects it might have on us."

"Hm," the Hellmarine grunted, pulling on his shirt and glancing at Seraphiel. "Did you?"

"I did," Seraphiel said with a nod of assurance. "I do not understand it, but I am also not the expert. She is."

"Alright," the Hellmarine agreed, looking at Mandy. "What should I be feeling?"

"It's not my job to tell you how you feel," Mandy chuckled with amusement. "You tell *me* how you feel and we work through it together. Guilt is a common response to such situations, but there are a myriad of other responses to such trauma."

"What about happy?" the Hellmarine asked.

"H-happy?" Mandy repeated uncertainly. "You're happy he's dead?"

"No," the Hellmarine answered. "I'm happy he got what he wanted. He told me it was what he wanted—to go out on his own terms. He told me this."

"He did?" Seraphiel asked, pausing as she put on her sandals.

"I objected," the Hellmarine added as a matter of course with a shrug. "But he insisted. He wasn't angry. He wasn't sad. He hit me."

"He...hit you," Mandy laughed a little, covering her mouth with one hand.

"He wanted everyone to know that," the Hellmarine said with an affirmative nod, finding a fresh pair of socks in the dresser and pulling them on.

"From the little I knew of him, he would not want us to mourn him overly much," Seraphiel remarked thoughtfully. "He liked to jest. To bring laughter to his companions. I believe asking you to tell everyone he hit you was for that purpose."

"Probably," the Hellmarine admitted as he grabbed his boots.

"Wait, where do you think you're going?" Mandy said, holding a hand out toward him.

"Need to talk to the captain," the Hellmarine said, lacing his boots up swiftly. "About Hawkins."

"What about him?" Mandy asked, glancing at Seraphiel for a clue, but the Angel knew as little about it as her.

The Hellmarine finished with his boots and stood, glancing between the pair of beautiful women. There was a part of him that wanted to just wile away the hours with them—have a day entirely of rest and sex in varying intervals. He missed the way Mandy liked to curl up in his lap and do her best to wrap her arms and legs around him, how she'd plant kisses so gently on his chest like she was hoping he wouldn't notice. And of course his sexual chemistry with Seraphiel deserved a mention too.

But there was still a lot of fighting to be done, and new fronts had opened up that needed to be addressed. "About Cosgrove and the Overlord. I'm pretty sure he's the one that orchestrated all of it."

CHAPTER 30

"IT'S A COMPELLING THEORY," Captain Horne said, rubbing his chin through his beard. "But I can't present this to Naval Command without some concrete evidence."

The Hellmarine sat back in the chair across from the captain's desk. Mandy sat beside him looking frustrated at the captain's inaction, but was unwilling to say anything about it.

"To be clear," Captain Horne clarified, holding a finger up toward the doctor. "I am in agreement with your hypothesis. But leveling such an accusation at a vice admiral requires a mountain of evidence. Especially against the one who has been holding together the fleet responsible for keeping the struggles of the Outer Colonies from becoming the struggles of the rest of the Alliance."

"It's already happening," the Hellmarine argued calmly. "Rifts and portals pulled into Hellspace become new attack vectors, captain."

"It's only a matter of time before the Demons discover one that bypasses the lines and goes into the heart of the Alliance," Mandy added. "Hawkins nearly accelerated that by creating the Overlord."

"Allegedly," the captain clarified, but her point was made all the same.

The holoprojectors in the corners of the room flickered as the Overmaiden appeared. "I believe I can be of assistance on this."

"Wonderful, another one," Horne sighed before the projector on his desk activated, showing a dump of information from the database of the Hammer of the Gods. It took him a moment to realize what he was looking at. When he did, he sat up wide-eyed, glancing at the hologram of the AI. "What did you do?"

"Technically, I did very little," the Overmaiden responded. "The Caretaker was more than prepared for me to attempt something against the vice admiral's systems. However, Greer is accustomed to using less conventional methods of obtaining information and managed to make contact with Dr. Cosgrove through a series of back channels he was...unwilling to disclose to me."

"Cosgrove just gave this up?" the captain asked, reaching out and scrolling through some of the information quickly. "Why?"

"It would seem that his service aboard the Hammer of the Gods is much more compulsory than we originally realized," the Overmaiden answered, glancing over at Mandy sympathetically. The Hellmarine did the same, realizing it must have come as a relief to know that her mentor was not the traitor they had believed him to be. It also raised questions about his safety, however.

"What does it say?" the Hellmarine asked, leaning forward in his chair once again. From his side of the desk, the information was an incoherent jumble of images of text.

"It would seem to confirm your suspicions," the captain answered, spinning the display around for him and Mandy to see. Much of the information was Cosgrove's own files, duplicated and transferred to the Hammer of the Gods, where they were further expanded into other tests.

"Project Upheaval," the Hellmarine murmured as he quickly skimmed the files pertaining to the Overlord. Because the theory of such an entity being postulated to occur naturally at some point in Hellspace, creating one came with a perfect cover. They'd injected a Soldier Demon with the modified serum before sending it on its way to begin wreaking havoc on Hell's hierarchy from within.

"This is why Hawkins tried to reassign us to the Orc thing," the captain concluded, anger smoldering behind his steely eyes. "The Overlord required time to gestate and gain strength. We had very nearly interrupted it with our own operation. He couldn't risk us doing so again."

"But he's the one that assigned us there," Mandy objected, confused. "Why would he send us there if he knew it was there?"

"He didn't," the Overmaiden said, her tone growing darker. "The Overlord was created in Hell, using the Hellrift on Taobos's moon that was supposed to be closed after our departure. Telemetry lifted from his probe indicates that the rift remained open for a time while Alliance tags traversed it multiple times."

"Likely, he didn't expect it to find a way out so soon," Horne suggested. "Then he saw the data and images from the battle of Vizuno and realized that the Overlord had already found its way back into standard space through a separate Hellrift."

"So what now?" the Hellmarine asked, his expression growing more intense. "We have the evidence."

"It's too dangerous to transmit," the captain said, glancing at the Overmaiden as he considered his options. "Gray is up for commendation and promotion, so we'll be pulling back to the middle colonies for the ceremony. He'll be made lieutenant. There, we should be able to meet with a trusted officer who can make use of the information back at Naval Command."

"Seraphiel will also be promoted," the Overmaiden added with a slightly more pleasant expression. "Miller is to be reassigned."

"How long will this take?" the Hellmarine wondered impatiently. He wanted action on things yesterday only to be told it was going to take more time before justice was served. Vengeance was a lot easier—more direct.

"Not long," the captain assured him. "We'll be making the jump in a matter of—"

The lights of the captain's office flickered as the holographic images projected in the room scrambled and disappeared entirely. With a furrowed brow, the captain tapped a button on his desk. "Ops, what the Hell is going on?"

"Not sure, captain," the officer responded. "Some kind of system-wide power drain. We're trying to track it down now."

Mandy and the Hellmarine exchanged glances as they rose from their chairs. The timing seemed incredibly suspicious. The comm squawked again, but it was little more than garbled words amid static. The captain jumped to his feet and stormed out of his office with the Hellmarine and doctor in tow.

Captain Horne stopped short as they arrived on the bridge. Vice Admiral Hawkins stood next to the captain's chair, his hands clasped calmly behind his back. "Captain Horne, I was just coming to speak with you."

"Vice Admiral Hawkins," Horne acknowledged, glancing at the rest of the bridge crew who appeared stunned into silence. None of them seemed to know what was going on. Even emergency lighting was struggling to stay online amid the darkness of the bridge. "What's happening?"

"Oh, I think you know," Hawkins responded coolly. "It seems some confidential information above your clearance level has found its way into your database. I've simply come to retrieve it and scrub it from your systems."

"Confidential information?" the captain asked, playing dumb as the Hellmarine slowly paced in a wide circle along the periphery of the bridge, poised to strike.

"Let's not play any more games," the vice admiral scoffed before pointing in the direction of the Hellmarine. "And you had best think twice before attempting anything. You're not nearly as stealthy as you think you are. Not with me, anyway."

"Meaning?" the Hellmarine asked, abandoning any pretense of subtlety as he entered the poorly lit center of the bridge. He noticed that the vice admiral wasn't wearing the typical uniform for the Navy. He was wearing something that stood between a power armor's undersuit and a uniform, completely black in color.

"Meaning that even with your enhancements, I've been in the stealth and secrecy game a lot longer than you, son," Hawkins clarified, motioning vaguely toward the lights. "The sensors of the Midnight Sea weren't nearly good enough to even see me coming."

"But I see you now," the Hellmarine warned, his hands balling into fists. "Big mistake."

"You ought to spend a little more time doing other things," the vice admiral laughed derisively. "Maybe poker so you know when you're not holding a winning hand, hm?"

"What did you do?" the captain asked, taking a tentative step forward. "Where's the Overmaiden?"

"Set to be decompiled, I'm afraid," the vice admiral replied calmly. A cocky smirk appeared on his face when the Hellmarine instantly cracked the table his hand had been resting on. "No hard feelings, big fella, I know she was basically your Mommy, always telling you what to do and making sure you made it to your appointments on time. She just knew too much. It's either that or we blow the whole damn ship, but we're over-extended as it is. Would be like cutting off my nose to spite my face."

"You expect us to just stay quiet about everything after all we've discovered?" Mandy asked incredulously.

"If you want Cosgrove to see another birthday, you will," Hawkins shot back. "Or if your helmsman's mee-maw is to avoid a tragic fall down the stairs or if you want Master Sergeant Gray's daughter to have a safe trip back home."

The vice admiral shrugged. "The choice is yours. I wouldn't come here personally without having a great deal of insurance to keep me safe around such a hulking monster."

"Right," Horne muttered. "And why exactly are you here? You seem to have the capability to have gotten in and out without us ever knowing."

"Excellent observation," the vice admiral chuckled, holding up a hand. "I came here to make a point."

"What point?" the Hellmarine growled, the veins in his arms swelling as he struggled to restrain his rage.

"First of all, to stay out of my business and stay in your fucking lane," the vice admiral snapped, staring daggers at the Hellmarine. "You've no idea what we're dealing with beyond the myopic view you were given in that serum. Demons are a blight, but one that will pass—a mindless procession of hordes that are ultimately rather straightforward to handle. But other alien species will still be here when they're gone. And when we're stretched thin from defending ourselves and the rest of creation against Demons, everyone else will move in for the kill. I'm looking beyond Demons—beyond the current conflict to the next one and the one after that."

The Hellmarine shook his head in disgust. In his view, this wasn't looking forward; it was looking behind. Hawkins wanted to use the confusion and fighting with Demons to make gains of his own before anyone else might think to do so. Either he didn't realize he was the only one spoiling for that fight, or he didn't care. He was going to do it anyway.

"Now, I'm willing to let you all off with a little slap on the wrist, as I still have a use for you out here. But know that I won't hesitate to be done with you should you decide to put so much as a toe out of line," the vice admiral snarled toward the Hellmarine and Captain Horne. "I guess the key point you should take from this is that the house always wins."

With the speed of a striking snake, the Hellmarine lashed out and seized the vice admiral by the throat and squeezed. "Not today."

To the Hellmarine's surprise, Hawkins only smiled. "If that's the way you want to handle it, go ahead," he rasped. "Don't think there won't be consequences, though. Every member of this crew and its Marine detachment has someone or something to lose should news of my demise reach the Onyx Tower."

"Don't," Captain Horne said, holding a hand out toward the Hellmarine with an expression as though someone had walked over his grave. "He's not fucking around."

"Captain," the Hellmarine objected, maintaining a firm grip on the smug vice admiral.

"Let him go," the captain said weakly. "That's an order."

After a moment of hesitation, the Hellmarine did as the captain said. Vice Admiral Hawkins coughed a few times and rubbed his throat but seemed otherwise unphased by his brush with the Hellmarine. He smiled back at them smugly, knowing that he not only held the winning hand—he held all the cards.

"Prudent decision," the vice admiral said, regaining his composure. "It would be unfortunate if we were to all lose our tempers. That's how mistakes happen. Best to let cooler heads prevail, hm?"

"You've made your point and recovered your data," Captain Horne growled furiously. "Now get the fuck off my ship."

"Very well," Hawkins acknowledged with a shrug. "Remember what I said. Keep your noses out of my business, keep your collective mouths shut, adhere to the objectives I assign to you, and there won't be a problem. So long as you remain useful and compliant, you have nothing to fear from me."

Hawkins paused to look between the individuals on the bridge to ascertain whether or not each of them understood the threat he'd issued them. Seeing it had been received the way he wished, he gave them a final nod before emergency lighting failed. When it came back online, followed immediately by standard lighting and normal power to the rest of the ship, the vice admiral was gone.

"Anything on sensors?" Captain Horne asked, seeming to know the answer to the question.

"Nothing, sir," the Helmsman muttered begrudgingly. "There's nothing out there."

The Hellmarine turned to Captain Horne. "Bring her back online. Now."

The captain looked pityingly at the Hellmarine, then around at the other faces in the room. "Hellmarine, I don't think I can."

"Then I kill Hawkins. Brace for the consequences."

The holoprojectors on the bridge flickered and came online again, projecting the Overmaiden at normal size front and center. "I'm very touched by your concern, but that won't be necessary at the moment."

"Overmaiden?" the captain asked suspiciously, raising a brow toward her. "Explain yourself immediately."

The Hellmarine's eyes widened as he took a step closer to the Ghost AI. "Yes, explain."

"What the vice admiral caught speaking with you was only a partitioned fragment of myself," the Overmaiden explained with a slight smirk. "During the battle, I had partitioned myself in several different directions to facilitate coordination on multiple fronts. While it reduces my individual processing power, enough of it remained between these disparate pieces to rebuild myself when the partition in the ship's computer was removed."

"Are you still you?" the Hellmarine asked, recalling some of the questions and concerns she had about the nature of herself when they had been alone.

"Yes," the Overmaiden assured him. "Much less of me was lost in the ship's computer than existed in these different places. Greer had some, my emitter in the Retreat had some, and even Twilight was holding onto some. All of these were air-gapped from the Midnight Sea. It took a moment for me to pull myself together once I was certain that Hawkins had left."

"That doesn't seem like enough to reconstitute you," the captain said doubtfully. "How do we know you aren't a version of the Overmaiden that Hawkins hasn't left behind for us."

"Well," the Overmaiden mused. "I suppose you could just ask Greer. He had me stored in the Malur ship's computer to assist with decryption. The storage space there is more than ample enough to contain the entirety of my matrix. But if you require something more personal, I could—"

"That will do for now," Captain Horne said, holding up his hand. "I'm convinced."

"The unconventional channels," Mandy laughed to herself. "He was using Malur carrier signals to reach out to people! The encryption is too tough to casually decrypt without considerable effort and likely went unnoticed by anyone in the area."

"Very observant," the Overmaiden responded with a little smile.

Despite their stroking of each other's egos, the Hellmarine remained in a sour mood, thinking about how the vice admiral had simply walked onto the bridge, rubbed their noses in everything, and walked away. He'd even attempted to murder the Overmaiden. Unacceptable. "Now what?" he rumbled.

The others grew a little quiet. Despite the fact that they still had the Overmaiden and presumably the data that the vice admiral had sought to remove, the threat he'd made still stood. If they were to do anything suspicious, an untold amount of civilians would be harmed as retribution. The Hellmarine looked over toward the captain again. "Why did you have me release him?"

"The Onyx Tower," the captain said, glancing uneasily between the various individuals on the bridge. "They're a secret, semi-rogue sub-section of Naval intelligence believed to be dismantled a few decades ago. They simply went underground. Very few people know that they ever existed or that they still do."

"How do you know about them?" The Hellmarine asked as he approached the captain, a look of concern on his face.

The captain waved a hand and heaved a sigh. "That's a story for another time, I think. What bothers me is that he somehow knew I would recognize the name drop and realize just how serious of a situation we were in. No one should know that I know about the Onyx Tower."

"But he did," the Hellmarine murmured. If they were as serious as the captain implied, then he had no reason to doubt that the vice admiral had the means to make good on the threats he'd made. It had to be assumed that anything tied to the Navy or the Alliance as a whole had to be compromised to some degree or otherwise known to the vice admiral. If he didn't know it already, he had the means to do so rather quickly.

"Gray to Captain Horne," the Master Sergeant's voice hailed over the comm system.

"Go ahead, Master Sergeant," the captain groaned, rubbing the bridge of his nose.

"Miller's gone, sir. We just did a head count and a ship-wide scan...he's nowhere to be found."

The Overmaiden crossed her arms over her chest in irritation. "I've got an idea of where he may have gone, as well as how some information about the ship was obtained."

Miller and Hawkins had similar beliefs on where things were going with the war. Miller had grown increasingly mistrustful of the Hellmarine and Seraphiel and chafed at having to work alongside them. He blamed them for the mishaps rather than the Demons that perpetrated them. The Hellmarine didn't doubt that Miller was with the vice admiral now.

"Here's what we're going to do," the Hellmarine said, cutting off any further wallowing in the state of their situation. "We're going to proceed as planned. But we're going to keep our allies close. That means the Zintari and the Arlier. They exist outside Alliance influence and wish to work with us, correct?"

"That's correct," the Master Sergeant said over the comm. "We made an impression on Cleric Quivara. She's inquired about staying on to assist us while Vex has floated a similar idea with her people."

"We get repairs and resupplied when we go into the middle colonies," the Hellmarine continued. "Determine who may be compromised by the vice admiral. The Arlier and the Zintari can assist us with our objectives, but we should see what inroads can be made with others who are also struggling to fight back."

The Overmaiden nodded in agreement. "It seems like a start. Many other species are struggling with the Demonic incursions in the areas bordering the Middle and Outer Colonies. If they were to receive assistance from us, they would likely view us much more favorably."

"Davis should be able to recover additional information for us that might be useful," Mandy suggested with a little shrug.

"And Twilight has said she wishes to assist, too, considering the state of things. Maybe all those tomes have some information on managing and navigating rifts better or just shut down Hell's ability to commandeer them as they do."

"Then what?" Captain Horne asked, clearly amused with the impromptu brainstorming session the Hellmarine had facilitated on the bridge.

"Then the mission continues," the Hellmarine responded matter-of-factly. "We destroy every last Demon we find."

The captain nodded in approval before sitting down in his chair. "Helm set a course back to Middle Colony space and prepare for rift jump. Everyone else, as you were."

The Hellmarine glanced at Mandy, wondering if it was too late for him to get her and Seraphiel together in his quarters for the additional activity the Angel had suggested earlier.

"Oh, by the way," the Master Sergeant said over the comm. "I need the Hellmarine down in the Armor bay to meet with the Armorer ASAP."

"She's finished the repairs already?" the Hellmarine asked, impressed with the speed and efficiency of the woman. What little he knew of her reputation didn't do her any justice.

"Oh, much better than that, Nature Boy, the Master Sergeant laughed. "You got an upgrade to a brand-new Hades Mk. III. Even threw in a little scented pine tree for you."

The Hellmarine's face split into a devious grin, perhaps the first that anyone on the bridge had ever seen from him. One of the worries lingering at the back of his mind had been the completely totaled nature of the Mk. II and whether or not it could ever be repaired. The Armorer had elected to just scrap it and start over, giving him a full suit of Armor that was already set to go.

"If we come across any Demonic activity on the way," the captain said from his chair. "I might be inclined to stop so you can take the armor out for a field test. But only if you get down there and run through all the initial calibrations first."

"Yes, sir," the Hellmarine responded enthusiastically, practically sprinting from the bridge with gory visions of tearing entire hordes of Demons to ribbons in his shiny, new power armor. Behind him, Mandy struggled to keep up, insisting that she had to be present to run all the necessary biometric scans. The Overmaiden similarly protested, insisting that the Phantasm Chamber would be a much more prudent and efficient way of testing the armor before dropping it into the field against actual Demons.

The Hellmarine ignored all of the noise, firmly holding the image of Demonic slaughter in his mind and focused on the battles to come.

Appendix

You have reached the end of the **Hellmarine: Book 1.** What follows is a lore appendix for those who are curious or want a refresher in preparation for **Book 2**. If you aren't interested in reading this part, then *now would be a good time to leave a review* and follow the authors on their Amazon pages. Please also consider sharing your love of the book on the various harem lit communities on Facebook and Reddit. Your support is incredibly valuable. Thank you for reading!

Equipment and Tech

Chiron Semi-Powered Armor Mk. II

A step above standard body armor but below true power armor, the Chiron power armor is worn by medics and various medical personnel in the field who require additional protection and mobility. The sensor array of the Chiron is specifically calibrated to monitor the biometric data of a squad at all times while possessing an extended range for biometric detection beyond the standard array given to the Orpheus power armor. The Chiron comes pre-loaded with a host of stimulants, analgesics, sedatives, and antidotes that are distributed through an integrated medical gauntlet. Some forms of the armor have been modified for other delivery systems or even with an additional medical gauntlet.

Hades Power Armor Mk. II

Claire Arleth designed this set of unique power armor to augment the unique biology and needs of the Hellmarine. Hades is composed of dense, ablative, lightweight alloys capable of dispersing a great deal of kinetic energy and withstanding extreme temperatures. The outer shell is polarized by an internal Arkane fusion core, further dispersing kinetic impacts but also offering resistance to energy weapons and similar attacks. The inner layer of the armor is composed of a sophisticated lattice capable of augmenting and reading the movements of the Hellmarine, operating as an entire secondary layer of artificial muscle that interfaces with the outer shell.

Other features of the armor include the ability to host assistant AIs, a HUD for environmental readouts and suit diagnostics, a hacking module, a communications array, magboots, wrist-mounted grapnel, and thrusters for zero-G navigation. The suit is completely sealed, allowing the Hellmarine to function in a complete vacuum as well as other incredibly hostile environments regarding temperature, gravity, and pressure.

Nemesis Semi-Powered Armor Mk. I

Constructed from the destroyed remains of Archangel armor, the Nemesis is designed specifically to cater to Seraphiel's needs and abilities after she becomes a Grigori. Created by Claire Arleth, this armor shares a similar composition to the Hades, using Elysian Steel instead of the standard lightweight alloys found in the Hades. This alternate construction reduces the weight of the armor while using the Angel's natural divine aura to power the suit, eliminating the need for an Arkane fusion core and allowing Seraphiel to use her natural magic and smiting abilities.

The Nemesis armor is not naturally sealed but uses a power field emitter to channel and redirect the divine aura into sectioned forcefields to offer additional protection to areas that would, at first, appear exposed. This technology works similarly to polarization but relies heavily on Seraphiel's natural stamina.

Orpheus Power Armor Mk. V

The Orpheus Mk. V is the standard issue power armor for all Marines within the Sol Alliance. The armor is powered by a miniature Arkane Energy reactor and augments the physical abilities of the Marine wearing it. Each suit of armor comes with a standard sensor array, HUD, and wrist-mounted grapnel as well as thrusters for zero-G navigation that have seen use in planetary combat scenarios. Though not as powerful as the Hades, the Orpheus is the next most powerful form of power armor available in the Sol Alliance and stands head and shoulders above any form of Semi-Powered armor besides the Nemesis.

Ryozo Riftdrive Engine

Named for its original creator, Sazama Ryozo, the riftdrive allows a starship to skate the dimensional barrier between universes. It uses the power of a contained stabilized rift in the engine core. The rift is maintained with an Arkane Energy reaction which, also provides power for the rest of the ship. The speed of a given ship is determined by the size and power of its internal engine reaction, allowing larger masses to transition into Riftspace at a time. Smaller ships can be fitted with "oversized" engines for additional speed, hastening their transition into Riftspace and the velocity by which they traverse it.

Spectravista Phantasmagoria V Phantasm Chamber

The most sophisticated Phantasm Chamber available on the market comes from Spectravista. Capable of interacting with all five senses, this Phantasm Chamber creates completely immersive hard light simulations limited only by the programmer's imagination. Numerous safety protocols are hardcoded into the system to prevent accidental death or dismemberment, but those implemented for military purposes include the option to have these protocols turned off.

The Phantasmagoria V is in service on various military ships but has also seen widespread use in the civilian sector to provide thrills ranging from high adventure and violence to satisfying the most sordid sexual fantasies.

Alliance Weapons

OT-5 Outsider

High-powered rapid-fire sidearm with magnetically accelerated caseless ammunition. The Outsider is one of humanity's most beloved and reliable weapons and is a standard issue in all branches of the military. The Outsider is magazine-fed with a standard 12-round capacity.

CR-3 Cerberus

A brutal pump-action shotgun originally used in colony worlds for "tunnel sweeping." Marines have adopted it for a similar purpose on hostile worlds. Though the weapon still makes use of shells like legacy models, the contents are magnetically propelled instead of chemically. It holds a total of 10 rounds at a time, each of which can be "charged" for an additional kick. This charge function can also superheat individual shots, effectively converting them into incendiary rounds on the spot.

R1-P Chainchete

Originally used as a way to breach armored vehicles, the R1-P has been put into circulation with Marines deployed against Demonic incursions. Highly effective in carving up the dense flesh and natural armor many demons possess, the R1-P has gained such a reputation for melee efficacy that schools of swordsmanship have sprung up around its use. The diamond-toothed chain of the blade is accelerated by a potent fusion-powered motor in a densely alloyed casing. Though it is rated for prolonged use, it can still overheat.

PR-60T Perforator Pulse Rifle

The bread and butter of the Sol Alliance Marines, the select-fire Perforator has a reputation for reliability and efficacy against close and mid-range targets. Loaded with magnetically accelerated, caseless, armor-piercing rounds, the Perforator has proven itself a force to be reckoned with against alien and Demonic targets alike. With a 60-round magazine, the Perforator is a favorite among those going up against Demonic hordes or Ghenzul raids.

RN3-D Renegade Marksman Rifle

Designed for longer-range precise strikes, the Renegade's lightweight design is ideal for marksmen who need frequent repositioning. The standard rifle is equipped with a scope for visual magnification and night vision mode. It holds 20 high-velocity rounds capable of penetrating polarized armor and some energy shielding.

B0-3R Bouncer Grenade Launcher

The Bouncer break-action grenade launcher is considered the most versatile single-shot launcher in service with the

Sol Alliance thanks to its multi-rail system for a variety of useful attachments and its ability to fire multiple 40mm grenade types. A smart-link function to a suit of power armor allows multiple shots to be set on extended delays. The weapon also features a highly accurate arc-assist readout along the back to help with firing trajectories.

HLS-0M Hailstorm Submachine Gun

The Hailstorm SMG is a lightweight weapon often wielded by those with a need to lay down heavy fire in close quarters and members of special forces. Its unique design allows it to empty its 60-round magazine much faster than the Perforator at a slight cost to penetration. The Hailstorm's design is also quieter than the Perforator and, when equipped for noise suppression, is perfect for infiltration and silent engagements.

PR0-3R Prowler Anti-material Sniper Rifle

Regarded as the most powerful anti-material sniper rifle in the Alliance, the Prowler is heavily favored by Marines with power armor capable of negating the drawbacks of the weapon's size and weight. The smart-link function featured in its onboard optics also allows for seamless integration with power armor HUDs, offering further advantages for Marines to enjoy. The Prowler has an effective range of 4 miles with a 10-round magazine capacity capable of firing explosive rounds in addition to its standard ammunition.

T3M-P5 Tempest Light Machine Gun

As a miniaturized version of the Cyclone, the Tempest is designed to be effectively carried and repositioned by individuals not wearing power armor. However, it has recently gained renewed purpose as a shoulder-mounted weapon for those in power armor. Linking into the sensor array of power armor, the Tempest can be set to automatically fire at enemies within a certain proximity or be manually directed through smart-link technology. The Tempest uses caseless armor-piercing rounds with a maximum capacity of 200 rounds. Shoulder-mounted models are difficult to reload, typically requiring assistance from another squad member to pull off in a timely fashion.

CL-N3 Cyclone Heavy Machine Gun

Due to its size and weight, the Cyclone is impractical for anyone to wield outside of power armor. For those with power armor, such as the Sol Alliance Marines, the Cyclone is a devastating weapon of war capable of heavy suppression fire while remaining mobile. With three barrels in a rotary configuration and a 400-round magazine of armor-piercing or explosive caseless ammunition, the Cyclone has been celebrated as one of the most effective ways to combat ground-level Ghenzul raids and Demonic incursions.

LNC-3R Lancer Rocket Launcher

Existing as a marked upgrade from the Pikeman in nearly every respect, the shoulder-fired Lancer has seen heavy use in the Outer Colonies against Demonic incursions thanks to its heavier payload, accurate aim-assist, HUD integration, and five-missile capacity. The Lancer is highly effective in breaking up dense horde formations and puncturing the heavily armored demons both on the ground and in the air.

SC-45 Scalder Light Blast Cannon

As one of the few blaster weapons in use within the Sol Alliance, the Scalder requires special training and certification to wield. Initially designed as a semi-stationary weapon attached via a power conduit to an energy source, the Scalder has been modified to function with the Arkane fusion reactors found in power armor. The significant power draw of the weapon requires a warm-up cycle before firing, followed by a cooldown period. When placed in the hands of experienced theurgists, both cycles can be reduced through subtle spellcraft for Arkane power manipulation. Due to their obscene expense, the number of Scalders in service is extremely limited.

SC-35 Scorcher Heavy Blast Cannon

Typically vehicle-mounted, the Scorcher is the "big brother" to the Scalder Blast Cannon, with a much higher power output per blast and longer beam duration. Both the warm-up cycle and cooldown cycles are longer than the Scalder, though they still benefit from reductions in the hands of a theurgist. The Scorcher's design integrates a powerful radsink to reduce the exposure to Arkane radiation on discharge but can become overwhelmed from sustained use, requiring a swap before continuing. Though the Scorcher can be powered by the reactor in power armor, its size and unwieldy design make it impractical to carry around for any length of time.

Titan Arms TA-12 Mining Gauntlet

A civilian tool for mining in the outer colonies, the TA-12 from Titan Arms has found a new use in hand-to-hand combat with demons. Augmenting the strength of the wearer while protecting them against impact, this gauntlet's default design comes with three polarized blades capable of penetrating the densest materials for mining. Though not officially rated for combat among the Marines, those who come across them in colony worlds often can't resist picking one up, especially if not equipped with a type of chainchete.

Alliance Ships

SANS Midnight Sea

Formerly a colony ship, the Midnight Sea has been converted into a light carrier and serves as the base of operations for the Overmaiden and the Hellmarine. The Midnight Sea houses numerous fabrication bays for constructing new ships, firebases, power armor, and other equipment critical to the crew's mission. The Midnight Sea also houses docking bays for various smaller crafts, such as interceptors and dropships. The ship is retrofitted with a powerful Mag-cannon as its main gun and bays of coil guns for ship-to-ship combat. Point defense systems are in place to defend against enemy fighters.

The two most important features of the Midnight Sea are its stealth array and the Overmaiden herself, who can integrate seamlessly with the ship's systems at any time to take control of any and all functions. Though slightly outdated, the stealth array serves the purpose of minimizing the ship's appearance on enemy sensors, often causing it to be mistaken as a lesser threat or less tempting of a target. The outdated nature of the array, coupled with the size of the ship, requires an inordinate amount of power that has to be re-routed from other systems when at full power.

Rain of Blood (Gunship)

Converted from another dropship specifically for Hellmarine missions, the Rain of Blood is armed to the teeth with weapons capable of clearing landing zones and defending against swarms of air-based Demonic threats such as Vespers and Terrogons. The heavier emphasis on the vessel's hull integrity forces it to move at slower speeds than other dropships while also increasing the prep time required for drops.

Shotgun Opera (Dropship)

The Shotgun Opera is the main dropship of the Midnight Sea and has been in service since the carrier's conversion. The Shotgun Opera is built for speed and maneuverability but sports light weaponry for defense and fire support. Primarily in service to Master Sergeant Gray's squad, the ship is often considered "his" by crew members of the Midnight Sea. The fact that the ship's name reflects the Master

Sergeant's preferred weapon type in the field only adds further weight to this belief.

SANS Hammer of the Gods

Heavy Cruiser capital ship typically used as Vice Admiral Hawkins' flagship in the Outer Colonies. As a Heavy Cruiser, the Hammer of the Gods is heavily armed and densely armored, capable of laying down devastating fire with multiple Mag-cannons, coil guns, and point defense systems. It bolsters a modern Ryozo Riftdrive that is faster than previous generations, even when making jumps to other layers of the multiverse. Much of the Hammer of the Gods has been converted to serve as a command ship, with advanced communications arrays and staff to coordinate fleet movements while conducting its own defensive maneuvers. Though not typical for other fleets of the Sol Alliance, the nature of the Outer Colonies often necessitates such a strategy.

SANS Tides of War

One of the Heavy Frigates damaged in the battle of Gephidus. The Midnight Sea returns to assist it after leaving the Hellmarine and Gray's squad behind to conduct the assault on the Voivode of Aonus. As a Heavy Frigate, the Tides of War is equipped with a formidable selection of Mag-cannons and coil guns, allowing it to engage in sustained fire against enemy ships or for planetary bombardment. It has limited fabrication bays, allowing it to effect its own repairs quickly while offering assistance to other ships in the fleet.

Worlds

Aonus

As an Outer colony of the Sol Alliance, Aonus is a rugged but beautiful world with an abundance of natural resources, both conventional and unconventional. While much of the planet's economy revolves around mining these precious resources, there is a secondary booming industry of scientific research that studies and examines what the various mining companies unearth.

Dirilia

Serving exclusively as a trading post to connect the Outer Colony worlds to one another, Dirilia is one of the few Outer Colonies to employ its own military independent of the Sol Alliance. Controversial as it was to have a dedicated military, the Dirilians were quicker to respond to a Demonic Incursion than most and would eventually go on to serve alongside the Alliance in defense of their world.

Elyndor

The original homeworld of the Zintari, Elyndor was nearly destroyed in a magically fueled nuclear war that caused the collapse of the global ecosystem. A secondary effect of this Cataclysm was rifts being blown through the fabric of reality, creating unstable throughways between worlds and universes. Slowly, Elyndor's life recovered, though little of it was the Zintari themselves. Today, Elyndor has a unique collection of species that have mutated and evolved from the original species that populated Elyndor in ancient times. Elyndor has a potent mixture of Arkane and Quixotic Energy sources and magic.

Gephidus

Gephidus is an Outer colony of the Sol Alliance consumed by a Demonic horde despite the Navy's and Marines' best efforts. The relatively dense population centers of the colony provided ample prey for the horde, which used their souls and flesh to expand rapidly. Soon after, the horde constructs ships from this planet, clashing with the Sol Naval ships assigned to contain the threat.

Itaris

The Sol Alliance has considered Itaris a friendly world for a few centuries. It is located somewhere outside the Milky Way, though its inhabitants have ventured to the Milky Way and even the Sol System. A handful of visitors from Earth have been allowed to visit Itaris over the last few centuries, but the world remains relatively isolated. Itaris is a world of darkness and rain with a plethora of exotic flora and fauna that have adapted to the specific conditions present on the planet. The most prominent species native to the planet are known simply as the Itarians, who always appear to members of other species as one of their own through a complicated form of psychic projection.

Lilles

A minor planet of the Outer Colonies and the site of the first Hellrift targeted by the Midnight Sea during the first world-hopping blitz. Lilles was in the early days of colonization before the incursion, providing only a limited amount of living material for the horde to expand. Much of the planet has not been properly surveyed, but was earmarked as a valuable colony location due to the large amount of its landmass being located in a temperate zone perfect for agriculture.

Numedha

Once a world comparable to Elyndor in terms of population and magic, Numedha is now a mere shadow of what it once was. Centuries ago, Numedha suffered from a Demonic incursion that persisted for years before finally being pushed back. Unfortunately, the damage to the world was so severe that it has been slow to recover ever since. Ruins dot the planet's landscape, with only a few strongholds of sentient life that thrive. Many of the underground dwelling species were wiped out in the original incursion, namely the Dwarves, who were blamed for releasing the horde in the first place.

Numedha was technically the first planet Earth colonized, albeit secretly, with a single military outpost to counter the Demonic threat. Since then, the Sol Alliance has taken over responsibility for the outpost and a few others to ensure the horde doesn't return. The Outpost was originally established by the founding members of the Advance Defense

Agency, a spin-off from the Department of Homeland Security in the United States.

Taobos

Gas giant in the Outer Colonies that hosts a multitude of moons primed for mining materials critical to constructing starships and other heavily armored vehicles in use by the Sol Alliance's military. Control of Taobos and the other moons allows replacement parts for such ships to be fabricated in the Outer Colonies until a proper shipyard can be constructed.

Vizuno

A major trading hub located at the farthest end of the Outer Colonies, little of Vizuno's sophisticated infrastructure remains after being hit by a Demonic Incursion and near-complete infernaforming of its surface that followed. Before these terrible events, Vizuno had begun to emerge as a site of valuable scientific and magical research.

Regions of the Multiverse

Celestial Space

Situated close to the very top of the multiverse, Celestial Space is the place where all of the divine worlds reside. Each world within Celestial Space has been responsible for different aspects of hope, altruism, and all things good found within the species of the multiverse. By inspiring these qualities in other sentient species, the goal is to increase the density of life in every layer of the multiverse.

Esoteric Space

Esoteric Space is meant to encompass all points in the Multiverse that sit outside of the conventional established layers. Regions of Esoteric Space vary widely in size and don't necessarily connect to one another. Powerful magic users across the Multiverse have been known to create pocket dimensions and private planes of existence, only for these floating islands of creation to be abandoned after their deaths.

Hellspace

Once a near-empty void known simply as The Pit, Hellspace is one of the last layers of the Multiverse before reaching Oblivion. Hellspace was renamed when the world of Hell came to power and began spreading its corruption throughout its universe while pulling worlds of other universes into it through a process known as infernaforming. Now, Hellspace is filled with rancid, corrupted worlds slowly devouring themselves to sate the hunger and hatred of the hordes that inhabit them.

Riftspace

Riftspace is less of a fixed place and more of a generic term for the spaces "between layers" of the multiverse. Riftspace is relatively chaotic but can be navigated safely by following marked paths set up ahead of time. The first of these stable riftways was established by using Zintari gates and rifts as a means to provide accurate mapping. The same process that created the gateways—and later the rifts—is also responsible for "clearing the way" for these first riftways. Later riftways would be established through other means, with iterative versions of the riftdrive becoming more accurate over time. However, blind jumps are still not recommended.

The Stack

Another term used for the general structure of the entire Multiverse. The Stack was originally coined in reference to a crude model of the multiverse that equated the layers of reality to a stack of pancakes covered in syrup. In this model, Divine Energy was the syrup and was meant to demonstrate the limited mobility it possessed as it got farther from its point of origin.

Standard Space

Every known layer of the multiverse that exists between Celestial Space and Hellspace is referred to as Standard Space. In Standard Space, the rules of physicals remain largely similar to the layer directly next to it, with some layers even existing as minor iterations of one another with the smallest changes. Standard Space was created as a way to propagate Arkane Energy, with each layer reflecting a different approach and design philosophy of ancient and unknowable beings.

Metaphysical Energy and Magic

Arkane Energy

Arkane Energy is the essence of life and magic which flow through the whole Multiverse. The closer to the upper portions of the Multiverse a single universe is, the more Arkane Energy it has freely available to it, making magic and other supernatural abilities more possible. The closer to the lower portions of the Multiverse a universe is, the more mundane the laws of physics become.

Divine Energy

Divine Energy originates within Celestial Space and fuels its inhabitants' supernatural and magical abilities. It is capable of creating life, smiting evil, and performing a host of other "administrative" functions in every region of the Multiverse. Such magic allows the user to tap into the underpinning functions of the Multiverse to alter, create, or destroy. For example, the act of "Smiting" is generally an administrative override to "Delete" a target from existence. Divine Energy is rare in other parts of the multiverse due to how slowly it moves, necessitating the proliferation of Arkane Energy. Even in layers of Standard Space where Divine Energy can be found, the means to wield it is typically beyond most sentient species.

Eldritch Energy

Eldritch Energy is a mysterious and rare form of energy created from "reclaimed" Profane Energy by mysterious entities of the Multiverse now long forgotten. Eldritch Energy is most often found in the lower portions of the Multiverse that had first contact with Hellspace. Eldritch Energy is capable of many of the same feats as Arkane Energy but can be taxing to the minds of younger species that are not equipped to handle it. Though it lacks the corrupting properties of Profane Energy, its entropic effects are sometimes viewed as equally detrimental to the Multiverse.

The side effects of Eldritch Energy can by bypassed by sophisticated machinery with redundant processing. Biological Organisms can overcome the entropic effects through singular focus or clarity of purpose, effectively "burning" the entropy before making contact with their consciousness.

Profane Energy

Profane Energy originates from Hellspace and is created by harvesting and corrupting the Arkane Energy from universes higher up in the Multiverse. Most of the energy harvested comes from the souls of the corrupted and the damned. The corrupted are any of those who have been tempted or coerced by the promises of Hell, while the damned are those who have been cast into Hell by others—be they demons or the corrupted. Those taken against their will are tortured and twisted in Hellspace, creating the conditions to produce more Profane Energy. Though not as potent as Divine Energy, Profane Energy is capable of incredible feats and abilities and moves at a much faster rate, making it incredibly dangerous to the Multiverse as time goes on.

Quixotic Energy

Believed to be created by the Ancient Zintari, Quixotic Energy is a form of energy created by reaping Arkane Energy and refining it into something more potent. Zintari store this energy solely within themselves, refining it further with each soul or source of Arkane Energy reaped. Quixotic Energy was created after an extended study of Profane and Eldritch Energy in hopes of creating an alternative to both.

Quixotic Energy requires a "resting" period to refine. If not given the proper time to process, Quixotic Energy can become unstable, creating excessive emotions and desires within a biological organism or poisoning living creatures in an area surrounding a refinery. Quixotic Energy can be created from Eldritch and Profane Energy but in both cases requires an extended period of "resting" to process.

The side effects of Quixotic Energy are believed to be at the root of the Zintari Cataclysm that befell Elyndor. While some Zintari showed restraint in using such power and used it benevolently, many took in too much too quickly, eroding their desires and morality. Such Zintari often viewed themselves as "more than" other species, even going so far as viewing non-Zintari as mere imitations of their glory or things populating their world solely for their amusement.

Angels

Angel is the general term for Celestial beings hailing mainly from the planet of Heaven. They have many varieties and ranks that make up their strict hierarchy. Like demons, the existence of Angels remains relatively static, with very few being capable of ascending to new positions or ranks.

The hierarchy of Heaven is organized into three triads with varying responsibilities. Those with whom humanity has had the most contact are from the Third Triad, with some scattered contact with the First. Though the Second Triad's existence and theoretical responsibilities are known, they've had nearly no direct contact with Humanity over the course of its entire history.

Each third of a Triad is further subdivided into Choirs, which have different physical areas of responsibility across the multiverse. In the place of surnames, Angels will identify themselves by their Choir, though particularly high-ranking Angels may choose to use their Triads or Thirds. Thus, Seraphiel could be addressed in full as Seraphiel of the Third Choir of the Third Triad, and this would technically be correct.

Demons

Demons are the creatures spawned from Hellspace, created by flesh and energy stolen from the layers higher up in the Multiverse. When created, Demons become very static in their existence, with few ever changing their roles or ascending in the hierarchy of a horde—the standard army or population of Demons in a given area. Hordes are typically controlled by a single Voivode, a type of general that oversees the movements and objectives of Demonkind through a series of subordinates. For hordes not actively engaged in expansion, Barons are typically employed for administration, manufacturing, and production for hordes that are.

Devourer

Devourers are bipedal demons with no forelimbs, eyes, or ears. They track entirely by scent, taste, and motion. They stand half as tall as the average man with short, stout bodies and skulls dominated by a mouth consisting of a bony beak and mandibles, all of which are sharp and serrated. Where Hunters are dispatched to track down prey, Devourers are used as attack dogs and guard dogs. The stomach acids of Devourers are incredibly acidic, allowing them to consume staggering amounts of meat far in excess of their own weight in a very short amount of time. Though tough, Devourers are some of the most unintelligent demons in any horde and have been known to be slaughtered by higher-ranking demons as food when they've reached the proper "ripeness".

Drone

Drones are the lowest form of worker among Demonkind, usually accompanying hordes to infernaform worlds being invaded. Drones operate as hives, with a Queen coordinating the efforts of the swarm in its duties. Drones are insectoid in appearance, almost like centipedes, with large acidic mandibles and long tails ending with a twin pair of deadly stingers. Each Drone is only about the size of a large cat, but swarms are capable of reshaping enemy territory with alarming speed.

Duke

Dukes are the collective lords of Hellspace, responsible for the creation of the first demons through the twisting and corrupting of mortal souls. Though their existence is known through their Warlocks and Voivodes, few concrete facts are known about Dukes and what they are truly capable of. No record exists of a human encountering a Duke and living to tell the tale.

Archduke

More mysterious than the Dukes of Hell is the Archduke, who sits atop the entire hierarchy of Hell's sprawling Empire. The Archduke is believed to be the original source of all hatred and corruption, even though it's unknown how such an entity could have come into being at the bottommost layers of the Multiverse. The Archduke is believed to commune only with the Dukes, possibly issuing their orders to expand the might of its Empire.

Forsaken

Made from the husks of humanoids slain by demons, the Forsaken resemble putrid rotting zombies as they shamble around in the aftermath of incursions. The flesh of the Forsaken can be harvested for demon technology, processed to create new demons, or left to fester and engage with enemy stragglers in their zombified forms. Some Forsaken are possessed by the larval forms of other demons, while others are animated purely by Profane Energy. Those harboring larval demon forms are often faster and stronger than their counterparts but appear almost identical to one another.

Hijacker

When the brute force of a Fulgis isn't enough to bypass a computer system, Hijacker's are employed. Resembling large floating, saggy balloons of pustule-ridden flesh with cybernetic implants protruding at odd angles, Hijackers are highly intelligent demons capable of humbling even the most hardened hacker. Hijackers appear deceptively fragile but are actually quite hardy and even dangerous to those that don't get the drop on them. Not only does a Hijacker have a devastating bite filled with all manner of filth, they are capable of releasing energy beams from any of their many eyes. These beams can target independently of one another or focus on a single target to generate a single powerful blast. Hijackers are usually seen on more technologically advanced worlds.

Hunter

Used as scouts and trackers, Hunters are eyeless quadrupeds with highly acute senses of sound and scent. Their tongues are lethal weapons when not used to scent the air, functioning as deadly harpoons capable of penetrating flesh and bone as well as light body armor. Each of a Hunter's limbs ends in powerful claws that allow them to climb walls and run across ceilings.

Ignis

Ignis (plural Igni) are powerful creatures composed of fiendish bone and hellfire. Resembling legless humanoids with large boney horns and a "mask" in place of a face, these demons revel in burning anything they can get their searing hands on to a crisp. Igni have been known to "speak" in a language that seems independent of the common infernal tongue, but attempts to decipher this form of speech have failed due to the limited sample size. Igni are used to raze large structures that aren't suitable for infernaforming or destroying crops to gut the food supply of their enemies.

Fulgis

Similar to Igni, but composed of metal and living lightning, Fulgi will often serve a similar roll when a horde descends upon worlds with highly developed technology. Fulgi are capable of shorting the most protected systems, projecting their consciousness into networks for a limited time to burn through firewalls and other security software. The Fulgi reputation for burning through energy shielding with EMPs and negating the benefits of polarized armor makes them priority targets even for other advanced alien species.

Juggernaut

Juggernauts are hulking masses of Demoni flesh and infernal iron in the shape of giant arachnids. Juggernauts are half Demon and half mobile fortress. Various cannons mounted along the front of the structure, resembling the forward legs and fangs of a spider, spit volatile molten iron in various directions. The face of the creature contains numerous "eyes" that function as enormous disruptor cannons. The grotesque abdomen of the abomination houses a host of reinforcements for the horde in forward positions which can be dropped into the field at a moment's notice. Because they lack any sophisticated intelligence of their own, lack decision making capabilities, and require "pilots", the Alliance often considers Juggernauts to be vehicles similar to Demonic starships rather than an independent variety of Demon in their own right.

Knight

Standing around seven feet tall, knights exist as the horde's lowest 'officer' class. Knights are formidable combatants in their own right, covered in blackened metal mined from Hell and forged in profane crucibles. However, they truly excel in commanding the movements of Soldiers, Hunters, and Drones. Knights revel in the chaos and destruction their forces wreak on other worlds and jump at the chance to demonstrate their own might in single combat with enemies that catch their attention. No mortal has ever seen what a knight looks like under their armor due to the fact that it is securely fastened to their flesh and—in some cases—to their bones. Knights are capable of the same fireball technique as Soldiers, albeit much more powerful, and possess swords wreathed in hellfire for close combat.

Cavalier

Similar to knights in appearance, Cavaliers lead portions of the horde that are mounted or function as vehicles. Cavaliers are typically armed with polearms instead of swords, each of which is capable of launching powerful disruptor blasts fueled by the Profane Energy the Cavalier carries within itself. Unlike knights, Cavaliers prefer to function on the front lines, leading charges of other demons into enemy lines astride armored mounts to devastating effect.

Akuus

Akuus are rhino-sized, six-legged Demonic steeds with deadly racks of horns to assist in charges that their Cavalier riders execute. Each Akuus leaves behind a flaming trail of prints that burns for several minutes before extinguishing. Like most hellfire, these flames resist conventional means of extinguishment before their duration expires. Akuus are not defenseless without riders and have been known to trample armored vehicles and breathe fire when enraged.

Larvae

Demon Larvae are composed of the unholy, blasphemous fusion of cleaving Profane Energy to the tattered remnants of twisted souls. In order to mature, the metaphysical essence of the Larvae must be placed in an incubation pod constructed of repurposed flesh. This pod can take many forms depending on the type of Demon desired, with some even incubating within the bodies of the Forsaken.

Soldier

Soldier Demons are the backbone of any horde. They possess natural armor in the form of thick bone plating and natural weapons in the spikes that protrude from them. Soldiers are deployed en masse to soften up targets ahead of commanders. Soldiers are bipedal, standing roughly the same height as the average male human. Their mouths are filled with sharp teeth that drip with highly corrosive acid. If unable to get into close range with the enemy, Soldiers will pepper them at a distance with fireballs conjured in their palms and thrown.

Tanker

True to their names, Tankers are large demons the size of armored vehicles capable of taking a great deal of physical punishment. A marvel of Demonic technology, the Tanker is a fusion of flesh and metal, with arms like cannons capable of firing varying types of ammunition at a moment's notice. Though balls of hellish napalm are the most common form of attack, Tankers have been known to switch to disruptor and blaster rounds when needed. Other forms of specialized ammunition have been reported. Tankers resemble twisted centaurs and are believed to be made from the tortured remains of the near-mythical creatures. Tankers are typically deployed to counter heavy enemy armor or breach enemy strongholds.

Warlock

Warlocks are the willing supplicants of Hell, granted the secrets of profane magic through their covenant with the

Dukes of Hell. Usually recruited and trained by Vidames, warlocks are much more numerous and lack the diverse spellcasting of their superiors. Warlocks paint themselves in the symbols of the Duke they have sworn themselves to and will frequently mutilate their own flesh as a show of devotion to their dark lords.

Inquisitor

Inquisitors are a variant of warlock that specialize in corrupting other mortals, making them vulnerable to the profane promises of Hell. Inquisitors will often take measures to blend in with other societies when undercover, either foregoing the mutilation of their flesh or using powerful illusions or mental influence to conceal themselves. Inquisitors seek out mortals steeped in a particular vice they prefer to work with, corrupting them to a point where they can be made into warlocks or otherwise offered as sacrifices to the horde. Some Inquisitors known as "Zealots" pride themselves on corrupting those who were in no danger of damnation, twisting them to their will and creating utter despair in their wake.

Vidame

Vidame are mortal creatures that have given themselves over to the influence of Hell, usually in service to a specific Duke. In doing so, their flesh changes, becoming more resistant to physical damage as they strive to emulate the tenets of their lords. Due to their time spent as warlocks, Vidame are incredibly adept at the profane magic of Hell and wielding its power. Vidame do not have uniform appearances owing to the fact that they aren't full demons, but they often adopt similar vestments to indicate their position and authority over the rites and rituals of the horde. All warlocks in a given horde report to a Vidame.

Voivode

Voivodes are the warlords of Dukes, commanding individual hordes assigned to incursions. Voivodes are infused with the power of their specific Duke, swearing an infernal Oath to become one of their order. Many will look similar to the Dukes that they serve, using their shared traits to inspire hate and fear in their enemies in the name of their lord. Voivodes rule through fear and have absolute authority over any horde their lord places them in command of, with only Dukes and Archdukes possessing the means to override it. If a Voivode is slain while in command of a horde, the horde temporarily loses its cohesion and command structure, forcing many of the demons to turn on one another or fight for dominance until a new command structure can be established.

Xenos/Aliens

The Arlier

The Arlier are an advanced species of religious elves that revere the cosmos as a living entity. The Arlier are from the same layer of the Multiverse as the Sol Alliance and were one of the first species encountered by humans during their exploration. The Arlier reverence for the cosmos originates in their part of space being one of the few places in their layer of the Multiverse where Divine Energy can be found in its natural state, providing them with a direct conduit to higher layers and their knowledge.

Initial conflicts with the Arlier began as simple border disputes, eventually escalating to all-out war when the Sol Alliance attempted to lay claim to a vein of Divine Energy. Numerous conflicts have been fought between the Alliance and the Arlier. The intervention of the Alliance against a Ghenzul invasion on the Arlier's behalf has led to a formal peace treaty.

The Arlier recognize other Elven species as distant cousins and welcome them with open arms, even allowing other species to refer to them generically as elves in recognition of the greater ideal of "Elvenkind". Despite this warm relationship, there are various physiological differences between the Arlier that set them apart from other species of Elves, chiefly of which is their natural ability to commune with Divine Energy. Arlier possess a longer lifespan than most other species of elves and possess keener sight.

Ghenzul

The Ghenzul are a terrifying species found predominantly in the layers of Standard Space, occurring more frequently in the lower layers before reaching Hellspace. Despite their proximity to Hellspace, the Ghenzul have no affinity for demons nor demons for them. Ghenzul exist to feed and reproduce, the latter of which is accomplished through a process known as transfiguration. This process is incredibly painful, using the biomass of other species to "build" new members of the Ghenzul based on pre-determined designs.

Ghenzul resemble large bio-mechanical skeletal humanoids wrapped in layers of dark latex. Their heads have large, flat, bony crests that house various sensory organs that replace their apparent lack of sight. They possess powerful psychic connections with one another despite lacking a true language or any thought independent of the desires of a Queen. These abilities are capable of occluding their presence from other psychic and magical detection while also dampening the efficacy of other abilities in sufficient numbers. This psychic ability amplifies fear responses in other species, causing them to behave irrationally.

The Ghenzul have invaded the space of numerous other species, but their place of origin has yet to be discovered. They are capable of surviving in the vacuum of space for extended periods of time, provided that food is still available, and are highly adaptive to numerous other environments. Those they are not immediately familiar with can be adapted to through the process of transfiguration. The vanguard of Ghenzul invasions focuses on the consumption of other creatures until sufficiently "primed" to begin producing through the transfiguration process.

Interdictors

Interdictors are a specialized form of Ghenzul that exist solely to amplify the suppressive nature of the hivemind, dampening all forms of magic and metaphysical power sources. The more Ghenzul present within a hive, the more powerful this effect becomes. Interdictors are only found on vessels that have been completely converted from a starship and are used to prevent prospective prey from escaping with riftjumps.

Queens

Queens are the source of control for a hive's collective intelligence. Everything that a member of the hive sees or experiences can be seen and experienced by the Queen. The Queen is many times larger than the typical Ghenzul, with a significantly larger crest, sharper claws, and a deadlier tail. Particularly powerful Queens have been known to infiltrate the minds of careless psychic individuals, reserving them for a specialized form of transfiguration known only to them.

Malur

The Malur are a hostile species of aliens from another layer of standard space that came into conflict with the Sol Alliance during their attempt to colonize worlds within the Milky Way Galaxy. The Malur are shorter than humans with white or gray skin. Despite their shorter stature, they have a formidable command of magic and Arkane Energy as a whole. Their society is divided into a strict caste system, dictating which areas of magic that an individual may pursue. First contact between the Malur and humans was specifically with the science caste, which is responsible for the extensive study of other species and universes prior to invasion. These abductions are where the term "little gray men" or "grays" came from.

Malur are cold and dispassionate in a way that humans often equate to sociopathy, with a select few even showing sadistic tendencies. Malur regard other intelligent species as inherently inferior and a source of impurity in the flow of Arkane Energy. Any species capable of working magic or wielding Arkane Energy is often prioritized for extermination to reduce their impact on Arkane purity. Though Malur technology remains considerably more advanced than that of the Sol Alliance, the Malur reproduce at a much slower rate than most other known species of the Multiverse. This relative limitation often leads to them being outmanned when not taking an enemy by surprise.

Malur regard the death of one member of their species as far greater than thousands of any other species, placing it on the same level that many species would reserve for entire genocides.

Orcs

Orcs are a warlike species of tusked humanoids that battle one another almost as much as they battle other species. Orcs are divided into clans and tribes across the multiverse, many of which have small physiological differences between them. Every clan vies for dominance among this diaspora to prove which among them is the most worthy to lead them—the pinnacle of Orc kind. Though this appears at first to be an obsession over genetic superiority, Orcs dismiss this idea. Instead, they view it as a complex system of beliefs and familial ties, which sometimes coincide with genetic traits—but not always. An Orc of Numedha could be accepted among the Orcs of Elyndor if their beliefs align and they're willing to forge bonds with one another.

As a whole, Orcs venerate the concepts of warfare, competition, and struggle. They believe that conflict breeds stronger Orcs and that peace breeds weaker ones. Even the most peaceful of tribes engage in regular ritual combat or extreme competitions to prove their worthiness to one another and whichever gods they worship.

Orc technology isn't typically as advanced as that of the Alliance, but it gets the job done. Orc battles usually occur through tactics and numbers rather than technology, proving formidable opponents through their pursuit of glory. Orcs do not possess their own form of FTL, opting to strip such forms of travel from other ships they come across and retrofitting them to their own ships. Though this once served as the source of numerous accidents in the past, the species as a whole has become highly adept at quickly adapting different technologies to working with one another. This hodge-podge of technology often makes it difficult to anticipate tactics in battle, which is another reason that orcs have stuck with it for so long.

Links to Follow

*PLEASE **REVIEW THE BOOK** and follow Alphonse and Virgil's Amazon Author pages! For more Harem Lit, LitRPG, and Monster Girl content check out the following:*

https://www.facebook.com/groups/haremlit
https://www.facebook.com/groups/haremlitaudiobooks
https://www.facebook.com/groups/haremlitbooks/
https://www.facebook.com/groups/monstergirllovers
https://www.facebook.com/groups/dukesofharem
https://www.facebook.com/groups/MonsterGirlFiction/
https://www.facebook.com/groups/1324476308314052
https://www.face-
book.com/groups/404822691240858https://www.face-
book.com/groups/2561978977185003
https://www.facebook.com/groups/LitRPG.books
https://www.facebook.com/groups/litrpgforum
https://www.facebook.com/groups/LitRPGReleases
https://www.reddit.com/r/litrpg/

https://www.facebook.com/groups/LitRPGsociety
https://www.royalguardpublishing.com
https://www.facebook.com/RoyalGuard2020
https://www.royalguardpublishing.com

Made in United States
Troutdale, OR
12/29/2024

27367129R00345